Series By Michele L. Coffman

The Alpha Evolution Series

The Battle for Liberty Series

The Universal Guardian Series

THE UNDERSTANDING

BOOK TWO
THE ALPHA EVOLUTION SERIES

MICHELE L. COFFMAN

Launch Point Press
Portland, Oregon

Launch Point Press
Portland, Oregon
www.LaunchPointPress.com

THE PURIFICATION CAST OF CHARACTERS

Civilian Survivors of the Apocalypse

- Christina Burgos–Young woman born and raised at CDC in Fort Collins
- Dr. James Burgos–Virologist, Christina's father
- Eva–Dr. James Burgos's wife, Christina's mother
- Jennifer–Trish and Christina's seven-year-old daughter
- Dr. Jenkins–Trish's Genetics instructor
- Karen–owner and weekday bartender of the longest running club in Rapid City
- Samuel (Sam)–Child rescued from mutant attack
- Olivia Stonleigh–Lead Veterinarian for Rapid City
- Olivia's Veterinary Staff–Tracy, Tylor, April, and Justin

Colonel Aralyn Williams' Militia

- Captain Trish Webber–Julie Webber's daughter, conceived and raised in a NORAD bunker
- Colonel Aralyn Williams–Head of Rapid City's Militia, Trish's godmother who was Julie's "best friend"

- Major Rebecca Thomas–Aralyn's Second in Command
- Staff Sergeant Jason Givens–Weapons specialist
- Captain Carlen Strong–Specializes in electronics and programming
- Captain Susan Travis–Specializes in medicine
- Sergeant First Class Stan Phillips–Specializes in maintenance and explosives
- Staff Sergeant Perez–Guard on Trish's team
- Sergeant Davis–Guard on Trish's team
- Staff Sergeant Young–Medic on Trish's team
- Sergeant Janet Simmons–Guard for Rapid City's HQ

Additional/Deceased Characters

- Betty–Waitress at Hometown Cuisine
- Old Stan–Lead farmhand on one of Rapid City's animal farms.
- Corporal Eric Leonard–In charge of Supply, youngest team member
- First Sergeant Todd Stevens–Weapons specialist
- Dr. Julie Webber–Trish's Mom, scientist who specialized in Biochemistry and Molecular Genetics
- Christina's friends from school–Stephanie, Adam, and Gabe

The New United States Characters

- Dr. Frank Webber–Trish's father, virologist
- Lieutenant Waska–In charge of locating Trish Webber.
- General Princeton–Director of Military Forces for the NUS government

To my daughter Ashley and my son Phillip
for filling my life with meaning, my heart
with love, and for always having faith in
me.

And to my granddaughter, Michele, whose
extraordinary personality engulfs my heart.

CHAPTER ONE
JUNE 5, 2090

"Steady…relax your arm…focus on your target…" Trish remained low and analyzed Jennifer's stance. She adjusted the girl's bow-arm and patiently waited.

Sheer determination caused Jennifer's brow to turn downward with burning concentration. After a few seconds of holding the tension, Jennifer's tiny elbow slowly shook past her wavy-brown hair. She released the string, and the arrow shot off, striking firmly in the target. The arrow hit several inches closer to the center than the last three.

Jennifer's big brown eyes gleamed at her mom. "How'd I do?" she asked, then waited for the praise she knew she'd earned.

Standing, Trish let out a long whistle. "Not bad," she said, trying to keep her pride concealed. "If it were a deer, you would've nicked the hoof, maybe even the lower leg." Trish shrugged in a way to suggest she couldn't decide on which one.

Jennifer squared her shoulders toward the target. "Not true. That shot would've killed it." She moved forward, closer to the point of impact. "If it didn't go down right away, it would've been badly wounded and easy to hit again."

"So, you're just going to keep shooting the poor animal full of arrows until you drop it? Doesn't sound like a pleasant way to go."

Sighing, Jennifer stepped up to the target and hunched over in front of the arrow. She held her hands above her head, stiff fingers outstretched like antlers. "See? Look. It went straight through the heart. Killed it. Dead."

"Yes, a deer two feet tall. Not much meat for supper."

When Jennifer turned her agitation to her mom, Trish could no longer hold in her amusement. Jennifer stared at her for a moment until finally she gave an unappreciative smirk. "It's only funny when you tease Mother."

Trish casually rubbed her nose and laughed. "I know." She headed over and helped the seven-year-old retrieve the arrows in and around the target. "We better go see Grandpa before Grandma and your mother leave the restaurant."

"Why are Grandma and Mother still mad at Grandpa?"

Trish opened her mouth but closed it. She almost said it was because the Burgos temperament afflicted both women, but the idea of Jennifer repeating this in front of Christina alarmed her. Even if Trish was worlds stronger, physically, in the confines of their relationship, she knew who the dominate was, and it most definitely wasn't her. "They love Grandpa. Your mother and grandma are only worried about him."

"Because of his work?"

Trish nodded. The aged wisdom of her daughter both thrilled and terrified her. For one so small, Jennifer had a way of grasping the conflicts of life. Of reading between the lines of grownup affairs, which all too often unfolded around her. "Like Grandpa said, don't stress over it. Sometimes people need time and space to work through things."

With her crossbow and Jennifer's bow loaded, Trish climbed into the vehicle and removed a few aspirins from the child-sealed container, intending to take them with the hope of diminishing her growing headache. After popping the pills, she swished around a mouthful of water and waited until Jennifer had her seatbelt fastened. Once Jennifer gave the required thumbs up, Trish tossed Jennifer her own bottle of water and pulled the armored vehicle away from the pond.

As Jennifer went through the playlist, they drove over a beaten path surrounded by open fields of tall weeds. She selected a familiar tune to listen to before settling in her seat. Evidently, as with this morning, their entertainment on the drive back to Rapid City would be done with the beat of classic rock.

Lowering her window, Trish removed her Kansas City Chief's ball cap and shook her short hair against the semi-cool breeze pouring in. She kept her eyes trained on the robust terrain while observing her daughter in her peripheral. Jennifer lowered her own window and shook out her thick, wavy hair, mimicking her mom. Trish suppressed a grin. She wondered if a more precious child had ever existed. Frankly, she doubted it.

Today was the first Monday of June. Life had cruised by since Trish awoke from her coma over six months ago. The construction in Kansas City, Missouri, finished last month with the rail line clear and the midway reclamation center in Nebraska walled-in and freed of Gramites. Salt Lake and Rapid City now stood at close to thirty thousand survivors each, while Kansas City accommodated over sixty thousand.

The governors of both Salt Lake and Rapid City selected this larger number of citizens for this one community to help with the startup of the Midwest sister-city, whose colossal walls encompassed over five hundred square miles of remodeled buildings, land for farming, and several manufacturing plants. Even without the generous relocation bonus, many of the citizens were eager to go. They also sent Major Reilly and a pre-selected committee to govern. Thankfully, the major's son, John, a.k.a. Scruffy-beard went with him.

Trish tapped her thumbs on the steering wheel as Jennifer strummed the seatbelt strap. A few minutes later, she pulled their duo band onto the highway, driving past the work the construction crews were doing to New Underwood. Trish shifted uncomfortably. She knew the outer wall was close to being finished, which meant soon she would have to tell Christina what the plans were for the overhauled town. Or to be more accurate, what her role would be.

The newly constructed fortress was intended so Trish and Doctor Burgos could study the creatures in a safe environment, away from the citizens of the city. Their mission would be to observe the Gramites, gain a level of understanding, run various tests, and maybe one day, if they were lucky, develop a vaccine to protect survivors against infection. Thanks to Trish's godmother, Colonel Aralyn Williams, and the governors of Rapid City, the soon completed outpost came fully supplied with vehicles, high-end equipment, and added personnel assigned to aide in this challenging and hazardous endeavor.

Pulling up to the first gate surrounding the valley of crops and animal ranches, Trish waved off the salute from the soldier guarding the entrance. "Sorry, Captain Webber. I keep forgetting this outer wall is a no-salute zone."

Trish offered the nervous kid a friendly smile, while inwardly wishing her godmother would forgo the salutes altogether. "Not a problem, private. Happens all the time."

She drove the vehicle across the freshly grated gravel, which snaked toward the main gate a few miles away.

"Mom, we wouldn't really shoot a deer, would we?"

Surprised by the sudden question, Trish peered at her daughter, then focused on the road. "Yes, if we needed to for survival. I'm not saying anything bad will ever happen to what we've built here, but if it did, you need to know how to live off the land. We all do." She weighed her next thought carefully. Jennifer was old enough to make her own decision. "Next fall, Jason and Phillips said they'll take us out hunting for a few days to teach us how to properly track, kill, and skin one, but only if you want to go."

After a brief silence Trish looked at her daughter.

Jennifer was staring straight at her. "I'll go if you do," she said. Her head drooped slightly, then slowly rose. "Mom, I may also cry, but just a little."

Trish knew how hard this task would be for them both, but Phillips was right. Learning to survive off the land was crucial in today's world. "I may cry a little more than you, but we'll cry together when no one else is around. Agreed?"

She could see the instant relief in her daughter's face. "Agreed," said Jennifer with a serious nod.

The sun was still a few hours from setting by the time they pulled into the driveway of Doctor James Burgos's lab. They got out and proceeded up the stairs.

When Doctor Burgos opened the door, he was newly shaven and, thankfully, not sporting his hideous checkered bathrobe. He'd worn the overly washed, tattering robe every day since Eva kicked him out of their house. Watching his emotional struggle these last two months had been difficult. But as always, Christina's father dove into his work for a needed distraction.

"Grandpa." Jennifer beamed and jumped into his outstretched arms.

"Chiquita! How was your first week of school?"

Jennifer rolled her eyes.

He chuckled while carrying Jennifer down the hall past the front room and library. Probably heading off to give her an unhealthy snack which would ruin her appetite before dinner. "Tell me all about it," he said, sounding both proud and supportive.

Enjoying their normal exchange, Trish followed the two through the house. She grunted when she entered the humbly decorated yet clean kitchen to a plate of huge, homemade cookies James was holding out to his granddaughter. Trish held up a finger, signaling one to both sets of pleading eyes.

"Is it in your office?" Trish asked.

Doctor Burgos dipped his head as he poured Jennifer a small glass of milk. Once the pair seated themselves comfortably at the table, where Jennifer began her lengthy spill starting from Monday, cookie in one hand, milk in the other, Trish left the room.

She ran up the stretch of stairs and deviated to the first room on the left into his cluttered office. Spotting the long, plastic container resting on the piles of documents covering his desk, she made her way over and undid the latches on each end. The container held a high-powered rifle with an attached scope and several clips of ammo imbedded in the foam interior. She removed a clip, extracted one of the unusually shaped bullets from the end, and rolled it back and forth between two fingers. The casing was smaller than she expected, but with what Captain Carlen Strong and Doctor Burgos had said, what it contained would help their mission greatly.

Replacing the items, Trish fastened the latches and headed outside to her vehicle. She concealed the weapon case under her prepacked gear in the rear storage area. Closing the hatch on her Gladiator, she inspected both freshly mowed yards. Even though James and Eva were temporarily not on speaking terms, Trish was happy to see Doctor Burgo had tended the lawn surrounding his lab as well as his and his wife's house next door. With her long hours managing and working the restaurant, Eva would have no time to mow.

Wanting to give the two inside some personal space, Trish made her way to the shed in the backyard and retrieved the hedger.

Lowering the serving dishes onto the counter, Christina spotted the newly sliced cantaloupe rinds and apple cores sitting inside the compost container. She smiled and went to the kitchen window to peer out into the backyard. She visually searched through the open space past the shed, then released a giggle when she found what she was looking for. Kneeling in the far corner of the fenced in area were Trish and Jennifer. Each held out tasty offerings to the robust groundhog, who sat hunched over beside the whitewashed fence chewing on a morsel of juicy cantaloupe.

Her heart gave its usual flutter. Her veteran, monster-killing wife and their brown-eyed daughter were one and the same. They each had a heart bigger than one would deem possible in a world full of such turmoil. Seeing the pair in their matching flannel shirts and jeans brought a heightened wave of love to course through her exhausted body. She kissed her fingers and touched the glass before turning from the scene.

The day had been a long one. From helping her mother with early morning prep, serving their normal breakfast and lunch crowd, and working half a dinner shift until the evening cook, who forgot to set his alarm for the third time this week, had finally made it in. She heated the double oven, carefully placed each dish inside, and headed to the backdoor. She was tired but ready to spend what remained of her long day with both her girls.

"Buck, you know what? I think you finally picked the right one." Trish nudged Jennifer's shoulder.

Still suspicious of the two humans, the fluffy groundhog, at seeing Christina approach, let out a squeal and scurried off to one of its many holes. "You've finally come up with a name for the fat rodent," Christina said, shaking her head at the two.

Trish stood and kissed Christina fully on the lips. "Fat rodent…and you wonder why Buck doesn't like you."

"What happened to the two names I suggested last week?" Christina asked, her body melting into the strength of her wife's arms. Trish had a way of always making her feel safe and loved. "Yard Destroyer or Garden Killer. They both have a truthful ring," she murmured, bringing her hand up and gliding a finger gently over Trish's soft lips.

"Mother—" Jennifer stood with her hands on her hips. "Buck has feelings, you know."

Christina rotated to her daughter. "Dear, it's called a stomachache. From everything he's been eating in my garden and the snacks you two feed it, I'm surprised he can still fit in his den." Her heart gave a slight spasm when Trish snorted. Christina lowered her head on Trish's chest and slowly inhaled the outdoor aroma of her lover. She blinked herself from the euphoric state and pointed to the house. "Speaking of eating, both of you need to go get cleaned up. Dinner will be ready soon."

Trish planted a tender kiss on her neck, then another, sending goosebumps along Christina's shoulders and neckline. Trish released her and bent forward to scoop Jennifer up in her arms. Christina followed the talkative pair through the yard toward the house.

Nearing the cobblestone patio, she suddenly came up short. "What is that?" she asked, turning her nose up to a red contraption by the toolshed door. The prehistoric device had a long handle and round wheels at the base, with woven blades twisting between the two.

Trish stopped, tossed Jennifer onto her shoulder, and glanced at where Christina was pointing. "Oh, our new reel mower. Jennifer and I found something safer and less stressful for Buck than the riding mower."

Christina swayed her head in disbelief from the two-acre yard to the unmotorized device. She figured the cutting width couldn't be more than a foot. "Do you realize how long it's going to take you to mow all that with this?" she asked. She held her arms out to their enormous yard to validate the reasoning behind her question.

Trish did a casual inspection of the yard. "A couple of hours longer, no big deal."

Christina gave a slight humph. "If you say so." She moved up the steps and held open the door. "Let's get one thing straight. Yard Destroyer will never be allowed in this house." She stepped inside just in time to notice the amused expressions and shared winks between Trish and Jennifer. "I saw that," she mumbled and closed the door behind her. "I'm serious."

When neither responded, Christina winced. She could almost picture round rodent turds throughout every inch of their beautifully kept home. The thought was repulsive.

Once dinner was over, they followed their regular routine. Jennifer took her bath, and both moms read and tucked her into bed before Christina made her way to the master bathroom to take a much-needed shower. She let the water run cooler tonight, aware of how tired her aching body was. No matter how her eyes kept trying to close, she wasn't about to give in. She knew what was waiting for her in their bed.

Every night after she and Trish crawled under the blanket together, the love that emerged always sent Christina's mind, body, and soul toward unexplored frontiers. Their passion ended with an elevated degree of blissful sleep, as their spent, naked bodies intertwined collectively, arms encircling the other. An experience unlike anything one could comprehend from reading the best romance novels ever written.

Trish didn't merely know where all her hidden secrets lay, but she had a way of reading Christina's holistic self to understand exactly what she needed under the sheets. Slow, passionate love, down and dirty sex, a quicky, or to take things slow—whatever her body craved, Trish provided. On the rare occasions when time wasn't an issue and Jennifer was staying overnight with a grandparent, Trish would stretch out Christina's building orgasm in a cascade of limitless pleasure before evoking a grand finale of explosions. Trish was her king in bed, who pampered Christina as a treasured queen.

The bedroom was by far Trish's area to control. Christina relinquished the reins every night, knowing Trish would steer them on the precise course they needed to go. Thinking of what that might be tonight heightened her building ache. She toweled off and ran a brush through her hair. The second she opened the bathroom door, her heart briefly fell out of rhythm, and her anticipation faded. The bed was empty. The room was deserted. She headed to her side of the walk-in closet, tossed on her robe, and made her way across the bedroom.

"Going somewhere?"

Christina's heart leap at the love in her wife's penetrating, blue eyes. She let out a long sigh and angled the left side of her lips into a smirk. "I was thinking you forgot about me and decided on sleeping with Yard Destroyer." She watched Trish's cocky grin curl upward, and her stomach fluttered. God, could Trish be any sexier?

"I thought about it but realized what I'd be missing if I did." Trish lazily shrugged. "Might sneak out later once my wife's asleep." She moved inside the room, placed a small box on the bench at the base of the bed, and locked the door.

"Are we requiring toys now?"

Trish held her arrogant smile, as she pulled back the covers and removed her shorts and T-shirt. Christina felt childishly nervous at how confident her lover had become. An experience that happened occasionally when Christina wasn't sure what to expect. Her mouth watered and the dampness between her thighs intensified when Trish stepped closer and pulled Christina against her nicely chiseled body.

"The way you're acting, one would think this was our first time." Trish's voice was husky, seductive.

"Every night we're together feels like our first time," Christina murmured.

Trish's hands slowly slid against the skin on Christina's shoulders and down her arms before removing the robe from around her. As the fabric fell to the floor, exposing her nakedness, Christina's body let loose a tiny shudder. Trish's smile widened, and she bent down to meet the hunger of Christina's mouth with her own. Frantically, their tongues searched, tasting the sweet combination of flavors the two offered together. Without breaking the connection or the level of passion, Trish picked Christina up and carried her the few steps to bed.

Christina tried to guide Trish down onto the king-sized mattress with her, but Trish's body remained unmoving, their lips being the sole connection. She tightened her grip and pulled, but her effort was useless. Trish grasped Christina's hands and dropped them onto the bed seconds before their lips pulled apart.

Christina pushed herself up onto her elbows and frowned as Trish turned away. "Where are you going?" She pouted.

Trish didn't answer right away but went to the bench past the edge of the bed. She picked up the box. "Would you like me to rush to the end and read you the last few pages, or let this story unfold on its own?"

Christina stifled her giggle, dropped her head to the pillow, and waited. Trish moved over and flipped off the light, casting the room in almost complete darkness. Christina opened her mouth but thought it best not to protest twice in one night, and definitely not within the same minute. She remained still, eyed the movements of Trish's shadowy silhouette, and listened closely to the unfamiliar noises in the room. It sounded as if Trish opened or gently smacked something next to her, and Christina's curiousness kept her fatigued eyes parted a little longer.

The stereo powered on to a low rhythm, with no vocals joining the gentle beat of soft musical instruments. Christina's eyes, still threatening to close, blinked several times as her body sank more into the bed's softness. The startling touch to her foot sent an alarmed jolt through her, and she pulled her foot back reflexively. Trish's hands held on and braced Christina's foot in place. Seconds later, Trish worked a thick lotion into her foot's aching arch, and the tension in the leg relaxed. Her toes extended slightly, grateful for the craved attention to their throbbing soreness.

The long minutes dragged peacefully by. Trish's skilled hands worked out each foot, then slowly upward along both calves, over Christina's thighs, and down her right and left arms. Trish rolled Christina's body gently over and trailed the deep massage along her neck and shoulders and twice throughout her upper and lower back. Each time Trish kneaded out a knotted muscle, her hands discovered another not far away. Every spasming knot Trish massaged transformed Christina's vocal releases from fluttering gasps to long, drawn-out moans. Surprised, Christina wiped at her mouth when she realized she was drooling on the pillow.

Once Trish finally rolled her around, Christina's entire body felt like a spoonful of gelatin, and she closed her eyes. When they flew opened, she was frantic. Did she fall asleep? She couldn't see Trish any longer. Had she gone? The moment Trish's shadow moved beside her, her mind eased and the muscles in her body returned to a restful state. Without warning, Trish's firm hands stroked a lighter lotion over her left breast, then her right. Her lover's mouth followed. A warm, moist tongue fondled both nipples, one right after the other. The tingling from this new lotion was enticing, as Trish continued the rubbing sensation down Christina's stomach and along the insides of each thigh.

Trish pulled Christina's legs farther apart, and Christina felt her pulse double in speed and strength. Enjoying the pampering, her body relaxed further, while she forced the reflection of sleep as far away from her mind as she could. A sound emerged again resembling a click from a lid. When Trish's hand slowly spread a cold gel over and through the lips between her thighs, Christina arched her hips and moaned. The sensation of coldness transformed into an intense heat, and Trish's hand caressed the cream firmly between Christina's dampened lips and over her swelling mound before pushing firmly through the tiny hairs.

Trish climbed on top of her and pressed a strong thigh between her legs. Their kiss was fervent, Trish's mouth as warm and wet as her own. Christina brought her fingers down, touching the sheer dampness between Trish's own legs. Christina's eyes rolled pleasurably upward at the proof of how aroused Trish grew by massaging her body. Feeling a ravenous need, Christina's fingers pushed in, searching to breach her lover's opening.

Jerking her hips away, Trish removed Christina's hand and cooed against her wife's demanding protest. "Stop," Trish finally whispered. She kissed Christina along her cheek and neck. "Close your eyes and relax."

Trish drifted her mouth downward, directing it below Christina's bellybutton. She spread Christina's legs out again, this time farther than before. Tasting nothing else, Trish's mouth covered Christina's wetness completely, her lover clearly hungry for what her body offered. Both the throbbing between her legs and her breaths intensified with each long stroke of Trish's tongue. Her back arched, her hands clasped tight to the backboard, and her feet flexed upward. As the minutes slowly passed, each gradual sway of her hips and every harmonious caress from Trish, gliding her tongue up against Christina's swollen mound, brought the building pressure of her approaching release to higher levels.

When Christina's muscles tightened and her Spanish flowed thickly out, Trish changed gears and pressed her tongue in, working it vehemently around, strengthening the power of the organism seconds before Christina's body produced a phenomenal eruption.

Yes… Trish was her king…

Christina rolled over and searched for the arms which always encircled her when she awoke in the mornings. Once she realized the bed was empty, she kept her eyes closed and slightly lifted her head. She yelled toward the bathroom, "Honey, please hurry. I need some early morning snuggling before my alarm goes off."

She shifted farther under the down comforter and waited. After a few seconds of silence, she flipped the thick covers off and shouted out, "Trish." Her eyelids blinked against the light engulfing the room through the parted curtains. Unnerved, she spun to the clock on the nightstand. Damn, the time was already after eight. She was on the schedule to help her mother prep the kitchen at six this morning.

With heart-racing haste, she leapt from the bed. When her feet touched the floor, she swayed a bit, as she tried to blink away the groggy fog blurring her thoughts. Her body felt off-kilter and her mind confused. Where was Trish and why didn't she wake her?

Mentally rushing through the morning list, she quickly decided what needed to get done and what she could skip from the daily ritual. Like her time-to-wake-up shower and the cherished two cups of coffee she consumed before leaving the house. She tossed on her robe and raced from the room to wake Jennifer. Opening her daughter's door, she saw the empty bed, the mermaid bedding neatly made, and Jennifer's missing schoolbag. Even more confused, she hurried back to her room. On a closer inspection, she spotted a folded piece of paper sitting beside the alarm clock. Christina scrambled forward and snatched it off the nightstand.

My dearest love,
Heading to the restaurant to help your mother open. Susan is showing up at seven to get Jennifer and take her to school. Sleep in as long as you need. I took the entire day off. I'll see you when you arrive at the restaurant. FYI, your mother and I would sure love a cappuccino around noonish.
Love your wife...Trish

Christina clutched the note to her chest and brushed at the corner of her eyes. Trish never ceased to amaze her. She pressed her lips to the paper, overwhelmed by the profound love she had for her wife. She swallowed down a lump in her throat, as she folded the paper and placed it tenderly in the top drawer of her dresser.

When her eyes swept past her closet, over the stereo system sitting on the dresser, and to her bathroom door, a surge of unfamiliar delight coursed through her veins. How long had it been since she had a morning all to herself? Weeks or months? Today she faced no strict schedule and no feelings of dread at having to rush so all of them would be on time. There were no morning responsibilities to tackle, and she wouldn't have to shout out every five minutes for Jennifer and Trish to "hurry!" The only dilemma she faced this morning was...where to start?

She searched through her playlist, found a song she hadn't heard in months, pressed play, and made her way into the bathroom. A nice, hot bubble bath was the perfect way to begin a morning as wonderful as this.

Popping some aspirin into her mouth and chewing, Trish added more pots to the soapy water and adjusted her hairnet. She wasn't sure why she needed to wear one. Her hair was short, she barely handled the food, and it wasn't like the health department was around anymore to make surprise inspections. When familiar arms slid around her waistline, she temporarily closed her eyes and fully took in the feeling of warmth they offered.

"If you're planning on doing anything perverted, you'll need to hurry. My wife will be here soon." Trish rotated and stared into the emerald eyes of the most beautiful woman in the world. Sucking in air, she acted startled. "Christina, what are you doing here so early?"

Christina shot her a playful scowl. She retrieved the disposable coffee cup from the counter behind her and brought it to her lips. "For that, I'll drink your cappuccino."

Trish frowned. "Fine. I quit. Find someone else to wash your damn dishes." Trish untied her apron. She was about to remove it from around her head until Christina passed her the drink. "That's what I thought," Trish grumbled with a sly grin.

Christina threw her arms around Trish's neck and placed kisses all over her face. Trish laughed and held the cup at arm's length so it wouldn't spill. The other arm she wrapped around Christina's waistline and lifted her until her wife's feet were off the floor. "I guess you enjoyed yourself?"

"A full-body massage, mind-blowing sex, and a bathtub experience of warm water, bubbles, and Cher. I would say I most definitely enjoyed myself. Unfortunately, I passed out before I could return the favor."

Trish eyed her suspiciously. "You better be referring to the rubdown and sex I gave you last night, and the actual singer who died years ago. If I find out there's a woman going around the city with the name Cher, I'm going to be pissed."

Christina wiggled from Trish's embrace, stole the hot beverage, and took a sip. She returned the drink, gave Trish another kiss, and headed to the employees' locker room.

"Hey, woman," Trish called out when the door opened. "Which Cher is it?"

Christina flipped her the bird seconds before the door closed.

Shocked Christina would display such an improper gesture on the off chance her mother might have noticed, Trish turned to the sink and suppressed a giggle. She plunged her hands into the soapy water and bellowed out the words to "Gypsies, Tramps, and Thieves," while wondering if she should call in tomorrow as well. Best not, Phillips would track her down and kill her if she did.

CHAPTER TWO

Wiping the sweat from her forehead, Trish opened the bottle of aspirins and shook out several. She consumed them with a mouthful of water. She debated chewing on a few more but thought better of it.

"Still getting the headaches?" Sergeant First Class Stan Phillips asked, as he loaded the last of the duffel bags into Trish's Gladiator.

Shoving the bottle into her pocket, Trish pulled the warehouse door closed to the grating sounds of squeaking metal and engaged the lock. They constructed the two-level building behind the old hotel a year ago when the teams emptied every supply bunker from here to Kansas City. After already filling the armory and supply basements at each of the four barracks in Rapid City, this structure became a swiftly erected necessity.

She engaged the alarm and headed for the vehicle. "Occasionally. It gets worse when I leave the city."

Phillips gently seized her arm. "Have you told Doctor Burgos you're still getting them?"

She shook her head. "He has enough on his plate to worry about. With Eva and Christina being upset and overseeing New Underwood's completion this week, I don't need to add a simple headache into his mixture of other crap."

"Trish, a simple headache? We almost lost you. You were in a coma for over a year, and since you've woken, you've had headaches so bad you look as if you're going to be physically sick. Don't think I haven't noticed." He shook his head in frustration.

"Until you talk to the Doc, no more lifting weights or doing twenty-five-mile runs."

"Phillips, I really am fine."

Phillips sighed. "Let him give you a full physical and maybe another EEG. Keeping you alive is top on our priority list, even above our mission." He rubbed his hand over the base of his neck. "I wish you would have said something before your run this morning. Damn, I had you lifting over twenty-five-hundred pounds today. Why didn't you tell me?"

"It's a headache, you big softy. Nothing more." Before he could protest further, she headed to the Gladiator. "Aralyn's taking me somewhere for my birthday tonight. I'll go see Doctor Burgos first thing tomorrow."

"Oh, that's right. You're nineteen today. Happy Birthday, Trish. Sorry. I forgot."

Trish eyed him evenly. "Are you sure you forgot, or are you covering for a surprise party this evening?"

Phillips's scowl affirmed she was right.

"Jennifer has a sleepover on a school night. All my friends, extended family, everyone has other plans. Even my wife and mother-in-law are too busy with a last-minute catering job at the restaurant, and all this is after I completely lost my eighteenth birthday from the coma last year. Easy to figure out—" She flicked a simple hand gesture his way. "You're all lying."

"Well, damn," Phillips grumbled. The edges of his eyes wrinkled. "Christina and Susan have been organizing this since Christmas. You better act surprised."

Trish opened the passenger door. "I will. Can you please tell me one thing? Will Jennifer be there? The idea of celebrating my very first birthday party without my daughter is heartbreaking."

Phillips's face relaxed on the side of uncertainty. He opened the driver's door and snatched his uniform overshirt from the seat. "Didn't they throw you a covert one in NORAD? Aralyn and the others in section A were planning you a party for your seventeenth birthday."

Trish climbed into the Gladiator. "My father had me sedated in his lab for two weeks before Aralyn could break me out. I slept right through my birthday. They packed my gifts but no party."

"Yeah, that's right," Phillips said, fastening the last button on his camouflage jacket. He slid behind the wheel. "Yes, Jennifer will be there but for an hour at the most. Then she'll spend a spoiled evening with Grandma Burgos. Apparently, Christina has afterparty plans for the birthday girl." He gave an exaggerated shudder and followed it with an elaborate illustration of a few dry heaves. She punched his arm, and he laughed. "Seriously, picturing you having sex isn't a pleasant visual. How would you feel if the roles were reversed?"

She closed her mind before any unwanted images of him with a naked unknown emerged. "Good point."

He flipped through Trish's playlist and selected one of the soft-rock hits of 2060s. "When're you planning on telling Christina about New Underwood and our mission?"

"A day or two after the party." Trish rubbed both sides of her head in the hopes of relieving the building pressure. "I don't know. Maybe tomorrow or Friday. I want to give us as much of this weekend to get past the expected arguments as I can before our team starts on Monday."

Pulling away from behind the old hotel that was headquarters for Aralyn's militia, Phillips finally let out a long sigh. "I'm glad. The woman deserves to know."

Silently, Trish agreed.

Christina fastened the last of the streamers to the ceiling by the bar and climbed off the ladder. She stood in silence, as she inspected the finished product. With all Trish's other birthdays being uncelebrated by a loveless father in NORAD, Christina couldn't wait until she experienced what a real birthday celebration was like. One full of love, family, and friends. It all needed to be perfect. Her amazing wife deserved nothing less.

She placed the roll of tape on a nearby table and took the fruity drink from Karen, the owner and weekday bartender of the longest running club still left in Rapid City. Since many of the short-term citizens headed to Kansas City to build a new life outside of the bunkers, the two largest adult establishments closed, which were by far more elaborate than this low-lit, subtle dwelling.

This club was by no means inadequate. The structure itself housed two fully stocked bars, a decent-sized dance floor, a game room with a pool table and dartboards off the kitchen, and a DJ booth for the weekends. With the original citizens coming in during the weekdays to have a simple burger and fries for lunch or a relaxing drink with friends, Karen continued working the bar herself with one server and cook on staff. On the weekends, her younger business partner and additional employees turned the down-to-earth atmosphere into a dance club. Because of the shuttle service the club provided to each of the four militia barracks throughout the city, this bar was usually the go-to spot for Aralyn's soldiers, especially during the busy weekends.

"You and Susan have done a remarkable job decorating," Karen said. "Place actually looks cheerful."

Christina scanned the decorations one last time. "If you ever came by on Friday or Saturday nights, you would see a complete transformation to your place."

Karen grunted. "I'm more than done with weekend hangovers and sharing my bed with a man whose name I can't remember the next morning. Give me a good book to read, a crackling fire, and a blanket to snuggle into, and I become as content as a hibernating bear in winter."

Christina took a few sips of her drink as she watched the hired DJ hook up the karaoke machine on the stage beside the dance floor. "A blanket to snuggle into. Is the blanket named Jason Givens by any chance?"

Karen gasped. "That man cannot keep a secret to save his life."

Christina's swell of success amplified, and she lowered her glass. "He actually said nothing. I figured it out last month at our wedding. You just now affirmed it. The way you both acted around each other that night, I'm sure there are others who suspect the same thing."

Karen seemed perturbed but not surprised. "I was afraid of that. We both had more to drink than we planned." She squeezed Christina's forearm. "Please keep it to yourself. Jason's worried Aralyn will kick him from Trish's team if she finds out, and that would break his heart."

Christina felt a tug of uncertainty work its way in. "Why would Aralyn do that?" The second she asked, the voice inside her head shouted. Deep down she already knew the answer.

"With the danger of the mission your father and Trish are preparing for, Aralyn hand-selected their team from the soldiers who were unattached. I almost asked Jason to turn down the assignment, but he would never forgive himself if something happened to Trish and he wasn't there. She's like a daughter to him."

Christina bit back a cry as every nerve in her extremities tingled from her sudden sense of panic. Her father and Aralyn's original plan. They were going through with it, and Trish hadn't told her. How long had it been since Trish agreed to their dangerous proposal? Days, weeks, months? Was it before or after their wedding?

"Christina, your hands are shaking. What's wrong?" Karen moved a chair around and guided Christina into the seat. "Here, let me hold your drink before you spill it all over yourself." Abruptly, Karen's hand jerked up and covered her mouth. "You didn't know," she muttered, sounding both surprised and worried. "Christina, I'm so sorry. Stay here. I'll get Susan."

Christina remained unmoving as every part of her felt strangely frightened and utterly alone. When this discussion was first brought up during the New Year's celebration, Christina had demanded Trish refuse the ludicrous proposal. Trish's responsibility was now to her family. She needed to stop being so reckless with her safety and put their relationship and daughter above her own need to fix an unrepairable world. One in chaos, filled with dangers which had almost claimed her life the prior year.

Then two months ago, when her father had insisted on approaching the topic to Trish again, Christina had given him an ultimatum, drop this hazardous proposal, which was sure to get him and whoever joined the foolish crusade slaughtered, or continue his irrational campaign and become shunned from his daughter's life until he came to his senses. When he didn't agree, Eva, just as upset as Christina, had kicked her stubborn, reckless husband from their bed and home a few days later. That night, Christina and Trish had gotten into a heated argument, lasting for several days. Eventually, Trish dropped the matter.

Captain Susan Travis hurried over. She was holding a half-empty package of deflated balloons that still needed helium. "Christina, Karen said you wanted…Christina? What's going on?"

Surging with wave after wave of fear and anger, Christina fought to stabilize the trembling in her body. "Did you know?"

Susan knelt beside the chair and clasped a hand over Christina's. "Know what? Christina, what's happened?"

"Their mission, Aralyn and my father, they're going through with it, and so is Trish. Did you know?" she asked, her words pleading to the woman beside her. "I need you to be truthful, Susan. I can't take anymore dishonesty. Did you know?"

Wide eyed, Susan shook her head. "No Christina, I didn't know. Ever since our disagreement at the New Year's party, Aralyn stopped talking about it. I figured the issue was settled." She spoke to Karen, who was still holding Christina's drink. "Please radio Sergeant Phillips for me. He needs to come here at once."

Trish exited the vehicle and followed Aralyn to the side entrance of the club. She felt a burst of excitement at knowing she was about to celebrate her very first birthday party with her wife, daughter, and extended family.

Beaming with pride, Aralyn motioned her inside.

Upon entry, the place appeared unnaturally deserted. No music played and other than the dim lights hanging over the main bar, complete darkness shrouded the place. Captain Carlen Strong, Staff Sergeant Jason Givens, Phillips, and Karen were sitting in huddled discussion at the bar, which was covered by a piling mess of discarded balloons and party streamers. When Karen veered her attention in their direction, she signaled to the others. All rotated in their seats with downcast expressions. At once, Trish's chest tightened.

"What is this?" Aralyn more of demanded then asked. "Where is everyone?"

Phillips stood from his barstool. "Ma'am, Christina and Captain Travis canceled the party an hour ago and sent everyone home." Givens kept his attention on his lap as Phillips sheepishly said, "They know about New Underwood."

Hustling up the moon-cast steps, Trish dug for her keys and unlocked the front door to their home. From the enclosed porch to the open floorplan of the front room and dining room, all lights were off. Not bothering to toss her keys in the bowl, Trish rushed upstairs. A sliver of light pierced the blackened hallway from the open slit of their bedroom door. She could hear the rhythmic beat of Adele's "Rolling in the Deep" thumping from the other side of the gap. Not losing her measure of urgency, Trish hurried forward and entered the master suite.

Her heart went from a thundering knock to a sluggish ache. Red, puffy outlines from excessive crying encircled Christina's emerald eyes. Christina had a half-drained bottle of wine in her hands and an empty bottle sitting on the nightstand beside her chair. She raised the bottle to Trish, a form of twisted salute, before refilling the crystal glass her other hand was clasping. Downing the burgundy-red liquid with one gulp, she refilled her glass and slammed the bottle on the table with enough force to vibrate the items resting on its surface. Slowly, she climbed to her feet.

Trish hurried over to help steady her swaying wife. Christina jerked her arm away and forcefully shook her head against the offering. "Leave. Sleep downstairs tonight. I can't bear to look at you."

With her mouth partially opened, unable to figure out a way to ease her wife's anger, Trish watched Christina head to the dresser. She pressed the button on the stereo to replay the song, then the repeat button so it would restart once the track finished. She spilled a splash of wine when she lowered her glass to the dresser's surface. Pivoting unsteadily around, her eyes locked with Trish's momentarily before she turned her head away and cried.

Trish had never seen Christina's body shake so violently or her tears spill over so completely as what she was witnessing now. Her bottom lip quivered, and she stepped in and wrapped Christina in her arms. Christina's arms flailed and swung out against Trish's chest, growing wild, insistent that she not be touched by the same embrace that encircled her every night they slept together.

The moment Trish removed her hold, Christina brought her hand up and slapped a hard smack across Trish's face. Trish took a startled step backward, surprised green and blue eyes staring at one another. Christina raised a shaking hand and covered her damp lips. Her eyes closed against her building grief.

Without saying another word, Trish fled the room. Feeling a surge of emotions rush in, Trish paced around the front room. She wanted to cry, scream, and lash out at every object she saw. Fighting to control the heartrending emotional rollercoaster, She kicked off her shoes and removed her socks, stretching out on the couch. She decided to count from one to as far as she needed until sleep overcame her or her tears finally fell. At this point, she would gladly take either.

Trish wasn't sure how long she had been asleep when she felt hands unfasten her belt buckle and unclasp her jeans. She opened her eyes to Christina's silhouette hovering above, her fingers desperately working the zipper downward. The powerful aroma of alcohol filled the air. Trish reached out, but Christina pushed her hands away and wrestled at trying to lower the thick material past Trish's hips. Trish's heart ached at the pain her own lack of candidness had caused.

Giving over control, Trish raised her hips and brought her hands down to help Christina with removing her pants. Again, Cristina forced away her hands. Leaving her hips raised, Trish brought her arms up. She covered her face and fought against her regret. Whatever Christina needed her to do to help her work through her heartache, Trish was going to oblige.

Once Christina threw her jeans to the floor, she yanked at the boxer-briefs with heightened determination. Trish heard the fabric rip, and they too slid down her legs and were pulled over her feet. Christina struggled to yank off the shirt and sports bra. Trish adjusted her body, hoping to assist her wife's inebriated efforts while not causing additional protest.

When Christina lowered herself against Trish's nakedness, Trish realized Christina wasn't wearing any clothes. She wanted to reach out and touch her wife, but she knew this would spark another heated reaction. Instead, she kept her arms up and away from the woman she longed to embrace.

Christina roughly ran her mouth over Trish's breast, sucking in the fullness and biting the hardening nipple. A surge of pleasure replaced the rush of pain, and Christina drew Trish's breast farther into her mouth, as if she were angrily starving for the taste it offered. The fierceness in which Christina's mouth worked over her stomach and thighs both frightened and stimulated her. She parted her legs seconds before Christina's mouth covered the top of her wetness and plunged several fingers deep inside.

Trish's release took only a few minutes, with an emotional force pressing past the boundaries of lucidity. She shuddered against the impact of her convulsing muscles, her vocals surrendering a boisterous, vibrating moan. The intensity of the ripples against Christina's unyielding tongue and finger thrusts caused her brain to swim in a sea of rolling blurriness, which was beyond imaginable.

When Christina broke the connection, Trish's drained body slumped against the couch. She reached for her love, but the outcome didn't change. Christina shoved her hands away and climbed off. Before Trish had time to react, she felt Christina's thigh brush against her cheek as her determined wife climbed over, straddling her wetness onto Trish's mouth.

Trish's surprise was overshadowed by her aching need to bring Christina to a release of her own. In doing so, maybe the orgasm would soften some of the hurt and anger hardening her wife's affections. She tried working her mouth around slowly, but Christina swayed her hips to her own rhythm, as she pressed herself fully onto Trish's moving tongue. When her hands encircled Christina's thighs, Christina didn't brush them aside. Instead, she firmly guided them up to each of her breasts. Christina didn't speak, only rocketed herself around until her body stiffened, followed by an overflowing outcry. The instant she finally dropped onto Trish's legs, Trish realized with a heightened sense of sadness, Christina was crying.

She reached for her, but as if expecting it, Christina jumped up and staggered from the room. Alarmed, Trish got to her feet and followed her up the stairs, her heart heavy with worry. The moment the bedroom door slammed shut, Trish heard the click of the engaging lock. She rushed in and gently knocked on the door.

"Go away," Christina's trembling voice called out from the other side.

"Please open up." Trish lowered her forehead down and painfully listened to the muffled whimpering. "I love you, Christina. Please open the door so we can talk."

After a few minutes of no response, Trish moved away from the cool surface and headed defeatedly to the solitude of the couch.

Bringing her hand up to the throbbing above her eyes, Trish squinted out the light from the window above her. She removed the throw blanket and struggled to her feet, while trying hard to keep her balance. She had to take a few breaths to steady herself, as she retrieved her clothing from the floor and made her way upstairs. Her brief excitement at seeing the bedroom door standing ajar faded when she noticed Christina wasn't in the room. Unable to console the unsettling nausea, she rushed to the bathroom. She barely made it to the toilet before her body expelled the rising sickness.

Once her stomach convulsions finally ceased, she lowered herself onto the cold tile and closed her eyes. If one could experience the sensation of death while still being alive, this agony is what the experience would feel like. Trish was sure of it. She remained unmoving for what felt like hours until she believed herself strong enough to stand without the twinge of nausea pulling at her stomach. She reached out for the sink, retrieved several aspirins, and choked them down with a handful of water from the faucet.

The warm shower brought with it a level of clarity, which helped soothe the ache she felt all over. Trish toweled off, brushed her teeth, and moved through the bedroom to go change. It was during a brief inspection of the newly made bed that she spotted the envelope propped up against her pillow. Her name was written on the front in her wife's graceful handwriting. She held her breath as she stared at the poised, blue sway in each letter. For some reason, the idea of touching the envelope, much less opening it and reading the contents, terrified her.

Slowly, she made her way over, grasped the edge of the envelope, and peeled open the flap. As her hands unfolded the single slip of paper, her eyes focused on the wording inside. Sucking in a deep breath, she raised her hand, clasping at the sharp stab in her head and dropped onto the bed.

Trish,
I can't do this anymore. You have hurt me deeply. I don't know how, or if, I'll be able to trust you again. Please pack the things you need and leave. Don't contact me, I must have some time to work through everything. I spoke with my father. He said you can stay with him until we figure out where to go from here. As far as Jennifer is concerned, I know she's also your daughter, and this will be hard for her. If you would like to see her, please go through my mother to arrange contact.
Christina

After Trish read through the letter a second time, she reached for the radio on the nightstand. Her hand was shaking so violently, she struggled to press the button to open the link. Once the line finally engaged, and the voice of her godmother answered, Trish's words came out scarcely audible. "I need you," she breathed. She dropped the handheld.

Aralyn rushed into the room when she saw Trish lying in a huddled ball beside the dresser. Her nose had bled out onto the carpet, but not enough to be too concerned about, and the red streaks above Trish's lips were already drying.

"Trish," she said, rubbing at the towel along Trish's shaking back. "Trish, sit up and let me look."

When Trish obliged, Aralyn noticed the crumpled-up paper her goddaughter was clutching. "Sergeant Phillips," she called out, and once the extra set of hands came forward, they both managed to get Trish onto the bed.

"It's over," Trish said and sniveled. She pushed the wadded letter toward her godmother.

Aralyn's heart broke, seeing the battered defeat embodying her goddaughter. Trish was the strongest woman she'd ever known, even more fierce than Julie, Trish's mother, was. Yet, here she sat ragged, in a state Aralyn never would have believed was possible. Opening the letter, her features transformed into a heated scowl. With the night she had, arguing with Susan, this hateful note reopened the freshly closed wound, refueling her anger all over again.

"What is it, Colonel?" Phillips asked.

She passed him the paper. As he read it, his face turned downward.

"Sergeant Phillips, I'll get her dressed and take her to see Doctor Burgos. I need you to call Captain Strong and Sergeant Givens. I want everything of Trish's packed and moved to New Underwood. Put her in the suite next to mine and have Captain Strong move to the other side. Tell her what's happened. She'll know what needs to be done."

Proceeding with urgency, Phillips left the room. Aralyn turned to Trish. "Honey, let's get you up and moving—" Her words broke off as a paleness washed over Trish's face and she reached out for the wastebasket by the bed. She handed it to Trish seconds before her goddaughter vomited. She rubbed Trish's arm and waited, thinking of how spiteful and spoiled the women in their lives were behaving.

CHAPTER THREE

"Your labs came back normal, for *you* anyway, Trish," Doctor Burgos wittily commented, apparently trying to lighten her disheartened mood. "As for your EEG, it's, well—"

"Oh, for the love of…James, will you stop dragging this out and simply tell us?" Aralyn insisted.

Trish squeezed her godmother's hand, as Aralyn shifted uneasily beside her.

Doctor Burgos cleared his throat. "Yes, of course." His eyes darted from Aralyn to Trish. "Your EEG has drastically changed since the one I took after your coma. Parts of your brain appear more active than before. I think this has something to do with the headaches and the nosebleeds you've been getting."

"How do we correct it?" Aralyn asked.

"I'm not sure if we can. However, I do have a hypothesis on what may be causing this. Yet, given Trish's irregularities, my belief is but a loose-stretched theory." When neither spoke, he went on. "I feel that what happened in NORAD is one of the rare gifts your mother's compound bestowed on you. That night your brain opened Pandora's Box in its own kinda way. With the damage your ability caused, we all insisted you replace the lid and never open the box again. Unfortunately, I think the entity inside doesn't just want to remain out, it wants to be utilized."

Trish frowned. "Okay, now I'm picturing a radioactive goo floating around inside my brain, seeking to destroy the rest of humanity and take over the world."

James laughed. "Maybe I was being overly dramatic when I threw out my theory."

Aralyn snapped out her disappointment. "Do you think?"

Doctor Burgos hurriedly said, "From the video Carlen gave me on what happened that night, and the damage to, not only you, but Frank's men, I believe your brain used one of your gifts as a defense mechanism when it sensed your need and the danger of those you were trying to protect. Being as how you've never used this component of your brain before and considering the strength in which the ability activated, you gravely injured your brain. Repairing the vast amount of damage was why your body remained in a coma for so long. Now, this ability is trying to function, but you're suppressing it and, in doing so, building up pressure on an untapped resource. Hence the headaches and nosebleeds. With the stress you were in last night, your mental strain added a rawness to this pressure."

Aralyn sighed. "*That* makes a bit more sense. So, what is this gift of hers?"

By the uncertain way he considered the question, Trish wasn't sure if Doctor Burgos was going to answer. He swiveled his seat around, powered down his processor, and spun back. "I also have a theory regarding this. Several actually. But until we get Trish to New Underwood and are in the newly erected vault, which is what I call it, then her ability isn't safe to test to see how accurate I am." He stood from the rolling stool, as if to say they were done.

Aralyn grumbled. "Your theory?"

He raised his brow. "Oh, right. I think her ability has to do with either high or low-frequency sound waves. Somewhat resembling what dolphins or whales use, yet different. There might even be a form of telekinesis hidden there, but until we get the chance to test my theory safely, it's all a waiting game for a few more days. The work crews are scheduled to finish by tomorrow tonight and return to Rapid City. I think the fewer people around when we experiment with this ability, the better."

Trish clambered from the bed and followed Aralyn and Doctor Burgos from the room. The idea of them intentionally provoking what happened in NORAD didn't merely make her uncomfortable, it frightened her.

Christina recoiled from the pain and sent the scalding pot to the ground with an echoing clatter. Bits of red sauce splattered outward, the rest covering several of the black tiles along the floor of the restaurant and encircling the soles of her shoes. Swirling puffs of smoky heat rose from the piles of spaghetti sauce. She jumped from the mess and rushed to the sink, right as her mom flipped on the cold water. Cursing to herself, Christina submerged the reddening appendage while her mother hurried off, fetching the ointment to doctor the burn on her throbbing hand. No one said a word, but Christina felt the servers and several patrons had heads pointed in their direction to see what the new wave of commotion was.

"Want me to tell them it'll be twenty more minutes on their order?" one of their servers asked.

"What the hell do you think?" Christina spat with angry tears streaming down her cheeks.

"Christina!" her mother barked, before nodding to the wide-eyed teenager. "Yes, Betty, thank you." She directed her scowl at her daughter. "I know the last few days have been hard on you, but that's no excuse to take it out on others."

Christina glanced upward to the drop-in ceiling, as she fought to manage her tears. She couldn't speak, yet, for fear of losing control altogether. She had gone through two nights of sleeping alone, two days since she saw Trish, and random bouts of Jennifer's half-answered questions had turned into youthful defiance. Every part of her wanted to rush off and find her wife, who wasn't staying with her father as Christina had assumed. Trish was instead unreachable, as Phillips and Givens had informed her when she inquired about her wife's welfare.

"I'm sorry, Mom. I'll apologize to Betty later."

Eva's scowl softened. "Do you need to go home? I can cover your orders until Jeremy shows for dinner."

"I'll be fine. Honest. Staying busy helps."

Eva studied her daughter briefly and signaled toward the backdoor. "Why don't you take out the trash? Enjoy a few minutes of fresh air, and I'll remake the sauce until you return."

Blinking away the dampness, Christina kissed her mother's cheek and did as she suggested. The moment she stepped outside and lifted her head toward the clear sky, she felt somewhat better.

"Hey, are you okay? Here, let me toss that for you."

Christina jumped sideways, startled by the woman's voice. The unknown individual abruptly snatched the trash bag from her grasp. Shifting her eyes away from the sky's hazy brightness, an average height woman with wavy, red hair came into view. Christina took a few deep breaths to calm her fight-or-flight reaction and politely did her best to return the soldier's friendly greeting. This was the same soldier who had come to Trish's aid the night her wife awoke from the coma. "Corporal Simmons, isn't it?"

The woman transferred the bag to her other hand to offer a handshake. "It's sergeant now, but you can call me Janet."

Christina shook the hand Janet held out and motioned to the trash bag. "I can throw it away, but thanks for offering."

Janet waved her off. She moved to the dumpster sitting on the far side of the all-brick alley and hurled the bag in. She jerked her head to the side and wrinkled her nose at the rotten smell that drifted out.

"Sorry, it only gets picked up every other weekend. A few days before they take the garbage, the smell's quite repulsive," Christina said.

Janet promptly closed the lid and moved away from the container. "Repulsive is an understatement."

When the woman winked, visions of the past came crashing in. Christina pivoted with the image of hers and Trish's first kiss together. She felt her eyes water, and her finger brushed away the dampness before her tears spilled.

"Is everything all right? Do you want to sit and talk? I'm a great listener."

Christina shook her head slowly. "No, I'll be fine. I need to help my mother with finishing lunch. Maybe some other time." Without waiting for a reply, Christina headed into the building.

The second Christina stepped inside the restaurant, she spotted her mother holding the phone receiver. With a hefty amount of excitement, Eva waved her over. She covered the handset and asked Christina if Trish could pick Jennifer up after school and drop her off around eight tonight. Then pick their daughter up tomorrow and bring her home on Sunday evening.

With a ripple of relief blending with delight, Christina vigorously signaled her consent.

Eva spoke into the handset. "Of course, dropping her off at eight will be fine. If you want to pick her up here at the restaurant tomorrow, eight in the morning works as well." When the conversation ended, she hung up the business landline and smiled at her daughter. "I hope this means you'll stop burning yourself for the rest of the afternoon."

Christina giggled, blinked against the redeveloping tears, and gave her an ecstatic hug.

"I don't understand. If you just tell Mother you're sorry, you can come home."

Trish averted her eyes from her daughter and directed them at the ducks in the pond. Three were snapping and cackling over the remaining pieces of bread Jennifer had tossed to them after she finished her dinner. Her daughter was too young to experience a breakup like this. The reality of the pain Trish had caused her family was hard to endure. She gazed at her daughter tenderly. "Honey, some things are more complicated than saying you're sorry. Now please, tell me more about school. What did the teacher do after the boy threw the eraser?"

Jennifer's face turned inward. She stood from the picnic table and angrily stomped her foot on the ground. She was teetering on the edge of crying. "I don't want to talk about school. I want you to come home. If not, then I want to stay with you."

Trish gave her daughter the same look Aralyn had used on her when she was younger and underwent a bout of youthful boldness. As always, it worked. Jennifer lowered her eyes and apologized. Trish tossed away the tiny rock her fingers were toying with and picked Jennifer up in her arms. They held each other for the longest time until Jennifer kissed her on the cheek and told her mom she loved her.

Trish fought against the sudden swelling in her throat. "I love you, infinity times that." She wrapped Jennifer in another embrace. "Please, baby girl, be kind to your mother. Especially now when she needs you the most. If I find out you haven't been, I'll be disappointed. Do you understand?"

"Yes, Mom."

"Good, now let's pack up dinner. It's about time we got you home. I don't want your mother to worry."

Fidgeting with the open book still left unread, Christina glanced out the window, then to the antique grandfather clock Susan and Aralyn had given them for Christmas. Ten minutes until eight. By the excitement and anxiety fusing throughout her body, one would have guessed years had passed since she last saw either of her girls together, not a couple of days. The way Trish doted over Jennifer was heartfelt. Jennifer's big brown eyes staring up in admiration at her tall, strong, charismatic mom was breathtaking. The visual brought a heightened sense of anticipation at seeing the pair step through the doorsill and into their home.

At home, together, this was where the three of them belonged. Whether she had been or was still upset with Trish, kicking her wife from their home should never have happened. She saw that now and had paid the cost repeatedly these last few days. With heart-wrenching tears and sleepless nights, the experience left her feeling lost and alone. Damn her own stubborn temper.

The secret Trish had kept from her was painful. Infuriating even. The one woman she could always depend on—how dare she conceal something so important from their relationship. Granted, Christina understood why Trish had been reluctant to talk, why she put this discussion off to the last minute. Fear of an argument still didn't make Trish's lack of honesty right. They needed some time to work on things, to discuss the issues, even argue throughout the night again, if needed, until Trish saw reason. But not to spend more time apart. Surely Trish felt the same way.

Again, she brought her gaze to search for vehicle headlights along the sporadically lit streets. Not seeing any, she blew out a bout of frustration, veered her eyes upward and away from the darkness. As she was getting ready to reach for her coffee, the double glow of headlights appeared through the window toward the adjacent block. She held her breath and mentally begged for this vehicle to be Trish's. When the tinted-windowed Gladiator halted at the four-way stop with its blinker signaling in her direction, her excitement rose. Once the robust vehicle turned, less than a half a block away, she noticed the distinct outline as being from the same armor-plated Gladiator Trish drove, with the same framed-in-weaponry resting on top.

She jumped to her feet, straightened her silky black shorts and spaghetti strap top, which happened to be Trish's favorite outfit Christina wore before stripping for bed, and nervously fluffed out her long, wavy hair. She took a step toward the door but made a sharp beeline to the couch to collect her book. It would be best not to look too eager, she thought, hiding a grin.

With her hand tight against the doorknob, she watched the headlight's beam travel through the window, along the far wall, before stopping as Trish pulled into the driveway. The second the knock vibrated through her pressed hand, she took a deep breath and encouraged herself to count to ten. Forcing her smile to drop a bit, she rotated the handle and stepped aside with the door wide so her girls could enter.

"I love what you're wearing. Is this a bad time?"

Wide-eyed, Christina's startled expression shot to the woman with red hair. Seeing Janet standing directly inside the doorway with a bottle of wine in one hand, and probing eyes searching the full length of her outfit, or lack thereof, Christina instinctively covered her chest with her arms. "What are you doing here?" she asked, examining the militia vehicle sitting in the drive. Janet wasn't dressed for duty, but instead she was wearing a pair of black slacks, loafers, and a red button-up shirt. How was she able to sign out a weaponized vehicle? With her rank she couldn't have been issued one like Trish and the other limited number of officers had.

"Oh, I was talking to the guys, and they said you and Trish broke up several days ago. After seeing you today, I figured you could use this and possibly some company."

She passed the wine to Christina, but instead of taking the bottle, Christina eyed the offering suspiciously. She knew the gift wasn't poisonous, but her consciousness still deemed the offering toxic. Not only that, she and Trish didn't break up. They were undergoing a brief time apart. She couldn't believe how fast fictitious rumors in the militia spread.

Janet frowned and pushed the bottle even closer.

Wishing for this exchange to be over, Christina seized the wine as she stole a looksee outside. Seeing another set of headlights turn right in front of the house, her heart raced, and an instant dampness formed on both palms.

Panicked, she stared at Janet, who was also watching the second armored vehicle pulling along the curb out front. Of all the people for Trish to see standing in their home, why did it have to be *this* woman? Her eyes widened further as she assessed her own sleeping attire. Christina immediately passed the wine bottle to Janet, then the book. Desperate, she told Janet to "wait here," and she nervously stepped out onto the enclosed porch and shut the door behind her.

Seeing Trish through the rolled-down window, her heart leapt with excitement until she noticed how Trish's eyes swept over the vehicle parked in the drive. Her stomach clinched, and she wondered how Trish was going to react when she came inside and spotted Janet looming in the entryway. Christina prayed her wife could see this unusual situation for what it was, an unexpected happenstance. Maybe they would laugh later over its absurdity and drink the wine, toasting it to the bizarre evening.

She grew worried as she watched the brief exchange between Trish and Jennifer. Trish wasn't planning on leaving, was she? Stepping to the edge of the porch, her heart dropped heavily when Trish opened her door and lowered Jennifer to the ground while she herself remained seat-belted in. With their daughter approaching, Christina caught Trish's gaze. She gave her wife an exuberant wave. After a brief pause, Trish returned the exchange. Christina's hope lifted when she saw Trish undo the seatbelt and step from the vehicle. God, her wife was stunning.

When she heard the door behind her open, everything shifted. Jennifer stopped walking toward the house. Trish froze next to the vehicle, her adoring expression painfully fading.

"Did you want me to uncork this?"

Christina's breath caught in her throat at the sound of Janet's words. In horror, she painfully noticed Jennifer's surprise swivel into a scowl. Christina's hand gripped her chest when she saw her daughter pivot and rush to Trish. Trish lifted her up and spoke to the protesting girl. When Trish finally lowered their daughter to the ground, she knelt beside her, not stopping her comforting gaze or the calm flow of words. Trish's eyes went from Jennifer to Christina as she whispered to Jennifer. During her last glimpse at Christina, Trish eyed the woman standing on the porch beside her. Christina saw Janet look in the yard, as if she were seeing the new arrivals for the first time. She brought the wine bottle up, using it to wave a simple hello to Trish.

Trish's expression hardened, but just as fast, it softened. She gave Jennifer a long hug and nodded toward the house. As the girl moved forward, so did Christina. Without turning for another look, Trish climbed into her vehicle and forcefully shut the door. She pulled away from the curb, not even bothering to latch her seatbelt. Jennifer stomped up the stairs, her brooding eyes not peering in her mother's direction. She moved past both women and headed inside.

Christina spun to Janet as anger flowed from every pore. She balled up her fists and closed her eyes, her lungs grasping for a steady breath.

"I take it this is a bad time."

Was the woman serious? With a somber grunt, Christina headed to the door. "Take your wine and leave. I need to go speak with my daughter." She stepped through the entryway, closed the door, and latched it. Overwhelmed by the sting of sharp disappointment, she couldn't help but cry.

The moment Trish was clear of the main gate, she pressed on the gas pedal, surging the vehicle toward the outside gate a few miles away. She needed to get free of this place, make it before the sergeant-on-call deemed it too dark out to open the barrier and let her leave the outer perimeter. She couldn't stay inside the city another night. Maybe she would head to New Underwood early and see if Carlen had programmed in her gate access. After all, her things were there. Or maybe she'd pitch a tent and take her chances with the infected. Anything was better than this.

Pulling up to the last gate, a guard waved her vehicle a few feet forward as another stood off to the side. She lowered her window and pointed to the exit. He peered at her and dropped his eyes to her chest. She was about to reach out and backhand him until he slowly shook his head. "Sorry, Captain Webber. I can't let you pass without the proper gear."

"Come again?" she said, scowling.

"Order came down from HQ this morning. Troops need to be in full battle-rattle before exiting the last gate in the evenings."

She peeked over her shoulder and turned back to the corporal to ask, "Do you not see the mounds of gear in my armored vehicle? I believe I'm prepared enough, don't you?"

Ignoring her comment, he assessed his wristwatch, and peered upward to the sliver of reddish-orange skyline fading from view. "Sorry, ma'am, orders. Seeing as how you won't have time to return here properly dressed, it's best you wait until morning to head out."

Angered, Trish jerked the transmission in park and climbed out.

Receiving her full-on glare, the corporal took two steps nervously away and swung his anxious gaze toward the other guard.

She jerked open the backdoor, before kicking off her shoes and unfastening her jeans. Stripping off her clothes, down to her sports bra and boxer briefs, Trish snatched the body armor from the top bag and adamantly yanked the suit on. She slipped into her boots, not bothering to lace them. She strapped on her loaded utility belt and moved her rifle and helmet to the front passenger seat. After throwing the items she previously had on into the vehicle, she slammed the door, climbed behind the wheel, and forcefully shut the driver's door. She glared at the corporal and his subordinate, who had moved directly beside him. Both had their mouths hung open in disbelief.

"Oh," she said, then attached her seatbelt. She pointed to the gate. "Now, if you both would be so kind." When neither moved, she growled. "I swear you'll either open that gate and let me out, or I'll be driving both of you straight to the hospital myself. Which is it?"

The corporal swiftly nodded to the private, and in less than a minute, her Gladiator was racing beyond the two-story, concrete barrier. With one actual destination in mind, she headed to New Underwood, close to twenty miles away. She used the bulk of the short drive to settle her hurt and anger and focus on the road ahead.

Still ten miles to go, she noticed the doming light off in the distance. Even with the work crews already having vacated the outpost, and with nobody yet living there, the minimal glow from the seven square mile structure grew more impressive with each closing mile. The city had not only powered on the electricity to this section of the grid but also contributed generously to the wall panels and towers erected throughout the entire circular stretch.

Approaching the gate, Trish couldn't tell which structures remained behind the looming barrier with Concertina wire running along the top and which were torn down. She hoped the crews had demolished the gas station, where the Gramites had slaughtered Adam and Gabe, and left the police department intact, where she and Christina had first fallen asleep together.

Thinking of their recent encounter, Trish's mind flashed to the excruciating view. She squeezed her jaw muscles together, her soul angered by how fast her wife had moved on. Christina in her nightclothes, the replacement grasping a bottle of wine, smirking.

Trish slammed on the brakes, put the vehicle in park, and swiftly jumped out. She let loose a building scream in the hope of easing the agonizing burn forming inside. The angrier she got, the more the painful pounding grew beneath her forehead. She stumbled forward, mind spinning with rage. Was this the reason Christina had kicked her out so easily? So, she could date other women? Trish bent over, leaned her butt against a cluster of boulders, and tried to get the images to leave her thoughts. It didn't work.

Without thinking, she whirled to the rocks and punched hard into the closest, stony surface. She wasn't sure if she was attempting to bust up the boulders or her own hands. As she struck out with her fists and chunks of rock flew off, she gritted her teeth to the sting, realizing she was doing both. She didn't care.

Experiencing the hurt in her hands was better than feeling this ache in her heart.

Without warning, the familiar surge of danger coursed throughout her body. She pivoted smartly around, her eyes searching the horizon for a new target to destroy.

CHAPTER FOUR

"Michael, the mud's not working. They're still tracking us," Debbie said through her panting, as she clasped tight onto the little boy's hand.

Once they reached the top of the hill, her boyfriend glanced behind them toward the shrilled sounds heard in the distance. He spun and pointed toward the glow in the valley below. "We can make it." He motioned for her to follow.

Without lending a hand with the child, she watched Michael sprint down the slope, surprised by his own selfish need for personal survival. She bent over and focused swiftly on the boy. "I know you're tired, but we have to push harder. Understand?" Debbie asked, as she fiercely rubbed at the stitch in her side.

The muddy-faced boy nodded and clutched tightly to the strap of his backpack. She offered his arm a reassuring squeeze, clasped his hand in hers, and ran. The sprint downward wasn't as bad as the dash forward once they left the decline. Her body was sore, her legs tired, and she was struggling to take laborious gasps of air while pulling at the child.

When she made it to the paved road, Michael was standing there, perturbed. "We're still about two miles away. You need to leave him behind. He's slowing us down."

Us, she wanted to scream, but she bit her tongue. If she angered him now, she was convinced he would go off and leave them both here to be slaughtered. In the New York bunker, he had been strong, handsome, a well-respected man. Like others, she found herself instantly drawn to him. Out here, when the real danger surfaced and the need to band together to aid in the group's survival mattered, he had shown his true colors. He had left the rest in the abandoned town to fight the mutated monsters alone, and like an idiot, she had gone with him.

For this reason, she had agreed to take the boy. Give him a chance at survival. But she knew to keep the boy safe, she would need Michael's help now more than ever. "Maybe if you carry him for a bit. Give his legs a break. We'll go faster."

The way Michael's features screwed inward, one would think she'd thrown cow feces on his dinner plate. "He's not even our kid!" The angry way he shouted caused the boy to move behind her. When she turned in the direction they had come from to comfort him, she saw the first set of bright-orange eyes scowling right in their direction.

Apparently, Michael saw it, too. In a movement resembling desperation, he reached for the kid and snatched him roughly by the arm. He balled up his fist and sent it straight into the seven-year-old's face. The boy went flying. She screamed out in protest, her fists striking Michael's chest with whatever energy she had left.

Michael grabbed her arms tight and shook her like a ragdoll. "If he's injured and can't move, they'll go after him. Don't you see? It'll give us more time to get away."

When he spun toward where the boy was lying, she jumped around Michael and threw herself over the child. She watched as Michael's face went from angry to expressionless. He shrugged his broad shoulders, stepped forward, and smashed his foot down on her lower leg. The sound of a loud snap charged the air, and pain unlike any other shot through her. She cried out in agony.

"That's it, darling. Howl as loud as you can." He threw her a toothy sneer, rotated, and hurried off.

In shock, Debbie bit hard into her bottom lip, tasting copper through her sobs. She wiped her tears and squinted around in the moonlight. Spotting the generously rusted vehicle several hundred feet away in the opposite direction Michael had gone, she reached out and seized the boy by the arm. "Samuel, you need to head over there and hide in the car. I'll distract them."

Wiping away the blood under his nose, Sam shook his head no and pulled on her backpack to get her to stand. She jerked his hands away and gripped tighter to his shoulders. "No, the only way you can help me is by hiding. Please, Samuel, please do as I say."

He stared at her for a moment, then nodded.

"Good," she said. "No matter what you see or hear, you stay hidden until sun up. Then I want you to head in that direction to where the lights are. Understand?"

Again, he nodded, and this time, he ran.

With her helmet sucked in and her night vision set to auto, Trish fought against the painful shake of her swelling hands and peered through the binoculars, searching for any signs of movement. She spotted a broad-shouldered man hovering over a petite woman, and the three Gramites running on all fours down the hillside a half a mile directly behind them. Her heart raced. No, these orange-eyed infected weren't Gramites. They were mutants, like in NORAD, and she was sensing them. Her mind flashed to Corporal Leonard and First Sergeant Stevens. Heaviness weighed on her chest until she pushed their lifeless images away.

She stood when she saw the man smash a foot down onto the woman's leg, sneer, and run off. By the look of her anguish, Trish figured the woman's leg was broken. Sending out a few choice cusswords at the man, Trish jumped into her Gladiator and peeled out, casting dirt and tiny pebbles up to rapidly ping against the vehicle's undercarriage. The voice deep within told her she wouldn't make it to the woman in time, but she was sure as shit going to try.

Less than a mile out, she spotted one of the infected break away from the other two heading for the woman and dart on all fours after the man. Fighting against the pain in her hand, Trish reached inside the glovebox and searched around. She found her backup knife, unsheathed it, and lowered her window. Seconds before reaching the guy waving her down, Trish leaned out, flicked the knife into the ground beside him, and shouted above the gusty airflow, "Good luck, asshole!"

When she passed the infected, it veered a bit off course, but promptly continued its pursuit of the frantically shouting man. She removed her pistol from the holster, held it out the window, and fired, trying to draw both beasts away from the woman. Every squeeze of the trigger sent a shooting pain through her swollen fingertips to her elbow, the glove on the suit stretching in size. Trish focused harder. She fired three more times, working at hitting the one not between her and the woman. Two of her bullets struck the creature in the back, the other scarcely missing the woman when the Gladiator wheels pitched to the right against the uneven terrain.

Confused, Trish studied closely the woman's swaying arms. She was calling the creatures to her, not struggling to get away. Suddenly, the farthest creature stopped and growled. Its eyes squinted into the headlights' blinding brightness. Trish pressed the pedal and shot forward, smacking the front end into the creature. She slammed on the brakes, threw it in park, and leapt from the vehicle, as her hands yanked her rifle with her.

The scaly-faced creature lying on the cracked asphalt twisted and struggled to get to his feet. She rushed forward, not giving the mutant a chance to rise. Two rounds and it stopped moving. One more she sent to its head, and she was positive the thing was dead. She spun as the other creature snatched up the woman and lifted her high in the air. Trish pulled the trigger and yelled, not bothering to count how many bullets she fired into the mutant. The beast dropped the crying woman and flailed face first onto the pavement. Trish stepped up, pressed the rifle to the base of the creature's head, and pulled the trigger several more times.

Certain the mutant was dead, but still feeling the heightened sense of danger, Trish spun. The mutant chasing the man had more than likely won the battle and was now advancing to their position. She scanned toward the direction of New Underwood, but the woman's cries pulled Trish's eyes away from the shadows past the headlights. Trish shifted to the woman and lowered herself down. She inspected the woman's forearm where the acid from the creature's ruptured pustules were eating at her flesh. "I've got something to help. I'll return shortly."

The woman tried to protest, but Trish was already on her feet and moving. Judging by the amount of damage the acid had already caused, she needed to act fast to save the woman's arm. She headed past the lights to the storage hatch, while keeping an eye out for the last infected. The second her hand grasped the container of clear fluid, her warnings flared to new heights. She heard movement behind her and adjusted seconds before the orange-eyed beast lunged. She raised her weapon and squeezed the trigger, not stopping until the creature and her threat perception both ceased quivering.

Before closing the hatch, she spotted her knife sticking out of the creature's shoulder. She moved forward, pulled it out, and poured some of the solution over it. Throwing the damp blade inside, she closed the hatch.

When Trish returned to the woman, her heart sank. She dropped to her knees beside the injured woman and stared at the light shade of orange appearing in both eyes. She lowered her head and retrieved the knife from her boot. "I'm sorry," she said, and she brought her hand up and placed it on the woman's cheek.

The woman reached out and grasped hold of her arm. "Samuel—car—save," she growled, right before she narrowed her eyelids at Trish.

With a heaviness in her chest, Trish's shoulders slouched. The transformation was complete. There was nothing left Trish could do. The woman who had spoken seconds ago was now gone, lost forever to the mutation.

Trish stuck the knife into the base of the woman's head with one hand and closed the woman's eyelids with the other. She stood and gazed upward, to the bright radiance of the moon. This woman's death—those mutants—both of her parents were responsible for all this suffering. This conviction was a truth she carried each day since she awoke from her coma. This world, the misery it held, this problem was her legacy to resolve, but like with tonight, she was failing. Miserably.

She took a few steps away and thought about what the woman had said. The man who broke her leg must have been Samuel. Why would she want me to save him after what he'd done to her? Feeling a brief twinge of guilt, she twisted toward where the direction the man had run. Whether she considered his actions immoral, shouldn't she have tried to save him? Would she have felt comfortable with a man like him roaming around the Rapid City with those she loved inside? The voice telling her no to each of those questions unsettled her. She gave him a knife, her conscience shouted, but its reasoning didn't ease the truth of what she'd done.

Clearing her mind, Trish headed to her vehicle and poured some of the solution over the pulley system the creature's body had struck. She couldn't tell if any of the acid was on the mechanism, but she figured it was better to be safe than sorry. She replaced the fluid in the Gladiator's storage area and dug through the piles of gear until she spotted where her backup knife had landed. Once she was seated, with the knife sheathed and returned to the glovebox, she pulled forward and steered the vehicle in a wide circle.

Spotting the rusted-out car in her headlights, she pressed the brake and waited. Trish removed her helmet as her eyes searched for any signs of changes inside the weather-beaten interior. All was quiet. She drove closer before powering everything down, including the headlamps. The moon's radiance was more than enough for clarity. Stepping from the vehicle, Trish made her way over and listened for even the slightest bit of noise.

She called out the name the woman had mentioned. "Samuel?" Patiently, she waited. When a tiny head finally popped up covered in both caked dirt and smeared blood, Trish's heart pitched sharply. The only thing clean on the child was the whites of his eyes, and even they appeared bloodshot. He couldn't have been much older than Jennifer, if not the same age. The sight of him brought a heightened sense of maternal protection to course through her and she fought with herself against rushing in, which would certainly frighten the poor child.

She bent over, still a good twenty feet away, and spoke in a soothing voice. "Are you hungry?" she asked.

The boy didn't answer straight away, and when he did, his reply was but a scarcely visible nod.

Trish stood, went to her vehicle, and searched for a few items from the storage area. Then she went to the rear passenger door and after a few minutes of sifting through the piles of tossed in bags and unorganized equipment, she found the rest of what she was after. Placing the items on the ground, she first unfolded two low-seated chairs, close to ten feet from where Samuel ogled her from the battered car. She set a ration tray and bottled water on one seat and slowly approached the wide-eyed child. She placed the other prepackaged food tray and water on the weeded ground at her feet.

"If you've never heated one of these and need help, let me know," she said. She waited for a moment, then headed off in search of kindling. Returning close to ten minutes later, she dropped the pile of twigs and rubbish on the ground and arranged it all inside a makeshift firepit. As she worked at prepping the fire, her eyes drifted casually over to the ration tray and water she had left by the car. Both were gone. She kept a straight face as she continued with her task at hand.

She had spotted the skepticism of the child when they first locked eyes with one another, which informed her he had gone through too much grief at such a young age. For how long, or what he'd suffered through, she did not know. What she could see was his level of trust in strangers was minimal. Trying too hard or forcing any kind of connection too fast would heighten his distrust. He needed to be in control and allow Trish in, but he wouldn't do so if he felt she was a threat.

Thanks to her isolated upbringing, unloved and unwanted by her own father, lack of trust was one emotion she could relate to. With the time she'd spent being loved by Christina and Jennifer, experiencing stability in the strength of their family, both her low trust in others and inadequate self-worth were becoming a thing of the past. A painful memory soon to be forgotten. Yet, over the last few days, by how rapidly the foundation of her life had crumbled, how easily Christina had thrown her away, she felt a familiar detachment work itself in. Her trust in others, in the faith that she was worthy enough to be loved, had been nothing more than a fantasy. An emotional concoction she had created from a yearning to be good enough. To be loved for whom she was.

With a start, she realized she was crouching over, staring blankly into the cold firepit with her mouth slightly parted, flint in one hand, steel striker in the other, neither moving. Trish blinked a few times and forced herself out of the mental hole her endless reflections had pulled her into. She swallowed down a bitter dryness and noticed the boy observing her. Feeling foolish, she focused on her battered hands and struck together the flint and steel striker.

Once the surrounding night was set ablaze with crackling heat, she went off to hunt for more fuel to burn. Striking pay-dirt in a downed tree near the temporary camp, Trish broke up the offering. She made several trips to pile armfuls of wood by the pit. With the rest, she found her entrenching tool in the overpacked vehicle and went farther away to create a larger firepit to burn the bodies of the infected, their stench already pervading the area. She cautiously dragged all three corpses to the pit, making sure not to get any of their acidic sludge on her armored bodysuit.

After the second fire was kicking up flames, Trish headed to her seat to fill up on some much-needed calories. She picked up the water and ration tray and plopped into the chair. She opened the outer package and peeked over the flames to see a set of eyes staring from her to her food. He must be as hungry as she was.

Fascinated by the concentration of his gaze, she lifted the package. His eyelids widened a little farther. Concealing her amused emotions, she held the ration tray and water out in his direction. "I tell you what. You clean up your trash, toss it into the fire, and I'll give you what I'm holding. Deal?"

The boy continued to stare, but he showed no sign of moving from his corroded shelter. She shrugged and pealed open the outer plastic, which protected all the individually wrapped food packets inside. At once, the boy bent over and shifted frantically around in the car. She watched curiously, wondering what he was doing. When he stopped moving, he gazed at her briefly, then slowly pushed open the creaking door. Her heart soared at seeing the many empty packages clasped in his tiny hands. He took a few steps forward and tossed the trash into the firepit. He retrieved a few that had fallen to the ground and threw them into the sizzling blaze.

"Thank you," she said and held the items out in front of her. When he didn't move to claim them, she relented to his apprehension and tossed both onto the seat beside her.

He looked from her to the chair, less than five feet from where she sat. He didn't move.

She sighed, climbed to her feet, and hauled her seat farther away, toward the other side of the pit.

She headed to the vehicle and retrieved two more ration trays and a few additional waters. Retaking her seat, she tore into the first bundle. She removed the package holding the main dish, opened it, poured in some water and the flavored tablet, and resealed it. She gave the pouch a few brisk shakes. As much as she wanted to look, she intentionally kept her eyes off the child now sitting in the chair across from her.

Instead, she glimpsed above the dancing flames ancient patterns, brandished throughout the plethora of stars. Her mind turned to Jennifer. She knew how much her daughter would love this view. Like with her, the beauty this planet offered fascinated Jennifer. From the critters that roamed the earth, to the various sceneries captured in the many photos they collected, to the sky above, all were blessings in their eyes. They had spent hours planning out different road trips they would someday take. Gramites, mutants, none of it mattered when one could see the magnificence past the horrors.

Once she consumed both of her high-calorie meals, she threw her trash in the licking flames and grabbed her miniature shovel. She dug the woman's grave close to the abandoned car, using it as a kind of headstone. As soon as she finished, she went over and spoke to the boy. With his lack of tears from her death, Trish didn't believe the woman was his mother or someone he had known for a long time, but she had still given her life to save him. Maybe their relationship was more than it seemed. "Is she your mom?"

The boy examined the body beside the hole. He averted his eyes. Slowly, his head shook.

"What was her name?"

Peering up, the boy softly spoke. "The man called her Debbie. The woman I was with asked her to take me with them this morning. She didn't make it either."

Trish pointed to the dirty blood left smeared and dried around his swollen nose. "Did the man do that?"

The boy squinted at the food packets he was holding. "He said if I was injured and couldn't move, they'd be able to get away. Debbie stopped him from hurting me again."

Trish felt her eyes fog over. She wanted to rush forward and throw her arms around the child and tell him he was safe, that no one would ever lay a hand on him ever again. To find the man's dead body and beat him until her anger subsided. Instead, she cleared her throat.

She headed to her vehicle and located her sleeping bag. Moving with care, she made her way over and draped it around the boy. Thankfully, he didn't protest. She went to the grave, carefully placed the woman inside, and refilled the cavity with the loose piles of dirt. After she finished, she spotted the child snuggled into the bedding, fast asleep. Adding a few broken-up branches to the fire,

Trish went to the vehicle and retrieved her rifle. She gazed up and inspected the speckled horizon. With no cloud formations in any direction, she forwent the tent and let the boy sleep in the chair while she kept watch.

Her eyes drifted to the tattered backpack beside his chair. It sank inward, the top half empty, and from what she could see past the smeared in dirt and filth, it held the design of a cartooned soldier on the front. She gently picked it up, surprised by the unexpected weight of the object. Heading to her seat, Trish unzipped the fastener. As she sifted through the meager articles of clothes, her soul ached. The extra pair of jeans were as stained and filthy as the ones he had on, with holes and shredded tears running throughout it. Two T-shirts were in the same condition, and she found no extra socks or underwear packed. She wondered if he had either on now. She doubted it.

What she found beneath the clothing deepened the level of empathy she felt for the child. At the very bottom sat a thick photo album packed full of pictures of the child, with a striking man and woman posed in most. From how each picture told his childhood story, they were his parents, and they had loved him very much during the youthful years of his life. Many of the background scenes led Trish to believe that they had lived in a bunker and both his parents were in the medical profession. Whether they were still alive, she did not know, but deep down, she knew the possibilities were slim to none.

In a side pocket of the bag, she found a woman's decorative hair comb and a man's wallet. She fiddled with her mother's locket around her neck while picturing the jewelry box from her childhood. Where was her wooden heirloom now? Still sitting on the mantel in her house. Or had they moved it to New Underwood with the rest of her things? She replaced every item carefully into the bag, fastened the backpack, and rested it against the boy's chair.

Thinking of Jennifer, she silently watched his tiny chest rise and fall, while considering how to plan out her day tomorrow.

The next morning, Trish pulled into the driveway of Doctor Burgos's lab at seven twenty-eight. She spent several agonizing minutes coaxing the boy from the passenger seat, knowing that if they didn't hurry, she would be late picking Jennifer up from the restaurant. The idea of running into Christina after yesterday was excruciating, but not seeing Jennifer—the painful concept was even worse.

She was glad she had radioed Doctor Burgos earlier, before she even cleaned up their campsite and loaded the vehicle. She had given him a brief rundown of last night's events and how the boy refused to go to the hospital when he woke. Doctor Burgos gladly agreed to watch the boy while she went to the outlets to buy him some clothes. Once she returned, they could figure out what to do. It took the entire drive in to persuade the child to stay with Doctor Burgos for a couple of hours until she returned.

Doctor Burgos greeted them at the door with the smell and sound of sizzling bacon lingering in the air. The succulent odor immediately peaked the boy's interest. Trish led Samuel into the bathroom on the main level and pointed to the smallest hospital gown Doctor Burgos had already set aside. "I promise I'll return as fast as I can. Until then, please trust me when I say you're in safe hands."

For a split second, it seemed as if the boy were about to hug her before she left. Thinking better of it, the boy turned away, and she closed the door. She spun to Doctor Burgos and thanked him again for helping.

"Just so you're aware, I contacted a psychiatrist after we spoke to come assess the child."

Trish forcefully shook her head. "Trust me, he won't go for it. At least not until he feels safe within these walls."

"I understand, but with what you've told me, I think this woman will be a good fit for him. She has a way of dealing with traumatized children."

Trish sighed and rubbed at the ache in her head.

Doctor Burgos inhaled sharply as he pointed to her hand. "What'd you do?"

Trish rotated her hand around with a shrug. "I had an accident. The pain's much better than last night. So is the swelling."

He gently seized a hand and examined it. Then the other. "Trish, I'd say you broke most of the bones in your hands. You may be stronger, with a trickier bone density than any other human, but you're not invincible." He lifted the other. "See how these two curve to the side? I'm afraid, with your increased healing speed, several of your bones have already set misaligned. I can try to re-break them, but it'll be painful."

Trish checked her watch. "Fine, but it'll have to wait until I return. I'm already running late," she said.

With not having to worry about congested traffic since many of the citizens were unable, or didn't want to pay the twenty-five thousand credits for a vehicle, the bulk of the populous used public transportation to get to wherever they needed to go. Trish made it to the restaurant in record time, but she was still ten minutes late.

She parked under the canopy of Eva and Christina's restaurant, Hometown Cuisine, located along a stretch of attached, red brick buildings. The restaurant was one of three businesses open along this strip of road. Two doors to the left a combined coffee shop and bakery stood, and across the road was one of the other nightclubs, which was where most of the newer residents spent their late nights and weekends.

Trish climbed from the vehicle and tried to peer through the window to see if Christina was serving any of the patrons. She saw Jennifer sitting at the long counter which separated the dining area from the open kitchen. Eva believed people felt more at home when they could watch their meals being prepared. Plus, it gave folks a level of confidence with knowing nobody accidentally dropped their food on the floor before consumption, or worse.

Right as she pressed on the door, Trish squinted at the figure two seats down from her daughter. Janet, dressed in her camouflaged uniform, was attempting to get Jennifer's unsolicited attention by tossing something in her direction. Jennifer kept her head down and hand working feverishly on the counter.

Trying to relax the tightening muscles of her jaw and shoulders, Trish stepped through the doorway and headed toward the counter. Janet threw a french fry, which landed next to Jennifer. Trish watched with pride as her daughter halted her crayon movements on the paper and threw the stick of red wax straight for the woman. Trish kept her face expressionless when the tiny item struck Janet's chin and triggered an inflated flinch from the surprised woman.

"I don't want to talk to you," Jennifer angrily said, her stern voice causing every eye to turn in their direction.

Trish swiftly reached out for Jennifer. The moment she touched her, the fury in Jennifer's large brown eyes turned toward her. Jennifer's refocused glare immediately registered her mom's presence. Jennifer shrieked with excitement and jumped straight into Trish's arms for a heartfelt hug. Trish lowered her to the ground and whispered in her ear.

Slouching her shoulders, Jennifer turned toward Janet with a voice barely audible. "I'm sorry for throwing my crayon at you. I was being rude." She paused, and loudly added, "You shouldn't have thrown food. It's gross and not polite either."

"Jennifer—"

The girl peeked upward at her mom, then to the floor. "I'm sorry."

Janet stood and bent forward. "Not at all. You were right. It was rude of me. I shouldn't have bothered you while you were busy." Janet held a slight smirk on her lips when she spoke to Trish, loud enough so those around could hear. "Sorry about last night. I hope me being at Christina's wasn't uncomfortable for you."

At Christina's? Last Trish knew, her name was also on the deed. Trish wanted more than anything to punch this woman. Break every bone her battered fist connected with. Instead, she moved to the opposite stool, grabbed Jennifer's backpack, and tossed in the crayons and drawing Jennifer had been working on. She then retrieved the red crayon lying on the ground by Janet's stool. She straightened when she heard Eva calling her name.

"Trish, we were beginning to worry," Eva said, crossing the kitchen from the office. She came around the counter and embraced her.

"I'm sorry I'm late."

"Trish, what happened to your hands?" Eva asked.

Trish spotted Christina exit the office and head their way. At once, Trish asked her daughter if she was ready to go. When Jennifer said she was, Trish spoke to Eva. "If you need to get ahold of us, I'll have my receiver on." Without waiting, she scooped up Jennifer and left before Christina reached them.

After Spending the last few hours going through the second largest shopping center in the city, Trish felt drained when she pulled into Doctor Burgos's drive. "Don't forget what I told you about the boy."

Jennifer unclasped her seatbelt. "I know, Mom. He's been through a lot. I'll give him space, and I swear I won't ask personal questions."

Trish gauged her daughter with a deep sense of pride. The clear-cut way Jennifer saw people, how she handled life's dramas, she was wise beyond her years. "I love you, baby girl. Now, help me with the bags, and I'll let you use my pole today."

Without hesitating, Jennifer sprang from the vehicle and loaded her arms up with packages.

Trish kept her tickled expression inward as she retrieved the rest of the bags. She silently acknowledged they may have gone overboard with their purchases. Normally, the experience of shopping would have been a dreadful event, emotionally straining in so many ways. Yet, as they went through each-and-every clothing store, Trish found the entire trip, with her overly committed daughter, doable, and even somewhat enjoyable.

Once she told Jennifer about the boy, her daughter had taken on Christina's role as the clothes-shopping-caregiver. She was insistent with picking out the best outfits they could find. Between Trish's militia pay and the occasional bonuses from the governors of the city, along with Christina's share of her and her mother's thriving restaurant, credits were never an issue. They combined everything they both made into one joint account.

A sudden blow of realism belted her hard in the gut. They would soon have to meet and discuss when and how to separate the life they had built together. Surely, Christina would want Trish's name off the deed to the house, and as far as their joint credit account, she would want that separated as well. Stopping by the steps for a moment to collect herself, Trish let out a long breath of air in the hopes of easing the crushing pressure on her heart. Her wife, their life together, everything was now gone. Forever over.

"Mom, you can cry. I won't tell anyone."

Startled, Trish looked to the top step, where Jennifer had dropped her bags. Her daughter returned to the step above where Trish was standing. Trish brushed at the wetness of her eyes with her gloved wrist. "I'm fine, sweetie. I'm a little tired is all."

"Mother said that woman just showed up last night. She didn't invite her over," Jennifer said, clearly trying to ease some of her mom's heartache. "She loves you, Mom, and I know she's sorry for fighting. She said that you, more than anyone, knows how stupid her temper can be."

Trish gave a slight grin and motioned toward the door. "Baby girl, I promise I'm okay. Please, I don't want you worrying about your mother or me. This grownup stuff, it'll all work out the way it should. Just know we both love you more than anything."

Jennifer hugged her and ended the embrace with a kiss pressed on Trish's cheek.

Trish dipped her head toward the door. "Let's get this stuff inside. Your grandpa's probably wondering where we are."

The moment they entered, Doctor Burgos waited until Jennifer dropped her bags and picked her up with his normal greeting. Trish's eyes drifted to the sound of soft music playing in the kitchen. She spotted Samuel, newly cleaned, sitting at the kitchen table, swallowed by the hospital gown. He was flipping through a magazine and chewing on a treat he found quite enjoyable. With the mud washed away, Trish could see the bruising circling both his eyes. Whatever guilt she carried last night was completely gone. A man who could do this to someone so young deserved what he got.

Trish headed into the modest front room and deposited her bags on the couch. She turned her head upward when the last song ended and a new one strummed out twangy vocals. She didn't know Doctor Burgos listened to country music. Maybe the boy was the one who picked the songs. Either way, Trish tuned out as much of the slow beat as she could, and she went to where Jennifer's bags sat, forgotten.

She grabbed the bags, pivoted, then froze the instant she spotted the faded western hat lying on the kitchen table directly past the doorframe. She leaned over, seeing slender legs stretched out and crossed under the table, in faded jeans and a pair of well-worn cowboy boots. Her forehead pulled downward until she remembered Doctor Burgos had mentioned calling in a psychiatrist to come and analyze the child. She expected someone in a stuffy suit with a white lab coat, like the one her father had her see six months after her mother's murder. The head doctor had grilled her for hours over several long weeks, more intent on finding out what she remembered than helping her cope with the loss of her mother. She had never trusted the profession since.

Trish was about done organizing the clothes and packing the boy's newly purchased duffel bag and backpack when Jennifer and Doctor Burgos entered. Jennifer, chewing on a piece of chocolate, beamed at her mother. "I like Sam. He has kind eyes."

Trish straightened. "Shouldn't you two let the head doctor and Sam have some alone time together?"

Doctor Burgos waved her off. "Not how Olivia operates. She wants to observe him, without seeming like she's observing him. She says it'll make him feel more relaxed and open that way."

Trish didn't respond. It sounded deceitful to her, but this wasn't an area she specialized in. Give her a cotton swab, a Petri dish, and a microscope, and she'll dissect what's growing down to the tiniest of details. This mental mumbo-jumbo—let others with more patience handle the invisible workings of the mind.

She held up a pair of jeans, tennis shoes, and collared shirt to Jennifer. Jennifer shook her head. "Not for camping and fishing, Mom. It's too nice. Here," she said, picking up a flannel shirt closely matching the one she was wearing. She selected a pair of hiking boots with a darker shade of blue jeans. After a moment, her tiny fingers worked open the package of white T-shirts and she pulled out one, adding it to the pile. "Olivia said it gets chilly on the farm at night. Maybe we should keep out this jacket for later and I can put it with ours."

They had been at Doctor Burgos's for less than ten minutes. How could their plans have changed so fast? "What's going on? I thought you and I were planning to go fishing and camping at Milberg Pond. What's this about Samuel and a farm?"

"Mom, he likes to be called Sam. Olivia said her farm has a bigger pond with way more fish, and no one will be there."

"Jennifer…" Trish sighed and knelt beside her daughter. "Look, we don't know this person, and I don't even know where this farm is—"

Doctor Burgos piped up. "She lives on a twenty-five-thousand-acre cattle ranch along the north stretch between the inner and outer wall. I've been there before when I watched her and a few of the other veterinarians round up the cattle for vaccinations. Seeing her work, you'd think she was born in a saddle."

Trish stood. "Wait, is she a vet or a head doctor?"

"I actually specialized in veterinary medicine."

Trish twisted toward the hallway. A woman, who dressed in more denim than Trish owned, was standing in the front room entryway. "My parents were two well-accomplished…head doctors, who insisted I take enough courses to get my feet wet in mental health," Olivia said politely and crossed the room. "I believe they were hoping I'd give up veterinary medicine once I began my studies. Instead, I've used it toward assisting in the emotional wellbeing of animals, and on rare occasions, children." She extended her hand. "Now that the resume's concluded, my name's Olivia, or Doctor Stonleigh if you prefer."

Trish felt suddenly awkward. "I'm Trish, Jennifer's Mom," she said, shaking the woman's hand. She wasn't sure if she should apologize or not. Was calling a psychiatrist a head doctor rude? It probably was.

As they stood there, still shaking hands, Trish noticed how the hazel eyes of this woman studied her busted hands and glided upward with a closer assessment. Trish wondered if Olivia was trying to analyze her mental state. Trish knew, with swollen, partially disfigured fingers, still wearing her body armor from yesterday, and almost certainly having bags under her eyes from staying up all night guarding hers and Samuel's makeshift camp, this woman's initial evaluation on her emotional wellbeing would be low.

"Is that the boy's outfit?" Olivia asked. She ended the handshake and pointed to the clothes Jennifer had picked out. "He's asking to change. Apparently, he doesn't enjoy wearing dresses."

Amused at someone else referring to the ugly hospital gown as a dress, Trish inelegantly snorted and promptly blushed. She played it off by motioning to Jennifer. At once, her daughter handed the pre-selected outfit to Olivia.

Trish's eyes moved downward to the faded, red T-shirt the woman was wearing underneath a loose-hanging denim overshirt. The T-shirt was two sizes two big, yet tied cleverly in front, showing off her low-riding jeans and shapely waist. Her long, light-brown hair was tied in a tight ponytail. The woman's distinct confidence and down-home beauty were both appealing. From the movies Trish has seen and Christina's many collectors' magazines which Trish had read through, if they were living before the virus, Olivia would have been the girl next door who dated the quarterback throughout high school. She was maybe a few inches shorter than Trish's five-ten build, and in her mid to late twenties.

Trish realized the woman was watching her gawping with tickled interest. The woman held up the outfit in a "thank you" gesture, pivoted, and headed toward the kitchen. Trish shifted uncomfortably. Thankfully, neither Doctor Burgos nor Jennifer had picked up on her uneasiness. Instead, they were going through the bags, removing and inspecting the folded outfits Trish had neatly packed.

Rolling her eyes, Trish headed to the door.

"Mom, where are you going?" Jennifer called out after her.

Trish waved a hand toward the kitchen. "It appears I need to reorganize the vehicle and make some room for Samuel—I mean Sam. Your grandpa too, if he's planning on joining us."

The two gazed swiftly at one another. The pounding in Trish's head kicked up at the thought of an all-night camping trip with Doctor Burgos, who was terrified of anything that crawled, especially spiders. When they both bobbed their heads in unison, the offer, which was actually meant to be a poor attempt at irony, became a sudden nightmare. "Great," she said, forcing a smile. "Just great," she muttered, heading out the door.

"Don't forget, I need to get x-rays and reset your hands," Doctor Burgos shouted, causing Trish to head straight to the glovebox for some needed aspirin.

After taking several pills, she radioed Aralyn to see if she could head over with a cooler and multiple bottles of the locally brewed beer. She also asked whether she could store some of her supplies in her godmother's Gladiator until they unpacked them in New Underwood on Monday. By the time the call ended, Aralyn, who was with Strong, Phillips, Givens, and Karen, were now *all* planning for a day of fishing and a long night of camping.

CHAPTER FIVE

Fighting through the renewed pain in her hands after having all but two bones re-broken and set, Trish worked at reorganizing her vehicle. The disarray of both rows of rear seating, along with the chaos in the storage area behind the hatch, were playing havoc with her compulsive need to keep her life neat and organized. Yet, with hers and Christina's recent breakup, Trish hadn't cared much about anything, except for spending time with Jennifer.

How could her entire world spin out of control so fast? Until a few days ago, everything about life was perfect. Even how she and Christina shared household responsibilities was an ideal fit. Christina took up the task of keeping their family fed and did all the shopping, whether for food, clothes, or something the house needed, not relating to home renovations. Trish kept the house in order, inside and out. From cleaning, doing the laundry, the yardwork, and any needed or requested home projects. The two rooms Trish didn't clean and organize were Christina's office and the kitchen. Unless Christina had added a specific item to the honey-do-list, these were areas her wife had reigned dominion over, and Trish stayed clear. In turn, Christina let Trish choose how she decorated her own office, and she rarely stepped foot in Trish's orderly toolshed.

The constriction of her chest was sudden, causing the air in her lungs to turn hot with grief. She bent her head forward and inhaled slowly, steadily, driving Christina's image as deep into her mind as her consciousness would allow. Her eyes grew blurry, and she struggled to keep her tears in.

"What the holy hell did you do to your hands?"

Trish's head jerked upright as Phillips stepped forward. It surprised her she hadn't heard Captain Strong's Gladiator approach, but the militia vehicle was parked along the curb less than ten feet away. "I punched a few boulders last night," she muttered.

Phillips gave a slight chuckle, but as he studied her changeless expression, his face stiffened. "Seriously?"

The moment Carlen Strong approached, hers and Trish's eyes met. "Trish, I spoke with Susan earlier. She said Christina radioed her at the hospital after you left the restaurant this morning. Susan believes her when she says last night was all one big misunderstanding. She's not seeing anyone. Your wife is very much in love with you."

Trish covered her face with her hands, which were swaddled by many finger-splints, and fought against her tears. Carlen moved closer and wrapped her in a motherly embrace. She could hear Phillips shuffle his feet close by, and occasionally he added an awkward pat when her stifled crying grew louder. A minute later, he excused himself from the women and finished with repacking Trish's vehicle.

By the time Aralyn showed up, Trish managed to suppress the rest of her tears, but her headache remained. She brushed along her nose the one finger on her right hand not bandaged, thinking she felt wetness from a nosebleed. Carlen's words of comfort had helped her heartache ease some with the hopeful idea that hers and Christina's relationship was only in need of some loving work and renewed trust. Trish knew, after living through the pain from these last few days, she'd never keep any more secrets from her wife. From now on, if an issue arose, they'd work through the dilemma together until they resolved the problem, whether their discussion turned into a head-pounding, heated argument or not.

"You look like shit. When was the last time you slept?" Aralyn asked, passing Trish a cold beer.

Trish fabricated an upbeat vocal response, hoping to ease her godmother's concerned appearance. "You sound like Susan."

Aralyn cringed at the name.

Trish's chest felt the familiar sting of her own heartache. "You guys still haven't worked through this?"

"Nope, she's being downright hateful. I think the long surgical hours she's putting in at the hospital aren't helping her moodiness." Aralyn shrugged. "I don't know, maybe this temporary leave she's on to gain surgical experience is happening at the right time. I couldn't imagine what it would be like having that anger-driven defiance on our team right now. Not with what we're getting ready to do."

"Are you still staying at home?"

Aralyn shook her head. "I wouldn't be able to get any work done if I were. Major Thomas put me up in a spare apartment at the old hotel. I tried going to New Underwood, but the scanner is not programmed in yet." She briefly shot Carlen a look of frustration. Refocusing on Trish, she gave her a curious look. "I heard you did too but got sidetracked with rescuing a kid. What is it with you and children?"

Before she could explain how the events of last night transpired, Doctor Burgos's lab emptied with the rest of those left inside. Jennifer rushed forward and hugged her Grandmother Williams. She climbed into the second row of seating with Sam, giving her grandpa the front seat. As the veterinarian headed down the steps visually assessing her, Trish was happy she had taken a shower and changed before Doctor Burgos worked on her hands. At least now she didn't feel so self-conscious around a person professionally trained to analyze the mental welfare of others.

She gestured from Aralyn to Olivia.

Aralyn waved her off, showing no introductions were necessary. "We already know each other." Aralyn said. "She treats our working dogs which patrol the outer fence line."

"Actually, Trish, you are the reason we first met," Olivia said. "It was almost two years ago when you were in a coma."

Trish frowned at both women. "I'm not following."

Olivia explained. "Doctor Burgos wanted me to go over some of your lab work since the results resembled certain animalistic qualities. He was hoping I could give him some insight on why you weren't waking," she said, glancing suspiciously toward Aralyn and Trish. "To be honest, I've never seen anything like it before. Even your blood type is unusual. Like a totally different species altogether containing unknown antigens. They wouldn't tell me much, but even now, I have a growing curiosity to stick a needle in your arm just to see what I'll discover."

Trish couldn't help but find that last part amusing. "Then I'll stay away from you when there're needles around."

Olivia's features turned playful, shifty, even. "Probably safer if you did."

Aralyn motioned to her vehicle. "Wanna ride with me, Doc?"

"If it's not too much trouble. Tracy has the vehicle today. She's checking on the pig farms and won't be finished until later tonight."

"No trouble at all, seeing as how we're heading to your place, anyway. Thanks for letting us use your pond." Aralyn patted Trish on the back. "We're all kinda needing an evening to relax and have a few beers."

If Trish could call an area so close to a walled-in city spectacular, this farm would be it. The three-story colonial house sat on a lush, grassy hillside with a breathtaking wraparound porch. The soft red and brown colors of stone pillars and tan siding walls matched with the outer buildings and both barns. A swimming pool and covered patio sat parallel to the house in a backyard enclosed with a four-foot picket fence. What really added to the beauty was the three-acre pond resting below the hillside. An acre of trees shaded the east end area where the dock sat, and the grazing pasture stretched out past the north with a third of the immense pond, the house, and the surrounding structures cleverly fenced-in to keep out the many head-of-cattle.

Trish removed a fish from her hook and displayed it proudly to the cheering group. She knelt beside Samuel. "Wanna name your fish before I release him?"

"Are we not going to eat this one, either?" Samuel asked, puzzled.

Jennifer wrinkled her nose and gave her fishing rod a slight flick with her wrist. "No, silly. That's why Givens, Phillips, and Grandpa are grilling. We're eating burgers and steaks, not the fish."

"Sam, these two might act tough, but when it comes to actually killing anything, they're a couple of babies," Carlen said, tapping her beer bottle against Aralyn's. "Honestly, I'm not even sure why you guys are talking about taking them hunting. Phillips, you know they won't kill anything, and if they do, they'll cry the entire way home. Might as well come here and camp. Going hunting for Bambi's parents? No, not with these two."

"We wouldn't cry," Jennifer insisted.

"Honey, it's not polite to lie, even to yourself," Aralyn plainly informed, the sound of their clinking beer bottles punctuating her words.

"I wanna name him Fish-sticks." Sam's words brought a bout of laughter from Carlen and Phillips, as Aralyn choked on her beer.

Jennifer gave Sam an upward eye roll and turned her agitated attention to her own pole.

"Okay, Fish-sticks it is," Trish announced. She lowered the flapping catfish into the water and waited until the lucky creature swam off in search of a way to celebrate his near-death experience.

She twisted her upper body when she heard the deep neighing behind her. Spotting the horse and rider approaching, she returned Olivia's wave, headed to the shade under a large oak, and pulled a cold beer from the middle of three generously stocked coolers.

Olivia dismounted beside a smaller tree and hitched the tall, chestnut-red horse to a low-hanging branch. Trish saw the pride in the horse's eyes, thinking she'd never seen a more beautiful animal in her life. His mane and tail were both jet-black, and he swished the long strands of hair on his tail around, batting away the flies swooping over from the pond.

Trish offered Olivia the beer. "He's gorgeous," she said, gawking at the animal.

Olivia politely declined the drink. "His name's Buck. He has a nasty, spirited side to him, so be careful."

"Our groundhog's name is Buck," Jennifer announced. She had reeled in her line and made her way smartly over. "We named him Buck because of his teeth."

Olivia's brow turned downward to Trish in a look of amused questioning at hearing they had a pet groundhog.

Trish shrugged. "He's more of a yard ornament than a pet."

Olivia stroked Buck's muscular neck. "His name's Buck because of his personality when anyone besides myself tries to ride him," she informed, admiring her own horse. "He's a big teddy bear once he lets you in."

"I bet my mom could ride him."

"Oh?" Olivia held out the reins. "Would you like to give it a shot?"

Trish shook her head and laughed. She bent over and picked up Jennifer. "Hon, I've never ridden a horse before. No matter how high you place me on that pedestal of yours, even I have weaknesses."

"I'm heading over to one of the southside farms to check on the goats and chickens. Wanna go? I can saddle another horse. Wouldn't take long."

Aralyn stood and stretched out her lower back. "Trish can, but not the little ones. Captain Strong and I are taking them to shoot off some arrows later. I bought Sam his own bow set, and Jennifer said she'd help us show him how to use it."

Jennifer dropped her eyes, her building excitement dwindling.

Olivia's good-natured laugh brought the girl's chin up. "My horses aren't going anywhere. There'll be more opportunities for you to ride later if your mom's okay with it."

Jennifer turned her eyes pleadingly to her mother.

"If Olivia say's it's fine, then I don't see any reason we couldn't," Trish said, throwing her daughter a wink.

Olivia slowed Buck enough for Trish and her horse to catch up to their brisk gallop. "You're a natural in the saddle," she said, reducing Buck's speed even more.

"Now I know you're lying," Trish replied, as she patted Pudding on the neck. She kept her eyes focused on the beauty of the beige mount. Pudding, with her tannish-white mane and tail, was as beautiful as she was gentle. Trish leaned over to check to see if the mare's jaws were relaxed. She couldn't tell, so she rubbed her mount a little longer.

Olivia laughed. "Will you stop worrying? I never should have told you the warning signs on a horse. Pudding likes you. To be honest, that mare likes almost everyone. She and Tracy don't really get along, but Tracy's a dog and cat gal. Not much on farm animals."

Trish gave Pudding another pat and eased back into the saddle. "I'm waiting for her to realize I'm a fraud and don't know what the hell I'm doing up here."

Olivia clicked her tongue at Buck again to increase their pace. "She has enough confidence in her own abilities to keep you both moving safely forward. She senses and likes your personality, and Buck here is a good lead horse for her to follow. You need to sit back and enjoy yourself. Let her feel you trust her, and in turn, she'll help you build up your confidence in a saddle."

Trish constantly adjusted her posture to Olivia's continued suggestions, passing through one of four farms producing this year's food crops. On the other side of the vast acreage, before the first of three animal farms, stood acres and acres of freshly grown feed for the livestock. Olivia said the city planted these corn, barley, and oat fields, destined for the animals, to separate the farm animals from the city's grown food source. It helped to keep the fresh fruits, grains, and vegetables from being contaminated by animal waste.

When Olivia sucked her lips together, the sound took Buck and their ride from an up and down bumpy trot to a wind-blowing sprint. Trish gripped the reins and leaned forward, focusing on keeping herself centered on the horse. At one point, when she slightly closed her blurring eyes, she thought she could hear Olivia laughing off to her left. She wasn't positive, and being so close to death, she really didn't care.

Olivia slowed their sprint to a gallop, then to a trot when they drew closer to the sound of chickens and barking dogs. Olivia pulled up on her reins and brandished her arm high in the air toward the largest of four barns. When a man waved in their direction, Trish heard him shout out for one of his dogs, who stopped its intense pursuit toward the new arrivals and headed reluctantly to its owner.

"Sorry. That scroungy Saint Bernard is one of the meanest dogs I've ever met. Molly goes after anyone who steps foot on the farm, including the horses. Buck hates her. Usually that breed is pleasant to work with, but old Stan lets her run wild, undisciplined."

Trish picked up on Olivia's distaste when she mentioned old Stan. She wasn't sure if there was additional reasoning behind it, or if the vet's sole disdain was from the unchecked temperament of the man's dog. She didn't pry but remained seated as Olivia directed Buck on where to go, as Pudding followed close beside.

They pulled up to the barn, dismounted, and Olivia showed Trish how to hitch the reins so Pudding wouldn't bolt off to her own barn if spooked. Old Stan greeted the women with a grunt and continued with his task. Olivia rolled her eyes and motioned for Trish to follow.

Olivia moved through each of the barns, inspecting the feed and cleanliness of every structure and the animals inside and out. After she removed some items from her saddlebag, she headed to the chicken coops. Trish watched her examine the shells and internal shading of various eggs with a light source. She completed her inspection by sifting through several piles of droppings on the ground.

On their way to the main barn, old Stan met them with a circling of his finger. "Do we pass inspection, or are you guys citing us again?"

Olivia gave the man a lengthy sigh. "Stan, like we've told you many times, these farms, including the animals living on them, belong to the city. We're here to make sure your team is properly caring for the animals and land. If not, then we will help you with the corrections. This has nothing to do with *you* personally but with making sure the process is safe and runs smoothly." She pointed to the stretch of chicken coops. "You need to keep up with the feces removal on each of the coops, and I noticed an unlisted pig in barn D."

Stan eyed her evenly. "I've told the city I'm down two hands, but to appease you, I'll make sure the coops are…'properly' cleaned out myself," he said, with an elaborate display of quotation marks with his fingers. "The pig is for us here on the farm, not for the city."

Sensing a sudden threat to the right from inside the barn, Trish sidestepped seconds before the Saint Bernard sprinted from the doorway, heading straight for Olivia. The veterinarian jumped backward with her arms held up as a shield right as the robust dog lunged forward, preparing to sink its teeth into flesh. Trish caught hold of a fistful of fur and the massive dog jerked backward with a startled yelp. Pain shooting from her fingers to her elbow, she slammed the animal to the ground with a thump. She hunched her body over the protesting animal with one newly throbbing hand pressing the dog's head firmly down and her knee keeping the flapping body from moving out from under her.

With demanding barks, the two other canine companions came rushing over, ignoring Olivia's wide-eyed commands.

Trish squared her shoulders, held up a splinted finger on her other hand, and in a forceful voice, shouted, "No," to both dogs.

At once, they stopped their hurried pursuit to intervene. They stared at her until she pointed toward the house. Without hesitating, both did as Trish's finger instructed.

"Hey, get off my dog! You're hurting her!"

"She's doing nothing of the sort," Olivia said. "We've warned you that if you didn't get her under control, we would have to remove her from the farm."

"What are you gonna do? Put my dog down? Kill her?"

Trish could hear Olivia steadying herself through paced breathing. "She's not *your* dog. She's here to help watch over the livestock. But thanks to your lack of discipline, she's grown too aggressive to do the job we trained her for."

The dog's wide eyes zigzagged at the sound of their loud bickering. The canine jerked her body between the packed dirt and Trish's leg, trying desperately to break free. Trish spoke to the heated pair. "Can you both do this somewhere else? I need a moment of calm before I let her go."

Olivia studied the dog and with a stern gaze directed Stan toward the house.

Once the commotion subsided, Trish slowly exhaled, and the dog stopped fighting. She studied the dirty animal. With her free hand, Trish rubbed along the dog's partially matted fur, whispering to the trembling dog. *Molly*, she thought. "You're not as mean as you lead people to believe, are you?" She moved her hand upward and scratched behind an exposed ear and under the jawline.

Molly let out a fleeting whimper.

"You're a beautiful girl. After a bath and good brushing, I bet all the other dogs in this city would gawk at you in awe."

Molly's next whimper was more of a long, drawn-out whine, as if saying she agreed. Her shuddering lessened, and after a few more strokes, Trish removed her knee and loosened the pressure of her hand. Molly didn't move, other than to flick her tail slowly against the dusty ground. Trish continued to stroke her. Close to five minutes later, she removed her hand completely. Molly stayed resting on her side, with her head motionless. Trish scratched along the ears and muzzle and rested her hand over Molly's eyes. Molly's tail flicked a few more times, and her legs stretched out into a relaxed posture.

Trish stood. She studied Molly, unsure of what to do or what to expect from the dog. Molly slightly raised her head to Trish, then lowered it after they locked eyes. This animal was gorgeous. Her eyes were wild, yes, but they were highly intelligent. It would be a shame if old Stan were right, and Olivia was forced to remove Molly to euthanize her.

Trish squinted at Buck, who was watching them both with a sideways stare. An idea struck her. At once, she headed toward the horse. When she whistled, Molly jumped to her feet and followed. Trish gently spoke to Buck as she approached. She noticed how the horse's ears whipped from her verbal cooing to the sound of the advancing dog. Trish held out her hand, and she touched Buck's shoulder. His muscles trembled slightly under her bandaged fingers. She slid her hand upward and stroked the horse's neck.

"I heard you two don't like each other." She motioned to the dog sitting a few feet away. "As you can see, she's as big of a teddy bear as you are."

Trish called the dog closer than she placed a hand between Buck's eyes and dragged it downward toward the unflared nostrils. She unfastened the reins around the post, and she took a few steps backward, with Buck following. "If I climbed up on your saddle, and we go for a gallop together, will you try to buck me off?"

Buck neighed and bobbed his head up and down.

Trish couldn't help but laugh. "Gee, thanks," she said, patting the horse on the neck. "At least you're honest."

Trish stopped walking and spoke sincerely to Buck. "I know I'm not your mom. I only want to make sure Molly will behave when you're running. If I make it a brief ride, will you keep your distaste for me to a minimum?"

Buck wobbled his head about and flapped his lips against his hefty exhale. She tipped her head, with a polite, "Thank you."

Before she could chicken out, Trish placed a foot in the stirrups and pulled herself up, straddling Buck to the sound of stretched leather. So far, so good, she thought. She looked at Molly. "Are you both ready?" she asked, gripping onto the reins. "To that tree and back, okay Buck?"

As if understanding her, Buck unexpectedly shot forward, with Molly right behind. Trish's body jolted backward in surprise, but she quickly gained control, leaned forward, and held on tight. Feeling the powerful muscles beavering under her legs was invigorating and scary at the same time, as the swift pounding of hooves struck rapidly onto the ground. With the wind whipping wildly, and keeping herself centered, she had a difficult time watching Molly moving hastily beside them. As far as she could tell, the dog was running with the horse and not at the horse.

When they reached the tree, before Trish had mentally gone through the steps on what rein commands to use, Buck shifted to a half-stop, swiveled, and shot in the direction where Pudding and two wide-eyed individuals were now standing by the fence, watching them.

Buck finally came to a four-legged bouncing halt close to the head-bobbing Pudding. Trish's insides felt like thickened jell, yet her adrenaline was running wild. She struggled to dismount with the slight shaking of her limbs.

Olivia's hands reached out and guided her down. "Are you okay?" Olivia asked, as Trish leaned her forehead against the saddle.

Trish swiveled her body around, and she spoke excitedly to Olivia. "That was both thrilling and terrifying at the same time." She patted Buck on his neck. "Your boy can really fly." She then pointed to Molly. "If you're planning on putting her down, please don't. I'll take her."

After asking again if Trish was okay, Olivia gave a slight hmph, and glared at Buck. "Traitor," she said with a grunt, leading the horse to the hitching post.

"Lieutenant Waska, we've located more carcasses close by. We believe they're the mutants we were missing."

Waska ran his fingers over the loose mound of dirt, a length suggesting someone fashioned a grave for an adult. He gestured to the recently constructed resting place and two of his men unfolded their shovels and dug. He stood and followed his subordinate past the remains of a firepit to an area several hundred feet away. He kept his face fixed even though the charred stench of rotten decay filled his nose. Lowering himself to his knees, he saw how someone with enough wisdom had dug out a burn-pit so the weeds around wouldn't catch fire. What looked to be three disfigured creatures were tossed into the opening of the earth before burning their hideous corpses.

One of his soldiers approached. "We found the woman's body inside the grave, Lieutenant, not the boy's."

"Did you scan her? Was she infected?"

"Yes, sir, but the creatures didn't kill her. She has a stab wound at the base of her skull."

"Take some samples and recover the body. Make sure the grave looks exactly like you found it," he ordered. He opened his communicator, articulating clearly to the woman on the other end. "Two miles outside of a deserted walled-in compound, what appears to be New Underwood, we located the bodies of the three missing test subjects. They had been killed and burned by unknown individuals. The two adults who got away are both dead. The child, still not accounted for."

He squinted off into the distance, beyond the walled town of New Underwood. "Requesting permission to continue toward Rapid City. Please advise."

A slight pause filled the other end, and he knew she was relaying his request up the chain.

"You've been granted authorization to proceed. Lieutenant Waska, your orders still stand. You are to observe from a distance.

If your team or your mission becomes compromised, you and your men will be subjected to harsh disciplinary actions."

Lieutenant Waska motioned with his hand to his troops, signaling for their promptness to pack up the gear. "Understood."

Once the call ended, Waska headed to the lead Gladiator, and informed his driver to take the backroads along the hillside. He opened his wrist processor and traced the trail of emptied supply bunkers along his map with his finger. Aralyn was not as competent at command as she believed herself to be. With the trail of breadcrumbs they had been following for the last few weeks and the brand-new wall panels encircling New Underwood, Waska knew this could be his day of triumph.

When the vehicle came to a stop at the top of a ravine, Waska stepped out, seeing the might of the city off in the distance without even using his binoculars. The walled-in farmland surrounding the additional walled-in city was by far better than Colorado Springs, or any of the other cities the New United States were busy constructing.

He removed his binoculars from the pouch attached to his utility belt and scanned across the miles of structures throughout the valley below. At various key places along the city's outer edges, he spotted laser weapons and heavy artillery positioned to aid with the city's defenses. At the far left side fence line stood an area housing over two dozen helicopters. Presumably the same ones from the NUS aviation outpost which had been attacked not long after Aralyn and her team broke into NORAD and downloaded vital information. The stolen data had contained the coordinates to where both the NUS's hidden aviation compounds were located. Thankfully, they assaulted the smaller of the two. Still, this additional arsenal could pose a grave threat if his chain-of-command went about attacking the city the wrong way.

He signaled for his second-in-command, ordering him to capture video, and focused imagery of the entire area. He squinted through his binoculars one last time. Right before he moved away, his heart gave a swift beat. His pulse race as two women on horseback came into view. He leaned closer, focused the magnification on a stronger setting, and patiently watched. The time ticked slowly by. It wasn't their highly engaged conversations with one another or the intermittent bouts of laughter from each that kept his attention. No, his sole interest clung to the view of the woman with short hair and piercing blue eyes.

He leaned in even farther and focused on her smile. In the photos, she had long hair, a downcast expression, and dressed in the fifth-level bunkers unflattering uniform. Here, outside NORAD, the woman was beyond stunning. Her short, neatly cut hair accentuated her high cheekbones, with its slightly longer, windblown length styled on top. Her grin was genuine and her outfit, the white T-shirt, flannel overshirt, and blue jeans, as crazy as it sounded, made the woman's extraordinary physique even more striking. Like a woman who wore her man's oversized dress shirt around the house with nothing else on underneath.

He jumped up and rushed to the Gladiator's console. When he opened the link, he fought to keep control of his rising excitement. The second the woman answered, he spoke slowly, clearly. "Inform Doctor Frank Webber and the committee, I found Patricia Webber."

At the sound of the woman's sharp intake of air, Lieutenant Waska silently praised his good fortune.

CHAPTER SIX

"What's with the campers down by the pond?"

Kicking her feet to the music, Olivia spun right as Tracy dropped her items on the kitchen table and plopped on the chair. "Aralyn's group wanted a night of fishing before heading out on an assignment on Monday. They were pretty tightlipped with where they were going, but it sounds like they'll be gone for a while."

Tracy's surprise was evident. "Aralyn, like as in the head of the militia, Aralyn? Since when were you two friends?"

Olivia shrugged. "I take care of their working dogs. You remember when I had to go give my two cents on her goddaughter's lab work? We first met then."

Tracy rubbed at her neck, looking worn after her full day of pig wrestling. "That's right." Her eyes suddenly widened. "Oh, did you hear about her and her wife?"

Olivia leaned over and pressed the tiny button to reduce the music volume. "I didn't know Aralyn and Susan were married."

"No, not Aralyn," Tracy said, waving her hand through the air. "Trish, her goddaughter. Her wife kicked her out earlier this week. I guess they're getting a divorce."

Startled by the unexpected news, Olivia went to the table and sat down beside the other veterinarian. The way Trish occasionally spaced off throughout the day, as if working through a troubling dilemma, well, it all made sense now.

"You know, with how the townsfolks talk about Trish, you'd think the woman was immortal. Word has it, she once dove into a hole full of the infected and single-handedly pulled two guys out.

Oh, and the Gramites badly ripped into her, but she's immune to the infection."

Olivia snorted at the absurdity. "Don't believe everything you hear." She picked at the checkered tablecloth, trying to act as casual as she could. "Why did her wife kick her out?"

"Not sure, but rumor has it, Christina's already seeing someone else. A woman who lives at the main barracks by the east gate. The one with red hair. We met her a few months ago."

Olivia wracked her brain, trying to think of a lesbian with red hair.

Tracy sighed in her frustration at Olivia's lack of recollection. "She was dating Tylor's friend, Stephanie."

"Who Janet?"

Tracy snapped her fingers together. "Yep, that's the one."

Olivia slowly shook her head. She had spent several hours talking to Trish. She wasn't just visually delicious, the woman was smart, fun to talk to, and she had an uncanny way with animals. Janet? "I don't believe it. Her wife would be a fool to go from Trish to Janet. It'd be like having a scoop of homemade strawberry ice cream, then wanting to consume a bowl of roundworms after."

The thirty-six-year-old vet wrinkled her nose. "What a gross comparison." Tracy lowered her arm to the table and narrowed her eyes. "I take it Trish is with your group of campers?"

Olivia comically stretched out her response. "Maybe…"

Tracy snorted and Olivia laughed. She playfully threw the tablecloth at Tracy as she headed to the counter. She turned the music up and worked on finishing the generous container of snacks. "I think I'm going to ask Trish if she wants to camp here another night before they leave on Monday."

"What about the bonfire tomorrow?"

Olivia shrugged. "She can go. It might be good for her to get out and mingle with others."

"How's a toddler going to mingle at the adult table? What is she, twelve?"

"Hilarious. I believe she's nineteen."

"Exactly, a nineteen-year-old hanging around an older, more sophisticated class of people. I mean, does she even have an equivalent to a high school diploma?"

"Can you be anymore catty?"

"Olivia, our entire group is caddy, including you. It's what makes us so incredibly unique."

"She's seven years younger than me, whereas you're ten years older. Doesn't stop you from climbing into my bed between your passionate flings."

"Yes, but your seven-year age gap is filled with a doctorate in Veterinary Medicine with a Minor in Child and Adolescent Mental Health." Tracy stepped behind her and peeked her head over Olivia's shoulder. "What are you doing? Is that for smores?"

Olivia finished adding in the final scoop of mixed berries. She placed the lid on, sealing it tight. "Yes, the kids have never made them before. I figured I might as well prepare enough for everyone." She pushed Tracy away with a butt thrust. "At the bonfire tomorrow, you'll be nice to Trish, understand?"

Tracy made an x-sign over her heart. "I'll be super nice and use small words, so she'll be able to keep up with the conversation."

Olivia huffed. She collected the smores container and placed it in a sack with additional snacks from the counter. When she turned to go, Tracy was carefully studying her. "Are you coming to my room tonight?"

Olivia shook her head. "I won't be in until late. Oh, Tylor, April, and Justin went to the club, so you'll have the place all to yourself. Enjoy." Without waiting for a response, Olivia walked from the kitchen, wiggled into her jacket, and left the house.

Trish and Jennifer pulled away from Mrs. Johnson's children's home at half-past seven. Thankfully, she had taken Doctor Burgos home first. At his lab, she showered and changed into a fresh pair of jeans and tucked in a black T-shirt. Once she had thrown on her belt, socks, and the one designer shirt she had packed in the vehicle, she laced up a black pair of hiking boots. Since the button-up shirt was also black, Jennifer informed her mom she needed to replace her black T-shirt with a white one. She had given her daughter a sheepish look and did as instructed. Where would she be without her fashionable daughter to help guide her?

With knowing she was getting ready to see her wife, her mixed excitement and apprehension grew tenfold. She wasn't sure if she should drive around for half an hour or head inside the restaurant early. She and Jennifer had already had dinner, but maybe one of Eva's pies would be a pleasant treat after their long day of romping around on the farm, fishing, and shooting off arrows at a makeshift target attached to a bale of hay.

"Mom, do you think Sam will be okay?" Jennifer asked.

Surprised by the unexpected question, Trish assessed her daughter. "You watched the way Mrs. Johnson and the others doted over him, and you've lived there yourself. Didn't you like being around the other kids?"

Jennifer let out a tiny sigh. "I did, Mom, but it's different not having your own family. Can't he live with us? I know Mother would love him and having a brother would be kinda cool."

Trish studied Jennifer's brown eyes a moment longer before she turned her attention back to the road. It's not that the idea hadn't crossed her mind more than once. But with her and Christina's relationship being unstable and the work she was getting ready to do, taking her away from the city for days at a time, adding Sam into the mix would complicate things. Plus, the boy wouldn't have the required stability he needed.

Also, there was an entire process to go through before a child was ready to be adopted. They spent months inside the home around the other children and under the care and guidance of a well-trained staff. They did their own assessments and provided a solid routine for each child. The children attended the local school, kept up with homework, and blended in socially with others their own age. This system met each of the children's required needs through emotional support, structure, and a caring atmosphere.

Still, Trish couldn't shake the guilt she was feeling for leaving the boy, nor the sadness in her daughter's eyes the second they headed to their vehicle. "You know, soon he'll be starting school. You might even be in the same classroom together, but even if you're not, you'll probably see him every day." She put on her blinker, deciding on the pie. "Maybe we can talk Mrs. Johnson into letting us take him fishing on our next overnight camping trip."

The suggestion brought with it a lifted mood from Jennifer. She relaxed in her seat and bobbed her foot to the musical beat coming from the speakers.

They spent the last few minutes in verbal silence, each in their own line of thoughts. The idea of not seeing her daughter this week was painful. Maybe Christina would be okay with her stopping by for a few hours during the week, hopefully even letting Trish crash on the couch. Perhaps then they would have a chance to talk.

The commotion of the weekend club crowd picked up as they drew closer to the restaurant. With plenty of open parking spaces, Trish pulled into her usual spot, while returning the waves through the windshield to a few greeters. Shutting off the vehicle, Trish promptly inspected her reflection in the mirror. Not the best likeness staring back, but it'd have to do.

"Mom, you know everybody thinks you're cool."

Trish grunted at her daughter. "Hon, in this town, everyone knows and acknowledges others the same way. I'm no different and definitely not special." She nodded to the people passing by. "Most of them are more than likely waving at you."

Jennifer's eyes widened, and she gazed around at all the beaming faces. "Really?"

Trish laughed. She pulled her daughter onto her lap and opened the door. "Come on, Queen Elizabeth. Let's not keep your subjects waiting."

The moment they entered the boisterous atmosphere, the savory smell of seasoned meat and the familiar garlic and herb tomato sauce greeted them. Trish saw the piles of spaghetti on many of the plates, letting her know what tonight's special was. She nodded to Betty and pointed to one of the few empty tables in the restaurant, next to the bay window. Betty waved and gestured her approval.

The moment Betty finished with a table's order, she hurried over and gave them their customary hugs. "You two look amazing. So, what'll you have tonight? The usual?"

Trish spotted Christina working behind the grill. Her heart leapt. She focused on Betty, raising her voice above the pre-club clatter. "We've already eaten. But if you have any pies left, we could each go for a slice."

"I think I might be able to scrounge up a couple. Any particular one in mind?"

Jennifer shrugged.

"Surprise us," Trish said, letting her eyes drift to Christina. Her stomach fluttered, and her excitement rose tenfold.

When she pulled her eyes away, she realized Betty was watching her with a heightened level of amusement. "I'll let her know you're here."

Trish reached for Betty's arm as the young girl was leaving. "Please don't. I can see she's busy. Let's wait until some of these people finish and head across the street."

Not losing her upbeat persona, Betty headed off, and Trish swung her attention once again to Christina. Her wife had her hair bunched up in a hairnet, and the area around her eyes were slightly darkened. Even as Christina's face glistened with both grease and perspiration, Trish knew her wife was by far the most beautiful woman she had ever met. Her heart ached, as she watched Christina shuffle to the sink and back to the grill. She could tell by her wife's movements her feet were hurting.

"Mom, you should go kiss her."

Startled, Trish let out a snort and bent sideways, planting kisses all over Jennifer's forehead and cheeks. The girl giggled, pushed her hands against her mom, and rolled her head to each side. When the door dinged, still smiling, Trish turned her attention toward the entrance. Her entire body stiffened. She watched the woman with long, wavy red hair zigzag through the crowded restaurant with purpose, heading straight for the counter.

Betty arrived at their table and placed a slice of pecan pie down in front of each. Trish didn't glance up. Instead, she kept her eyes glued to Christina, who turned to the woman who was now calling her over. Christina stared at Janet for a moment, then at the book Janet was holding out to her. Christina covered her mouth, and when her hand dropped to her chest, she was blushing. Trish's insides compressed together. Her breathing felt dangerously constricted, as painful ripples of anxiety strained every gulp of air. She watched Christina walk over and take the book, and as she did, Janet touched her arm in a way suggesting they had been friends for a long time.

"I should let Christina know you're here." Betty sounded nervous, but Trish couldn't take her eyes away from the heart-wrenching scene by the counter. Janet was laughing, and she pointed to the book now in Christina's hand, while still holding onto her arm. Trish's eyes narrowed to the book and her insides grew hotter, burning with tortured anger. Janet had handed off the same book Trish had given Christina a few weeks ago. A romance novel her wife hadn't yet had the time to read. Christina let Janet borrow it?

"Mom…"

Trish couldn't look at her daughter or at Betty. She spoke, shifting her gaze to the glossy pecans covering the pastry. "Can you get Eva for me, please?"

"Mom, just go talk to her."

Trish leaned over to her daughter and kissed her gently on the forehead, trying hard to keep her emotions from spilling over. This battle, she was worried she would lose.

When Eva showed, her warm welcome distorted to concern. She seized Trish's wrist and directed her outside the restaurant, motioning for Jennifer to follow. "Trish, what is it? What's happened?" she asked once they were away from the bulk of the crowd.

Trish went to the backseat of the Gladiator for Jennifer's bag. She handed the backpack to Eva. "Can you see if I can have Jennifer next Saturday for another camping trip?" Trish knelt, holding her daughter in a tight embrace. She brushed Jennifer's bangs off her face and winked a watery eye at her daughter. "We're wanting to go fishing again." When she stood, she spoke hurriedly to Eva. "I'm sorry, I can't stay. I forgot, I have someplace to be tonight."

Ignoring Eva calling her name, Trish got into her vehicle and left. She drove in silence while fighting away the release of her tears.

"Olivia, didn't you hear my question?"

Olivia yanked her attention from the darkness surrounding the road which led to the city's main gate and onto Tylor's amused smirk. He waited for her response at the center of the horseshoe seating arrangement around the bonfire. "I'm sorry. What'd you say?"

"Seriously, child, where's your mind tonight? I asked what the deal was with the tent, and why is a dog resembling Mangy Molly lying beside it?"

Olivia flashed her attention to the dog. The view of the canine's transformation was captivating. "We have a guest joining us tonight who enjoys camping. To answer your second question, it's because the dog *is* Molly. Yet, as you can see, thanks to the two seven-year-olds who gave her a bath and brushed out her coat this morning, she's no longer mangy."

Several sets of eyes stared first directly at her before resting on the transformed dog. Ignoring their openmouthed disbelief, Olivia aimed her attention in the direction of the gate. With a jolt of excitement, she sat straighter in her seat. She was positive she had seen headlights flicker over the far hillside before dropping off into darkened seclusion. She doublechecked to make sure she brought out every cooler she'd personally packed.

Trish had said one of her favorite beers was a pale, wheat blend from the local brewery. Olivia had gone there personally after the visitors had left to pick up two cases. She had purchased a few mixed cases of the other blends for the off chance that Aralyn and the others changed their minds and showed.

"Honey, I know that's not Molly. Do you know how I know?"

"Because the dog's not trying to kill us," Justin said, answering Tylor's question.

"Exactly." Suddenly, Tylor's head lifted higher in the air. "Looks like whoever you invited has finally arrived."

Olivia peered at the headlights and glared at each of those present. "I swear you all better be nice to her. She's going through some issues, and she doesn't need any farcical attitudes thrown her way."

Tylor leaned forward. "Honey, you've pricked my curiosity. Who is it?"

"Trish Webber, Colonel Aralyn Williams's goddaughter," Tracy muttered, bringing her wineglass to her lips.

"No, really?" April asked from the far side of the spitting inferno. She adjusted her slouched posture, acting too eager for Olivia's comfort. "I met her once before. Have you all seen her in a tank? Absolutely scrumptious."

"Honey, you believe everyone's edible. I'm really surprised you're not fat from the wide variety of people you dine on." Tylor stood and removed the wine from the container of ice. He busied himself with refilling each of their glasses. His eyes narrowed at Olivia playfully, as the vehicle came to a stop between the tent and bonfire. "Is she even old enough to drink?"

Hearing the snort from Tracy and the group's combined laughter, Olivia stood, as her unsettling agitation rose. "I swear, if you don't stop, I'll close the bonfire down for the night."

Tylor's forehead wrinkled, but Justin didn't lose a beat. "Oh, I think someone's got your panties all sweaty, and I believe it happens to be that sexy creature heading in our direction."

Olivia threw him an added glare. She went to the cooler and retrieved a beer. As Trish walked closer, Olivia marveled at seeing Molly trot smartly to Trish for a sought round of praise. Trish gave the eager dog a generous rubdown and motioned for Molly to heel once she continued toward the group seated around the bonfire.

As Trish drew closer, Olivia spotted the drained expression in Trish's eyes. She wondered if Trish had been crying recently. Suddenly, the idea of Trish being around this callous group of vultures in a clear vulnerable state worried her. Fighting to hold her laid-back greeting steadfast, she passed Trish the cold beer. "Are you okay? Do you want to go somewhere private to talk?" Olivia whispered, but apparently not soft enough.

"Oh, no, you don't. Trying to hog the guest all to yourself." Tracy stood and moved forward. When she reached out for Trish's hand, the Saint Bernard bared her teeth and snarled. Fearful, Tracy leapt backward.

"Damn, that really is Molly," said Tylor, taking a few steps away himself.

Trish calmly turned to the dog and dropped to one knee. Her jugular inches away from Molly's muzzle, she tapped a wrapped finger to the ground in front of her and at once the dog laid her body down, rolled over, and exposed her belly to Trish. Trish spoke to Tracy with a hand resting on Molly's snout. "I'm sorry. If you want to come pet her, she won't bite."

Without skipping a beat, the older woman shook her head no, her eyes anxious. Olivia had to work hard to hold in her laughter.

Trish nodded. She stood, blushed slightly, and tilted the lid of the bottle in Olivia's direction. "Would you please open this for me?"

Olivia jumped. "Oh, I forgot about your hands. Of course," she said, twisting off the clasp, and letting it dangle. "You know, you never did tell me what happened."

Trish's soft lips cocked to the side. "You wouldn't believe me if I did." Trish took a long drink and licked a drop of beer from her bottom lip.

Swallowing hard, Olivia pulled her eyes away. What made Trish even sexier was the fact that she didn't seem to realize just how sexy she was. Olivia silently wondered if Trish had been ill-treated when she was younger. This would explain why Trish kept her personal and past lives closely guarded, leaving their recent conversations generic in nature.

Olivia motioned to the open chair away from Tracy and sat in the empty seat beside her. Molly came over and dropped her head into Olivia's lap for a pat. Surprised, Olivia obliged and watched in amazement as the massive dog plopped to the ground between hers and Trish's feet.

Olivia's gaze fell over the gathering of people, some with their mouths slightly opened, but all staring directly at Trish. Trish shifted uncomfortably before raising her bottle high in the air. "Noroc," Trish said, before taking a drink. She did a stunning half-chuckle and peered awkwardly at those sitting around the bonfire. All were closely ogling her. "I take it none of you are Romanian?"

Mesmerized, Olivia couldn't help but laugh. She raised her wine and said, "Noroc," and tilted her glass toward her lips. A few of the others did the same. Around those on her team, Trish had been confident, blending in well with conversation and companionship. Around strangers, Trish was clearly uncomfortable, uncertain in her own self-confidence.

Tracy didn't raise her glass. Instead she lowered it onto the log beside her. "Okay, so what does it mean?"

"Good fortune…cheers," Trish said.

Tracy gave an elaborate nod. "Fluent in Romania, or is your vocabulary limited to a few cusswords with the added knowledge of how to toast?" she smugly asked, as she retrieved her drink.

Olivia bit her tongue, imagining all her own choice cusswords she was planning on utilizing on Tracy tomorrow. She was wracking her brain, thinking of something to say to assist Trish in her predicament until she spotted Trish's half-rounded grin. "I can ask for directions on where to take a piss. Does that fall into the category of cusswords?"

A few among the group laughed. April leaned forward and tipped the rim of her glass in Tracy's direction. "As active as Tracy's bladder is, you might wanna teach it to her. Noroc," she ended and drained her wine. She winked at Olivia. "Mind if I switch to beer?" April stood and headed to the cooler. Bending the upper half of her body at a ninety-degree angle, she pulled out a few bottles, twisted her head, and left her butt pointed in Trish's direction. "Anyone else craving something a bit saltier?" she asked. She slowly stood and passed out bottles to those signaling for one.

Olivia wasn't a fan of the way April had sprung to Trish's aid or the young vet's heavy flirting, but what she really didn't like was the suspicious glare Tracy was giving Trish between her sips of wine.

Tracy said, "I'm guessing one of the teachers in your bunker was Romanian. Am I right?"

Trish casually shook her head no. "Unfortunately, I didn't attend the classes in NORAD."

Here we go, Olivia thought, noticing how Tracy's distorted expression locked onto Trish's statement. Without waiting for Tracy's snide comments to flow, Olivia stood and motioned for Tracy to follow. "Can I have a quick word?"

Tracy ignored her and remained seated. "Really, so you didn't even go to school. Interesting…" she said, dragging out her last word.

Trish didn't return Tracy's stare as she took a long drink, her gaze never leaving the depths of the bonfire. "I was tutored."

Tylor was the one who asked the next question. By the sparkle in his eyes, Olivia could tell he was trying to keep Tracy's sketchy ball rolling. "You lived in a bunker and didn't even go to high school? How is that possible?"

Tracy continued with the prodding, not waiting for Trish to answer. "Exactly how much education do you have?"

Trish downed her beer and placed the bottle beside her chair. When she was about to stand, Olivia waved her down and went to the cooler. Irritated, she pulled two bottles from the ice. She was growing agitated with Tracy for showing her demeaning ass, Tylor for egging it on, and herself for subjecting Trish to this group in the first place. She tossed her wine into the fire, glass-and-all, then opened a bottle for Trish. The other she opened for herself. "You don't have to answer," she muttered, her agitation hinting toward anger. She turned to Tracy. "I need to speak to you. In private."

Tracy's laugh was fleeting, humorless. "Sorry. Olivia feels I'm being 'caddy.' You do know what caddy means, don't you?" she asked condescendingly.

"Tracy," Olivia snapped, her eyes narrowing. Tracy reciprocated the glare. The long seconds both women glowered at one another, the only sounds came from the occasional snapping and hissing from inside the fire.

Trish cleared her throat, causing both women to drop their visual daggers. "It's actually pronounced catty, not caddy, and yes, I do know what it means." Trish stood and rubbed at her temple. "Thank you for the beer, but I'm gonna take off. If you don't mind, I'll break down my tent in the morning before I leave the city."

Olivia pivoted suddenly. Her hopefulness of being Trish's physical, unemotional, and unattached rebound later tonight disappeared. Now she was only left with a heightened urge to pull Trish aside to make sure she was okay. "Please don't go."

Trish looked at Tracy and Tylor. Slowly, her head shook at Olivia. "I don't belong here."

"Would you like to go swimming?" Olivia asked, desperately grasping for anything she could think of. She wasn't ready to see Trish leave, and having her head from the bonfire upset made Olivia feel miserable inside. "It's a huge pool. We can bring the drinks, put on some music, and the house has plenty of room. You could crash in the spare bedroom tonight."

The way Trish's blue eyes examined her, working out Olivia's friendly offer, their intensity came close to truly taking Olivia's breath away. She fought to keep her shudder hidden from the probing eyes of those around them. Trish made a cute, scrunchy face, and she pointed to Molly. "I will if Molly can sleep with me, and I get to pick the music. Sorry, but I can't stand country."

Olivia found herself fascinated by the request. "Yes, to Molly staying, and I'll allow you to pick every other song."

Trish countered with, "I pick five songs and you can choose one."

Olivia squared her shoulders. "Two songs and one."

"Two and one, but your songs have to all be from female artists. It'll be less painful that way."

Olivia thought for a moment, holding in her building enjoyment over the unexpected banter. "Deal," she finally said.

Grabbing the cooler Olivia pointed to, Trish called for Molly and lumbered her way to the house. With a brisk bark and a generous shake of her tail, Molly obeyed. Once Trish was out of earshot, Olivia glared over at Tracy, and she openly released her scowl. "Sleep someplace else tonight, and maybe tomorrow as well. I'll probably be too pissed to be around you for a few days." She snatched up the handle on the wheeled cooler and followed Trish and Molly up the hillside.

CHAPTER SEVEN
JUNE 12, 2090

Popping a few pills in her mouth and chewing, Trish chased their bitterness with a swig of water. She steered the vehicle up the steep incline a few miles away from the city's outer gate, while wishing the sun would show its rays through the thickened clouds. On a clear summer's day, the vibrant colors along this outer hillside had a way of lifting the beauty of this carefully chosen site, which made Trish temporarily forget about the creatures and their inward horrors plaguing the land past the wall. It was a gift, if only for a moment.

Pulling over to her usual spot, Trish tenderly selected a handful of bright, colorful wildflowers and bound them tightly with a sheet of red wrapping paper. With Molly at her heels, she walked the rest of the way, feeling a pull of guilt for not paying her respects these last few weeks. Even with her life spiraling out of control, she knew that was no excuse not to come and share the news regarding both men's extended family.

Reaching the top of the hill, Trish halted at the sight of those already gathered around the two graves. Phillips, Givens, Carlen, Perez, Young, Davis, and Aralyn were all holding hands, with an open spot between the two women. Doctor Burgos was standing to the side clutching his hat, his head hung low, as if in prayer. The other five soldiers, attached to Trish's team were keeping guard around the three vehicles and Aralyn's helicopter, a few hundred feet away. Their placement to secure the area wasn't because these soldiers didn't hold a level of respect for the two fallen souls who had died nearly two years ago. They were newer recruits. They'd never had the privilege of knowing either man. Trish approached the group. She locked hands with those she would gladly give her life for. They were her family. Their love for the two fallen would never falter, no matter how many years passed over the hillside they forever slept on.

Aralyn was the first to share her feelings, brief but heartfelt. Once she finished, they all took turns offering their respects. When it was Trish's time to speak, Aralyn squeezed her hand. Trish cleared her throat, not bothering to wipe the dampness from her eyes. She lowered her head and spoke from the heart toward those they had lost.

"First Sergeant Stevens, even if others don't understand why we've chosen this path, I know in my heart you do. You were the toughest, deadliest sonofabitch I've ever known, and the closest person to a father I'll ever have. You chased down and took out three mutants by yourself to try to save the life of one of our own. Those bastards weren't strong enough to bring you down, but the infection was. All because of one tiny scratch."

Her gaze moved slowly over those around her. Her heart ached at the thought of losing anyone of them, but she knew they were all prepared to sacrifice themselves for the greater good. "I don't know if this mission will be a success or a dangerous waste of our time. What I do know is, we can't hide behind a wall for the rest of our lives, waiting for the creatures to kill those we love, or an aged death finds us. Shame on us if we try to pass this burden down to the generations who follow. These Gramites, the mutants, we need to discover a way to stop this spread. With my mother's research, what's inside me, and this unstoppable team, I believe we're the closest hope humanity will ever have for a future free of infection. We can't sit idly by and do nothing. I refuse to do nothing."

Her words broke off and Aralyn pulled her in, giving her a hug. Carlen was the next to join the embrace, then one by one, ending with Doctor Burgos, the group stood huddled together in each other's arms. Aralyn offered an uncharacteristic prayer, asking whoever was listening to watch over this group whom she loved and help aid them with bringing peace to the world her unnamed entity so generously created.

Once those gathered added flowers and trinkets to the graves of both men and the last of the shared feelings were spoken, Aralyn addressed the entire group. "It's time to head to the vehicles, everyone. We still have a lot to do to get the rest of this gear unloaded and our new outpost up and running."

Crossing a street still smelling of fresh asphalt in front of the row of newly constructed concrete dorms, Trish scanned her hand on the wall panel. She stepped through the reinforced door of the highly secured building and looked over toward the area where the cell to the old police department once stood. Even though they had demolished every building in the town, replaced them with solid, generously supplied structures and high-tech machinery, and surrounded them by seven square miles of two-story walls panels which spanned out in the opposite direction of Rapid City, she could still picture the cot she and Christina had first shared.

Doctor Burgos waved her over from across a room filled with long workstations and built-in processors. She maneuvered around the outer row of leather seating and security monitors to join him. He nodded to the team's medic, Staff Sergeant Young, who brought over a tray and placed square, sticky pads on her chest and back, underneath her jumpsuit.

When he finished, he fastened the suit and gripped her arms. "I know if First Sergeant Stevens were here, he would tell you how proud he was of you. He would also tell you not to push yourself too hard. If you feel overwhelmed with the tests, or as if you're losing control, think of First Sergeant's stern voice, and stop whatever your body's doing." He hugged her and placed the makeshift halo sensor on her head.

Both men followed her toward the basement, as Carlen, her godmother, and the others remained motionless, monitoring her dead man walking procession. "One would think I was heading off to be executed," she said to both men, as they descended the concrete steps.

Right before Trish went through the steel door at the bottom, Doctor Burgos tapped her shoulder. She pivoted, noticing the fear in his eyes. "Trish, please take these tests slow. Do what Young said, and don't push too hard. I'm hoping the more we study this new gift of yours, the more you'll be able to understand and control it, which will make it safer for you in the long run. But don't rush through these tests. You don't need to master this overnight." He sighed. "None of us can bear the idea of you falling into a coma again, or worse."

Trish touched his forearm gently. "Believe me, I know the risks. I'll follow your instructions to the letter."

Appearing satisfied, he beckoned her through the doorway. When she stepped inside the room, she saw the various cameras and monitors surrounding a concrete enclosure directly in the center of the wide open basement. She moved forward and waited while Sergeant Young opened a thick, reinforced door. Inside sat more cameras in every corner, a stool in the center, and a long table off to the left with bolts attaching each leg into the concrete floor. On the table was a handheld machine that resembled a nineteen eighties boombox, with speakers on both sides and a monitor housed in the center.

She slowly headed in as Doctor Burgos went to the center console and connected the system to those assessing the readings from upstairs. Young closed and bolted the door, the metallic click elevating her heartbeat.

Doctor Burgos's voice filled the enclosure. "Trish, everything's fine. We've got you. Please don't worry. Remember, we're taking things as gradually as possible until we have a better understanding of what we're dealing with."

Nodding toward one of the cameras, Trish placed her hand on the icy surface of the stool before sliding her keester onto the hardened metal. As she waited patiently for the instructions from Doctor Burgos, a chill originated out from between her shoulders, moving down through her legs to the tips of her toes. It was as if the temperature had dropped ten degrees in seconds. A pressure formed in each ear, sending a wave of popping sounds every time she flexed her lower jaw muscles.

"Okay, Trish. Let's begin. Now I want you to focus on the sound sensor on the table in front of you. Do you see it?" he asked.

Tilting her head to the side, Trish glared at the camera. Seriously, how could she not see it? Other than the table and silver stool her butt was planted on, the sound sensor was the lone item that stood out in a room doused in white. Hell, even her jumpsuit was white.

"Okay. Now I want you to mentally focus on the device. Try giving it a nudge with your mind."

Trish centered her eyesight on the sensor. She took a deep breath and shook the anxiety from each of her limbs. Blocking everything else out wasn't hard since everything she saw was colorless. She squinted her eyelids halfway closed and tried to visualize the boombox contraption sliding away from her on the table. Nothing happened. Her lids narrowed more, and this time she imagined the device smashing forcefully into the wall behind the table. Still nothing.

She let out an exasperated sigh, and Doctor Burgos's voice echoed out. "It's okay, Trish. Don't get frustrated. We're just beginning. It could take days, weeks, even months before we see any results. Now, relax yourself and try again."

Months, it could take months. Her mind recollected the time her father had her under sedation in his lab. For two weeks she'd slumbered so the soulless man could run his experiments on a daughter unwilling to be his guinea pig.

Suddenly, she felt her eyes roll upward, and her entire body grew lifeless, as if ignoring the burden of gravity in the room. She could smell burning wires and hear a far-off cry as someone called out to her, beckoning her to them. Was that Christina's voice? Wanting desperately to see the image of her wife, Trish fought with her inner self, struggling to control her eyes' involuntary movements. It felt like hours had passed until, finally, her eyes rolled downward again.

She jerked when she saw the smoke and flames surround the sound sensor. Doctor Burgos's voice screamed for Trish to wake up and for Sergeant Young to step away from the door latch. Trish jumped off the stool so fast, the metal chair fell backward with a loud, vibrating clanking of metal when it bounced against the concrete floor.

"Trish…are you with me? Give me a sign to let me know you understand."

Trish glowered toward the camera behind her. She threw up her thumb, signaling to Doctor Burgos she was mentally present, even though she figured this should have been apparent the moment she stood.

He informed Young the room was safe to enter. The door burst open, and the sergeant came rushing in with a fire extinguisher to douse the flames. Once he had the fire out and a smoky residue wafted above the table, the concerned Young pointed to Trish. His expression held both wonderment and worry. He directed her toward the door. "I'm calling it for the day. Let's head upstairs to the infirmary. You're getting an EEG, CT scan, blood draw, the works."

Trish's shoulders slumped. She opened her mouth to protest, but the worried voice of her godmother broke the silence first. "You heard him, Captain. Now go."

When Young said she was getting the works, he wasn't kidding. By the time she entered the briefing room, the sun had already set, and she felt poked, prodded, and drained of whatever blood she had to spare. The others were waiting for her around an oblong, shiny black conference table, and thankfully, so were several ration trays and a few bottles of water. She took her seat and opened the first package.

Doctor Burgos waited until Aralyn signaled for him to proceed before he ran his palm over an embedded console in the center of the glossy surface. The blue holographic image that appeared was both feminine and familiar. The imaged processor smiled warmly at Doctor Burgos, and he returned the friendly greeting. "Please pull up the video of Trish's time in the vault and a side capture of the sound sensor readings."

"Yes, Doctor."

Trish scooped a bite of the semi-warm chicken Alfredo into her mouth, too hungry to nurture the idea of heating it longer. She would take extra care of the next meal. She waited as Doctor Burgos sped through the video, past her entering the vault and the door being sealed behind her. When she was seated on the stool, he slowed the video to the point she saw herself focusing intently on the sound sensor. Finishing off the last of the creamy dish, she licked her spoon and opened the package containing the pound cake. She dumped in the required water and flavored tablet before sealing and shaking the package.

Doctor Burgos directed them all to the semitransparent display of the sound sensor. "The device captured a few seconds of soundwaves and frequency right before Trish's eyes rolled upward here." Trish lowered the warm package containing the expanding cake inside. Her eyes in the video grew haunting the way they rolled skyward to where all she could see was white. She averted her gaze and swallowed a few times, feeling her stomach growing unsettled at the view.

Doctor Burgos paused both screens at the same time. "When we get to this point, the sensor can no longer register the high-level pitch Trish's mind is sending off, and a few seconds later, the wires within the sensor began to melt."

"Why couldn't we hear anything?" Carlen asked.

"The hertz she started with was over fifty thousand, way above anything human ears can pick up, and once her eyes rolled upward, the sensor could no longer detect it either. Before the sensor malfunctioned, it recorded an ultrasound well above two hundred decibels."

"Not possible," Young said. The concern on his face was mimicked by several people around the room. "At the levels you're suggesting, Trish, hell, even those of us who were around the vault, should have been injured or even killed. I gave her a complete physical. Her lungs are fine, hearing, everything is normal."

"That's precisely it," Doctor Burgos said. "Nothing about this is normal, but not only is Trish able to generate these high-level frequencies, but she's able to focus them on specific targets like the sound sensor." He tapped on the display and brought up a third video. When Trish saw the dimly lit cavern of NORAD, she knew at once the video feed was from the night Aralyn restarted her heart and her body had sunk into the slumbering abyss of her coma.

She swallowed a few more times at seeing herself standing with an arm raised, Givens savagely beaten, and Christina yelling for her to stop. She saw her father, Frank, clutch his right eye, his nose profusely bleeding, as he stumbled from view of the cameras. Her hypnotic body fell to the ground at the same time her father's soldiers dropped dead, and Givens and Christina were both knocked backward. The video feed went static and stopped.

"Do you see how Trish's mind can use this ability to pinpoint certain targets while leaving those she loves unscathed?"

Those she loves unscathed, the words soaked in with a sickness rising in her chest. What if Christina had been harmed or even killed that night by her body's sudden use of this…weapon inside her. Her ability. Wasn't this what it truly was, a dangerous weapon, one which she and the others had little to no understanding of?

Feeling the overwhelming need for fresh air and solitude, she left the rest of her meal untouched, as she rose from her chair. Aralyn nodded to her and held up a hand to silence the unasked query forming on Phillips's worried features. Trish turned from the table and left the room.

By Friday evening, Trish's mind felt drained, yet free of the severely recurring headaches. Pressure flared up occasionally, but nothing that didn't go away after a few minutes of steady breathing. After a full day of testing while encased in thick, white painted concrete walls, Doctor Burgos informed her that until Phillips could gather the parts to repair the pile of sound sensors her newly tapped ability had disintegrated from the inside out, this next week they would focus on finding the clusters of Gramite hordes living throughout the area. They were planning to tag a handful and begin the crucial process of monitoring behaviors and running various tests on the creatures' vitals.

She now had an entire weekend off. Trish was debating on driving by the restaurant to see if Christina was working. After a week of struggling through the dilemmas of their last few encounters, she hoped Carlen was right and she was reading Christina's and Janet's connection all wrong. She had done as Christina had requested in her letter by not contacting her, but the long days and nights without even catching a glimpse of her wife's face were growing too difficult to endure.

Molly jumped into the back and barked to let Trish know she appreciated the added legroom from the cleaned-out Gladiator. Trish lifted a brow at the dog's reflection in the mirror. "I know. I like things to be organized as well."

Molly barked again and jumped into the next row of seats. Trish laughed and pulled a bone from the container beside her seat. She flexed her recently unbandaged fingers, tossed the treat behind her, and listened as Molly adamantly searched both rows for her treat. "One left, girl, but don't worry. Olivia said she'd restock your supply tomorrow if we go camping. No, stay out of the storage area. I don't need you trampling all over my things."

Trish felt fortunate she had met the veterinarian when she did. She'd never had an actual best friend before, well, other than

Christina, but that was different. Christina was her wife. Christina knew everything about Trish, things that others didn't know, including how Trish hated looking at her own reflection in a mirror. With Olivia, their conversations were different, jaunty even. They didn't go into great depth with their discussions involving their past lives, but the lighthearted conversations were constant, flowing easily between the two. No expectations, just friendship. It surprised her that a camaraderie with a straight, feminine woman could be so enjoyable.

She pulled the vehicle into the usual spot and told Molly to stay. She opened the door and stepped out into the rain. When she was under the canopy, she peered through the glass at the few patrons in the restaurant. Thankfully, none were Janet. Mentally rehearsing the one excuse she could come up with for the unexpected visit, the whereabouts of her mother's jewelry box, Trish steadied her nerves and headed inside.

Christina was talking to one of the waiters, her demeanor still appearing as tired as it had last weekend. When the bell on the door chimed, Christina's attention swung her way. Trish stopped beside a grouping of chairs, their eyes locking directly on to one another. Trish wasn't sure, but her wife's emerald eyes appeared to hold a deep sense of longing, and Christina's hand shot to her chest. She watched Christina take a step forward and reach her other hand out for the counter, as if to steady herself.

Trish's heart melted. She gave a clumsy wave, trying to keep her own emotions in check. Christina rotated toward the man, who was still talking. Trish couldn't hear what she said, but the exchange resolved the issue. The man pivoted and went to a couple sitting at the other end of the counter. Wiping her hands on her apron, Christina hurriedly moved forward, meeting Trish halfway through the scarcely occupied dining room.

The familiar contact of Christina's hand pressing firmly on Trish's chest, directly over her heart, sent a warm tremor throughout Trish's body. Without thinking, Trish bent forward, and brushed her lips softly into Christina's, soaking in the heat with each of her wife's accelerated breaths. Christina clasped her hand on the nape of Trish's neck, taking their connection to an unexpected, different level. Their lips pressed urgently together, each of their arms encircling the other. The clattering sound of silverware striking the floor brought their heads apart, but their eyes didn't break contact. She could see the reddening color grow on her wife's honey-beige cheeks, making her glowing skin even more beautiful.

"I love you, Christina," Trish muttered, not wanting to release her grip around her wife's waist.

Christina closed her eyes and whispered sweet words of Spanish. Sensual ones Trish had heard many times before. When Christina's eyelids parted, Trish's heart ached at the tears lining the lower lashes. "Why haven't you returned any of my messages?" Christina asked, the deep green searching the piercing blue for an answer.

The simple question took her off guard. "What messages?"

"The ones I left every day with the sergeant-on-call. Each morning I open the restaurant, and every evening before picking up Jennifer, I called the desk sergeant on duty, but you've never replied."

"I haven't received any messages." Trish was beside herself. "I would have gotten in touch with you if I knew you wanted to talk. You know I would've." She brushed at a tear as it rolled slowly down Christina's cheek. "Tomorrow I'll contact HQ and find out what's going on."

"It's okay. I only needed to know you were safe." Christina's soft features were full of love and longing. "I have about an hour until the dinner crowd comes in. Wanna go into the office and talk?"

The slanted grin on her wife's lips let Trish know Christina wanted to do more than talk. With the dilemma of their relationship over the last week and a half, Trish's libido had taken a drastic nosedive into oblivion. Yet, with the feel of her wife's body against hers, and the matching need etched in Christina's features, Trish's libido didn't climb, it soared. She eagerly nodded.

Christina's eyes brightened. She seized Trish's hand and led them as casually as possible through the dining room toward the kitchen. The rubbing of her jeans as she walked, while gawking at her wife's shapely backside, sent tiny shivers between Trish's legs. The thought of touching her wife's nakedness, tasting her soft flesh beneath her tongue, the anticipation was maddening. Thankfully, Christina maintained a swift pace.

The second they stepped into the office and the door closed, they lunged together, mouths hungrily devouring. Christina fumbled with the handle, working to engage the latch, as she pulled at Trish's belt, trying to work the clasp free. Stifling grunts and moans urgently released between the two, they ignored the sporadic bumping of Trish's elbow into the filing cabinet beside them and the light pounding of Christina's butt hitting the door. Trish pulled off Christina's apron, her stiffened fingers fiddling with the buttons on her work blouse.

The clicking of the lock sent both of Christina's hands to desperately work free Trish's belt, the clasp, and the zipper of her jeans. With still a few buttons left to undo, yet losing patience with her fumbling fingers, Trish untucked Christina's blouse and reached around, unclipping her wife's bra. Trish's hand pushed the loosened cups up, as she reached toward an exposed, shapely breast.

Christina released a trembling moan and arched her chest to Trish. "Oh, my love. I've so missed you."

"I need you," Trish pleaded, her own voice crackling in the shadowy room. Trish's fingers continued with the buttons on the blouse while she sucked a nipple firmly into her mouth. When the last button finally gave, she yanked off both blouse and bra, each one dropping to the floor.

Christina pulled roughly at Trish's shirt, while Trish's mouth slid to the other stimulated nipple. Trish swallowed, feeling her own need build into an uncontrollable state. She jerked Christina's slacks down with her panties, the dampness of the lacy material brushing against her arm.

Christina's next moan was Trish's breaking point. She gripped her wife's thighs, easily lifted her, and moved both their trembling bodies a few feet forward to lower Christina onto the surface of the desk. When her fingers rubbed through the wet hair between her wife's thighs, Christina adamantly pushed various papers and items to the floor and leaned on the desk's hard surface.

Their desperate cravings drove them both on, frantically straining to quench the severity of their combined thirst. Trish tried mentally fighting against her ravenous ache, to slow things down, to savor their overdue lovemaking, but her efforts were useless. Her soul was starving for this connection, and it sought to consume. Trish's fingers parted the dampened lips, caressing and teasing the swelling mound lying within the tiny curls of hair. Her mouth nibbled and sucked from one breast and the other, as her fingers worked just enough to stimulate before shifting to other locations every time Christina's rocking hips and tiny whimpers signaled she was close.

Christina spread her legs out wider, begging Trish to enter. Trish pulled Christina's butt toward the edge of the desk, loving the heady fragrance the room already was taking on—the sweet smell of bodily sweat mixed with the rewarding essence of sex even before Christina released her first orgasm.

"Please, my love, don't tease." Christina moaned, leaning on her elbows to slide her hips even closer.

The moment Trish's fingers entered her, Christina's stomach quivered. Trish knelt and covered Christina with her mouth, her tongue sliding as her fingers stroked against what lay inside. The release didn't take long, and it coated Trish's fingers in a thicker wetness than before. Christina's legs trembled, her body jerked, and Trish's tongue pulled the juices into her mouth, satisfying her greedy appetite.

When Christina's hips stopped moving, she touched Trish's head with her usual gesture, signaling for Trish to stop. She had reached the point where additional stimulation would be too much for her newly sensitive area. Instead of stopping, Trish pushed herself in deeper, faster, hungrily searching with her mouth for every ounce of taste offered.

"Trish, Trish…what are you doing?"

Christina's legs swiftly closed in around her, but Trish removed her hand from Christina's breast, and she pushed Christina's legs farther apart, refusing to be denied her needs. Christina's body shifted from trying to stop her to slowly thrusting her hips to a new rhythm. "Trish…oh god, Trish—" Christina shouted. Her hand came up, suppressing her next outcry. She lay on the desk, her feet pressing onto Trish's shoulders, her body swaying with each stroke. Her hand pushed on Trish's head, sending the pressure of Trish's tongue in with force. The next release that came was long, delivering wave after wave of shudders through Christina. When Christina's body finally slouched against the desk, Trish rose, and she pulled her trembling wife into her arms, where she belonged.

Trish pulled up her boxer-briefs and reached for her jeans. For the second time, Christina yanked them down. Trish groaned at her giggling wife, who was still lying naked on the couch. "I'm serious, babe. Get dressed. Your mom will be here soon."

Christina threw her arm above her and pouted. "Honey, the door's locked. Come lay with me for a few more minutes."

Trish sighed loudly as she glanced at the door. She shook her head and dropped herself into her wife's arms. "Fine, but don't say I didn't warn you."

"Woman, stop worrying. The door's locked. Even if it wasn't, you're my wife, and we both needed this. She'll understand."

Trish's head jerked upward. "The door is locked, right?" She moved to stand again, but Christina refused to let her go.

"Yes, it's locked." She laughed, placing kisses and love bites all along Trish's neck. "I love you."

Trish's body trembled, and her heart lifted even higher. "I love you too," she murmured, tasting the flavor of sex on her wife's full lips. "If we don't stop this, you know what'll happen. Not that going in for round three would be a bad thing, but we'll most certainly get caught."

Christina grunted, and she playfully pushed against Trish's sports bra. "Fine, you big chicken, get up. We can finish this later tonight in our own bed."

The idea of holding Christina all night swelled in her throat. She had gone too long not being with the woman she loved—talking to her, sharing in their life and love with one another. She stood, retrieved her jeans, and slid them upward, fastening them around her waist. She grumbled under her breath as she dressed. "I'm calling HQ first thing in the morning. I don't know why your messages aren't getting to me, but I'll damn sure find out." She stepped into her hiking boots and sat on the closest chair, lacing them tight, as her feeling of agitation rose.

She flung on her baby-blue T-shirt and tucked it in. "I'll also talk to Carlen about getting a long-range communicator placed in our house. It's like the one here, but the reach is over a hundred miles, so you'll have no problems contacting me throughout the week," she said, shaking out her collared shirt and tossing it on. When she turned, she was surprised to see Christina standing there, half dressed. "Babe," she muttered, bending over, and retrieving Christina's blouse from the floor. "You need to hurry."

Christina's face pulled downward, scowling. "You—" She closed her eyes and took a steady breath. "You're not still planning on continuing with your mission at New Underwood, are you?"

Trish straightened, startled. "Well, yes. What we're doing is important." She stepped forward and held Christina blouse out to her. "But I'll try to be home every weekend, and even during the week if I can." She wanted to say, if she wasn't out studying the Gramites, but with the alarm on Christina's face, she knew that wouldn't go over well.

Christina's fear blended with anger. "For four hundred and fifty-four days I watched you lying unconscious on that damn bed, worried you'd never wake. Every tiny twitch of a muscle gave me hope you would, but you didn't. Why? Because you had injured yourself to the point your body struggled to recover. My love for you and our daughter kept me going, but I can't go through that again."

"Christina, don't you understand? I have to do this."

"Why, because of some twisted God complex you have to change the world?" She jerked her blouse from Trish's grasp.

"God complex? Is that what you think this is?" Trish felt a wave of hurt and anger stab violently into her heart. "Do you even know me?"

Christina's eyes shot upward, her face recoiling as if Trish had slapped her with her words. She threw on the blouse and fervently yanked at the buttons. "I give up. Until you drop this foolish charade, I don't want to see you again."

"Another fucking ultimatum! Those are becoming second nature for you!" Trish whirled, heading to the door. "Fine, I'll pick Jennifer up tomorrow like we planned."

"No, she's busy tomorrow. If you ever bothered to check your messages, you'd know she's going to a birthday sleepover this weekend."

Trish spun, tasting the bitterness in Christina's words. "Christina, I haven't seen her all week—"

"Because of your own idiocy. What are we supposed to do, stop living our lives when you're away playing fixer-of-all-things?"

"Damnit, Christina, don't do this."

"She'll be free all next weekend. If you have time in your busy schedule, you can pick her up at the house on Friday. I'm off the entire day."

"Fine," Trish muttered, spinning from the anger spreading thickly between them. If she didn't leave now, she was sure she would say something she'd regret later. With the door unlatched and swung open, she veered right instead of left, heading out the backdoor, away from the glimpses of prying eyes.

Olivia slowed Buck to a trot and gave him a vigorous rub. Buck whipped his head while bellowing out his gratitude for their run. "I know," Olivia said to Buck, "but it's been a terribly busy week. I told you it would be. I promise, next week we'll go out twice as much as we usually do. Agreed?"

He pumped his mane up and down, expanding his chest beneath her legs. He let loose a lip-smacking, *thank you*, and she replied with an effulgent, "You're welcome." Both their heads shot up with the sound of shouting over by the outer gate, directly past the hillside. Her heart raced, thinking maybe the Gramites had been spotted close to the outer wall again.

Since Trish had awoken from her coma six months ago, the Gramites had stayed away. Olivia never connected the two until the uncanny events of last weekend with Buck and Molly, and the haphazard way Trish answered her questions when they went swimming. To Olivia, Trish seemed to have a mysterious link to the animal world, but were the Gramites animals? The more the week played out, the deeper Olivia's psychoanalytical mind crossed into the realm of fantasy. The gossip of the fearless blue-eyed goddess diving into a hole full of infected, injured, yet unchanged was an infamous story her friends had kept reliving since the bonfire. What really got her mind spinning was recalling Trish's sidestepping at the pool, in which she didn't affirm, nor deny, the incident had occurred. Trish's lab work from a year ago was an additional clue something strange, yet magnificent, was going on. A secret Aralyn and the others, even Trish, were adamant to keep hidden.

A bit concerned by the continued sound of commotion, Olivia directed Buck up the hill, still staying far enough away not to be noticed or so that she could cast Buck into a sprint if needed. The moment they reached the top, Olivia's eyes squinted at the two guards arguing with someone in a militia vehicle. Her eyes narrowed to the vehicle and the arm of the person sitting behind the wheel. Even from hers and Buck's location, Olivia was certain the fitted shirt was attached to Trish's perfectly molded body. The moment the door flung open and the heated driver got out, Olivia's heart leapt. She signaled Buck into a run, and he darted toward the commotion.

"Look, assholes," Trish shouted, motioning for Molly to stay. She headed to the tail-end of the vehicle. "I've got everything I need, and then some."

Buck kicked up gravel once they hit the road, and she slowed him as they drew closer to Trish's raised voice. The guards spotted their approach before Trish, who was too set on her objective to be easily dissuaded. Olivia watched Trish throw open the hatch and point forcefully inside. Trish eyeballed the guards and turned abruptly, spotting Olivia bringing Buck to a full stop.

Olivia saw the same sadness in Trish's eyes as the night of the bonfire, yet the blue was also seething with an added splash of icy anger. She had a good feeling Trish had met with her wife and the outcome had ended badly. "Hey, stranger. Buck thought he heard your voice, and he was insistent on coming over to say hi."

With pressed lips, Trish refocused her agitation on the guards.

Olivia waved to each of the soldiers before dismounting. "Is everything all right?" she asked.

"I'm trying to leave this damn city and head to New Underwood before dark, but *Thing One* and *Thing Two* claim I need to change first." She glared at the privates. "Even though I wore this a few hours ago on my way in here." She then pointed to the bulging duffel-bag and rucksack sitting neatly in the vehicle's storage area. "As you both can see, I'm well equipped for a twenty-mile drive."

Olivia also noticed the generous supply of camping supplies on the other side of the open space. Trish really did enjoy camping.

So, their mission was at the whispered construction site of New Underwood. Those in the city said the work had finished the previous weekend. Of course, why didn't she piece this together herself? Olivia moved closer, not losing her smile. "I happen to have several bottles of beer in the fridge. Wanna hang out tonight, maybe even go for a swim?"

Trish peered from her to Buck. Her eyes softened. She stepped forward and ran her hand over Buck's neck and muzzle. Olivia watched in awe as Buck's eyelids slowly dropped, soothed by the woman's tranquil yet firm touch. Olivia had a sudden belief Trish probably gave the most amazing back rubs. She swallowed and nervously scratched behind Buck's ear.

"I really don't want to be a burden," Trish finally said.

Olivia huffed. She headed to Buck's side and climbed easily up into the saddle. "I already told your stubborn ass. You don't need permission to camp at my place. I've officially told my friends and colleagues that the few acres in front of the pond to the trees are yours. If they want to orchestrate another bonfire, they must go through you to do it."

Trish's throat released a short-lived snicker, and she followed it with a clearing of her throat. She moved over and closed the hatch. Olivia watched with amusement as both guards saluted Trish, but instead of returning the hand gesture, she stopped and glared until each soldier pivoted around and hurried off to their tower.

Olivia laughed. "Do you know, before we met, I was told you had a pleasant personality. I think I've been lied to."

Trish shrugged. "My life's growing too complicated to maintain a cheerful persona. Grumbling is becoming my new pastime."

When Trish climbed into the vehicle, Olivia let out a soft giggle. Like last weekend, Olivia would work her magic through lighthearted conversation, good food and drink, and a restful atmosphere to release the tension on Trish's adorable lips.

CHAPTER EIGHT

At hearing the familiar beat of Shania Twain's song, "Any Man of Mine," kick on behind her, Trish lowered her book and shifted her head toward the stables' open door. She checked her watch. Seven-fifteen in the morning. Life on the farm seemed a lot like the militia in the sense that hard work kicked off early and ended late, three meals a day was an unwavering part of life, and whenever you had a moment to yourself, you filled your downtime with hobbies you enjoyed. Around here, entertainment came in the form of country music, bonfires, swimming, and drinking.

Trish dropped the book, stood from the collapsible lounge chair, and made her way to the barn door. Pudding greeted her with a pithy neigh and a flick of her head, which Trish returned with a generous neck and muzzle rub. She peeked toward the rear of the barn, where she could hear a gush of water and see the slithering of a hose along the wet concrete slab, past the farthest set of partially opened doors. She kissed Pudding's nose, and headed down the row of empty stalls that smelled of fresh hay and leather. Two aromas Trish realized last weekend, she greatly enjoyed.

The early Saturday morning sun hit her the moment she stepped from the shaded building. She leaned against the wooden panels and watched the way Olivia kicked her boots in the puddles to the beat of her favorite song. Molly lay in the grass with her head cocking from one side to the other at the lively display from the dancing woman. On Olivia's next kick-turn-combo, her hazel eyes whipped around, and she leapt with a startled gasp. She brought her hand up to her checkered shirt and let out a bout of panting laughter. "Trish, you scared the crap out of me."

Trish casually shrugged. "What are you doing?"

Olivia directed the nozzle onto the patiently awaiting horse. "Giving Buck a bath. What does it look like?"

Trish slowly took in the surroundings. "The slab's wetter than Buck, but if you say so."

Olivia narrowed her eyes. "Your hair's damp, but I didn't hear you come in this morning. Please tell me you didn't bathe in the pond."

Trish straightened and called Molly to her. She knelt and scratched along the dog's fur. "Okay, I won't tell you," she said, not raising her eyes with her poorly suppressed chortle.

"Trish, I told you to use the first floor bathroom. You'll smell like fish all day."

Trish stood. "So, I can run into Tracy again? No, thank you." She raised her arm and took a big whiff. She moved around Buck to the amused Olivia. "Plus, do I smell like fish?"

When Olivia leaned forward, her nose brushed along the softness of Trish's neck as she inhaled. Trish snickered, jumped backward, and scratched at her goosebumps. "Okay, punk, that tickled."

Olivia raised her eyes and bit her lower lip. "Punk?" She pointed the hose suddenly at Trish.

Trish's arms shot upward, as her entire frontside became drenched in water. Trish laughed wholeheartedly as she ran inside the barn, with a stream of water following close behind.

She heard Olivia call out, "Now go inside and shower…punk."

Turning off the shower valve, Trish stepped out into the spacious bathroom to the smell of fresh, cooked bacon. Her stomach growled. She moved to the lengthy granite counter surrounding the double sink and frowned. Where were her clothes? She searched around the sink and by the shower. Nothing. Her eyes scanned carefully through the entire roomy bathroom. She spotted the faded blue outfit sitting on the chair by the door. When she retrieved the denim shirt resting on top, her nose scrunched. "You've got to be kidding me," she muttered.

Gripping onto the towel enveloping her body, she opened the door and peeked her head out. Her mouth watered at the wonderful aroma of a Southern fried breakfast, hopefully the same one Olivia had made for her last Monday before she left. She was about to call out for Olivia, to insist her outfit be returned, when she heard the distinct sound of Tracy and Olivia arguing. Hastily, she closed the door.

She rubbed her hands on her forehead. Frowning, she snatched up her sports bra, boxers, white T-shirt, and socks and put them on. Reluctantly, she dressed in the matching jeans and denim overshirt. The belt buckle was way too big, and the faded boots appeared as worn as the rest of the outfit. Sitting on the toilet for a moment, Trish debated if she should remain in the bathroom for the rest of the day or go eat first before returning here to hide.

Sighing, she left the belt on the sink and rose to her feet, surprised by how comfortable the boots felt. Even the jeans hugged her in all the right places, strangely making her feel more in tune with herself than the designer ones she normally wore. It was the same welcome feeling her beloved flannel shirts or the colorful board-shorts and flip-flops offered.

She leaned forward and cracked the door. The sound of the heated arguing was gone. She exited the bathroom and entered the kitchen to Tracy sitting at the table red-faced and agitated and Olivia cooking with no music on. Something was most definitely up. Trish was about to head out to her vehicle for a ration pack, which strangely enough, now sounded better than crispy, cooked bacon, until Olivia spun from the stove and pointed toward the table. Trish gave a slight shake of her head. Olivia placed her hand on her hip, and Trish slumped her shoulders.

"You look good, by the way. The outfit suits you," said Olivia, breaking the silence. She visually inspected her. "Where's the belt?"

"In the bathroom where it'll remain, and I feel like one enormous pair of jeans from my neck down. By the way, where are *my* clothes?"

Trish could tell Olivia was struggling to hold down her enjoyment. "In the wash. They smelled of fish. Now sit."

"You may as well take a seat," Tracy said. "She's in a freaking mood today." She stood and crossed to the sink to rinse off her plate. She twisted her upper body toward Trish. In a snide voice she added, "Seriously, you can sit at the grownup table. I promise I won't ground you."

"Tracy!" Olivia shouted.

Tracy's condescending tone struck a nerve. After the week she'd had, ending with the verbal fight with Christina, Trish had hit her breaking point. She gave an amused snort, which was followed by a surge of forced laughter. Trish moved to the cabinet for a coffee cup. She breathed out, "adult table," as she poured her coffee. Suddenly, she eyed the black liquid in her cup, then Tracy. Her expression animated into panic. "Does this really stunt your growth?"

Tracy puckered her brow. "What?"

Trish shrugged. "What are you, five-three, five-four? If I drink this, will I grow up short like you? Cuz, I'd rather be tall like momma Olivia."

Surprised, Olivia let out a bout of laughter.

Tracy scowled, balled her fist, and stepped a few paces toward Trish, her bruised ego demanding blood to mend itself.

Olivia's laughter fell silent.

Trish placed her cup on the counter, rested her butt against the sink, and casually crossed her legs.

Tracy didn't say a word, but her eyes were gliding over Trish, as if assessing her competition. Clearly, the five-foot-six woman wasn't threatened by the several inches of height or muscle mass Trish had on her.

Trish sighed. "Do you really want to do this, Tracy? At your age?"

Wide-eyed and with a new ripple of anger, Tracy rushed forward, brought her fist up, and swung straight for Trish's face.

Trish seized her arm, kicked Tracy's foot out from under her, and slammed the off-balance Tracy easily to the ground, knocking the air from her lungs. As Tracy struggled to catch her breath, Trish did her best to assist the gasping woman. "Breathe slowly," Trish said.

The instant air found its way in, Tracy took in several rapid breaths. She swayed to her side and knocked Trish's hands away. Trish kept her hands raised in surrender as she straightened, and she turned to add sugar to her cup. Tracy climbed slowly to her feet. Even though her eyes now held uncertainty, she was still livid.

Trish took a sip, placed her cup down on the counter, and the spoon in the sink. She moved forward a few feet from Tracy. "If it'll make you feel better, take a swing. I swear I won't block or hit you in return."

"Stop this, both of you!" Olivia shouted, but they ignored her.

Tracy narrowed her eyes. "Bullshit you won't."

"I promise," Trish said. "What do you have to lose?"

The jab to her nose was instant.

Unwilling to show her surprise, Trish stood her ground. She clicked her tongue against her teeth, somewhat impressed that Tracy wasn't all bark and no bite. "Weak. You were too hasty. Take your time and try again."

Olivia moved forward in protest, but Tracy tossed her a glare, insisting she stay out of it. She adjusted her footing. The next fist she sent was with solid force directly to Trish's cheek. It landed hard, cutting the flesh below her left eye and drawing blood.

Trish casually brought her hand up and brushed at the point of impact. She inspected the red smear of blood on her fingers. "Much better," she said with a wink. "Now, are we done?"

Olivia moved in and pushed herself between the two. "Damnit, I said enough." She spun on Tracy. "Get out. Don't come back until you're ready to apologize."

Tracy opened her mouth and glowered at them both. She fixed her glare fully on Trish. "That'll never fucking happen." After a few long, awkward seconds, Tracy pivoted on her heels, seized her bag from the table, and left the kitchen.

Olivia frowned. "What the hell, Trish?"

Trish sighed. "I'm sorry for egging her on. I wasn't in the mood for her snippy comments today. I'll go pack up—"

Olivia clenched her teeth together. "I swear, if you mention leaving again, I'll be so pissed at you." She pointed toward the table. "Now, sit."

Trish reluctantly did as Olivia instructed. Olivia headed out of the room. She returned a few minutes later with a sizeable first aid kit. She placed it on the table and rushed to the stove.

"I'm fine, Olivia," Trish said, eyeing the army-green bag with a bright red cross on the front.

Olivia flipped off the gas burner and removed the last of the bacon. "Tell that to the cut under your eye. I swear, what was the plan? Stand there like a punching bag and hope for the best?" She removed a kitchen towel from a side drawer and soaked it with hot water from the faucet. Olivia pulled a chair over beside her, seated herself, and opened the bag.

"Honestly, I didn't think Tracy had the balls to hit me." Trish wiped the drying blood on her fingers along the outside of her pantleg. "I guess I was wrong."

Olivia narrowed her eyes at the door Tracy had left through. "Trish, that woman can be downright nasty, and she's never lost a fight. Please, until things calm down between you two, stay away from her."

Olivia used the damp towel and cleaned the blood from Trish's cheek. When Olivia touched the cotton-ball drenched in rubbing alcohol to the cut, Trish flinched. "Crap, Olivia! I really am fine."

"No, you need stitches. Now hold still."

Trish knew in a few hours the cut would have sealed itself. Realizing this, she adjusted the way she was sitting, as if this would help ease her sudden feeling of dread. How would she explain her body's rapid healing speed to a skilled doctor? "Look, I don't like needles. Can't you throw some tape over it and call it good?" Mentally, she kicked herself in the butt for verbally spurring Tracy into action.

"I'm trying to keep you from scarring."

Trish stared directly at her.

After a moment's pause, Olivia threw up her hands. "Fine, I'll bandage it, but if you end up looking like Frankenstein's creature, don't come crying to me."

Trish laughed. "I won't."

Olivia busied herself with selecting what she needed from the bag. "I've set up the spare bedroom next to the bathroom for you.

It's yours, you can come and go as you please. The bed's more than big enough for you and Jennifer, but I can make up another room if you think she'd be more comfortable having her own space. I placed several outfits in the closet and drawers, similar to the ones you're wearing. They're sturdier than the designer outfits you normally dress in, for when you're riding or fishing out at the pond." She gestured toward the front room. "I also placed a spare key in your hiking boots next to the coffee table."

Surprised, Trish wasn't sure how to respond. She pulled her eyebrows together, feeling instantly uncomfortable. "Olivia, I camp because it's peaceful being out in the open. I'm not in need of anything. I have more credits than I'll—"

Olivia raised a hand up. "Trish, this isn't charity. This is one friend helping another friend out while they get their life together. You need a place outside of work to call your own."

Trish inhaled sharply. "Is this why you and Tracy were arguing?"

Olivia covered the Steri-strips with clean gauze and adhesive tape. "What did you hear?"

Trish kept her head still while Olivia worked. "Raised voices is all. I closed the door as soon as I realized you two were having a heated discussion. Believe me, I've lived through enough yelling lately to last me for a while." She wasn't sure if she should say anything or not, but decided, due to the day's events, she probably should. "You do know Tracy's a lesbian, right?"

Olivia's eyes widened. "Yes, Trish, I know that. From what I've heard, so are you."

"I know, but with Tracy, I think she has a crush on you. With me being here, it's probably making her jealous."

Olivia applied the last strip of tape on the gauze. "I can handle Tracy," she said, eyeing her work. "Now you need to hurry and eat.

We have a full schedule today of riding and teaching you how to line dance later. Which is why I switched out your outfit."

Trish forcefully shook her head. "I don't dance. I'm not any good at it. I do love how the clothes fit, though. But I refuse to wear the belt,"

Olivia headed to the counter to prepare both plates. "Line dancing differs from other types of dancing. Like the clothes, I'm positive you'll love it." She placed the plates on the table and retook her seat. "I won't force you, but it would be nice if you at least tried it."

Trish sighed. "Fine," she said with a grumble, taking her first bite.

Trish dived into the water, enjoying the refreshing wetness as her muscles worked at pushing her forward. After doing a lap, she swam to the deep end and allowed her body to sink downward in the water. She rolled into a ball, kicked off from the bottom, and shot herself toward the edge. She loved swimming. She only wished her dense bone structure allowed her more mobility. With her weightiness, her movements were vastly limited.

"Trish, what are you doing? I said no swimming."

Trish gripped onto the side of the pool. "You were still at the barn, so I decided to come kill a few minutes until you finished."

Olivia bent down and removed the soaked gauze from Trish's cheek. "Trish, the tape isn't supposed to—" Olivia's words broke off.

Realizing her dimwitted blunder, Trish turned her head away. She kicked off from the wall before diving under the water. God, she was such an idiot. When she came up to the other side of the pool, she looked over right as Olivia finished stripping off her clothes, down to her matching bra and underwear, and dove in.

"Fuck," Trish whispered, moving farther along the edge. Fleeing was no use. Olivia was well skilled in swimming and holding her breath underwater for long stretches. She popped her head up right beside Trish.

Olivia extended her hand outward and stroked her thumb over Trish's cheek. Trish lowered her eyes, averting them away from Oliva's full breasts floating under the red, lacy material. Olivia slowly peeled at the corner of a Steri-strip and worked it free. Again, her fingertips rolled over the spot of the cut, or where the cut once stood. "There's nothing there."

Gripping onto the edge of the pool, Trish sighed. "Please don't ask me to explain." She avoided Olivia's searching eyes.

After a brief silence, Olivia agreed. "Since we're already here, we might as well enjoy a swim."

Trish could hear the confusion in Olivia's voice, and she knew many unasked questions were spinning around in the veterinarian's mind. She pulled herself up and out of the water. "I'll get the beer," she called over her shoulder, praying the subject wouldn't be brought up during the rest of their weekend together.

CHAPTER NINE

JUNE 30, 2090

Pulling the trigger, Trish watched through the rifle scope as her bullet struck the Gramite in the back, the impact jerking it forward. The creature swung an arm blindly outward, hitting nothing but air. It turned wide-eyed in every direction, narrowing its eyes with hatred toward a subordinate over twenty feet away. It screamed out a ferocious protest, causing the startled Gramite to drop itself down into the weeds, cowering as the others surrounding the area looked on. Trish watched the male pound its massive arms into the ground, grunt a few times, and eagerly return to feasting on the deer carcass at its feet.

"That's it, you big brute. Stop throwing a tantrum." Trish lowered the rifle and her visor, as she spoke to the others in her helmet. "I finally tagged the leader of horde-three. You were right, Phillips, he came out of the den when the others dragged in the deer." She gazed through the scope. "We're naming this one Scarface."

"Got it, Scarface," Doctor Burgos repeated.

"Really? Scarface? That's the best you can come up with. All these names suck, and you owe me twenty credits by the way," Phillips said.

Trish shook her head, as she glared into the hologram image of Phillips on her display. "We said ten."

"No, ten for the hunting party bringing the deer to the den and not eating it themselves, and another ten that the leader would be an ugly sonofabitch."

Trish sat up and searched the hillside. She was roughly twenty miles from New Underwood, and two miles from this cluster of Gramites. "Are you following me?" she demanded as she retrieved her binoculars from her utility belt. She raised her visor and peered inside the eyes piece. She searched the hillside, stopping on the dark-haired man to the far edge of the hill, with peppering-gray above both ears. He was standing by one of their militia vehicles, waving to her.

Dropping the visor, Trish fought to keep her voice calm. "I said I didn't want anyone out here with me. You're a distraction I now have to worry about."

Phillips argued, but Trish muted his link. "Colonel," she slowly said, climbing to her feet. "We agreed I would oversee this part of the mission from the beginning. I'm requesting you to send Sergeant Phillips to New Underwood asap. I have work to do."

"Captain Webber, you've been out there for three days straight." Trish could hear the worry in her godmother's voice.

"Colonel, we had an agreement," Trish insisted.

Aralyn wasn't even supposed to stay at the outpost for more than a few days a week, but with her and Susan still being at odds, Trish knew why Aralyn didn't remain in Rapid City longer than a couple hours each day. This Trish was okay with. However, out here amongst the creatures, this hazardous landscape was Trish's domain. The last thing she needed was to worry about the safety of one of her teammates while she performed this part of their critical tasks.

Trish unmuted Phillips's link in time to hear Aralyn order him to head to the outpost. She grinned, knowing the man was saying a few choice cusswords under his breath. She peered into the eyepiece, flashed him a toothy snicker, and sent him an elaborate wave.

Feeling satisfied with herself, she headed toward the tent by her Gladiator. She changed from her bodysuit into her running outfit and did a simple stretch on the trampled patch of weeds in front of her tent. Slinging her rifle strap over her head like a sash, she refilled Molly's water and instructed her to stay in the shade while she was gone.

This beautiful day was Friday, June thirtieth. The last two weeks had consisted of long hours working on honing her abilities inside the vault, finding and tagging a few Gramites in the three located hordes around New Underwood, and spending last weekend with Jennifer and Sam. They camped and fished at Olivia's pond, with a few breaks dedicated to horseback riding and line dancing lessons for her and the kids from the overly patient Olivia.

After the heated exchange between her and Christina when she dropped Jennifer off on Sunday, Trish had done all she could to keep her anger and anxiety to herself. With the two veterinary trucks already in use from the other four veterinarians on Olivia's staff, Trish and Jennifer offered Olivia a friendly ride to collect the horse feed after they dropped Sam off at the children's home. When Trish had walked Jennifer to the door, Christina saw the outline of the woman sitting in the Gladiator and instructed their daughter to go to her room. Christina then verbally lashed out, criticizing Trish's mothering abilities. Trish had told Christina she was being ridiculous, and Christina informed Trish she wasn't allowed to have Jennifer when she was hanging out with her bimbos. Fuming with rage, Trish silently drove Olivia and the bags of feed to the farm. Trish had apologized profusely when she dropped off Olivia for pulling the veterinarian into their family drama. She then headed to New Underwood a day early, even after Olivia told Trish she was fine and insisted that Trish being alone in her state wasn't a good idea.

Trish visually searched over the brown grass, colorful wildflowers, and rocky patches mixed throughout the rolling green for miles surrounding her. She thought being alone was exactly what she needed. She headed off along the hillside, doing a second twenty-mile run of the day. Next week she would be stuck in the testing room, blowing through the repaired sound sensors again. Until then, she was going to enjoy the last few days of this week on a hillside of peace and quiet while observing the Gramites of this horde.

Eva passed it along to Captain Strong on Tuesday that even though Christina would be working, Jennifer would be unavailable this weekend. Right after Carlen reluctantly gave Trish the message, Trish had suffered through the worst feeling of pain she'd ever experienced before. She felt as if she were losing her daughter. Even though Olivia was expecting her to show up later, Trish decided to forgo this weekend of riding and line dancing lessons. Instead, she wanted to study the Gramites and be free of other people.

Trish woke up early on Saturday and packed. She kept a cold camp to help hide her location from the Gramites, so she had little to tear down. There was an unusual, tingly sensation off to the north, and being as how her intuition was usually spot on, she rolled with it. She drove twenty miles, passing the outline of New Underwood to the left, and traveled ten miles more toward Rapid City. She pulled her vehicle over and climbed out, unsure of what her intuitive mind was picking up.

When her wrist processor beeped, Trish opened the door, leaned over the seat, and powered up the Gladiator's mainframe. Scrolling through the holographic commands, she connected to the verbal link and turned up the volume.

Doctor Burgos was on the line. "Trish, we're checking in to seeing why you've changed locations."

Confused, Trish climbed in behind the steering wheel. "Doctor Burgos, why are you working on Saturday?" she asked, switching to the hologram display. She saw others move around the room behind Doctor Burgos's video feed. "Who's there with you?"

He peered over his shoulder and at her. "We all are. No one went home since you decided to stay out in the field."

Trish gripped her hands on the steering wheel, as a wave of guilt and agitation surged through her. "What the hell," she said, grumbling.

"Complain all you want," he said adamantly. "Everyone made their own decision." His blue figure drew closer to the screen. "So, why'd you move?"

Trish studied the area, not sensing any danger, yet something didn't feel right. "I'm not sure. I'm going to drive around a bit. If I don't spot anything in the next half hour, I'll head in so everyone can go home. Our guards need some time off." Trish deactivated the link and powered down her processor. Her groan was short-lived, but her agitation lingered. Why did Doctor Burgos and the others have to make something simple so dang complicated?

Once she had her armored vehicle moving again, Trish drove up the steep hillside. She lowered her and Molly's windows and inspected the terrain for movement. "Now, if you see anything, bark. Got it?"

Molly yelped out her affirmative and stuck her head outside, allowing the wind to flip her tongue wildly about. Trish chuckled at the sight.

She scratched along Molly's fur, as her eyes searched the valley below. Rapid City was nestled in the distance, giving off a stunning view. It was the ideal setting for a pre, end-of-the-world souvenir postcard. They continued slowly forward, drawing within several miles of the concrete exterior wall. Once the rocky terrain finally became impassable, Trish brought the vehicle to a halt next to a steep drop-off. Her eyes skimmed over the outer rim, which resembled a man-made ravine, horseshoeing around for close to half a mile. She pulled out her binoculars and studied the landscape, spotting a weed-infested pathway marked by old metal signs along the far side of the cliff.

The drop-off on her side was too dangerous for any type of vehicular traffic. Or so she thought. Stepping out to get a better looksee, she noticed multiple tread markings on the ground. Her eyes shifted along the dirt trail, where she recognized several sets of wide tire treads. They were a perfect match for the Gladiators her own militia used. With the rain on Thursday, these vehicles had to have been here yesterday or earlier this morning when the sky was still too dark to see clearly. Because of the swift drop-off, she didn't believe anyone would drive this stretch of the ravine with limited to no light visibility.

She headed to the Gladiator and threw on her helmet. She linked to Doctor Burgos and asked to speak to her godmother. Within a minute, Aralyn's blue holographic face appeared. She told her godmother about the tire marks and how the bulk of the city was in perfect view of this location. Aralyn said she'd verify with headquarters to make sure none of their vehicles had been out that way. She'd also have Major Thomas send a team up to place sensors along both sides of the ravine for future monitoring.

The second the connection ended, Trish's senses flared. She veered her concentration to the left, away from the city. She snatched her binoculars off the dashboard when she saw a stretched dust cloud moving down in the valley, heading in her direction. The instant she spotted the lead horse of a sizable herd, her excitement rose as she stood in awe at the unexpected phenomenon. She swiveled her eyepiece around, taking in the magnitude of the swiftly moving herd. Her enthusiasm plummeted. The yellow-orange eyes that followed the herd was what really made her heart race.

Olivia jumped from her seat by the pond at the sound of crunching gravel from an approaching vehicle. She flipped her fishing pole and grumbled when the front end of one of their own trucks emerged. She had thought about taking a drive to New Underwood to check on Trish when she didn't show yesterday, but her voice of reason told her not to. Trish needed space, and Olivia needed to respect it, whether the apprehension buzzing around in her stomach felt the same way or not.

She was getting ready to reach in the cooler when she saw their other vehicle and three of the local farm trucks following, all with horse trailers attached. She reeled in the line and propped the pole against her chair. Heading toward the house where the convoy of vehicles came to a stop, she saw Tracy leave the barn to meet the group.

Tylor exited the lead pickup, overly ecstatic. "The supply run heading to the Oahe Dam radioed an hour ago. A herd of horses is moving our way."

Olivia's heart skipped a beat, and she had to force herself to keep her voice calm and speak clearly. Not blabber out her question like an overexcited adolescent. "Did they say how many?"

He said, "Over twenty."

Olivia clapped her hands together, thrilled by the numbers. "Load in Buck and Pudding while we collect our things." She rushed up to the house behind Tracy.

Laying on her stomach overlooking the valley past Horseshoe Ridge, Olivia fanned the rifle scope around the herd for the third time. Before Olivia had even noticed the pursuing Gramites, she could tell by the way the herd was moving, something was wrong. They looked exhausted, as if they had been running for hours without a break. Once she spotted the yellow-orange eyes numbering close to twenty infected, her heart sank, pulling any excitement left down with it.

"Crap, they're heading into Horseshoe Ravine. Looks like this operation was a waste of time," Tracy grumbled beside her.

"They can't kill every horse in the herd. There's too many. We'll wait and gather up the stragglers when it's over," Tylor said, trying to sound hopeful.

Olivia lowered her rifle and dropped her head into the bend of her arm. This slaughter would be hard to watch. Still, Tylor was right. They might get lucky.

Her head lifted as the herd passed into the lip of the cavity, with no exit. The Gramite horde was half a mile away, running on all fours and snapping fiercely in thrilled excitement for the expected kill. The screams echoing out from both Gramite and equine mixed in a sickening unison off the rock walls under them. Dust hung throughout the herd like a dense cloud from the running, jolting, and anxious circling of the frightened animals. They were realizing what the people on the ravine already knew. They had nowhere left to go.

"What the hell? Is he planning on heading down there alone?"

Olivia's head darted to Tylor. He pointed to the ledge of the ravine across from where they were hiding. She peered into the scope and spotted the soldier dressed in the militia's armored bodysuit and helmet. The individual attached a clip from the Gladiator's pulley system onto a utility belt. Olivia's blood froze. She shook her head in disbelief. The soldier worked the controls on the device and pulled on the cable, as if trying to find the right tension.

Suddenly, the soldier sprinted forward, dived off the edge, and swung outward. He found instant footing when the line shot him into the rocky wall. He ran down the solid barrier as if running on a horizontal span of road. The cable didn't loosen and drop him, but pulled tight, causing the soldier to dig into the vertical rock surface to keep himself pushing downward at an elevated pace. Before he even hit the ground, the cloud of dust covered his final twenty- or thirty-foot descent.

"Idiot," Tracy muttered. "Even if he was planning on trying to stop the Gramite attack, the horses will trample him as soon as he hits the ground."

They all waited and watched as the Gramites drew closer. The horse's screaming softened and the Gramites bellows picked up in strength, almost drowning out the horses' cries all together. The dust surrounding the horses also kicked up less with the wind twirling around, carrying away some of the powered thickness that remained. They still jerked their heads around, a few in sight pawing nervously at the ground, but even these actions were lessening.

"Don't tell me they're giving up." Justin scowled toward the horses, while shaking his head in disbelief. "If they do, they'll all get slaughtered."

Olivia's eyes widened when the dark figure moved out from the cloud of dust. Her heart raced as the soldier turned and raised his hands to the horses. Olivia's stomach tightened, as her palms turned cold, clammy. She peered into the scope, silently praying other soldiers were around to help. She studied the rock ledge, scoping out the area for any other signs of movement. She saw none. The lone soldier pivoted to the Gramites and rush forward, heading straight toward the infected.

"Are we not going to do anything?" she heard April ask.

Tylor hissed, "Are you crazy? If we fire even one bullet, they'll know we're here and come for us next. Do you not see how many there are?"

Olivia knew Tylor was right, but her finger still drew closer to the trigger. The soldier dropped in speed to a jog the second the Gramites hit the opening of the ravine. Once the soldier's hands reached up and removed the helmet, she heard a wave of startled gasps on both sides of where she lay. Her eyes widened with shock, her body too numb and frightened to react.

They all watched as Trish sat her helmet casually on the ground. She unslung her rifle and placed it on the helmet with the muzzle end resting on top. She pounded her arms across her chest and squatted, striking the ground violently with both fists. She was mimicking what the creatures did before they attacked. Trish's deep, yet powerful cry bounced brutally off the rock walls. The line of creatures slowed but didn't stop. Olivia watched the scene with helpless fear. Trish went through the motions again, as if egging them on. This time her cry was deeper, harsher, more determined than before.

If she was trying to get the infected to take notice, it worked. Close to a hundred yards away from Trish, the leader in front halted his pursuit toward the herd, and those around it did the same. It bent forward and eyed Trish suspiciously. It pounded on the ground, and those around it repeated his movements while screaming and snapping at the air in her direction. She moved forward and circled around, directing each of their eyes off the horses and fully onto her.

Olivia swung her gaze to the horses. A tall, black stallion was standing at the front of the herd, eyeballing the exchange, with his head angled sideways. The rest stood behind, pawing at the ground. The dust had settled to the point that each of their heads were exposed. Nostrils flared, glares intensified, but their anxious prancing was gradually subsiding.

"Olivia, let me hold the rifle. I don't trust that look in your eyes," Tracy said, reaching over to take the weapon from her grasp.

Olivia spun her head to the side and glowered at Tracy.

Tracy had the good sense to yank her hand away.

Olivia peered into the scope. The leader sized up Trish and took a step forward. The infected stopped suddenly and tilted his head. He half-pivoted and barked at two Gramites next to him, which sent both towering infected to sprint toward Trish on all fours. When she saw the blue-eyed woman ready herself, holding no weapon of any kind, Olivia felt the sudden urge to be sick. This was it. The moment she lost Trish, the same way she lost her first love. She closed her eyes tight, dropped her head to her arm, and stifled her cry.

"Holy shit. Did that really happen?"

Hearing Tylor's words, Olivia couldn't help but peek at Trish, knowing full well that one of her limbs had probably been violently ripped from her body in a matter of seconds. She knew the Gramites had a taste for that.

She was beside herself when she saw both Gramites on the ground, and Trish standing over the closest, sending the infected a commanding yell. Olivia looked into the scope. One of the fallen Gramites slowly rose and shook the cobwebs from its head, as the other lay sprawled out, unmoving. It stumbled onto its feet, and Trish ran forward and jumped high in the air. She sent a fist with her body momentum right into its face. Its head snapped forcefully back, its legs wobbled, and it fell to the ground beside the other. Trish spun and screamed out to the leader. She pounded her chest and continued her motions at the horde.

"This is incredible," Tylor muttered next to her. "How is she able to physically do that?"

The leader glowered at his followers and roared louder to two more. They both rushed at Trish on all fours. As the first one reached her, Trish spun low, sweeping her leg around and into the cheek of the creature. Its face distorted to the blow and its powerful, yet graceless build tumbled onto the hard earth. She sprinted forward and hit the next one head on, flipping it high in the air and sending it to the ground with a wave of hard punches straight to its face. It reeled and cried out, as if unsure of what to do. Trish rolled backward suddenly, missing the flying claws from the first of the two. She pivoted and kicked a foot out, dropping the infected swiftly to its knees. After two more blows to the face, it fell, squirming on the ground in agony.

"Look," April bellowed, pointing to the right.

Every eyeball followed her finger past the line of Gramites. Three militia vehicles sat unmoving. Aralyn and a few others were standing beside their Gladiators watching the same events going on, and Doctor Burgos was on the hood of the lead vehicles, appearing to be recording the proceedings. When Arlen waved, her gesture wasn't to them, but to Trish, who casually swung an arm overhead to acknowledge their presence, before locking one Gramite in a chokehold.

"Why aren't they doing anything?" April asked, almost insistent.

"What are they supposed to do, April?" Justin responded. "Fire a bunch of rounds into the Gramites, and risk hitting Trish or the horses?"

"Does it seem like Trish even needs their help?" Tylor questioned, still sounding astonished.

As if on cue, Trish dropped the one wrapped in her arms and shouted again to the leader. The leader's anger was to the point of rage, but it didn't move. Instead, it grimaced from Trish to the militia vehicles behind it. It yelled out in Trish's direction, sending three of the Gramites slowly up and scurrying to the horde. The one on the ground by Trish's feet lay with its eyes closed, its body unmoving. *Was it dead? Did she snap its neck? Choke it to the point it stopped breathing?*

If one had told Olivia that events couldn't get any crazier, they would have been gravely mistaken. Olivia watched in awe with the rest, as Trish knelt and rubbed slowly along the tattered, filthy remnants of a sweatshirt covering the unmoving Gramite. Trish glimpsed over her shoulder, as if to make sure none were sneaking up behind her before she focused her attention on rousing the one lying motionless in the weeds. Its leg twitched, an arm, and suddenly its head spun with a glare to Trish. She calmly pressed her hand against it, stepped several feet away, and watched it tremble to all fours.

The leader yelled again. The creature next to Trish looked at her uncertainly and skittered unsteadily to its group. Trish squared herself to the leader. They exchanged no more noise between one another. The leader snarled toward the horses and at Trish. It pivoted and bolted from the mouth of the ravine with his followers close beside it. Trish waved to her godmother and retrieved her helmet and rifle.

"Well…I'll be damned," Justin said, twisting his head in Olivia's direction. "How the hell could you possibly have kicked Trish's ass two weekends ago?"

Olivia opened her mouth, confused. "What?" Suddenly, she realized he wasn't speaking to her, but past her. She spun, fuming with anger. "Is that what you told them, Tracy, that you kicked Trish's ass? You're such a fucking liar. You better be grateful Trish didn't hit you back." She pointed into the ravine. "She would've killed you."

Olivia stood, fighting to get her anger under control. They needed to go down and collect the horses, and hopefully, she would get some answers to all the unimaginable questions darting around in her thoughts. Before taking her first step, she gasped.

Phillips and Carlen were standing beside a tree, watching them. Phillips gave their group a casual hello, wave. "The Colonel would like to speak to you all." He motioned toward the path. "If you don't mind heading down to your vehicles and following us to the others, it won't take too long. I promise."

Over thirty minutes later, Olivia pulled the truck to a stop beside the militia vehicles, which were now moved inside the ravine, blocking the horses from leaving. Searching past the windshield, Olivia noticed Trish was nowhere around. Glancing upward, she saw how both the cable and Trish's vehicle were gone. Did Trish scale the full length of the cliff? Honestly, at this point, nothing about Trish would surprise her.

Aralyn was standing with Doctor Burgos, surveying the nervous shifting of the black stallion and the other horses. Olivia and her group of four veterinarians and four farmhands approached, unsure of what to expect from the intimidating commander. Doctor Burgos was the first to greet them, but Aralyn's stern persona was what Olivia was most concerned with. He held out his hand, and she slowly shook it. "I have a feeling you all have questions about what you saw here. Unfortunately, for safety reasons, we have no answers to share. What we can tell you is Trish and the event you just witnessed are protected by both the governors of the city and Aralyn's militia."

Aralyn said, "What James is trying to say is we would appreciate you not telling anyone else in the city what happened here today."

Hearing the vibration off the rocky walls, Olivia rotated with the others and saw another militia vehicle pull into the area. She bit her lip in kiddish excitement, as Trish jumped out with Molly right beside her. Phillips passed Trish a bottled water, and she downed it in three throaty swigs. Then he passed her another.

Before she could open the bottle, Givens put Trish in a head hold and ruffled her hair. "We were placing bets on if you were going to give the last one a kiss or not. Unfortunately, I lost forty credits."

Several of the surrounding soldiers laughed. Trish pushed him playfully off and chugged her water. The comradery of those in Trish's life was awe-inspiring to watch. They loved her, and she loved them.

After Trish drained the bottle, she and Olivia locked eyes. Trish waved with enthusiasm and Olivia's heart fluttered. Trish headed in her direction. "You guys made it here in record time." She pointed to the horses. "Look what we found wondering aimlessly around."

Aralyn said, "Trish, they were up on the other side of the cliff. They saw everything."

Trish pinched her lips together. "Oh." She glanced with concern, toward Aralyn, then Doctor Burgos, and back to Olivia. "Well, crap." She paused for a moment in thought. She spoke to Aralyn while giving a slight nod to Olivia's group. "They might as well load the horses and get them safely to the city. The leader moved his horde, but they're not far. I'm sensing a mile away at the most. I think they're waiting to see if we leave any horses behind."

"You can sense them?" Olivia released her question, as her eyes shot to Aralyn. "I'm sorry. I didn't mean to pry."

Ignoring her question, Trish signaled to the trailers. "How many can you haul in one load?"

"Twenty," Olivia said. "We brought two of our own horses to help with rounding them up."

Trish gestured at the herd. "There's thirty-four horses here. You'll need to load what you can and run the rest in. We'll follow behind in our vehicles to make sure the Gramites keep their distance."

"Olivia can ride Buck, I'll take Pudding," Tylor said. He headed around to the main trailer and unlatched the gate.

Olivia moved toward Trish and whispered, "Are we not going to talk about what happened here?"

Trish shook her head. "Not right now, but I do want to say I'm sorry I didn't show up yesterday. This has been a tough week."

"Olivia, Buck's in one of his moods," Tylor hollered. Buck confirmed this when his kick echoed from inside the trailer.

Olivia waved anxiously in Tylor's direction, but her eyes never left Trish. "Please stay over tonight. I promise not to hound you with questions, but I need to know you're okay." She saw the apprehension in Trish's blue eyes, and Olivia inwardly sulked. "I have more beer," she added.

Trish gave a slight smirk, and Olivia's hope rose. Trish crossed her arms over her chest. "You're a willful woman when your mind's set on something."

Olivia flashed a wide grin and moved to help Tylor. "Many would agree."

Olivia rattled the ice around in her glass and took a sip. She tipped her head to Karen. "You're right, this is smooth."

Beaming with delight, Karen headed into the house to deposit the last case of liquor, supplied by two of the nightclubs. Once the news spread of the city's good fortune, many townsfolk arrived on Olivia's farm to see the beautiful creatures dancing friskily around within the two-acre field. With the limited number of vehicles to share between the ten homesteads, and previously only having five horses at the city's disposal including the two assigned to the

Veterinary staff, this discovery would help animal care and crop production immensely.

If an individual wanted to go from one spot inside the outer fence, all the way along the entire perimeter, the miles covered would be roughly one hundred and fifty. The long trip would take a traveler through places which had once been called Keystone and Piedmont, South Dakota. Now, it all fell into the city limits of Rapid City. On horseback, the ride would consist of several long days for rider and horse, which was what the vehicles were for. Yet, to work the land and commute to neighboring farms, these horses were more than a blessing—they were life-altering.

Olivia looked out at the grills and smokers, the many tents lining the area by the pond, and all of the farmhands building up wood for tonight's bonfire. She knew the place would be in an uproar over the next few days. Filled with good food, hearty celebration, and the town folks coming in with various side dishes, beverage donations, and lighthearted company to add to the celebration. She also knew the ranchers would help the veterinarians separate and examine each horse. None would leave here until they were assigned and physically taking the horses to their individual farms.

What excited Olivia the most was Aralyn had talked Trish into giving their team a few days off to enjoy and help with the festivities. Olivia had already prepared her house for the new guests, even before the stubborn Trish conceded to their mini holiday. For some unknown reason, Trish appeared guilt-ridden afterward. As if taking time off from their mission would endanger those inside the city. This belief added more questions to Olivia's growing list concerning Trish.

Olivia was adamant about Trish's team not sleeping outside with the other farmers and tent-dwellers. After all, they were the reason the horses were still alive. Tylor, Justin, and April gladly gave up their rooms for a few days, while Tracy had at first refused. When Olivia offered to sleep with Trish and give Aralyn her bedroom instead, Tracy immediately agreed to stay at the neighboring farm with April.

"It's about time Sergeant Givens cut that mop on your head," Carlen told Trish the moment Trish exited the house. Carlen handed her a beer and inspected her outfit. "Not bad. I actually like this new wardrobe. You need a cowboy hat to complete the ensemble," she said, running her fingers through Trish's hair.

Olivia sipped on the scotch and eyed Trish's outfit. The boots were black, so was the tucked in T-shirt. Her faded jeans were a perfect match to the pale blue color of the short-sleeve checkered overshirt. The lack of material showed off a set of arms, which old-world censorship would have deemed pornographic by nature. A black belt wrapped nicely around her fit waistline. Her hair was perfect, and her blue eyes gleamed when she was around those on her team.

Normally, Olivia would have agreed with the hat comment, but Trish's hair was sitting too cute to cover. Once she realized she was gawking like an openmouthed schoolgirl, Olivia blinked a few times and averted her gaze. She chased the moisture in her throat down with another drink of scotch, savoring the cinnamon aroma in her nose.

Trish walked toward her as sexy and innocent as ever. Damn, why did Trish's heart belong to someone who clearly wasn't right for her? Why was Trish blind to the connection Olivia and she both shared, and why did Trish always look at her as a dear friend and nothing more?

Most slithered their greedy eyes over Olivia's shapely body, as if she were a feast their hidden fantasies were famished for, which always infuriated her. Yet, Trish, the one person she craved the ogling attention from, stared into her eyes and never toward any of the curves of her body. As if Trish was uninterested in having even the smallest of visual tastes.

"Is that the famous scotch Karen's talking up in the kitchen?"

Olivia rolled her eyes when Trish snatched her glass and downed the rest. Trish smacked her lips together, cocked a damn infuriating smirk, and sent a wink Olivia's way. If Olivia had any scotch left, she might have chucked it straight at Trish for looking so damn adorable and not even realizing.

Trish lowered the glass. "Are you okay?"

Olivia took a long breath and sighed. "I'm fine. It's been a long day." She pointed to the empty glass. "You owe me another."

Trish's concern vanished. She placed her beer on a nearby table and headed toward the house.

Kicking the toe of her boot on the concrete slab, Olivia groaned out her frustration. She swung her gaze over to April, talking to Phillips and Carlen on the other side of the pool, and snorted. April was chatting away, while intensely watching Trish's ass as she headed through the sliding-glass doors.

Olivia swung her annoyed attention away, only to spot Aralyn staring directly at her. Trish's godmother was standing beside Doctor Burgos, who was engaging the intense colonel with in-depth conversation. Aralyn was listening to him, yet her eyes remained glued to Olivia, as if she were studying Olivia closely, while trying to stay up to speed with the man's adamant discussion. The way she toasted her drink in Olivia's direction worried Olivia. Had Aralyn picked up on Olivia's attraction toward her still married goddaughter?

Olivia spun and peered toward the barn, very much alarmed by what Aralyn must be thinking. She silently counted to ten and leaned on the railing, trying hard to steady herself. The sun was still touching the horizon, but many of the lights surrounding the barn were already on. She needed to pull herself together. Stop being so obvious when Trish was around.

The moment Trish returned, she placed a hand on Olivia's shoulder and rubbed. "Seriously, woman, are you feeling okay?"

Olivia's entire body tingled at the touch. She dipped her head, no longer caring if Aralyn was spying on her or not. The long circular strokes to her back caused her to take sluggish, deep breaths, which paused each time Trish's fingertips brushed against her beltline. Her traitorous body let out a tiny moan, which caused her shoulders and neck muscles to tighten. "Sorry, I guess the day was longer than I thought."

"No kidding, you feel like one big knot. Here, let me give you a full backrub. It might help."

Olivia's head shot upward, and she jerked away, nervously giggling. "Ticklish," she blurted out, holding up her hand. "I'm good."

Even though a backrub from Trish was exactly what her body was craving, the excitement throbbing between her legs was growing too intense. If Trish pressed her vigorous hands deeper throughout her muscles, Olivia was certain this entire group would know exactly how attracted Olivia was to Trish. She grabbed the drink, while working hard to keep her trembling hands steady. She downed a few sips, chasing them with a generous swallow.

Trish eyed her carefully. "Are you upset I didn't show up yesterday?"

The question surprised Olivia. "Not at all. You're an adult, and you can come and go as you please. Honestly, I've been worried about you since the incident last weekend." She shoved her shoulder into Trish's. "I know you'll talk if you need to, but if not, you know I'm here either way."

Trish's features showed appreciation, yet also concern. Her blue eyes raked the area, as if making sure no one else could hear. Trish took a drink of her beer, and leaned her elbows on the railing. "I will not ask you a hypothetical question, because we both know I'd be lying. I have an issue, but I can't really talk to anyone here about it. They'll be biased and take my side." She stood and turned her heartbreaking eyes to Olivia, who wasn't completely sure how unbiased her own response would be. "I need some friendly advice," Trish finally said.

"Olivia, I've got the numbers."

Both women twisted toward the ranch hand heading into the yard. He waved a slip of paper around. Olivia flashed Trish an apologetic look.

Trish leaned closer. Damn, she smelled good. She had used coconut shampoo to wash. "We can talk later," Trish said.

Olivia tried to keep her disappointment in. She had a feeling later for Trish probably meant never. Trish wasn't one who easily expressed her feelings, and her sudden need for guidance may be short-lived.

Olivia skimmed over the writing on the sheet as fast as she could, not absorbing much of what was on it. Not until she saw the penciled in number beside the word stallion. "Four stallions in one herd," she muttered. She went through the writing again, and this time she carefully studied each line. "Ten mares are pregnant. This is wonderful news. Where did you move them to?"

The tension on the ranch hands' face was clear. "We think those numbers are right, but we can't separate the in-foal mares, or any of the others to tell. This list was Tylor's visual assessment. Ever since we unloaded the herd, that black stallion kicks up a ruckus whenever we get too close," he said, pointing toward the pasture behind the barn. "He's one mean bastard."

Trish headed over to the line of food tables and searched through the bountiful offering.

Olivia sighed heavily at seeing her go. She folded the paper in half. "The herds been through a lot of stress in such a short time." She waved toward the commotion surrounding the pond. "None of this is really helping, either. Maybe we should send folks home for a few days to give the horses time to adjust."

The ranch hand shook his head. "You know old Stan will jar everyone up into a tizzy if you do. He's already got some here convinced the city's gonna try to charge their farms monthly allowances for any horses they take. He's scaring people, hoping to get more than his share. Several of us know it. We aren't stupid."

"What an asshole," Olivia grumbled.

In her peripheral, she saw Trish leave the generous assortment of food with a simple apple. Rejoining the two, Trish bent forward, lifted her pantleg, and unsheathed a terrifying hunting knife from her boot, with a serrated edge running down the opposite side of the blade. When she held it to the apple, Olivia's eyes widened to the blade's length.

The ranch hand was just as startled. "God woman, do you always carry that thing?" he asked.

Trish sliced the apple in half, running the sharp blade through as she made another pass. She waved the tip around, signaling to the others enjoying the pool area. "All those on my team carry them," she said. She wiped off both sides of the blade so fast on her jeans, Olivia was afraid Trish had cut herself. Trish replaced her knife, the pantleg still intact. "Except Doctor Burgos. He's a pacifist, not into weapons. Guns, knives, he refuses to touch any of it."

Trish dipped her head toward the barn. "The stallion isn't mean, but high-spirited. He's simply trying to protect those he feel's responsible for." Trish leapt over the railing and headed for the gate on the picket fence.

Olivia handed the man the list. "Here, tell Tylor we'll work on separating the herd tomorrow."

Curious, she was eager to go after Trish and see what schemes Trish's mind was hatching out. Before she stepped off the concrete patio, Aralyn moved in with Doctor Burgos close behind. "Olivia, can we go somewhere private to talk?"

Startled, and somewhat apprehensive by the look on Doctor Burgos' face, Olivia eyeballed Trish, who was heading toward the barn. "What's this about?" she asked. She hoped the talk could wait. She really wanted to see what Trish was planning to do. She was also interested in finding out what dilemma Trish needed help with. She had a feeling Trish's problem had to do with hers and Christina's relationship, but she wasn't positive.

Aralyn plainly said, "We'd like to offer you a job."

Pulling her curiosity off Trish, Olivia focused more of her attention on the unexpected conversation at hand. "I have a job."

Doctor Burgos cleared his throat. "We understand, and believe me, the governors of the city know none of this would be possible without your remarkable vision and knowhow. Which was why we awarded you the deed to this farm instead of offering you a provisional contract like the others. Our way of saying thank you for what you've done for the city."

Olivia narrowed her eyes. "Are you threatening to take my house if I don't agree?"

The question clearly stunned Doctor Burgos. "Of course not," he said, wide-eyed.

Aralyn was fast to offer him some assistance. "Whether you take the job or not, you've more than earned this place. We're also not expecting you to stop your lead role here. Instead, we're hoping you'll hand off the bulk of your responsibilities to your staff to free you during the weekdays."

Doctor Burgos said, "The city has agreed to offer your farm two additional ranch hands as well, at no cost to your monthly allowance. They can help with the cattle and upkeep of this place while you're off consulting for us."

Olivia tried keeping her sudden burst of curiosity in. "For you? Do you mean for the city, or for this secret mission no one's talking about?"

The straightforward question didn't alter Aralyn's intimidating expression in the slightest. Instead, Aralyn gestured them away from the clusters of chatting people around the pool. "Yes, with your unique combination of animal knowledge, both medically and psychologically, and by the friendship developing between you and my goddaughter, we would like you to join our team as a consultant," she said, once they were far enough away from others.

"What does my friendship with Trish have to do with this position?"

"If you haven't already noticed, my goddaughter has issues with letting people get too close. When she's out in the field, she won't allow any of us to be with her, and we're her family. She stays out there for days at a time alone. With everything she has going on at home, well…none of us feel this solitude is heathy for her."

Olivia frowned. "You want me to leave my work here, for days at a time, so I can babysit Trish?"

"Good god, no," said Doctor Burgos. "The city wouldn't agree to pay handsomely for a glorified babysitter. With your background, we feel your insight would help our mission greatly. Also, Trish would have no good reason to disagree with you joining her."

"She doesn't know?"

"No," said Aralyn. "Trish doesn't know. Also, the mission is dangerous. You'll be with Trish, and I have no doubt she'll keep you safe, but you'll still be doing most of your work past the wall."

"Doing what exactly?" Olivia asked, feeling more than a smidge uncomfortable. The idea of working with Trish sparked her interest, but was the prospect of accelerating a friends-with-benefits relationship worth the danger?

Aralyn and Doctor Burgos locked eyes. After Aralyn gave Doctor Burgos a slight shoulder shrug, he spoke. "Study the Gramites. Figure out what's inside them, and see if there's any trace of humanity left to salvage."

"You hoping to cure them?"

"One day maybe, but now, we need to learn more about the actual virus inside and how it has mentally and physically affected the host."

"That's enough." Aralyn held up her hand. "I'm afraid we can't tell you much more until you agree. Even then, your understanding will be limited to the Gramites and the virus."

"Not Trish?" Olivia asked.

"I'm afraid not."

Olivia pursed her lips to the side in thought. Her mind unexpectantly flashed to the loss of Wendy and her family. She swiftly pressed the painful images away, hiding them deep within her mind. "Answer me this one question. Is what's going on with Trish related, in any way, to the infected?"

The manner in which both silently reviewed one another, Olivia had her answer. "Okay, I'll do it. On two conditions."

"Name it," Doctor Burgos beamed.

"One, besides my pay, the city gives me my own personal truck from their generous stash of unused vehicles."

Doctor Burgos' head gradually bobbed. "That can be arranged. What else?"

"Two, you tell me everything. If I'm going to put my life in jeopardy for the 'greater good,' then I need every piece of information you have, including what you're hiding about Trish."

"Absolutely not!"

"Aralyn," Doctor Burgos said, causing Aralyn to spin angrily away.

Olivia had never seen Aralyn upset before. The display was alarming. Yet, she forced herself on. "Believe me when I say, even the smallest of details could be the biggest of breakthroughs. I can't do my job effectively if I'm missing vital bits of data."

Aralyn rotated. "Fine. We have a contract for you to sign which assures your silence."

"Of course," Olivia said.

Aralyn continued. "We're adding the deed of your house into the contract. If you speak a word of what we tell you, or anything about our mission, you'll lose everything. Your house, your position, even your horses."

"Wait just a damn minute—"

Aralyn took a step forward, her brow strained in an unrelenting glare. "If you mention this to anyone, you'll place my goddaughter in danger. The prospect of losing your farm is a small price to pay compared to Trish's life."

Olivia took two steps backward, surprised by Aralyn's unexpected waver in her self-controlled temperament. She was seriously worried about Trish. What mystery could place Trish in this much danger? Was she sure she even wanted to know?

Olivia mentally weighed the pros and cons. She knew she would never share Trish's secret, so it really came down to placing herself in danger versus helping this team understand the virus and those infected. Maybe even assisting with finding a cure. When her brain cut through everything that didn't matter, Olivia's decision was simple. Yes, she wanted to know Trish's secrets, but no longer to gain access to a potential love interest. If they could work on finding a cure, then maybe this would give some meaning to the deaths of the loved ones who died so she could live. She squared her shoulders and took a step forward, staring directly into Aralyn's eyes. Olivia stuck out her hand.

Aralyn studied her briefly. With a scarcely visible lift to the left side of her lips, she clasped Olivia's hand in a firm handshake. "Okay. Doctor Burgos will have Captain Strong prepare the additions to the contract. In a few minutes, once we've all signed it, we'll tell you everything."

"I get to physically pick the vehicle. A Gladiator from the militia," Olivia blurted out, suddenly fearful of signing a legally binding document without dotting her i's and crossing her t's.

Aralyn's brow rose. "Anything else?"

"One of your armored bodysuits, a helmet, a rifle…the works. Oh, and one of those intimidating knives you all carry."

CHAPTER TEN

Lieutenant Waska activated his processor, momentarily surprised. He'd expected the call to apprehend Patricia Webber would have come from Doctor Webber himself, not the Director of Military Forces. He'd sent the video link to the entire committee, yet Doctor Webber's daughter was the one who had nosedived off the side of a ravine to fight a horde of Gramites by hand. Why shouldn't Doctor Webber be the one to issue the order?

"General Princeton, what can I do for you?"

The General's voice was rugged, commanding. "Lieutenant, first you can explain to me why you copied the link to Frank, who's not even on the committee?"

Waska's confident facade wavered in front of the blue holographic image. He stepped around his desk and signaled for his second-in-command to leave his tent. "Sir, I assumed, with Patricia Webber being his daughter—"

"You don't hold the rank or position to assume anything," General Princeton shouted. "For reasons which are none of your damn business, Doctor Webber isn't in the loop with issues relating to Patricia Webber…or Colonel Williams. You receive your directives from this committee, not from Frank."

"Yes sir. I'm sorry I overstepped. It won't happen again." Waska sat in his chair and nervously waited. This scolding wasn't the praise he had expected to receive.

"No, it won't, Lieutenant. From here on out, you will send your reports to me directly. I'll be the one who personally issues your orders."

"Yes, sir, of course, sir. Whatever the committee asks of me, I'll do. I'm an ardent patriot through and through."

The General scoffed at his remark. "I'm sending you your first order now. I'm warning you, Lieutenant, misstep again, and it will be the last move you make in your career."

The link ended and Waska stared blankly at the space where the holographic image had stood. No good job, no talk of praise or promotion, but a threat from the highest man in military command whose words still lingered heavily in the air. When his wrist communicator blinked again, he ran a hand slowly over his desk processor. The blue, semitransparent image of his order popped up before him, and he swiped his hand along the controls to visually solidify the document.

Reading through his directives, he felt his entire form go completely numb with what the committee was ordering him to do. They didn't want him to bring in Doctor Webber's daughter but add her into the tests the lieutenant and his men were conducting with the mutants. To see what she was capable of, if she could take on the added strength of the mutants as she had with the Gramites, and whether or not the experiments killed her.

He slammed his fist down hard on the surface of his desk. When two of his soldiers rushed in to make sure he was safe, Waska jumped to his feet and barked at them to leave. He slumped into his chair, feeling the weight of the undertaking the committee had forced on him. The slaughter of such an incredible being would soon be authorized from his own lips. No, this definitely wasn't the praise he had been expecting.

Trish waited at the main gate until those posted on the other side of the wall judged it light enough out to open. Even though this barrier was the inside gate, they each followed the same simple rule. If the sergeant-in-charge couldn't see the area surrounding the outside gate clearly, the gates remained closed. Today they opened the gate a few minutes after seven, those guarding it waving her inside the city.

She headed toward the restaurant first, making sure Christina was already at work for the day. The thought of driving by Eva's house to see if Jennifer was there crossed her mind, but the idea of a heated argument later with Christina kept her from chancing it. The last thing she needed was for Christina to stop all contact Trish had with their daughter.

Once she spotted Christina's vehicle parked underneath the restaurant's canopy, Trish headed straight for their house. She pulled in the driveway and told Molly to wait in the Gladiator. She removed the thick envelope from the glovebox and headed toward the enclosed porch. Saying a silent prayer, she slid the note inside the mail slot attached to the front door and gently placed her hand against the red painted barrier. She'd spent most of the night pouring her love and feelings onto several sheets of paper, and the rest of the night exposing every ounce of vulnerability she had left to give on several more sheets. Trish was certain she and Christina loved each other enough to work through anything. Even this.

She turned, not daring to use her key and go inside. She respected Christina enough not to infringe on her wife's place of safety and privacy. If Christina wanted to invite her in, fine. If not, Trish would abide by her wife's decision.

She stepped off the porch and visually inspected the tall blades of grass covering the yard. With Christina's busy work schedule, and taking care of Jennifer on her own, Trish felt a wave of guilt at not coming over sooner to mow.

With a sharp whistle, she called to Molly, who jumped from the window and followed. They proceeded to the backyard where the reel mower stood. Trish selected one of Christina's medium-sized containers she used for her garden and filled it up from the spigot with some water for Molly. Removing her overshirt, Trish prepared herself for several hours of mowing.

Christina threw the radio receiver down and let loose with a heated display of Spanish at the device. She spun, entered the office, and forcefully slammed the door closed. She headed to the couch and dropped straight to the cushion. Her heavy eyes shot up when the door reopened.

"Trish still isn't responding to your messages?" Eva asked.

Christina shook her head, as she focused on the ceiling, not her mother.

"Honey, you told me a few weeks ago she said she wasn't getting them. Maybe she still isn't. You both simply need to talk to one another. In person. I'm sure there's a good reason she's not returning your messages."

"Mom, I was so mean to her. The things I said last weekend, and with Jennifer present. Whether she's seeing that woman, I never should have let my jealousy impede on hers and Jennifer's relationship. I need to make this right."

"Christina, Trish is madly in love with you. She's not seeing anyone else. You know this. You're tired, and you both need some time together away from outside influences. Speaking of which." Eva lowered herself next to Christina. "I finally found another weekend cook for the restaurant. Once he starts work, we'll both be able to have our weekends completely off. No more of these crazy, long hours we've been doing."

Christina gave her mother a tremulous smile. It transformed into a cascade of tears the moment Eva pulled her into her arms. She rocked her daughter until Christina's sobs lessened. "I also loaded up my truck with the pies for the festivities tonight. I was going to run them to the farm during my lunch break, however, Jeremy asked me for some extra hours. Maybe you'd like to take them yourself and have the rest of the night off." She lovingly drew her daughter to an arm's length away. "You should go, Christina. Enjoy the celebration."

"No, I'm not going to *her* ranch, Mom."

"They said Aralyn and her entire team will be there."

Christina yanked her head upward. "Trish is there?"

Eva nodded. "There's a rumor going around that your wife dove off a cliff to save the herd. Knowing Trish, it's more than a rumor." Eva stood and pulled Christina with her. "Honey, take the truck and go. Physically go see there's nothing going on between your wife and the veterinarian, and please, work this out between you two. I'll drive your car and pick Jennifer up from the sitter after work. I have tomorrow off, so I'll take her shopping with me in the morning."

Janet slowly pushed around the last few bites of her pie while staring off in the direction of the office. The moment Christina and her mother emerged, Janet sat up straighter in her chair. Christina looked to be in a much better mood than when she'd ended her call ten minutes ago. Probably another message left with the desk sergeant at HQ. Janet wasn't worried. Twenty credits a day and that problem went away. The cost used to be ten until Trish had heatedly called the sergeant-on-call about the lack of messages and insisted he investigate the issue. Thankfully, with a bit more persuading, and double the credits, the man continued to find a way of misplacing Christina's messages.

She watched in silence as Christina went to the employee locker room for her things, gave her mother a hug, and headed toward the rear of the building. Damn, she was leaving. Placing her fork on her plate, Janet pulled up her check on the screen, paid for her tab, and turned to go. She halted when she saw Eva rush through the kitchen as she called out for Christina. Eva spun and yelled at Betty to head to the front and flag Christina down. When Betty returned, she shook her head to Eva.

"Is everything okay?" Janet asked the second Eva threw up her hands.

Eva held up a small set of keys. "I forgot. I took off Christina's spare house keys the other day when Betty borrowed my truck, and I never replaced them. Christina and I switched vehicles tonight so she could run some pies to the celebration dinner, but I forgot to give her the keys."

Janet's heart raced, but she kept her excitement in. "I'm driving past Christina's. Want me to drop them off?"

Eva's worry lines relaxed. "If it's not too much trouble." She offered a grateful pat to Janet's hand when she passed her the key ring. "Put them on the stool inside the porch by the door. And thank you, Janet. You've earned a free slice of pie the next time you come in."

"Sweet," Janet said. She tossed on her hat and headed to the door, beaming broadly, as she flipped the keyring around her finger.

Janet drove past Christina's house when she spotted the other militia vehicle sitting in the drive. She scowled, cursing against her unfortunate run of bad luck. She pulled onto the next street over and thought through the predicament. Christina left for Stonleigh Ranch, and here sat Trish's Gladiator. A new thought crossed her mind. Her forming plan was a long shot, but maybe.

Janet grabbed her militia hat and Christina's keys from the center console, locked up her vehicle, and carefully approached Christina's. She saw a massive dog running in the freshly mowed backyard and heard what sounded like someone chopping wood. Odd thing for one to do heading into the hot month of July. She continued along the other side of the street and crossed directly in line with the screened-in porch.

She'd already thought of a backup plan if her hunches were wrong, but her gut instinct told her she wasn't. She opened the screen and scampered to the front door. The deadbolt was still engaged. Mentally, she crossed her fingers. Inserting the key, she turned the handle and quietly let herself in.

As soon as she entered, she noticed an envelope lying on the floor with Christina's name on it. She retrieved it and removed the folded-up pages from within. After reading a few lines, she replaced the pages with a transfixed leer, folded it a few times, and shoved it inside one of her cargo pockets. The day keeps getting better.

She headed swiftly upstairs and located the master bedroom. Stripping from her camouflaged uniform, she rummaged through the clothing hanging in the master closet. The confidence in her plan grew at seeing the checkered robe dangling in the far corner. She threw it on, fastened it, and headed down to the kitchen. She searched inside a few cabinets, found a coffee cup, and filled it halfway with water, purely for mental effect. Before she stepped outside, she did a last-minute visual inspection. She spread the top of the robe enough to reveal she wasn't wearing a shirt. Then she removed her hairband and shook out her long red hair. Modestly messy, but not too much.

Her hand reached for the door. Taking a few steady breaths to focus on the surprised ambience she was striving for, she unlatched the deadbolt and threw open the backdoor. She gasped. "Oh, Trish. I thought I heard someone out here."

Trish stopped halfway in a swing, wide-eyed and speechless. Janet had to dig out all of her inner strength to suppress her laughter. The way Trish's face went from shock to pain, and swiftly to anger was priceless. She watched Trish's hand grip tighten on the ax handle, and Janet silently wondered if she had poked too hard at the wrong bear. When the massive dog came forward, it flashed a set of powerful fangs and growled.

"Molly," Trish hissed. At once, the dog silenced. Trish raised the ax and slammed it straight down, burying it deep into the three foot tall stump.

"Want me to tell Christina you stopped by when she gets home?"

Trish didn't say a word. She threw on her overshirt, called the dog to her, and headed angrily from the yard. Janet waited. The moment she heard tires peel out on pavement, she bit her bottom lip, reining in her delight. With a mental slap on the back, she headed inside to change.

Olivia squinted at the road when she heard the sound of an approaching vehicle. The truck wasn't Trish's militia vehicle, but one she'd seen before. Recollection swept in and she moved around Buck to get a better view. This mode of transportation belonged to Eva, Christina's mother. She noticed when the truck stopped and the driver got out, Eva wasn't driving. Christina was. Phillips and Givens both exited the house to greet her, but Carlen remained reclined in the chair by the pool, nursing her beer. Carlen was clearly upset at seeing Christina, and Olivia more than understood why. After the story Aralyn told her last night, she herself felt angry.

When Aralyn said she would tell Olivia everything, she wasn't lying. She had opened the hour-long tale with the death of Trish's mother, and how her father had murdered Julie Webber with the four-year-old Trish watching. She explained how Trish's father created the monstrous virus which killed off billions of innocent men, woman, and children. Julie, Trish's mother, found out about the mass genocide caused by the governments of the UWTF and the role her husband played. Julie intended to expose this corruption but had been shot by Frank Webber, although not until Julie first destroyed her life's research—a marvelous and dangerous serum which was accidentally injected inside Trish that very night. Aralyn explained how Trish's father stole part of his wife's older, unstable formula to aid in constructing the immunization for those inside the bunkers, Olivia included. Yet, when those with the immunization become infected by the creatures, or any blood-borne pathogen, they mutate into something far worse.

The unloved and emotionally abusive childhood Trish experienced growing up angered Olivia. The love Trish received from her godmother and those select few on Aralyn's staff soothed much of that anger. Aralyn told her about their escape from NORAD, how Trish met Christina and Jennifer, the few months living in the city and falling for her first love, and the painful events which occurred once they returned to NORAD, including Trish waking up from a coma what Trish had experienced since then.

Portions of the incredible story Olivia had heard before, such as the night she herself escaped Colorado Springs after the airing of Julie Webber's video. It caused her and those she loved to flee Colorado Springs. Yet, hearing Aralyn retell it, everything felt so overwhelming. Parts of the story were frightening, others gripped at Olivia's heart, and the rest brought her to appreciate the incredible woman who had come into her life.

Trish wasn't simply stunning, she was incredibly strong, highly intelligent, and had abilities Doctor Burgos and Aralyn's team were trying to help her understand and control. Trish had tested out of school at thirteen. She had a photographic memory, could read, and comprehend over five thousand words a minute, and had specialized in biochemistry and molecular genetics like her mother. She spoke seven different languages, one of which was Romanian. When Tracy had put Trish on the spot at the first bonfire they shared, Trish hadn't felt the need to justify her life's accomplishments or her higher level of education to others. That made her even more alluring.

The woman unloading pies with Phillips and Jason, she didn't deserve a woman like Trish. Yes, she was attractive, but she was also selfish and controlling. *What kind of person keeps a daughter from a mother? Throwing out ultimatums left and right.* No, these threatening stipulations were abusive in any relationship. All because her wife and this team were willing to risk their lives to make the world safer for everyone else. Hell, Christina even kicked her own father from her life. *Who does that?* What Olivia wouldn't give to see her father's loving face again.

Buck's head shook, and Olivia focused on her task. She apologized to his lip-smacking complaints and moved the brush to a different area on his back. She saw Christina head up to the pool and say something to Carlen. The tall woman stood, waved her arm in the air, and headed heatedly away. Good, Olivia thought.

She spoke directly to Buck. "Carlen's welcome here anytime. Isn't that right Buck?"

Buck snorted, and he bobbed his head.

She gave him a good rubdown before taking him to his stall. The second she latched the door, a loud commotion kicked up from the rear pasture. She swiftly rotated. A few ranch hands headed in through the sliding door, carrying in a muddy Tylor. He was holding his upper leg and cussing up a storm.

"The stallion kicked my leg," he grunted, wincing in pain.

Olivia spotted Justin rushing in from the pasture, also covered in mud. "How's his leg?"

Olivia pointed toward the house. "Justin, go find Young. I think he's by the pool. If not, check the grill area." She shouted the last part to the running man, as she directed the workers to lower Tylor gently to the ground.

After instructing the ranch hands not to let his leg move, she got up, fished her keys from her pocket, and ran toward one of the storage rooms. Selecting the right-sized battery from the wall mount, she shifted a few containers around and located the box containing the portable x-ray machine. Slapping in the battery, she powered it on, threw on a blue apron, and reached for another. Once she returned to the group, she draped the lead vest over Tylor and had the ranch hands move out of the way.

Young arrived as she finished capturing the last angle and waited for the images to load on the screen. "Yep, his distal femur has a hairline fracture," she said.

Young pointed to the imagery. "Not as bad is it could be. Looks stable. He might not need surgery." He found two adequately sized boards and some rope to stabilize the leg. "If someone's available to drive, I can go with him to the hospital."

Olivia nodded to one of the ranch hands. As the man headed off to locate a vehicle, Olivia returned to the storage room. She replaced the gear, retrieved one of the folding, large animal stretchers from the far corner, and locked the door behind her.

Once she hustled to the front, she noticed they had Eva's truck backed partway inside the barn. Heart racing, Olivia stopped mid-stride. Her eyes were staring directly into the probing emerald-green eyes of Christina. The woman's expression was wary, holding the same sadness Olivia had seen multiple times in Trish's own piercing blue gaze.

Suddenly feeling like a homewrecker seeking to destroy another woman's happy marriage, Olivia dropped her focus to Tylor, and she hurried forward. Their marriage wasn't happy though, was it? Christina had kicked Trish from her bed and home and had painfully dangled their daughter out in front of Trish like a carrot. She was even seeing another woman. From how the rumors went, Christina had left Trish's arms and headed straight into Janet's. Same day even. *Shit, who does that?* No, Olivia had nothing to feel guilty for.

She helped the men gently lift Tylor onto the stretcher and load him carefully into the bed of Eva's truck. This time, when she and Christina locked eyes with the other, Olivia didn't turn away. The sound of another vehicle approaching a few seconds later was what finally forced both to end their visual pissing contest. Olivia saw Trish and Molly climb from the vehicle by the pathway leading to the house, where Carlen rushed down and met her. The woman spoke with haste, and Trish veered her sadness toward the barn. Damn, she seemed on the verge of crying.

Trish said something to Carlen, and the woman followed it with a motherly hug. After Carlen said a few brief words, Trish squared her shoulders, instructed Molly to head to the house, and she moved toward the crowd gathered around Eva's truck. Olivia noticed how everyone else had also silently watched the exchange, even Christina. Olivia saw the fresh tears form on the cheeks of the woman standing with the driver's door open. For a brief second, Olivia felt sorry for her. But seeing the pain in Trish's eyes as she approached, her empathy for Christina vanished.

Trish moved around the other side of the truck, opposite Christina, and she headed to where Young was climbing in beside Tylor. "Carlen told me. How bad is he?"

"Hairline fracture. We're taking him to the hospital now. He'll be all right," Young said.

"I told you to wait until I returned before separating him from his herd," Trish said to Tylor, her voice husky and heated.

"We tried, but the natives were getting restless," Tylor said, his face sheepish. "Trish, old Stan and a few others mentioned shooting the stallion. I had to do something."

Olivia straightened. "What? Why didn't you tell me?"

Justin closed the tailgate. "You were out with Buck, dealing with the cattle issue." He headed toward the passenger door. "Now, do you two have any more questions, or can we take him to the hospital?"

Trish sighed out a frustrated "yes," and took off at a tempered stomp toward the rear pasture with Olivia following at a slower pace.

Olivia stopped when Christina ran around her. She angled a few steps to the side, trying hard not to listen to the two exchange muttered words.

Seconds later, Trish's voice rose, and Olivia's head snapped to the two. "Seriously, wearing my robe, Christina, and in our house?"

Christina reached out to touch her, but Trish yanked her arm away. Christina sounded miserable, even desperate, when she spoke. "I don't understand. What are you talking about?"

"I'm too upset to do this right now." Trish's body slouched. She tilted her head toward the sky with her eyes closed. Her exhalation was loud, shaky. "Make a schedule for when I can have Jennifer, and give it to Susan to give to Carlen. If you don't, or you try to keep our daughter from me, then I'll take this up with the governors personally and let them sort it out."

Without waiting for a response, Trish headed continued toward the pasture. Olivia moved forward, worried that Trish would try to approach the stallion in her current emotional state. The exchange could be dangerous. When she passed Christina, she kept her eyes forward.

"She's my wife, not yours."

"Then treat her better," Olivia snapped. She was planning to continue forward, but her temper flared. How those in Trish's life had mistreated her made Olivia sick with rage. Trish's own father through her youth, then this woman, her supposed first love, Olivia's anger was getting the better of her, and she knew it. She spun fully to the woman. "You say she's your wife, yet you have a strange way of showing it. Kicking her from her home, keeping her from her daughter—why? Because you want to live in a fantasy world where you think you'll be safe? Our world's not safe, Christina. It's a time bomb just waiting to go off. Trish, your father, this team, they're risking everything, hoping to make life better for everyone."

"You don't know me or Trish, or what we've been through together."

"Please enlighten me. Because, from where I'm standing, with your threats and abusive ultimatums, you're acting like a spoiled child. My father and those I loved died from the creatures outside the wall, and you stopped talking to your father. Why? Because he's trying to change that for others. What I wouldn't give to hold my father again. To tell him I love him one more time."

Christina moved forward, and Olivia did the same. "I wish you would," Olivia muttered through clenched teeth.

"Damn it, stop this, both of you," Young shouted, pushing himself between the two. "Christina, get in the truck. We've got to go. Olivia, go check on Trish."

"With her imprisoned childhood, Trish's never even had a birthday to celebrate with those who love her. The very first one you could've given her you took away because—"

"Olivia, go!" Young adamantly pointed toward the pasture, causing Olivia to glare abruptly at him. She darted her eyes to Christina and whirled on her heels to leave.

Olivia found Trish over by the far pasture, leaning against a section of fence, watching the black stallion prancing around his herd. Trish pointed to the horse with one hand, the other rubbed her neckline. "He's got a good heart. I can sense it."

"Trish, what happened this morning? Where'd you go?"

Trish's shoulders shook gently at her sluggish inhale. "I'd rather not say." She continued to study the horse. "Olivia, I'm so tired of crying. A month ago, life felt complete. Now…I don't know who I am or where I fit anymore." She patted her chest. "I feel like I have all these emotions flooding in and part of me is trying to flip off a switch, numbing me inside. This overwhelming sensation is frightening."

"No, so much has happened and you're under a lot of stress, so your body's working itself into an emotional fight-or-flight response. It's normal, but you need to acknowledge those feelings and work through them." Olivia took a step closer. "Don't pull away because you're too worried about dampening your eyes in front of others or feeling the pain. Heartbreak, yes, it sucks, but it's still a part of being human."

Trish shifted wearily from one foot to the other. Her eyes clutched at a grief which appeared to be utterly consuming. "Crying is all I seem to do lately."

"Well then, what's a few more tears?"

Olivia tenderly touched her shoulder and waited. When Trish finally shared the dilemma behind her pain—how Janet had emerged from inside Trish's house, body wrapped naked in Trish's own robe, Olivia reached out and held her as she wept. The woman who had dived off the side of a cliff and fought a horde of Gramites, all to save a herd of horses—this magnificent woman cried so violently, Olivia's own eyes moistened, and her heart ached to take the pain away.

Right as Trish's weeping settled, a cool breeze brushed against the dampness on Olivia's cheeks. She looked over, spotting rainclouds in the far distance.

Taking in a lungful of air, Trish peered skyward, she too noticing the storm rolling in. She gave Olivia a tender hug, telling her she appreciated Olivia listening to what she had to say. Trish backed away and motioned toward the stallion. "I guess I should try to separate him from the others. Could you get me a couple of apples or some other edible bribery you think he'd like?"

Olivia wasn't thrilled with the idea of Trish trying to coax the horse by herself. She knew Trish had a connection to the animal world none of them wholly understood. Probably not even Trish herself understood, but if she got too close, the ill-tempered horse could seriously injure, even kill her.

Olivia promptly headed off to the barn in search of horse treats. By the time she returned, Trish was standing a foot away from the stallion. Her hand rested on the softness of the stallion's nostrils, and she murmured something to the powerful creature. Olivia remained by the far fencepost and observed. Trish was speaking too softly for Olivia to hear from where she stood, mesmerized. Whatever Trish was saying, the proud horse, who threw up a ruckus when anyone else came near, remained with his head bowed, relaxed, and listening.

After several more minutes, Trish strolled toward the gate separating the enclosed pasture from the miles of fenced in grazing fields, and the horse followed. Olivia moved toward them when Trish signaled for her. As she approached, she saw the stallion flick his ears in her direction before his eyes turned toward her. She inched forward, keeping herself calm, but prepared to dash toward the closest fence and hop over it if needed. She passed Trish the horse biscuits and shifted a few steps backward.

"He likes you," Trish said, holding out the first offering to the horse.

Olivia remained silent, as the stallion nibbled the treat from Trish's outstretched hand. She waited for Trish to unlatch and swing the gate open. "He does, does he?" The thick layer of nervous amusement in her own voice startled Olivia. She had never been one to be jumpy around animals, large or temperamental.

"Wanna come say hi?" Trish asked, rubbing her hand over the horse's impressive chest muscles and down his front legs. He was definitely part thoroughbred and stood no less than sixteen hands in height. The way the horse acted, one would believe this striking creature had been Trish's sole companion throughout his entire life.

Olivia kept her strides slow when she approached, and she reached a hand gradually out until it rested on the muzzle. Out of all the animals she had ever touched, other than Buck, this powerful stallion was by far the most thrilling. As she worked her hand along the jawline and down his neck, she felt his muscles stiffen and relax under her touch. Trish passed Olivia a treat. The stallion sniffed the offering and snatched it, causing Olivia to giggle like a schoolgirl.

Once he finished chewing, Trish nodded toward the open pasture. "Like I said, your family will be cared for. You don't need to worry about them anymore." With her hand flat and palm turned upward, she presented the last tasty offering. The moment he seized it, he jerked his body forward and headed off at a tremendous sprint.

"How do you do that?" Olivia breathed, feeling a heightened level of adrenaline combined with admiration for the woman standing beside her.

Trish latched the gate, turned to her, and answered, as if the horse had personally confided in her. "He's been carrying the burden of protecting this group for a long time. Even a horse needs a moment of individual peace to enjoy the feeling of being alive and free." She motioned her head toward the pasture. "Can he stay there for a while until you guys get the others situated?"

Olivia nodded. "He'll be safe in there. Plenty of miles to run and untouched land for grazing. There's even a freshwater source the cattle use."

Trish waved to one of the ranch hands by the barn and pointed toward the rest of the herd. The man eagerly returned the wave and headed into the building. "What will you do with him?" Trish asked.

After the display she'd experienced with Trish and the stallion, Olivia already knew what she wanted to say, but until the governors approved the idea of giving Trish the stallion, she kept it to herself. In all honesty, she said, "Not sure yet, but I promise he'll have a wonderful home."

Seeing a forming group head from the barn with Tracy and April working to organize the gaggle, Olivia asked, "Do you want to go for a walk? They can handle the rest, and I'm not ready to head in yet."

Trish inspected the sky. "Sure, we have some time before the rain gets here."

Olivia guided them from the enclosed fencing, down to the gravel road, and away from the commotion. She slowed the pace when Trish bent over and picked up a smooth pebble. They continued forward while Trish swiped dirt off the tiny rock with her fingers. "Has anyone ever told you, you look like your mother?"

Trish stopped walking. As she searched Olivia's eyes, Olivia felt a tiny shudder at how the blue shade thoroughly captivated her. She wanted to move closer, lean in, and feel the fullness of Trish's lips on her own.

"So, you know who my parents are?"

Olivia could tell Trish wasn't thrilled by this. Part of her understood why. "Many of us here came from the bunkers. I knew you reminded me of someone, but I didn't put two and two together until last night. Your last name and your mother's beauty. I can't believe it took me this long." She decided not to share Aralyn was the one who had informed her. Now that Olivia knew the entire story, everything about Trish made sense. Aralyn had also told Olivia not to mention their chat or the job offer to Trish until they lined up everything and she was ready to start.

Trish tossed the pebble and placed her hands deep inside her pockets, but she didn't take her eyes away. "I'll understand if you no longer want to be in my life."

Trish's response was unexpected. "Why would you think I wouldn't want to be?"

Trish's outline didn't change. She remained steadfast, both mentally and physically. "Because of what has happened here. My parents are to be blamed for the deaths of so many people."

Olivia cocked her head, her mind evaluating Trish's peculiar verdict. "Yes, your father is at fault, as with those he works for, but your mother didn't know. She even died trying to stop it."

"My father used part of my mother's initial research. It causes a mutation that affects anyone who lived in the bunkers that were vaccinated against the original virus, which would include you. My mother toyed with an area of science modern advancement has scarcely grasped. She pushed it past the limits, generating a dangerous component my father ended up using."

"Trish, the crossbow you shot off a few weeks ago. If I stole it and headed into the city and randomly killed people with it, should the city hold Sergeant Givens responsible?"

Trish jerked her head to Olivia. "No, that's ridiculous."

Olivia tenderly touched Trish's arm. "Yes, it is. But he made it for you. Crafted it personally for your seventeenth birthday. So, from the logic you're using, wouldn't he be partially responsible?"

Seeing the edge of Trish's lips rise eased Olivia's concern. "Okay, head doctor, I see what you did there. You used my own convictions against me. I keep forgetting your psychological background." She restored their gradual walking pace, this time heading them toward the farmhouse. "Maybe you're right, but my father—" Trish's eyes darkened with her words. "My father, those he works for, the other governments involved. One day they'll have to answer for what they've done. We hoped my mother's video would have caused more people to break away from the governments in the UWTF, at least here in the States." She sounded disappointed. "I don't know. Maybe people in some of the other countries have taken control, overthrown those in power. I guess there's really no way for us to know for sure."

"Trish, my group left Colorado Springs the night your mother's video aired. My parents had a feeling they would increase security, prevent people from leaving, and we didn't want to wait to find out. You already know what those ruling the old government are capable of. Who's to say they aren't forcing people to stay? You're right—we don't know for sure."

"Maybe." Trish stopped walking. "You know, I believe this is the first in-depth conversation we've really had. I'm sorry. I guess I haven't been a good friend to you. I didn't even know you came from Colorado Springs." She sucked in a mouthful of air as if an idea suddenly struck her. "We lived in NORAD together."

Olivia's spirit lifted at the notion. They'd had this connection all along and didn't even know it existed. "I guess we did. They housed my family and me on the fifth level, section C."

Trish grew animated. "Seriously, I was in section A of the fifth level." Her head dropped, and she deepened her voice. "Hard work is a sign of strength and unity. Without it, our system will fall."

Olivia giggled at Trish's mockery of the forced-on propaganda from their past. She cleared her throat. "Laziness leads to disorder. Without order, we as a nation will not survive." Her own voice was mockingly intense. "Don't you just miss the old recordings?"

Trish placed a hand on Olivia's shoulder as she laughed. "What's really frightening is you sounded exactly like the woman's voice they used."

Olivia's giggling lessened. She held her breath. Trish was so close, her enchanting eyes obliterating Olivia's every thought. She felt an intense desire to pull Trish fully into her arms and kiss her. She wanted to have Trish look into her eyes as more than a friend. For Trish to offer Olivia the love she so yearned for. Her breathing grew faster.

"How long did it take your group to find Rapid City?" Trish finally asked once they were walking again.

Olivia kicked at the gravel, feeling newly flustered. "Almost a month. We fled with a group of eighty-seven and walked through the gates of this city with twenty-four."

"God, I'm so sorry. Your parents?"

Olivia lowered her head.

"Damn. What about any brothers or sisters?"

"I had an older brother, but he died trying to save our mother from the Gramites. I should have died that night too, but the infected killed my betrothed, who was helping my father protect me."

She heard Trish's deep sigh. "I'm really sorry for those you lost, Olivia. If you ever need to talk, I'm here."

"Thank you. I appreciate that."

Trish seemed a little uncomfortable, as if she weren't sure if she should talk more on the subject or not. "Your fiancé. What was his name?" she finally asked.

Olivia came to a sudden halt. "*His* name?"

Trish stopped with her. "You don't have to talk about the past if the memory's still painful. I guess I've been bombarding you with personal questions."

"*Her* name was Wendy."

Trish blinked a few times as the information sank in. "I'm sorry she died."

Olivia tried recalling their other conversations, realizing the topic of her being a lesbian had never presented itself. "It's been almost two years, and until now, I haven't talked about her to anyone."

"What was she like?" Trish waved a hand in front of her, regret clouding her features. "You don't have to tell me. I'm not good at the close friendship thing. I'm not even sure if asking questions on those you lost is insensitive. If it is, I didn't mean for it to be."

"No, it's okay. I don't mind telling you. What was Wendy like…" Olivia's heart felt lighter in her chest as her memories flashed to images filled with many of the wonderful times they had together before leaving NORAD. "Wendy and I didn't get along at first. I thought she was arrogant. It wasn't until much later, once I truly got to know her, that I discovered she was a kind, genuine woman who loved animals more than people. I was hooked. She was the first person I'd ever slept with, my first love. Since then, I've only been with Tracy."

"Oh wow, Tracy's distaste for me now makes perfect sense." Trish grimaced. "Olivia, I honestly didn't know. If I've done anything to disrespect your relationship, I'm really sorry."

Olivia stretched out her legs and hurried beside her. She grabbed hold of Trish's arm. "Trish, no. Tracy and I are not together. I've shared my bed with her a few times, but that's the extent of our relationship. I'm not saying Tracy isn't jealous, but that's who she is. Her bedroom should have a revolving door added considering the number of people she sleeps with. She's not necessarily jealous of the thought of you and I being together, but more of you as a person. You intimidate her."

"Why? You know what, don't answer that. I couldn't care less what Tracy thinks." Her displeasure switched to hesitation. "I seriously thought you were straight," she said. The last part came out almost to the point of disappointment.

"Good grief, Trish. I'm still the same person."

"No. Beforehand, I always pictured you as one of the guys. Someone who likes a cold beer, is easy to talk to, and enjoys fishing." Trish corrected herself. "Not that you're masculine, because you're not. Quite feminine, actually." The way her eyes darted to the ground, to the sky, and then toward the commotion surrounding the farmhouse, Trish seemed upset. "Now, I'm not sure how to picture you. I've never had a friendship with any woman other than my wife, but that's different. I don't really have anything in common with other women, except those on my team, and they're more mothers to me than friends. You know, this kinda sucks."

Olivia folded her arms over her chest. "Are you quite done with your rant?"

Trish made a feeble attempt at a smile. "I think so," she said, still uneasy.

Without waiting for a response, Trish increased their stride, while placing more space between them. That's when Olivia realized everything about her and Trish's close level of friendship was suddenly unstable. Trish had thought she was straight. Therefore, Trish thought Olivia was safe to be herself around. Would Trish pull away after learning she was a lesbian? Not wanting to chance losing Trish from her life altogether, she pushed away any notion of a kiss from Trish anytime soon. This would take time.

Olivia did her best to sound as much like a safe, guy-friend to Trish as she could. "Let's get something to eat. I'm starving. I could also go for a beer unless you need to cry some more. I think you left a dry spot on my shirt."

Trish jerked her head to Olivia, and her brows pulled together.

Olivia sent Trish a wink.

Picking up on the playful jab, Trish emitted an entertaining grumble. "Fine, but you're buying."

Olivia was grateful for Trish's small attempt at bantering. Her effort was a start. "I wouldn't have it any other way."

By the time Christina turned down her street, she was drained of every ounce of energy she had left. Emotional, physical, all of it gone, wasted away in the long, painful events of the day. The veterinarian wasn't only ridiculously beautiful, she also had strong feelings for her wife. Christina was certain. Whether this judgmental woman felt she was in love with Trish, or lusted after her, either way, Christina hated herself for placing her wife and their relationship on the path of a devious woman like her.

Her heart suddenly raced, and she sat straighter behind the wheel. Squinting, she drove slowly, trying to see past the tinted windows of the militia vehicle parked at the curb in front of her yard. Was Trish in the vehicle or had she gone inside their house? She prayed for the latter, wishing deeply to see her wife strolling once again through the dwelling they both called home.

Her excitement faded when Janet stood from the porch steps and waved a hand to Christina. Pulling into the drive, Christina's heart ached with a distinct sense of emptiness. She raised her window and groaned at seeing the wine bottle Janet was holding.

She stepped from the truck and spoke with weary effort. "Janet, I'm really not in the mood to be sociable."

"Yeah, you look kinda beat up. Listen, I'm simply dropping off these keys for your mom. Apparently, she forgot your house keys weren't on her keyring."

Christina grimaced. Beat up, what a great thing to tell someone. She opened her mouth to Janet, ready to stress her lack of needing the friendship Janet insisted on pushing in her direction until her tired gaze swept over the yard. She suppressed her cry. She had been putting off the mowing until her next day off, but at the restaurant, this never seemed to happen. The stressful chore had been moving steadily up that long Must-Do List, which seemed to never get done.

Christina bit her bottom lip, trying to keep her emotions in check. "You mowed?" she whispered. She brought a hand up and covered her face, hiding her tears.

"Yeah…uh, it wasn't a big deal. I chopped some wood too. I saw the stack was running low, and even with this god-awful heat, I figured, hey, why the hell not."

Christina placed a leaden hand to her stomach, breathed in slowly, feeling overly emotional. "I always have the fireplace going when I read a book. It reminds me of when I was younger. My mother used to read to me in front of the gas fireplace at the CDC." Christina wiped her eyes, knowing she sounded foolish for babbling. The heavy weight of stress faintly lifted. "Okay, one glass, After that, I've got to go to sleep."

Janet beamed. "Deal!"

CHAPTER ELEVEN

"All right, Trish. I've been thinking about this some, and I've decided we need to take a different approach. I want you to focus your energy at the rock I placed on the table, not on the sound sensor sitting to the left. Understand?"

Trish raised a thumbs up at the camera, wondering why a man who often told her she had a brilliant mind frequently spoke to her as if she were a toddler. She squared herself on the stool and gauged the rock. She'd noticed by the second week of doing these tests, triggering this ability wasn't the issue. Regaining her mental control once she was under was where she struggled. Each time she pictured Christina's face, she found her subconscious pull her toward reality, hoping to see the one she loved standing before her, calling her home. She knew, even though their chapter was ending, the internal desire to see those emerald eyes always brought her to a coherent mental state. Even though she was deeply hurt, she still loved Christina with every fiber of her being. Together or not, she wanted the mother of her child to be safe and happy.

The second she glared at the rock, as if it wanted to hurt those she loved, her eyes rolled backward against her mind's constant demand to keep them in place. She heard a loud pop and thought of Christina. When her vision came into focus, she saw sandy dust lining the area on and around the table of what once was the rock,. The sound sensor wasn't in flames, but the device was lying on the floor with the right half separated from the body.

"Great job, Trish. Do you feel like going again?"

She gave the camera a nod, which prompted Young in to switch out the rock and sound sensor.

Trish awoke early on Wednesday, climbing from bed slower than normal. Carlen had given her the schedule the night before for the times she would have Jennifer. She'd hoped for every other weekend, and maybe a weekday once or twice a month. Christina had agreed to every other weekend, with the addition of every Friday evening. If Trish approved of the arrangement, they would make the first exchange this Friday at six. Trish had wholeheartedly agreed.

Even though the proposal fit perfectly with her workload, after receiving the sheet with Christina's handwriting on it, Trish's emotions were all over the place. Love, anger, longing, heartache, betrayal. She had fallen asleep well after midnight, and the dream she'd had of Christina and Janet's naked bodies intertwined together while in *their* home, under *their* bedding, had caused her pillow to dampen from unconscious tears. Christina hadn't mentioned the letter Trish had poured her heart and soul into, which added to the firm belief Christina had moved on.

As the emptiness of life closed in around her, what propelled Trish into the shower, got her dressed for her morning schedule, and kept her moving one foot in front of the other to leave the serenity of her apartment, was her conviction for the importance of the work they were beginning. Those survivors inside each of the freed cities, her family, the children being raised on this planet: they were what mattered. Her broken heart would have to mend itself on its own, or she would need to learn how to live with the pain. Either way, she pushed herself forward, allowing the numbness to take hold.

After the last of today's tests were over, she would travel outside these walls to do recon for Gramite horde number four, the group that had gone after the horses the previous weekend. Ever since she spotted the female in the horde, she'd been champing at the bit to head out and locate their den. She wasn't sure if she wanted to tag the Gramite or kill her for the painful memory of Adam and Gabe's death. Trish felt a powerful curiosity to figure out which decision she would make when the time came.

Trish exited the mess hall and headed to where Phillips and Givens had been working on one of their armored vehicles since yesterday morning. "Could you guys keep an eye on Molly again?"

Givens jumped down from the top of the vehicle and baby-talked his way over to the ecstatic Saint Bernard. "Of course we will. Who's a good girl? Who's a good girl?"

Trish stared at the metal plate they were affixing to the top, where the framed-in weaponry normally sat. "What's going on?" she asked, peeking through the front window. She noticed they had removed the processor from the main console, and in its place stood a medium-range communicator and a stereo system. "Why are you guys dummying her down?"

Avoiding eye contact, Givens kissed the air and called for the bouncing Molly, telling her to follow him to get some water. Confused, Trish squinted up and briefly caught Phillips's discomfort. He flipped down the visor on his helmet and struck an arc to continue welding. Trish turned her eyes away from the brightness, as her hand searched out for his pantleg. Her fingers clutched tight and pulled barely enough to throw him off balance.

"Jesus, Trish, now my bead looks like shit."

She *hmphed* and pointed to the black rank on her collar.

He splashed his pithy chortle with bitterness. "Pulling out the ma'am card, are we? Let's see what happens when you wake up tomorrow welded to your bed."

"You can't weld flesh to metal, idiot."

"No, I would weld a few metal straps…oh, forget it." He was about to strike another arc when her hand snapped to his leg. "What!" he blurted out and followed it with a heated, "ma'am."

She pointed to the vehicle. "What's up with this?"

He knocked on the plate he was welding and pointed to the building. "I only work here…ma'am. You'll have to ask one of those nice, fancy officers inside."

He flipped his wrist and went to work. She spun away from the flash, this time a bit too late. With a bright-white streak, temporarily blinding a spot in her vision, she grumbled under her breath and headed for the building housing the vault.

As soon as she entered, she knew something was wrong. All eyes rotated in her direction. She moved farther into the room toward Aralyn and Carlen. The instant she spotted Olivia, her anxiety increased. "Is Spirit okay?"

Olivia chewed the inside of her lip, her voice amused. "Spirit. So you've named the stallion. It's a good name. It fits his high-spirited personality."

Knowing something was amiss, Trish spoke to Aralyn. "What is it? What's happened?"

"Everything's fine," Aralyn said. She gestured to Olivia. "I'd like you to meet the newest member of our team. Olivia will consult for us while you study the Gramites."

Confused, Trish scrunched up her forehead. "Consulting? I don't understand."

Aralyn held out an arm and motioned for Trish to follow. They headed over to Aralyn's corner office. Trish peeked over her shoulder questioningly at those on her team, who held expressions that were mixed with amusement and apprehension.

She shadowed her godmother inside the office and waited until Aralyn closed the door. "What do you mean, she's on the team? What exactly will she be doing and why? Or better yet…why wasn't I included in this decision?" she asked the last question with a building edge of agitation.

Aralyn threw Trish one of her infamous watch-yourself-soldier glares and took a seat. She gestured to an empty chair across from her desk. "With her animal husbandry and psychiatric knowledge, Doctor Burgos and I feel she'll be a big help during the next phase of the mission. Since you've done most of the tagging and Doctor

Burgos is analyzing the data the trackers are relaying to us, we need to turn our focus on studying the Gramite behaviors and characteristics, both individually and inside their hordes."

Trish sat on the edge of her seat, still feeling like she was missing something everyone else knew but her. "So, is she helping Doctor Burgos with the medical data and field reports that come in?"

Aralyn nodded. "Yes, she'll go over his assessments and compare them to her own, as will he with hers."

Trish relaxed in the chair. "That makes sense. With the gravity of our mission, I guess another set of eyes won't hurt."

"I'm glad we agree. She'll be doing in-depth reports from the field with you, and during the times you're working in the lab or perfecting your abilities, she'll help Doctor Burgos with analyzing both sets of data."

Trish rocketed to her feet. "No, absolutely not, Colonel. I work alone. That was our agreement from the beginning." Her protest was forceful enough that she could genuinely feel the pressure rise in her veins along both sides of her neck.

Aralyn drew her brows together. "Captain, don't push me today." Her voice was an octave above normal, which, for Aralyn, was anything but normal.

Trish stared at her godmother, knowing the ma'am card had been hurled in her direction. Did she care? Six months ago, Trish's mindset would have been an adamant, hell no, I never signed up for this crap. But at this point in her life, fitting into her role within the militia for these last many months, this deeper level of comradery felt like an extension of herself. An extra arm, or a leg, a part she didn't want severed. Realizing this certainty, she took her seat. Since when did this mental metamorphosis come about?

She peered up at her waiting commander. "I'm sorry for my outburst, Colonel. It won't happen again."

With a hint of surprise, layered with a sense of maternal pride, Aralyn gave a curt dip with her head. "I understand this will first feel like an added burden for you, with now having to worry about her safety on top of your own workload. Nevertheless, I'm confident you'll soon see how her skillset will push us along faster to reach our objectives. Her consulting position could take years off our work, which hopefully will save countless lives in the long run."

Trish sighed a few times. She fidgeted with a container of pens and rubbed her finger along the edge of Aralyn's spotless desk.

"For the love of—child, what's bothering you?"

Trish looked toward the door and pleading with her godmother silently, and not her higher-ranking officer. "Aralyn, Olivia's a lesbian."

Aralyn stared at her goddaughter comically, as if Trish had told her infected creatures roamed the planet. "And?" she asked, stretching out the word.

"What, you knew?"

Aralyn leaned back in her seat. "The entire city knows—well, apparently you didn't until recently, I take it?"

"Two days ago. My life is already spinning around inside a toilet, just waiting for the right amount of shit to flush it down."

"First, never say that to me again. Second, I'm not telling you to shag her. Believe me, I know you better than anyone else here. Your heart belongs to Christina. You're exactly like me, Trish. When someone holds your heart in their hands, nobody else can penetrate any part of you. I may as well have shacked her up with a devout nun, placing her with you."

Trish stood. "I'm not sure what my heart feels anymore, but I know this won't help it." With hers and Christina's marriage falling apart, life was complicated enough. She made her way to the door.

"Trish," Aralyn called out. When Trish turned, she saw empathy in her godmother's eyes. "This addition to the team is a good thing. Please, trust me on this."

Feeling defeated, Trish opened the door and left the room.

Trish packed the last of the extra equipment into her Gladiator and closed the hatch. With the most recent test inside the vault ending with a chunk of the concrete wall exploding behind the table and her nose bleeding soon after, Young had insisted on conducting a complete physical before letting Trish leave the outpost. The day had slipped away to a few minutes after five in the evening, and she grew impatient with wanting to locate the horde and set up camp before dark. At the rate they were going, this probably wouldn't happen.

She loaded Molly into the vehicle once Olivia headed over from the officer's dorm, where Aralyn and Doctor Burgos both had felt their consultant would be most comfortable. Trish cringed at the sight of the approaching woman dressed in an armored bodysuit. Olivia had her hair down, helmet on, weapon slung over her shoulder, and standard militia backpack strapped to her back while carrying an overstretched bag in each hand. By the time she made it across the doublewide street to the vehicle, her lengthy strides had dropped to a shuffle. "A hand would be nice," she said, dropping the bags by the rear tire.

This isn't going to work, Trish thought, pointing to the bags. "You know, we'll only be out there for two days. What's with all this crap?"

Oliva raised her visor, revealing a small bead of perspiration running down the right side of her face. She motioned toward the army-green bag housing multiple compartments. "Medical supplies which I've assigned to your vehicle." She gestured to the other bag. "This black one has my processor and office essentials for working on my reports as well as the video equipment and several reference books I thought I might need." She passed Trish her rifle and took off the backpack. "Rations, water, another bulletproof bodysuit—"

Trish waved her off and headed to open the hatch. "I know what's in the rucksack," she mumbled over her shoulder. She heard

Olivia chuckle as she flung the hatch up. Peeking around to where Olivia was shaking her head with her hands planted firmly on her waistline, she asked, "What?"

Olivia hoisted up her bags and smirked at Trish. "Phillips and Carlen both said you'd be a bear since I was tagging along. To be honest, I didn't believe them until now." Olivia stepped over and bullied her way into Trish's space, causing Trish to take a few steps backward. "I can manage simply fine with my own gear. I wouldn't want you to think I was a freeloader." She threw in the medical bag and heaved the black one halfway onto the pile with a swing of momentum,. She pushed it on top of the camping supplies. "I'll do my job, and you do yours. One of your tasks is keeping us alive, which I hope is top on your priority list."

Trish stepped forward and removed both the bags Olivia had loaded. "It is, but before we go, let's get a few things straight. Rule one, you'll carry all your own crap. Other than keeping you alive, I won't be coddling you. Rule two, this is my ride, so I'm in charge of how everything's packed. Each bag has its own designated spot. It'll help with us loading and unloading within minutes." Trish shifted some of the camping supplies around and cleared a small area in the center. She tossed in Olivia's bags. "This is your space. Mine is on the right. I'll stay out of your bags, and you keep out of mine. Go ahead and throw your backpack in. You won't need it until we make camp."

Trish went around and opened the passenger door. She could have sworn she heard Olivia mutter something about OCD, but she ignored it. She made sure Olivia's rifle was set to safe and attached the muzzle to the weapon latch protruding from the console. After she climbed in behind the wheel, she waited for Olivia to be belted in before driving.

"You're not going to secure your weapon?" Olivia sarcastically asked. She directed her amused stare toward Trish's rifle laying on the seat between them.

"I'm not worried about me accidentally shooting anyone," Trish said, pulling up to the gate to leave New Underwood.

"Oh, but you think I will?"

"Until I see how well you can handle yourself, I'm not taking any chance." She then gave Olivia her most serious glare. "I'm in charge. You do what I say, when I say it. No arguing."

Olivia tightened her lips together and threw Trish a two-finger salute.

With a scowl, Trish focused her impatience on the opening gate. *This is going to be a long two days.* Trish stretched out the tension in her neck. She powered on the stereo to her classic-rock playlist and increased the volume to flood out the possibility of additional questions. She threw Molly a treat and headed toward the ravine where she had last sensed horde-four.

Of all the times in her life she desired to be left alone, this week was at the top of her list. She'd long since learned about her own way of coping with uncontrollable stressors. Her mind required some peace and quiet to sort out and rationalize emotional health issues. If this arrangement was going to work, Olivia had to respect her need for silence, not only to mentally deal with the problematic predicaments enveloping her life, but to focus on the surroundings past the wall.

Still, the major dilemma bothering Trish was the way Olivia seemed to study her movements. Trish wasn't sure if this uncomfortable quandary was new, or if Olivia had been watching her for a while now. With recently learning Olivia wasn't interested in men, and how easygoing their friendship had become, Trish realized she could either be paranoid or have an unwelcome issue develop within their relationship. Whatever the case, Olivia needed to understand, with or without Christina in her life, Trish wasn't on the market for anything other than an arm's length friendship. Ever.

It didn't take them long to reach the ravine. They then headed twenty miles east, traveling away from the city toward Elm Springs, and turned north, moving past what was left of Union Center. Most of their drive was offroad over stretches of weeded landscape and dirt flats while weaving around a few impassable areas of terrain, both wild and notably beautiful. Trish veered west on Highway 34, steering across chunks of missing asphalt on a forgotten road long overdue for old-world maintenance.

Right as they passed a weathered sign showing five miles ahead lay Sturgis, South Dakota, Olivia let out a surprised gasp. Trish slowed the vehicle as both women gazed in awe off to the right. A few hundred feet from the edge of the highway, stretching out along the dusty brown grass with sparse patches of greenery, sat thousands upon thousands of rusted and battered motorcycles. The lined up and forgotten bikes were lined up for over a mile in both directions in an organized clatter of corroded metal and worn, muck-covered seats and sidecars.

Trish pulled the Gladiator off the road and parked. "What is all this?" she asked, more to voice her bewilderment than to ask Olivia. She climbed out and motioned for Molly.

"My father told me about this," Olivia said. "He said Sturgis used to be the place where avid motorcycle enthusiasts came together every year for the largest bike rally in the world. He had gone once, before he and my mother got married. From how he told, or didn't tell it, the festivities were a memorable kind of wild." Olivia's eyes sparkled as she relived her father's story. "Once the fuel reserves had hit a critical turning point, many brought their motorcycles here for one last rally. I guess they were trying to push for the conversion of privately owned motorcycles, from fuel to solar power."

Trish ran her hand along the first torn seat she came to. "I wonder why Rapid City's reclamation crews haven't scrapped all this metal."

Olivia spun, shocked. "Trish, don't you see?" she said, sweeping an arm out wide over the landscape. "This is a memorial for times lost. To show their convictions. People left a big part of themselves here. A contribution they deeply cared about. The time and money riders put into their bikes…to abandon them like this…" Olivia fully took in the view. "I can't imagine how hard it must have been for them."

Trish opened the loose flap on a saddlebag attached to a nearby motorcycle. Other than a collection of coarse dirt, the cracked-leather pouch sat empty. "They're vehicles. A means of transportation from one place to the next, nothing more."

"No, not to those who rode. My father said there was a sense of freedom with riding. Like being on a horse and thinking how easy it would be to head in any direction and leave everything else behind. All your stresses, worries—" Olivia's attention swayed from the view to Trish. "Every ounce of life's demands weighing on your shoulders, gone. To ride off into the sunset with the minimal necessities to take you someplace new, where no one knows who you are. I've seen that same look on your face several times, Trish, like now."

Trish stared at Olivia's investigating eyes, feeling suddenly vulnerable. That was exactly how she felt. To load up her vehicle and head off, leaving the pain of her life in her rearview mirror. To search for anywhere new, where her heart no longer ached. The idea was both soothing and terrifying. To leave her daughter, Aralyn, and those she loved, to never see Christina's face again, even if Trish wasn't the one Christina's arms were aching to hold. No, abandoning them was something she would never do. Could never do.

With a sudden ripple of sadness, Trish called for the inquisitive Molly. The Saint Bernard was already a hundred feet ahead of them, sniffing anything of interest. "The sun will be down in over an hour. We need to go."

Not wanting to chance either of them catching sight of additional distractions, Trish avoided driving through Sturgis altogether. When they were less than a mile past the city limits, Trish's senses sparked. She headed to the closest hillside and parked along a gathering of young trees shrouded by the shadowing limbs of their aged ancestors. She climbed out and told Olivia to leave her rifle. The horde was still a few miles away.

"How are you sure others aren't closer?" Olivia asked, more fascinated than concerned.

Trish removed the binoculars and peered at the area where her perceptions pulled the strongest. "I really don't know how to explain it," she said. When she spotted the first Gramite huddled by a fallen tree, she passed Olivia the binoculars and motioned toward the unaware creature. "When I'm close enough, it's like I can see them. Not visually, but inside me. More than a gut feeling. It's like an inner certainty of their presence."

Olivia lowered the eyepiece. "What? You're gambling our safety on a gut feeling?"

"No, it's more than that." Trish puffed out her cheeks and gradually exhaled. There was no easy way to explain her internal phenomenon. "I know this will sound crazy, but I feel like I'm connected to their emotions. Ever since one infected me, this feeling has grown much stronger." Trish headed toward the Gladiator and opened the hatch. "It was the same with the mutants. At first, I couldn't detect them at all. Then one scratched me. Now I can sense them. I think it's related."

Trish pulled out both tents and positioned each dwelling by the vehicle where she wanted them set up. She retrieved her helmet from the passenger seat, sealed it to her bodysuit, and lifted her visor.

Olivia studied her movements and motioned toward the tents wrapped inside their travel bags. "Are we camping here tonight? Kinda close, don't you think?"

"We're still a little over two miles away. Don't worry. I'll be able to tell if they come closer or spot us." She went to the rear of the Gladiator and removed the long-range rifle from its case with a magazine full of tracker rounds and one of Givens' specially made, hollow-point rounds. She placed both inside an ammo pouch on her utility belt. "While I'm gone, can you set up the tents? They're pretty easy. Shouldn't take you long."

"You're leaving me here...alone?"

"Molly will keep you company, and I won't go far," Trish said. She headed swiftly down the hillside. She knew their camp had a good vantage point, but she had a personal matter to attend to, and she wanted to do it unaccompanied. Hitting the bottom of the hill, she darted through a dense section of overgrown brush which was intertwined with sweet-smelling vines. She avoided as many spiderwebs as she could, trying hard not to disturb their habitat. She zigzagged until she finally penetrated Mother Nature's thick obstacle.

Trish dropped to a knee and peered through the scope on the rifle, scanning for movement. The area stretching out before her was an old softball field. Several brown, fifty-gallon barrels, each labeled trash in chipped, yellow paint, stood out from a carpet of tall weeds that blanketed the aged field in yellow and purple flowers. Toward the far right stood two run-down concession booths. Stenciled on the front of each was colorful faded lettering, listing the various food and drinks they once offered, and restrooms huddled between the two. Vine-covered, rusted fencing diamond-shaped outward through the area, with long, rotting bleachers lining the far fencing behind the catcher's box and running halfway down each side of the field.

She heard a rustling commotion of brush behind her and spun. Olivia stopped, half-crouched, and held up her hands. "Sorry for intruding, but as I was watching you leave, a thought occurred to me." She calmly gestured a finger between them both. "You and I are on the same team. I figured if there was something important you needed to do, I should be here when you do it," she said, hunkering closer.

Trish glared. She opened her mouth and closed it. Ten seconds later, Molly emerged from the brush, covered generously in spider webs. She dropped her stout frame to the ground and rolled around, trying to clean the foreign netting from her fur.

"You left your helmet and didn't bring your rifle?"

"You told me to leave the rifle."

Olivia's grin was infuriating. Trish struggled with the urge to call Aralyn and beg her to reconsider this arrangement. "Are you planning on picking which of my orders you aim to follow?"

Olivia made a sucking noise with her cheek. "That's the problem right there. This whole order thing. Yeah, I'm not keen on the idea of being told what to do." Olivia deliberately crossed her arms. "Now, if you asked me nicely, I may just listen. Don't forget, I'm not actually in your militia."

Trish was about to snap out a retort when she realized two things. First, she had once felt the same way Olivia did with the whole military mumbo-jumbo not too terribly long ago, and second, Trish knew she was being a complete ass. She softened her glare and brushed a hand over Molly, trying to help her remove some of the hard-to-reach strands of webbing.

She glanced at Olivia, who was searching Trish's body language for information. "I'm sorry. I'm irritable and taking it out on you. I promise from here on out, not to be such a dick." Trish was more upset with herself than this entire situation. "I'm asking you to please give me a level of space. I'm not feeling very keen on being around people right now."

Olivia continued to watch Trish closely. "I get it, I really do. I know you're the type of person who likes to withdraw into themselves when they're under a lot of stress. My father was the same way and a complete opposite to my mother. I'll keep my questions related solely to our work here." She pointed with her thumb over her shoulder. "Do you want me to head to the camp and wait?"

"You're already here. If you promise to remain quiet and do as I ask, you might as well tag along."

Once Olivia agreed, Trish signaled Molly to go to the vehicle. Seconds after the dog pranced through the brush, Trish made her way along the inner field toward the concession stands, with Olivia right beside her. They headed to the far corner and approached the wooden door of the concession building on the right. One good push against the door and the weathered clasp that housed the rusted padlock broke away from the splintering wood. Trish let the door swing out wide, casting the evening light into the darkened room.

"What are we searching for?" Olivia asked.

Staring around at the dusty stove, scattered plastic cups, and left-behind cardboard boxes along the far cabinets, Trish peered upward and pointed to the ceiling. "That," she said, directing Olivia's gaze to the hatch in the corner. She went over and jumped up onto a metal counter. Leaving distinct footprints through the grimy surface, she shifted directly underneath the metal box protruding from the ceiling.

"Do you think this old roof is strong enough to hold our weight?"

"There's one way to find out." Trish flipped the lever, pushed up onto the bottom of the roof access hatch, and tossed it open. Additional light poured in.

She noticed the worried look on Olivia's face. "If it makes you feel better, I'll go try it out first and pull you up after. If it can hold my 260-pound body, you shouldn't have any issues." She laughed at Olivia's shocked appearance. "Did they not tell you about my thicker bone density and larger muscle mass?"

"They did. I just never considered how it affected your bodyweight." Her mouth cocked to the side. "I guess this is the reason you kinda suck at swimming and you have a crazy-healthy appetite. I was actually starting to think you had a tapeworm."

Trish muttered, "I don't suck at swimming. I manage with the body I was given. Big difference." Trish unslung the rifle and passed it to Olivia. She pulled herself through the opening and once standing, she moved around the roof and checked the structure for weakness. The aged roofing was solid. At the access hatch, Olivia was already on the counter, and passing up the rifle.

"We're good," Trish said, placing the rifle on the roof beside her.

Olivia held her hands up for assistance.

Trish easily pulled her upward and onto the roof. She drew out her binoculars, but before scanning the area, she noticed Olivia's eyes were like saucers, staring straight at her. Trish gauged Olivia's astonishment curiously. "What?" she finally asked.

"You pulled me up like I was nothing. How much can you lift?"

"Well, three times a week Phillips and Doctor Burgos have me lifting several sets of twenty-five hundred pounds. Doing a onetime deadlift, maybe three thousand."

"My god, that's amazing."

Trish huffed. "Tell that to Doctor Burgos. He insists, like a gorilla, I can hit four thousand pounds. I believe my body's maxed out, though. It's been consistent for a few months now."

"But you're not a gorilla, and being able to lift four thousand pounds differs from doing a workout with that much weight."

Trish peeked through her binoculars. "Maybe you can add that to one of your reports, and Doctor Burgos will stop pushing so hard."

"I will," Olivia said.

Trish could hear the humor in Olivia's voice. Before she could respond, she spotted the leader of the horde a mile away. She passed Olivia the binoculars and pointed.

Grabbing the magazines from the pouch, she retrieved the rifle and tracker rounds.

"You're not going to shoot it, are you?" Olivia asked, sounding surprised and upset.

Trish pulled out one of the smaller bullets. "It's a tracker, which also sends Doctor Burgos various vital readings throughout the day. She replaced the round, inserted the magazine, and charged the chamber. "The rifle has a built-in suppressor, but you still should cover your ears."

"Will they be able to hear the noise?"

"We're closer than I usually shoot, but even at this range, it'll sound like a distant pop. They won't know which direction the sound came from. Don't worry. We're safe here."

Trish took her position, found her target, and readied her weapon. She pulled the trigger. They both watched as the tracker round struck the confused Gramite leader on his right shoulder. He spun swiftly. After an awkward stretch, he resumed eating. "Way to take it like a champ, big guy," Trish murmured. She closed her visor and connected to the active link.

Doctor Burgos came on. "I got it, Trish. Good work."

"This one's the leader of horde-four." She turned to Olivia and raised her visor. "Wanna name him?"

Olivia turned away from the direction of the Gramites. A smirk formed on her lips. "Champ," she said with a shrug.

Trish beamed brightly before dropping her visor. "This one's called Champ, Doc. Let Phillips know Olivia named him, not me."

"I'm sure she did, because this name I actually like," Phillips cut in.

Groaning, Trish raised her visor. She continued to search through the grouping of Gramites. This cluster appeared more laidback than the other three hordes. Maybe because they were smaller in number, or possibly the temperament of the leader played a part. Whatever the reason, the leader didn't bully himself into his flock as the others ate. No heads bowed low when he passed by. It was a casual evening of feasting on smaller game before the sun set. Trish studied the skyline. They would need to head to camp soon.

"The entire time you've been around Gramites, have you ever noticed any offspring?"

Surprised by the question, Trish said, "No. Doctor Burgos has a theory about the virus making the infected sterile."

"I believe his theory has been blown out of the water. Look over to the right, by the farthest oak with the bottom layer of bark missing."

Feeling a sudden rush of adrenaline, Trish shifted the scope and scanned for anything resembling a child. Her anger flashed the second her eyes locked on to the female she had come here to find. No tiny creatures were with her, but the second Trish adjusted the scope setting, she realized what Olivia was referring to.

Her palms grew clammy. She lowered her visor and linked in with the others. "Doctor Burgos, I believe we have a pregnant female here."

"Trish, are you sure?"

Trish said, "She looks pretty big in the belly to me, Doc."

"Trish, several factors could cause a distended abdomen that has nothing to do with pregnancy."

She looked at Olivia questioningly, and after a moment, Olivia held up five fingers. "I'm not positive, but she seems pretty dang impregnated to us. Olivia believes she's five months along. Do you want me to tag her? Will the tracker hurt a fetus?"

"No, it won't. Yes, tag her, but I don't see how this is possible. We might have to send Sergeant Perez and Sergeant Young out to you tomorrow. Maybe you guys can manage to get me some blood samples, even drug her long enough for an ultrasound. We'll discuss it tonight and contact you with a gameplan in the morning."

This changed things. Whatever anger Trish had been carrying toward this creature evaporated, replaced by an unfamiliar urge to protect mother and fetus. Even if this creature was an infected, wasn't the Gramite still considered a life, as was her unborn child? Trish raised her visor and the rifle, feeling suddenly hesitant to pull the trigger.

Olivia touched her shoulder and leaned in beside her. "I agree with Doctor Burgos. She'll be fine."

Trish found her mark along the center of the left shoulder. She held her breath and fired.

CHAPTER TWELVE

Olivia blinked sleep away. She was positive she heard movement outside her tent. Her heart raced when she realized Molly was no longer curled on the ground beside her. Olivia now found herself huddled in her sleeping bag on the firm cot all alone, lying under a dome of thin fabric for fictional protection.

Suddenly, a dark silhouette moved along the outside of her tent. Someone or something was intentionally rubbing against the stretched material, replacing the eerie silence with stroking fear. Her heart thundered as the figure drew closer to the door. Her eyes danced around in the darkness to the slow, serrated sound of her tent door unzipping. With the absence of Molly, there was no weapon in here she could use. Trish had said she wouldn't need one since her own tent was close, less than ten feet away from Olivia's, and she would wake before something came near.

Olivia closed her eyes tight, held her breath, and remained motionless, trying hard to slow the loud pounding in her chest. Whatever had worked at the zipper was now slipping inside. She wanted to scream out for Trish, but her scarcely working lungs wouldn't allow it. Her cot gave a slight creaking, and she felt pressure on her right side as the zipper on her sleeping bag moved downward, letting cool air inside the warmth of her all-weather cocoon.

When her eyelids parted, she gasped. Trish's mesmerizing blue eyes were inches away from her own. A warm wisp of breath poured from Trish's full lips, sending a shiver down Olivia's body. The thrill of Trish's closeness induced goose bumps along Olivia's chest and inner thighs. Trish's fingers gently slid through the opening of the sleeping bag, and Olivia was surprised to see Trish's own nakedness. Olivia's body shuddered when Trish bent closer and brushed their lips softly together, teasing their first kiss with the slightest of pressures.

The cot screeched louder as Trish climbed her own naked body onto the cot, their eyes locking lustfully onto one another. Olivia could feel her heart pound wildly as they kissed again, this time with more firmness, more taste exchanging between the two. Trish moved her lips downward to Olivia's breast, and Olivia arched into the gentle sucking as she kicked her legs out, exposing herself fully to the touch of this woman. She closed her eyes, brought her hands around, and caressed the ridged muscles along Trish's arms and back. Oh, how she had longed for this moment.

She could feel the raw strength in Trish's hand as it glided downward, parting Olivia's thighs gently, yet with assertion. Olivia groaned. She ran her fingers through Trish's hair as her body quivered with anticipation. Trish's tongue flicked over a nipple. Olivia licked at the dryness of her lips, while praying this moment would last forever. Trish teased her mouth downward, moistening a trail of warm flesh with her full lips and scraping teeth, before sliding her tongue between Olivia's legs.

A low growl caused Olivia's eyelids to spring open, and sudden fear gripped her. She jerked up on her elbows, as every muscle in her body tensed. Yellow-orange eyes peered in from the tent flat and darted from her to the woman sucking fully at her wetness. She tried to scream, but no sound came out. Olivia moved her hand urgently downward, struggling hard to push Trish's head away, to draw her attention toward the threat behind her, but Trish wouldn't stop her relentless pursuit, which caused caressing pleasure to combine with heart-stopping terror.

The Gramite leader of horde-four lunged its massive body straight at Trish, slicing its claws wildly into skin, muscle, and bone. Trish cried out, her blood flying everywhere, splattering against the ceiling and walls of the tent. Olivia watched in silent shock as Trish tried fighting off the massive beast, but she was unfocused, weakened by their moment of passion. Olivia shifted to jump from the cot and help her, but her body refused to move. A second Gramite entered. The pregnant female. Her animalistic rage frightened Olivia to the point of anesthetizing panic. She witnessed the horror as the female dove in, ripping her sharp teeth into Trish's throat.

When Trish's esophagus tore and she gurgled out her final breath, Olivia found her voice, and she screamed out as loud as she could.

The moans inside Olivia's tent shift into terrified screams. Trish dropped her coffee cup and rushed to the tent. "Olivia! Olivia, wake up. You're okay."

Trish fumbled with the zipper in the moonlight while hearing Molly's anxious whine from inside. Olivia pressed her hands hard against the fabric, distorting the walls of the tent and flipping the zipper out of Trish's fingers. "Olivia, I need you to calm down, move away from the door, and take a few deep breaths."

Once the tent grew still, Trish found the zipper, and she yanked the metal clasp upward. She could see Olivia's slouched form shaking, hear the stifled sobs echoing from inside. She made her way in, steadying the trembling woman in her arms. "Breathe slowly. Clear your mind. Everything will be fine."

Olivia held on to her tightly, her arms wrapped completely around Trish. "Trish, the dream was so real, so horrible."

"Believe me, I understand. I've had nightmares before," Trish said. "Let's get you outside, and I'll make you some coffee."

Trish reached a hand to the side and stroked Molly's fur. She motioned the settling dog from the tent. Once she helped Olivia onto her feet, they exited to the soothing burst of early morning air. The sun was still a good hour from rising, with a gentle haze of the glowing horizon giving their cold-camp shadowed clarity. The rhythmic calls of the surrounding insects kept the silence away.

"Still no fire?" Olivia asked with weak humor.

"I'm afraid not," Trish said, motioning Olivia toward one of the unfolded chairs. She headed inside the tent for Olivia's sleeping bag. Trish draped the bulky material around Olivia before retrieving her coffee cup from the grass and heading for the Gladiator. Hatchback raised, she flipped on the camping light she had hanging from a built-in ceiling clip. "When we're so close to a horde, I don't build a campfire. If they smell it, I'm worried they'll either abandon the area or come to investigate. Neither scenario is really what we're aiming for here."

Trish removed her black cargo bag from the camping pile. She opened the main compartment and removed a three-cup container.

Olivia moved beside her and searched through her backpack. She yanked out a pair of dark-blue sweatpants and a pale-blue sweatshirt, throwing them over her shorts and T-shirt.

"What are you doing?" Olivia asked, as Trish unpacked items from various pouches to add into the plastic canister.

"Making you some coffee. Would you like cream and sugar?"

Olivia's face distorted. "Is that the same coffee from the ration packs? No thanks. I've had more than my fill of that disgusting black tar in NORAD."

Trish laughed. "I've tweaked it with my own blend of flavors. You'll love it." She added two sugar tablets and one creamer. She shook it vigorously as Olivia skeptically looked on.

Trish removed a second coffee cup, popped the lid on the container, and poured the steaming beverage inside. She passed it to Olivia and prepared a new serving for herself. "At least try it," she said.

Olivia brought the cup up and carefully sniffed the rising heat. The moment Olivia touched the cup to her lips and sipped, her eyes widened.

Trish gave another brisk chuckle. "I told you." She pointed past the gear inside the hatchback. "There's several cases of water and a few duffel bags full of ration trays stored in the last row of seating. Unfortunately for you, they haven't been tweaked."

Olivia raised her hand. "The day we arrived in Rapid City, I swore off eating anything that doesn't have an expiration date. The coffee's fine, thank you."

"You'll get hungry soon enough," Trish said, shaking the heating blend. She filled her coffee and took her time to return each item to their proper compartments, first rinsing out the containers.

Before flipping off the light, she double-checked every compartment of the bag, making sure they were all closed. As she straightened Olivia's backpack, she noticed Olivia's amused, analytical eyes watching her. Trish feebly bobbed her head. "Yes, I'll admit to having a bit of OCD, but I don't see how being neat and organized is really a bad thing."

Olivia took another sip. "I'm not judging, just marveling at how alike you are to my father."

Trish quirked a brow and flipped off the light. "You father sounds like he was a very intelligent man."

Olivia responded with pride. "He was."

"Sir, we have the three test subjects loaded and ready to go."

Lieutenant Waska lowered the scope on his rifle and thought to himself. The second Gladiator had arrived at Trish's camp right as the sun hit the highest point in the sky. Now Trish and the woman with long, brown hair were watching the Gramite horde on a roof with two other men, both of whom Lieutenant Waska had never seen before. How skilled were these soldiers and how long were they planning on staying with the women? Having no answer to either of these questions troubled him.

He stood from his prone position and slung his rifle over his shoulder, casually inspecting the overgrown farmland attached to Crook City, South Dakota. They were several miles from the Gramite horde and had the wind at their backs. With Trish's high level of perception and the Gramites' advanced sense of smell, he knew setting up camp here was too risky.

"Have them drop the container over by those trees and leave the bait heading toward the horde and not Trish's camp. I want the door set to remote, not timed. We can't run our tests until those other two leave the area. They'll get in the way and impair our findings."

He moved toward his vehicle. "I'm heading with the others to locate a suitable spot to make camp. Keep an eye out and notify me once Trish and her companion are finally alone."

Sergeant Young raised his visor. "I don't think disturbing her now is a good idea. Her temperature and heart rate are both extremely elevated compared to the other Gramites we're monitoring. This could be normal with her condition, but I'd rather give it until next week to see if both readings improve."

Trish clicked off the vitals monitor on her screen and lifted her visor. "I'm with Doctor Burgos. I'm leaving this decision up to you and Olivia."

Sergeant Perez cleared his throat, bringing all eyes to him. "Like I asked Doctor Burgos at the meeting last night, is allowing this pregnancy really something we want to do? The idea of deranged toddlers with massive teeth and claws running at me is a terrifying thought I'd rather not live through."

Olivia lowered her binoculars. "These Gramites were once people like you and me. It's not like they wanted to be turned into this."

"I'm not saying the Gramites themselves should die. We're all going into this mission hoping one day Trish and Doctor Burgos might discover a vaccine and a cure if these creatures are curable. But that being said, an offspring from two infected, would it even have a soul to save?"

"Okay," Trish cut in, before Olivia could snap out the heated retort forming beneath her firmly pursed lips. "We're here to learn about the Gramites. The more we study, the better the understanding we'll have. Let's stick to the facts. One, none of us have ever seen Gramite offspring, so we're not even sure if they're able to carry a fetus to full term. What we now know is they're not sterile as we once believed. Two, as Doctor Burgos said, certain viruses can cause birth defects and miscarriages. If she's under distress, it could be the virus reacting to the fetus. So I say let's let nature run its course, and see what happens. If the fetus makes it past labor, we'll go from there."

They spent the next few hours observing the Gramites in awkward silence. Olivia jotted down notes and Perez remained glued to the scope on his rifle. This tension was another reason Trish didn't like anyone working with her. Their social uneasiness made Trish's intriguing task unenjoyable, even stressful. Thankfully, Young was a buffer to some of the stillness in the air.

Half of the Gramites left the area surrounding the two openings to the underground den, while the rest stayed behind and worked. Young and Trish discussed how several went through the lush foliage and gathered various nuts and berries. A couple of the others brought in different edible plants and what looked to be small apples, maybe crab apples. The one who was with child and a long-limbed male left and scurried in an hour later carrying armfuls of pre-stained clothing.

"They're actually changing their ripped clothes for new ones," Young said to Trish, as all watched one male tear off his shirt and struggle into a new one from the pile.

"Not much of an improvement," Trish said. The male's claws had sliced into the new T-shirt like the material was a thin sheet of paper. It heatedly protested before ripping the fabric off and searching for another.

The rest of the large group of Gramites finally returned, bringing with them several dead rabbits, squirrels, a young deer, and, from what Trish could tell, a fox. Soon after, the horde settled in for an early evening meal. It surprised Trish how the leader of the horde glared out at his followers, as it offered the pregnant female the first go at the food. Not that any appeared to object to the delay. A few even helped her with selecting what she was going to eat, and one stripped the skin off a rabbit for her.

"Do you see that?" Perez finally said, gazing into his scope. "They're doting on her."

Olivia and her binoculars were leaning halfway over the edge of the roof. She was just as enthralled as Perez. "Yes, they've been doing thoughtful things like that all day. Did you notice the other female took the clothes from her when she came in? It's like a close-knit family, loving, nurturing."

"So, they have empathy?" Perez asked. He was more than interested—his face held a deep level of surprise.

"Yes, empathy, but pay attention to everything else," Olivia said. "The traits and actions which make us human and not brainless creatures." Her words gained in speed as she pointed. "The one sitting over by the clothes. See how her features appear amused by the one beside her. She almost looks as if she's about to laugh. I don't see their lips moving, but it's like they're carrying on a full-blown conversation. Maybe it's through body language. I can't tell from here.

"This group, they have a strong tie to one another. All went out today and worked for the good of the community." Her voice lifted, becoming even more excited. "Take this meal for instance. Not only are they still like us, omnivores, but they are rummaging through the pile of meat and vegetation, choosing what they want to eat. Also, the one who's pregnant and the leader sitting beside her, even though there's plenty of food left, they finished eating once they had their fill. Several species of animals will do this, yes, but not all. I guess I assumed with their hostile nature, they would eat until the food was gone and would be aggressive with each other while doing so," Olivia said, frantically scribbling down her findings.

Perez snickered in Olivia's direction, and she shot him a questioning stare. "I'm glad you're here, Doc."

As soon as Olivia and Perez shared a flash of appreciation with one another, Trish turned her head to Young. Young sent Trish a "see, they worked it out," wink and continued filming.

Trish lowered her rifle and leaned her shoulders against the roof's miniature wall. She removed her canteen and checked her watch for the time. She too, was getting hungry. She didn't realize they would be out this long, so she didn't bring her backpack with her. She took a drink and examined the overgrown service road heading away from the sports field. They were far enough away from the horde not to be easily detected. They should have driven their Gladiators here. Next time.

She replaced her water seconds before Young nervously cleared his throat. "Umm, should I keep filming this?" Young asked.

"My goodness, yes. This is great for research," said Olivia, the pitch of her voice lower than before, but still reflecting her interest. "Make sure you show this video to Doctor Burgos as soon as you get to New Underwood. Their exchanged level of intimacy mixed in with their aggressiveness is significant."

Curious, Trish peered into her scope and skimmed the area. The moment she spotted the two Gramites off to the side heatedly mating, her face flushed, and she averted her eyes.

Olivia laughed. "I think your captain's blushing."

Trish grunted. "What are you…like twelve?" Trish said, uncomfortably climbing to her feet. "I'm going to head down and stretch my legs a bit. Are we almost done here?"

Olivia focused through her binoculars, then directed a casual smirk to Trish. "I'd say we're a good fifteen minutes away from finishing. As vigorous as this research is going, there may be a shared cigarette after."

Trish rolled her eyes and headed to the hatch. The moment her feet touched the floor, she heard the hearty laughter from above.

Pumping her legs through the overgrown grass, Trish shifted her body, adjusting herself to the dip in the terrain. This route wasn't the preferred choice for her evening run, but with Olivia out here in the wild with her, Trish didn't want to chance going too far away. Instead of doing her usual ten miles out and ten miles back jaunt, she ran in a wide circle around the camp, not going farther away than a mile from Olivia, who was waiting anxiously on the hillside for her return.

Before proceeding to the last stretch, Trish shook her head when she spotted Olivia standing by the tents. Olivia was out of her seat again, scanning for Trish through her binoculars. Trish waved her arm in the air so Olivia would see her and continued to concentrate on her stride. She picked up the pace for her last mile sprint, but right as she pushed herself harder, a great sense of dread overshadowed her mind. Something terrible was approaching—she could feel it.

Ignoring the complaining in her lungs, Trish struggled for every ounce of strength her burning legs had left, as she changed direction and rushed up the hillside. Olivia's uncertain expression met her when Trish raced into the camp and headed for the Gladiator. She skidded to a stop beside the door and jerked at the handle. She retrieved her rifle from the front seat, while rapidly sucking in raspy gulps of air.

"Trish, what's wrong?"

Trish moved around Olivia and pointed the scope toward the Gramites below. At once, she noticed how their anxiety also increased with the growing threat. Trish rotated the scope to the vicinity of where her rising warnings flared. Toward the far hillside, past the nestle of trees where horde-four had built their underground den, three hideous creatures with bright-orange eyes tore through the foliage, heading in a straight line toward the restless Gramites.

"Mutants," Trish said, lowering her rifle. Her mind raced, knowing the strength of one was bad enough but three might prove to be more than she could handle. *And Olivia…damn. What am I supposed to do with her?* Trish wracked her brain, trying to decide how best to handle their security situation and still help the Gramites. "I need you to drive," Trish blurted out as she rushed to her tent. After she snatched up her bodysuit, boots, and utility belt, she headed for the passenger seat.

"Trish, I don't understand." Olivia stood unmoving. She was scared.

"Please, I'll explain on the way." Trish pulled off her running shoes and stripped down to her sweaty boxer-briefs and sports bra. She called for Molly and wiggled herself into the armored suit. Molly jumped over the seat right as Olivia climbed in behind the wheel.

"On the far side of the hill, there's a service road. If you head to the right, it'll take us to the softball field. You need to drive fast, Olivia. Don't worry. I won't let anything happen to you," Trish said, adding the last part to ease some of Olivia's nervousness.

Once Trish fastened the suit, she worked herself into the utility belt and boots while riding through the jarring dips and bumps swaying her roughly in her seat. As soon as her boots were laced, she searched around for her helmet. Damn, she had dropped it in her chair before the run. Thankfully, Phillips wasn't here to see.

"Where's your helmet?" she asked Olivia, leaning over the seat to search the floorboard behind her.

"I left it in my tent. Trish, what's going on?"

"Three mutants are heading for the Gramite horde. I want you to drop me off by the concession stand and return to the camp for our helmets. Stay inside the vehicle close to the camp, where you can see me with the binoculars. Once I give you the signal, drive down, but don't get out of the vehicle until I tell you."

"Absolutely not—"

"This isn't open for discussion," Trish said, pointing toward the concession stand. "Don't worry. This vehicle is a tank. Keep the doors locked, and nothing will get in. If any creatures approach, leave and head to New Underwood."

Olivia forcefully shook her head. "I'm not leaving you out here alone. Your head's not even protected."

Trish glared out the windshield, feeling the level of danger increase expeditiously. The mutants had reached the Gramites. She was sure of it. Trish grabbed her rifle from the seat and spun her pleading eyes to Olivia. "Please trust me and do as I say."

Time felt frozen as both women gazed silently at one another. Things were going terribly wrong with the Gramite horde. Trish could almost sense their cries for help. She felt her heart race with the urgency to rush to the Gramites' aid, but she needed to make sure Olivia wouldn't do anything stupid to place her own life in danger. The veterinarian was at the top of her list of those she needed to protect. Then Molly, the Gramites, and at the bottom, was herself.

Olivia brought the vehicle to a stop at the side of the building. "Fine, I'll go wait up top, but if I feel you're in trouble and need to be pulled out, I'm coming to get you."

Trish could see by the fixed determination in Olivia's eyes, this less than appealing arrangement was the best she would receive without wasting any more valuable time. She clutched tight to her rifle and exited the Gladiator. She waited until Olivia had the vehicle heading away from the sports field, and she took off running, advancing right for horde-four.

When she was less than a half mile from the den, the screams coming from the area ahead were heart-wrenching. Her thoughts kept trying to turn to the pregnant female, but she continued to force them away. She had to keep her mind focused and judgments sharp. She would need clarity with the numbers she was about to face.

A quarter mile away, the merging forms in the shadows ahead separated into distinct images. Two mutants were in the center of the trees, the third was to the left. Three male and two female Gramites were fighting viciously against the lone mutant, who towered a good foot in height above them. That meant the mutant would be close to a foot and a half compared to Trish's own build. The mutants' muscle mass was more robust than Trish remembered. The remaining Gramites engaged the other two mutants. One mutant was viciously pounding the ground while the other was attacking any Gramite that came near.

She noticed all three mutants were about the same in build with robust arms and sharp teeth, longer than the ones she'd fought over a year ago. Their skin had shaded into a sickening green color and was scalier, with acid pustules covering their flash, mimicking a severe case of inflamed chickenpox. They had to have been infected for some time with their rate of growth. Was a few inches over seven feet their max height? Or were there even larger mutants roaming the planet?

Her eyes narrowed to the two directly ahead, encircled by protesting Gramites. The mutant wasn't striking the ground—he was pounding two fallen Gramites. Her heart raced. She could see by the torn brown sweats covered with blood that one was the leader of horde-four. Another male Gramite huddled over him, taking the bulk of the beating. A Gramite rushed in and the guarding mutant bit off a chunk of flesh, blood covering his mouth as he screamed.

Were the mutants planning on killing these two and any others who resisted them taking over leadership, or were they trying for a complete slaughter? Something told her their end goal was for the latter. This belief was more than just her sensing it or evaluating their sinister facial expressions. It was almost as if she could read their emotions, and what she felt was evil. Pure and utter hatred for the Gramites. No, not solely for the Gramites, but with each other, everything around them, even life itself. She shuddered the closer she drew to their inhumanity.

She was less than a few hundred feet from reaching the closest mutant. She knew she wouldn't have a shot with her rifle, not without taking the chance of hitting a Gramite from horde-four, and if she did, Gramite and mutant alike would rip her to pieces.

Despite that, with the listless movements coming from the two on the ground, she needed to do something fast.

When the Gramite in front of her dropped and pounded the ground, sending out a scream of desperation and anger, she caught a full view of the mutants and found her way in. She swiftly slung her rifle-strap around her head and onto her other shoulder. Slowing her run enough to unsheathe her knife, she regained speed while reaching for her pistol. Sprinting, she jumped up, bounced off the Gramite's shoulder, and lunged in the air at the mutant assaulting the two fallen Gramites. The mutant guarding the other one brought his head up and glared at her with disbelief. She plunged her knife into the base of the first mutant's skull before the other could react and landed headfirst into a roll that ended on one knee.

For a split second, the surrounding commotion grew silent with every yellowish-orange and bright-orange eye in the gathering directed at her. She gripped the butt of her pistol and forced her lungs to expel the trapped air. The mutant with her knife sticking from its head frantically clawed behind him, searching for the handle. The other dropped to all fours and roared angrily at her from several feet away. His battle cry caused a chain-reaction of hatred from the Gramites. They scuffled with the weeds, smacked the trees, and glared at one another. They grew fervently wild, as if the first feral cat had hissed and the rest had joined in—a heated hysteria. They pounded their fists on the ground and cried out to her and the mutants in the middle.

With her heart beating overtime, Trish couldn't tell who they detested the most, the attacking mutants or her—the woman who denied them the kill from their claimed horses a week ago. Trish remained still, keeping her expression motionless and her fear to a minimum. She would not make the first move. Her intuition told her this would be a mistake. The mutant screamed out again, and the closest Gramite drew closer to Trish snapping wildly, as if the Gramite had never tasted human flesh before.

Suddenly, the group to the left shifted, and a Gramite flew toward her from out of nowhere. Before Trish raised her weapon, the pregnant female landed beside the Gramite who was biting the air less than five feet from Trish. She swung with speed and pounded her arm straight into his neck. He staggered away, surprised by the force of the blow and with the one who had dealt it. He growled toward the pregnant Gramite, but his eyes didn't hold anger. They held emotional hurt.

Trish silently studied the female glowering to those from her horde. All had grown silent, baffled. Her throat gave a low grumble, and she raised an arm to Trish. When hers and Trish's eyes met, Trish saw the same sadness present as the night of Adam and Gabe's death, and like then, Trish felt an uncomfortable disturbance swelling in her chest. The rawness of the exchange was overpowering.

Trish slowly stood, and the female took a few steps forward. Trish could hear several Gramites send out grim, growling protests, and a few inched closer. Trish could sense how worried they were for this female. Trish held her gloved hand out, palm facing upward, and the female stared intently. She carefully closed the gap and gently brushed her hand against Trish's.

Suddenly, the mutant with the knife in its head fell to the ground, and the one beside him jumped forward, toward Trish and the female Gramite. With limited time to react, Trish knew she couldn't move out of the way. If she did, the mutant strike would be a full-force tackle at the female Gramite and her unborn child. Trish swiftly leapt in front of the female, as the Gramites around the circle screamed out their sounds of alarm. She pushed her body forward and met the impact with minimal momentum of her own. The blow knocked her off her feet, and she landed painfully hard on her side with the mutant directly on top. It smacked her firmly on the jawline and raised a clawed hand as it growled. Trish lifted her pistol to its forehead and fired. Its head jerked back, and as it rolled off her, she moved with it. She raised her pistol and fired several more times, each one directly into the mutant's temple.

The moment she rounded toward the mutant with the knife, a swift set of teeth flashed to her right, and she stepped sideways, seeing the last mutant rush directly at her. Without conscious thought, her body reacted. Her eyes involuntarily rolled upward, as casually as taking in a breath of air. Her mind locked onto the threat, and she felt a wave of intense heat on her forehead as her ability took flight. An excruciating scream emerged directly in front of her, followed by another. Something brushed against her foot, before all fell silent.

With her vision coming into focus, the first thing she saw was the dead mutant at her feet. Every orifice on its head was oozing with a dark-red thickness, not smelling of copper but of a putrid stench like meat that had turned rotten over an extended period of time. Next, she noticed the Gramites had moved away from her position, and uncertain fear had replaced their looks of anger. And then she spotted Olivia's wide-eyed reflection through the windshield of the Gladiator, less than two hundred feet from the tree line.

CHAPTER THIRTEEN

Olivia remained frozen as Trish approached the two Gramites lying on the ground. The leader of the horde was moving, but the other one wasn't. After instructing Molly to stay in the vehicle, Olivia threw on her helmet, climbed out of the Gladiator, and jogged to the hatch to remove her medical bag and a jug of clear solution. She headed to the front, where Trish met her beside the hood, clearly agitated.

"What do you think you're doing?" Trish asked. She opened the driver's door and motioned for Olivia to climb in.

"Trish, I'm treating your neck," Olivia said, as she unfastened the medical bag on the hood.

"I'm fine. I'll let you doctor me once I take care of the Gramites."

Ignoring her, Olivia poured out a generous amount of solution onto some gauze and cleaned the acid from the opened wounds along Trish's left cheek, all the way down her neck. Trish wasn't happy, but she didn't stop her either.

Before she could pack and cover the wounds, Trish protested. "Finish with me later. I really need to treat the Gramites. A few have burns worse than mine, and one of them," she paused to sneak a peek over her shoulder and winced in pain from the turn to her neck, "I don't think he's going to make it."

"Fine, but I'm going to help you," Olivia said, closing the bag. Trish sidestepped a few inches and blocked Olivia's way. She stood in front of her, arms crossed, with a glare of determination that told Olivia there was no use arguing. Trish's mind was made up, and her decision was final.

Olivia felt a shiver travel through her. She found herself mildly agitated and genuinely in awe of the woman standing before her. Trish wanted to keep her safe because this was who she was. She protected those she cared about, even a herd of horses or these Gramites who needed safeguarding.

With Trish at her side, Olivia felt empowered, and she wanted to help. "I'm the one with the medical training. I'm going with you whether you like it or not."

Trish's posture remained unchanging. "I know enough first aid to get me through this. You stay in the vehicle. If I have questions, I'll come ask."

Trish reached out a hand for the bag, but Olivia shook her head no and made a move to step around her. Trish seized Olivia's arm. Not hard enough to leave a bruise, but with enough force that Olivia couldn't shake herself free. Olivia raised her visor and scowled. "I'm a grown ass woman—"

Trish pulled her close, her face reddening with anger. "One tiny scratch is all it takes, Olivia." Her voice was low, her head bent forward, inches away.

Olivia's breathing caught in an exhale. She could feel the pulsating on her neck, and she was worried Trish could sense the increase in her heart rate.

"I'm immune Olivia, you're not," Trish said, a hint of fear in her voice.

"I have on the bodysuit."

"And if they get pissed and decide to all attack at once?"

Olivia shook her head. "They won't. I saw how they acted around you. You know it too." Her voice was scarcely above a whisper. "Plus, you'll be right there with me. I'm not worried."

Waiting silently as Trish worked out their impasse, she watched Trish's eyes flit from the Gramites to her. She could easily read the uncertainty in Trish's eyes.

"You will listen to *everything* I say. You will wear protective gear over the bodysuit and treat this like you're in a hostile warzone surrounded by a deadly virus, because that is exactly what we're walking into. You won't touch any Gramite until I give the okay, and you will not leave my side. You will disinfect your bodysuit thoroughly when we're done, whether or not you get any bodily fluids on it."

Trish's searching eyes reflected her racing thoughts. "Absolutely no touching the mutants. I'll need to take some samples and burn their bodies after, but you'll wait in the vehicle when I do. Do I have your word?"

Olivia nodded, and followed it with a verbal, "Yes," knowing Trish wouldn't take an informal headshake for proof of her agreement. True to her word, she stayed right beside Trish the entire time. They entered the corpse of trees to the sound of grumbling and grunts from the surrounding Gramites, who spent more time glaring uneasily at Trish than giving Olivia much of a look-see. Did they know she was weak compared to the poised woman beside her? Could they sense Olivia wasn't dangerous, had no phenomenal hidden abilities?

Trish first led Olivia to the pregnant female she had nicknamed JW, which Olivia found odd but didn't question. Olivia handed Trish the solution when she gestured toward the jug and watched her twist off the lid. She filled the cap, splashed the liquid on her neck, and pointed at the Gramites who were keeping their distance. JW's chin rose as if in understanding. She turned to those watching and moaned. When none moved, she bared her teeth and growled. Several shuffled reluctantly toward Trish.

"This stuff stings at first, so I'll treat the acid burns. After a few minutes, once their pain goes away and they realize we're trying to help, I'll assist as you treat the other wounds. Then you can examine the two on the ground."

Olivia nodded, too frightened to speak. She remained unmoving, not daring to make eye contact with any of the Gramites. She knew with gorillas—with most animals—they could take visual contact as a challenge. A plight for dominance, which Olivia wished to avoid. She noticed, by Trish's commanding stance and penetrating glare landing on any Gramite that moved, Trish didn't seem to share Olivia's concerns. Obviously, Trish wanted the Gramites to know she was the alpha.

When Trish's eyes darted from Olivia to the four Gramites who had stopped fifteen feet away, Olivia could tell she was trying to decide whether she should stay where she was or move with her. Olivia was about to let Trish know she would be all right when an interesting thing happened. The pregnant female moaned to Trish and cautiously shuffled closer to Olivia.

Trish stiffened, but Olivia touched her arm. "Wait," she breathed, grasping what was happening. JW positioned herself a foot away from Olivia and eyed her fellow Gramites, sending them a threatening growl. Olivia's excitement soared. Her hand squeezed Trish's arm. "She's going to protect me while you take care of them."

Trish studied JW briefly. Olivia tried to give Trish an encouraging shove toward those gathering with the burns, but Trish didn't move. "I don't like this," Trish mumbled.

"Please, trust me," Olivia said, her voice warm. The way Trish safeguarded her was profound. It sent a familiar intensity twisting inside her chest, one which Olivia hadn't felt in some time, and never to this degree. She averted her gawking away from Trish's eyes and focused instead on JW's protective stance, as she tried to grapple with so many overwhelming emotions rushing in.

Finally, Trish went over and treated the acid burns and the minor bites. The first one yelled out his protest and flashed his teeth. When Trish poured more on, she called him a baby. He stopped, scowled at her, but no longer complained.

Olivia found this intriguing. Could they remember what speech was like, or the meanings of certain words? Could he be sensing the teasing in Trish's voice? Whatever the case, none of the others showed any other further signs of weakness around her. One female even motioned to Trish, wanting her to douse her injuries with the stinging solution again, as if to show the others she could withstand the burning pain twice.

Trish's lips held a hint of a smile when she poured more of the clear liquid on the female's wounds. "Badass," she whispered.

The female twirled, held up her head to a few Gramites to the right, and growled. She then rushed on all fours to stand, hunched over with two other Gramites who were licking their injuries.

Trish returned and locked her gaze with JW. Their shared nonverbal exchange reflected an aged alliance. It held more than a traded, "thank you," for the kindness they both had shown the other. The experience made Olivia wonder where Trish's meaningful connection with this Gramite came from. She decided to ask Trish about JW later tonight, once they were safely at camp.

Olivia threw on a gown and latex gloves over her bodysuit and lowered her visor. Trish stopped her and personally checked to see the helmet was sealed, which it wasn't. After sealing the helmet and giving Olivia a full inspection, they moved to treat the larger wounds. The leader, who was resting on the ground watching the two humans curiously, was the next to be treated.

The leader had fewer injuries than the male lying unconscious next to him. Once Olivia's careful examination was over, she informed Trish that, from what she could tell without the proper equipment at her disposal, the leader had at least three cracked ribs, several deep cuts, and some massive bruising. The unmoving Gramite beside him had a broken arm, a possible concussion, and sustained injuries to several of the ribs on his right side. She had items for a cast and could doctor the other issues, but if the unconscious one had any internal injuries, there was a good chance the Gramite probably wouldn't make it without proper treatment.

By the time Olivia finished with the two and treated several more bite wounds, Trish had her take Molly and the Gladiator up to camp while Trish stayed behind to collect her samples and burn the mutant carcasses.

When Trish headed into camp, she noticed how the setting sun drew shadows across much of the sky, converting the last of the dazzling orange into a reddish-purple haze which filled the horizon. Between her run and the events at the Gramite den, she was physically and mentally drained and in dire need of food and water. Apparently knowing she would be, Olivia had two ration trays and several bottles of water already sitting out by Trish's chair.

Still holding her miniature shovel, Trish downed one water and opened another. "Thanks," she choked out before swallowing several more mouthfuls.

"I figured you'd need it."

Trish went to work on digging out the top layer of trampled grass far enough away from both tents. She could feel Olivia's questioning eyes on her as she exposed a wide circle of earth and dug two inches down into the soil. Once finished, she dropped the shovel by her chair and went around the area, collecting any decent-sized rocks she could find.

Trish could almost physically feel Olivia's excitement in her question. "Are we actually going to have a fire tonight?"

Trish kept her smirk hidden, even as Olivia gathered some rocks of her own. Trish knew Olivia had already figured out the answer to her question, but she answered anyway. "I don't see any point in hiding our camp."

Olivia stopped and squinted nervously around. "Do they know we're up here?"

"I'm afraid so. Before I finished burning the mutants, several had left the area. I'm not sure why. Maybe they're looking for a new spot to call home." Trish hoped this wasn't the case, but after what the Gramites had just been through, she wouldn't blame them. "A handful of the others followed me to camp."

Olivia scrambled to where Trish was arranging the rocks around in a circle. She dropped the ones she was holding beside the pit and crouched down low. Her eyes scanned the overgrowth along the hillside. "How close are they?"

Trish peered to where a small lining of basswood trees stood a little over a hundred feet away. She slightly bobbed her head, signaling the location to Olivia. "There's also one closer, hiding in the weeds past the tents."

Whining, Molly stood from beside the chairs and moved next to the women. Trish cooed softly and reached her hand outward, rubbing Molly's trembling fur. The dog, who wasn't afraid of anything, knew she had met an adversary she couldn't defeat.

"What are we going to do? Should we find somewhere else to camp?"

Trish finished adding the last of Olivia's rocks to the circular mound and stood. "No, they're only curious."

"Wait, where are you going?" Olivia jumped up and followed. So did Molly.

Trish spoke over her shoulder. "I'm planning to head into the tree line to gather firewood. Please trust me. You know I wouldn't do anything to place you in danger."

"Trish, I don't like this. Let's pack up and drive to New Underwood before something bad happens."

Trish stopped halfway to the Gladiator when she realized just how frightened Olivia was. "Like us with them, they're simply interested in who we are. I don't sense even the slightest trace of a threat." She cocked her head to the side. She could sense the excitement in the distance, which was mimicked by the Gramites close by. Her insides felt light, and her lips curved upward.

"What is it?" Olivia asked.

Trish tried to explain what she was feeling. "The group that left, I believe they returned to the den. Whatever they went to do, they had to have been successful. The outcome pleased all of them."

Olivia looked dumbfounded. "They're communicating with one another? How can you tell? I don't hear a thing. No screams, nothing."

This was a question Trish couldn't explain. "I'm not sure. I just know it."

Olivia looked at Trish, the tree line, and toward where horde-four's den was located. She was clearly working through the information. After over a minute of uncomfortable silence, she knelt and pulled Molly closer. The Saint Bernard didn't object. "Okay. Molly and I will wait here, but please don't take long."

Trish headed to the vehicle and removed her hatchet. She remained in plain sight, feeling the shift in the Gramites as she drew closer to their hiding location. She kept her eyes off their figures crouched behind trees and mounds of earth until she located a downed tree ideal for burning. She used the hatchet instead of breaking it up by hand with the hope it would be less threatening to swing a tool than displaying brute strength. Also, maybe the Gramites had memories from past lives. Even if they didn't, seeing a human using a basic hand tool could be entertaining for them.

Trish made three trips to camp, carrying armfuls of firewood. Once she finished, Olivia had Trish sit and eat, while Olivia doctored Trish's already healing injuries and got the fire ready. After a few minutes of Olivia striking flint to steel and adding in a few more pieces of kindling, both women sat in silence with Molly in the middle, all mesmerized by the flames.

Not long after, the surrounding area darkened, and night rolled fully in, casting shimmering stars and a glowing half-moon out past the yellowing haze of their camp. Trish worked at cleaning off the shovel and hatchet, as Olivia continued to stare in her direction. Trish dropped the hatchet beside her and gave Olivia her full attention. "If you have a question on your mind, you may as well come out with it. It's not like you don't know my secrets."

"Yes, your medical mysteries." Olivia's voice was low, her words chosen carefully. "You have a knack for keeping your personal ones heavily guarded."

Trish stood and selected a long stick from the kindling pile. "Seriously, what's on your mind." She ignored Olivia's last comment in a way she hoped Olivia would understand. Parts of her would always be off limits. Her thoughts ventured to Christina, but she refocused on the shades of the yellow flames outlined by a blazing orange. She poked the stick forcefully into the hot coals. The sizzling-crackle and rise of spitting embers helped to erase the images of her wife.

After a few more stabs, Trish dropped the stick and returned to her seat. Olivia's eyes lingered on her, but she still didn't speak. Trish sighed, knowing a question would soon be following. She retrieved the shovel and hatchet and headed to the vehicle. "Do you want anything?" she called out once she stored the tools and selected another ration tray.

"Some liquor if you have it, if not, a bottled water."

Trish could hear the humor in Olivia's voice, but she also noted the sincerity as well. She handed Olivia the water. "Sorry. Never occurred to me to pack alcohol. I'll do better next time."

A fleeting chuckle rolled from Olivia's throat as Trish retook her seat. "Please do," Olivia said before opening the bottle.

Trish tore into her tray but kept her eyes on Olivia. Patiently waiting, she heated her meal and took her first bite. She was halfway through her main dish when Olivia asked her question. "What if you're actually communicating with them and don't even realize it?"

Skeptically, Trish peered at Olivia.

"Hear me out," Olivia said. "Like the high frequency your body uses for defense, what if there's a lower form of soundwaves going on within these Gramites, and you can tune into them?" Olivia dipped her head to the area of trees off to the side. "I've watched the way they are around each other, and even though they seem to converse by body language and different shouts and screams when they're in a battle, they also appear to communicate silently to each other."

"Like telepathy?"

Olivia looked at her as if saying, *sort of.* "Whales use a method of communication many experts had believed is a form of extrasensory perception. Sound waves that stretch out for hundreds of miles under the water."

Trish finished her spaghetti and meatballs and tossed the trash into the fire. "If that was the case, the sound sensors in the vault would have picked up on it."

"Not necessarily," Olivia said, sitting forward in her seat. "You were not going through the tests to communicate, but rather to perfect what you did in NORAD. What if there's more to this? What if your senses are actually picking up on the Gramites' brainwaves, their special way of mentally talking with one another?"

Trish paused her search for the dessert package long enough to consider what Olivia was saying. "I don't hear words, but I experience their feelings, emotions," she answered. She removed the plastic pouch containing mixed fruit and continued her quest for what she hoped was her beloved pound cake.

"We as humans have a verbal language. There's also sign language, body language, drawing, writing, so many techniques which all have the same outcome, to express our thoughts, feelings, and information to others." Olivia stood and called Molly to her. She headed to the vehicle and motioned her inside. Reluctantly, Molly did as she was told, and Olivia headed to the firepit to retake her seat.

"What's going on?"

"I want to do an experiment, and I don't want Molly to be a distraction."

Trish pulled out the dessert package and grumbled. "Do you like fruitcake? I can't stand it. It leaves an aftertaste."

"Please take this seriously."

"I am, but I'm hungry."

"You're always hungry," Olivia complained right as Trish tossed the unopened package into the flames.

Trish frowned. "I burn three times as many calories as you do." She lowered the rest of her tray when Olivia rolled her eyes. "Fine, you have my full attention."

Perturbed, Olivia moved her chair closer and whispered. "Are they still near us?"

Trish raised her brow and jerked her head forward. "They're watching from the trees. A few others from the group that left earlier have joined them."

"What are their emotions telling you? Are they angry we haven't left?"

Trish relaxed in her seat and focused on the Gramites. "No, not angry at all. If they were, my senses would have warned me. I'm detecting curiosity, maybe a flicker of apprehension, but I know it's because of the fire."

"How do you know?"

"I felt their uneasiness the moment the first flame sparked to life."

"Yet, you don't think you're communicating with them?"

Trish shook her head. "Not in the way you're believing. It's more like sensing a dog is getting ready to bite or feeling desire from another person without hearing them speak it out loud."

Olivia shifted uneasily but soon settled. "Okay, I want you to open yourself up to this being its own kind of language. Try to say something to them in your head. Not really words, but more like a gesture of friendship, or think of the words to yourself and follow them with the meanings behind the words you used."

"You want me to communicate mentally and see if they react to what I'm thinking. I can try." She thought hard, attempting to come up with a way to test Olivia's unorthodox theory. Her eyes landed on the half-burned package of fruitcake inside the firepit. An idea struck her.

Trish retrieved the rest of her ration tray and strode to the vehicle. She opened several more rations and selected a few items to prepare. Once done, she took the three meals and headed off to the tree line. She stopped where the glow from the fire faded into darkness. Trish positioned one tray in the weeds and moved to the right ten paces. She lowered the next tray and after ten more paces, she placed the last one in a clearing beside a tree.

She retook her seat. Her thoughts turned to JW and the first tray. She concentrated and waited, not losing the images in her mind. A few minutes later, the pregnant female appeared a few feet beside the food, a heated bacon cheeseburger sandwich. JW sniffed the air, stared at the women sitting around the camp, and inched closer to the disposable dish. The moment her clawed hand reached through the weeds, Trish willed her mentally not to touch it. Trish's eyes widened when she felt the disappointment in the Gramite. JW stared at Trish and backed several steps away.

Trish scooted forward in her seat and her mind pictured the third tray awaiting consumption. She visualized the beef stew, and her thoughts went to the leader, Champ. She ignored the pull of Olivia's probing gaze and focused harder. Not long after, JW grunted in disappointment when the leader moved toward the stew. JW released a moan, sat reluctantly on her heels, and watched him eagerly devour the dish. Trish thought of JW and the sandwich again, and she mentally nudged JW forward to her first bite. The Gramite sniffed the cooked meat covered in bacon, cheese, and a sourdough bun, Trish's favorite meal. JW opened her mouth and nibbled. Once the juicy bite moved past her lips, JW's eyes jerked to Trish and with three huge mouthfuls, between minimal chewing, the cuisine was gone. Trish couldn't help but laugh.

"Are you controlling this?"

Trish briefly held up a hand to Olivia, gave a shrug, suggesting she might be, and her mind called to the leader and JW at the same time. She focused on the center dish, beef cubes in buttery noodles. She urged them both to share the meal. JW grumbled to Champ, who looked from JW to the dish. His head lowered slightly, and he moaned. JW retrieved the tray and made her way to the male, who raised his eyes. Champ brought his head forward and took a few bites. JW devoured the rest.

Olivia's voice was scarcely above a whisper. "I think JW might actually be the leader."

Trish blinked a few times, coming out of her concentration, and nodded. "I thought the same thing earlier." She allowed the full weight of this evening to settle heavily on her mind while her vision trailed over the two headed back into the trees' shadows.

Olivia pointed. "Did you do that?"

Trish nodded a second time, still feeling too overwhelmed to speak. She stood and retrieved the empty trays. After tossing the plastic into the fire, she retook her seat. "In my head, I suggested which dish was to be consumed and by whom. They listened."

Trish could feel Olivia stare at her for a long time. Olivia shimmied her seat even closer, with her eyes centered fully on Trish. "Do you realize what this means, Trish?"

Trish rubbed her gloved hands along the suit covering her thighs. She felt a powerful urge to be alone and think. To go for a long run or a drive. God, and to take off this damn bodysuit and stand under a hot shower for a day or two.

"Trish," Olivia said, touching her gently. The soft contact forced Trish's eyes toward Olivia. "You and the Gramites have more than a connection. A gift that runs deeper than the warning senses which flare up inside you." Olivia's gaze ogled the trees for a moment. "You're able to tap into their way of communicating and use it with them. Maybe it's the same with other animals, or possibly different, but whatever it is, you've unearthed an ability that gives you and the Gramites a peek into one another's mind. A profound degree of understanding."

When Olivia awoke the next day, she realized she was alone. Molly had abandoned her, and the light soaking into the material of the tent from the sun's rays was hot, thick, and stifled the surrounding air. She sat up and used her suited hand to wipe the sweat from her brow. She squinted at her watch. The time was already past ten in the morning, and Trish wanted to leave here by two, drive around where the other hordes were located, and make sure all was well. Olivia still had to finish writing her reports, pack, and spend more time studying the Gramites of horde-four while making use of Trish's newly revealed ability.

Olivia yanked her feet off the bed and sat on the edge of the cot, trying to clear the rest of the sleep from her sluggish body. She turned her mind to the questions she had asked Trish regarding her superpower—how it felt, how it worked, and anything else she could come up with through the late hours of the night. She thought of those personal questions she'd wanted to voice but left unasked before turning in. Why did Trish still love Christina after everything that woman had put her through? Olivia had seen it in Trish's eyes, as she watched her stoke the fire. A yearning which made Olivia's own chest burn. Olivia knew she was falling for Trish. She also knew Trish had been deeply in love with someone else, and a lost love like that took time to mend. Olivia still felt herself fall, even though her better judgement shouted out warnings.

Olivia wouldn't push it. She would give Trish time. All the time her heart needed to get over Christina. The possibility of a lifelong relationship with Trish was worth the months, even years, of waiting. Would it really take that long? Her own mind shouted, no! From what Olivia understood, Trish and Christina had known one another a few brief months prior to dating, then less than a handful of days of being in a relationship before the coma. A year and a half later, Trish woke up with a family. They married after five short months of living together, and a month later, everything fell apart. Exactly how in love could Trish truly be? Did Trish even know the answer to this question?

When the succulent aroma of cooked meat drifted in, Olivia's interests shot to the door-flap, and her stomach gave a sudden rumble. She unzipped the door and poked her head outside. Her mouth watered and she climbed all the way out to where Trish was busying herself around the campfire. Trish had rigged a makeshift grill, and the prepped meat of a large animal, possibly a skinned deer, was wonderfully sizzling above the red coals.

Trish turned her tired eyes to Olivia. She looked exhausted, yet happy. "You just missed a black bear coming in with that same hungry expression on his face." Trish pointed to the area of trees, and Olivia's brow snapped upward. Most of the Gramites were sitting outside the tree line, watching the camp. She shifted nervously closer to Trish.

"They scared him off as well as a mountain lion an hour ago," Trish casually said, as she continued to rub a yellowish-red liquid along the outside of the deep-red, cooked meat with spots of black crispy areas lining the outer edges.

"Is that deer?"

"Yep. Evidently, the group that left yesterday went off to hunt us a thank you meal for helping them out with the mutants and their injuries. I cleaned the carcass, rigged it over the fire, and once they sniffed the aroma of the roasted meat, I had an instant audience. I think they now want us to share." Trish rolled her eyes upward, but she pulled her lips into a grin. She cut off a strip of meat, inspected it, and passed it to the drooling Molly. She used two towels to remove the grilled deer from the fire and placed it on the grass beside the pit.

"What are you doing? Are we not going to eat it?" Olivia asked, her displeasure clear in her voice.

Trish headed to the vehicle and returned shortly with a ration tray and some water. She handed them over, and Olivia let out a lungful of disappointment.

"I understand you're tired of eating these, but the Gramites killed the deer. I will not chance the possibility of the infection passing from the meat to you. I skinned and cooked the meat for their horde as a sort of 'thank you' for letting us camp here. Since you can't have any, I won't either, even though the meat smells amazing."

Olivia snorted. "Fine, how about some of your coffee, then?"

Trish wittily pointed at the hatch. "No coddling, remember? The first night was an exception. Now you're on your own. Don't forget to clean up after yourself," Trish said over her shoulder.

Olivia suffered a sharp sense of annoyance when Trish headed off with the grilled meat to where the Gramites were anxiously waiting.

Once Trish returned, she told Olivia she had used every means of seasoning at her disposal, which was nothing more than tomato and onion soup, mixed with butter flavor tablets, multiple tiny packages of seasoning salt, and a few bottles of tobacco sauce. No matter how the unusual combination sounded, Olivia couldn't rid herself of the wonderful tang to vanquish her nose or the sight of Trish's happiness.

After they watched the horde feverously enjoy the cooked deer, the hours flew swiftly by. Olivia finished her daily reports, including in-depth data for Doctor Burgos of their interactions with the Gramites as well as Trish's way of communicating with the infected. Olivia stated several times how she believed Trish and the Gramites were using low-frequency soundwaves. Or to be more exact, infrasound. She listed the many animals who used this means of communication, such as whales, elephants, giraffes, alligators, and several other animals she pulled from memory. Maybe when they moved into the genetics aspect of the mission, they could use this information to pinpoint strands of DNA from these animals, and cross compare them with Trish and the Gramites to see if there were any links which allowed the use of this ability.

Tearing down her tent, Olivia straightened when Trish returned from checking on the injured Gramites from yesterday. She waited until Trish replaced the med kit before asking the question tugging at her thoughts. "Trish, I'm curious about JW. It's like you two know each other—"

Olivia let the rest of the question go when she saw Trish's body turn rigid. She slid her folded tent inside the bag, while keeping Trish in her peripheral. Trish's shoulders finally relaxed a bit before she lowered her tall frame into her chair. Olivia headed to the hatch and placed the tent neatly inside with the camping equipment.

Before she reached for her folded cot and work bag, Trish motioned to the chair beside her. Trish opened the conversation with the Oahe Dam run Christina, a guy named Adam and his best friend Gabe were on two years ago. Olivia noticed as Trish relived the story, her eyes were unfocused, hollow even. She told Olivia how she jumped over the wall to go find them when they didn't arrive at Rapid City before the gate closed. She shared what Christina had experienced during the time a horde trapped her on a gas station roof, and how JW had come into the horde. Olivia could see Trish's eyes were reddening at the memory that wasn't even hers. As if she had lived through the pain herself, through Christina's eyes.

Olivia almost asked Trish to stop. She didn't need to hear the rest if the memory caused Trish such heartache. Yet, she was too numbed by the vividness of the tale to even adjust her uncomfortable position in the chair, let alone speak.

Trish ended with how she had looked into JW's eyes, and let her go, but after finding what remained of Adam and Gabe, how she wanted to nothing more than to kill the Gramite. "To be honest, when I came here searching for this horde, it was solely out of a selfish urge to track JW down. I'm not even sure if I was going to kill her or not, but a rawness took over that gave me a fierce desire to find out." Trish dropped her gaze.

Feeling a longing to reach over and comfort Trish, hold her tight until her pain went away, Olivia blinked a few times and cleared her throat. When she spoke, her voice was low, scarcely recognized even by her own ears. "Why did you let JW go the first time? What did you see in her eyes that kept you from pulling the trigger?"

This time when Trish spoke, her eyes locked on to Olivia's. "A sadness mixed with a questioning hatred, like JW wasn't sure herself why or who she was angry at. I remember my mother's eyes when she died. At least I think this piece of my memory is real, untainted by years of time and my need to hold on to something, anything, relating to her. After my father shot her, I was there, right beside her. She had the same sadness, but there was also this questioning anger. I don't know if her anger was for my father who pulled the trigger, or for knowing her time was ending and she was leaving me with the man she was trying to protect me from. Whatever the case, I saw the same sadness and anger the night I let JW go free."

Olivia sat up straighter. "JW—Julie Webber!"

Trish nodded, and her vision drifted off to the spitting flames, as the red embers struggled against their last lick of fading fuel. They sat silently, neither talking, until a disturbance to the left brought both heads around. Trish scrunched her nose and looked away as Olivia shot to her feet and headed to fetch the recorder.

Trish stood and shook her head when Olivia started filming. "Isn't one sex scene a week good enough? Do you really need to film another?"

Olivia guffawed but didn't take her eyes off the display. "You really are a prude. If you stopped for a moment and looked past the sex to the emotions and feelings attached between these two, you'd see the beauty of the exchange and realize how important this is for research."

Trish peeked upward but spun toward the Gladiator when the male Gramite inserted himself into the other. "No thanks," she said.

Olivia giggled. Trish was heading off to put her newly folded chair into the vehicle. Olivia called out in a teasing tone, "They're really going at it. I guess someone's adamant about fathering a child." She continued to snicker under her breath when she noticed the redness wash over Trish.

"Kinda hard for him to do," Trish said, "unless male Gramites can also get pregnant."

Olivia directed her attention from the screen to the two she was filming. Her heart raced the second she understood clearly what Trish had meant. Both the Gramites were male.

CHAPTER FOURTEEN

Phillips's kindness sent a surge of relief sweeping through Christina, catching her by surprise. She was certain they would all resent her for what was happening in her and Trish's relationship. But other than the cold shoulder from Carlen, no one else batted an eye or uttered an unkind word in her direction. Christina thanked him for the coffee. She had missed Trish's extended family more than she realized. Phillips took the seat beside her, and both sat in silence as Christina's father and Jennifer worked the controls on the drone flying over New Underwood.

Phillips leaned closer. "I'm glad you and your mother are reaching out to him. Doctor Burgos has been struggling without you two."

Christina placed her cup on the workstation counter, while she fought to keep her tears in. "We—I've been a complete idiot. With him, Trish, all of you." Christina rubbed her face with her hands, feeling the drama of these past several weeks weighing heavily on her shoulders. "I didn't handle any of this well."

Phillips brought his arm around her shoulders and pulled her closer. She lowered her head onto his chest, and he rubbed her shoulder in comfort. "I get it, girl. You were scared. The thought of losing your loved ones, especially after we all almost lost Trish last year, was hard for both you and your mother. You wanted to keep your family safe." He placed a fatherly kiss on the side of her forehead. "I understand."

Christina returned his embrace with a one arm hug. Her heart sank even farther when she saw Carlen shoot visual daggers in their direction. Carlen flipped off her monitor, stood from her workstation, and exited the building. Christina slowly backed away from Phillips and cleared her throat. Being forgiven for her recent actions was going to take time, she knew that, but seeing the contempt in Carlen's eyes was still difficult to witness.

"Don't worry about Captain Strong. She loves you, Christina. She'll move past this. Give her time."

Christina was grateful for his optimism, even though she herself wasn't convinced Carlen would ever forgive her. She knew with Susan's temporary placement at the hospital, Carlen had taken up Susan's role as Trish's maternal caregiver. Which meant Carlen was the one who watched over and comforted Trish's broken heart. Christina also knew she was the person who caused Trish's heart to break the day she kicked Trish from their home. No, she had handled none of this situation the way she should have. With Trish, their relationship, even her father and those on this team, Christina had mismanaged everything. They were all trying to do what was right, to make the world safer for others, and she had thrown demands at Trish to stop it. What really made Christina berate herself was the knowledge that her realization hadn't come from her but from what the veterinarian had said to her on Sunday. A mere five days ago. The long days and nights since had dragged by, as she mentally relived hers and Trish's painful weeks of conflicts.

Aralyn headed from her office to where they were sitting. "I spoke with Major Thomas. She'll personally find out why Trish has received none of your messages."

"Thank you, Aralyn. I truly appreciate it." Christina peered at the monitor on the wall, which showed a perfect image of New Underwood's one and only gate.

An hour ago, Aralyn had explained how they had signed on the veterinarian as a consultant. Christina's heart had plummeted. Aralyn then informed her Trish and Olivia were out in the field doing research on the Gramites and how they had been out there since Wednesday. Christina's chest had tightened so forcefully, she found her next few exhales hard to manage.

Aralyn and Phillips had simultaneously picked up on Christina's distress, and both reassured her she had nothing to worry about. Trish loved her, and no woman would change this. The idea was inconceivable. Her father further justified the level of importance Olivia was to their mission and how Olivia's skill set would aid in the outcome. Christina knew he was attempting to comfort his daughter with why Trish and Olivia were working together, but his logic made her feel worse. Olivia wasn't simply beautiful with a charming personality this entire team seemed taken by, but she was also smart and had a higher level of knowledge in a skilled profession. How was she supposed to compete with a woman like this?

She had seen the way Olivia had looked at Trish on Sunday. The woman had feelings for her wife. She was with Trish right now, using her skills to help Trish change the world they lived in. To tip the scales toward the survival of humanity. What did Christina offer Trish? A high school education? A foolish temperament? Survivors needed to live life behind a wall for protection, and Christina whipped up food in a restaurant.

She lifted her coffee, trying to mask her growing torment around Phillips and Aralyn. Ever since they first met, Trish had always been there for her, loved her, protected her. She had let Christina make her own decisions, even if the decision placed her in danger. Now, when it came time for Christina to do the same, she had failed, and failed miserably.

Sergeant Perez stuck his head in through the half-open door. "They're here," he shouted. He shot Christina a wink and left.

Christina jumped to her feet, spilling some of her hot coffee onto her hand and the tiled floor.

Phillips chuckled and reached for her cup. "I've got this," he said, taking the drink from her. "We'll watch Jennifer. You go spend some alone time with your wife."

Thanking him, Christina hurried to the door. She headed from the air-conditioned building into the July heat. The sun was setting directly ahead, casting enough of its diminishing rays to temporarily obscure her view. She blinked downward and brought a hand up to help shield its intensity and to dim the bright glow of the all-white landscape so she could see.

Spotting where Trish had parked her vehicle beside the buildings across the street, where Perez and Givens were both waiting, Christina's heart raced. Trish opened the door and slowly stepped out. Christina's stomach fluttered and her love for Trish swelled just by her presence. They had been apart for far too long. The sluggish way in which Trish moved, the dark circles around her eyes, Christina could tell Trish was exhausted. Christina's body ached to provide comfort and remove the weariness consuming her wife.

Christina began her trek across the street when Givens waved her over. She had to fight down her eagerness to rush in and throw her arms around Trish. To tell her how sorry she was for the poor way she had handled their relationship. The last time they spoke, Trish was angry, hurt, and didn't want to talk. Christina silently pleaded to whomever was listening that this still wasn't the case. She hoped Trish would hear her apology for the strain in their lives she had caused. If anyone could forgive her, it would be Trish. Trish knew Christina better than anyone, and she had loved her unconditionally.

"Perez, where's Young?"

Christina stopped walking when she heard Olivia speak, seconds before the veterinarian came into view. The woman was wearing an armored bodysuit, had her hair pulled into a loose ponytail, and she was holding her helmet in one hand, rifle in the other. She also appeared tired, but she had an enthusiastic bounce to her step, which made Christina shift uncomfortably. Not daring herself to feel inferior to this woman, Christina defiantly raised her head and continued forward.

"He's over in the infirmary, getting everything set up to give Trish a complete physical. He should be here any minute."

"Good," Olivia said, heading to where Trish had the hatch open and was removing several bags. She leaned her body over and playfully nudged Trish. "This morning, the sex was even better than yesterday, Perez. The level of intimacy and passion was wonderful, and the rawness was…" she brought her eyes amusingly to Trish. "Breathtaking."

Trish threw her hand in the air, a scowl overshadowing her features. "Must you tell everyone?"

With the sudden urge to be sick, Christina froze in place. She saw Givens' gaze land on her with a level of nervousness that spoke volumes. *Breathe, damn you,* Christina's mind shouted to her rising panic. When Olivia followed Givens' gaze, the veterinarian turned fully to her. At that moment, Christina wasn't sure if Olivia was glaring triumphantly or not.

Christina pivoted to the building she had just left, finding the simple act of moving one heavy foot in front of the other difficult to accomplish. When she reached for the handle, a gloved hand from a black bodysuit came from out of nowhere and covered her trembling fingers. She felt the warmth of the figure standing up against her and she knew at once the person was Trish.

She couldn't move, couldn't look over. Her body had drained of all energy, her mind left empty of every thought but one. "Is it true?" she asked. She heard the shaking in her voice, but she didn't care.

"Christina, what are you doing here?"

Christina didn't know where the sudden burst of energy came from or the anger that reared up inside. Maybe from the way Trish avoided her question, or the unrelenting image of Olivia lying naked with her wife, kissing the lips, the body, the woman who didn't belong to her. She spun, giving herself a full view of Trish, needing to see the reaction as Trish either answered or avoided her question. "Is it true? Did you sleep with her?"

Trish was instantly taken aback. Without warning, Christina saw something flash in Trish she had never seen before. Anger—raw, unmovable anger, directed right at her. Trish's hand shot off the door so fast Christina wasn't sure what was happening. Trish gripped her arms tight and pressed Christina against the building. Christina's eyelids widened before she closed them altogether, not wanting to see that degree of fury in Trish. Heat filled Christina's neck and cheeks, and she could easily picture Trish's sneer inches from her ear.

"You fuck someone in our house, then come here believing you still have the right to question me about who I may or may not be sleeping with?"

Startled, Christina opened her eyes. Trish was furious, her face was red, her eyes teary. "What are you talking about? I haven't been with anyone but you."

"Janet. Sunday when I came over and mowed. She was in our house, not wearing anything but *my* robe."

Christina's lips slowly parted. "When you mowed?" she asked, feeling herself going numb. She was in a daze, as she watched Perez and Givens rush in. Both men struggled at pulling Trish away. Phillips all but flew out of the building to assist.

"When you mowed?" Christina whispered again, not understanding what Trish was saying or what was going on around her. She no longer felt attached to her body, like the world was playing out, but she was merely a bystander observing her own life from a 3D perspective.

Trish's anger left her as fast as it erupted. The surprise, pain, even disbelief pouring from Trish was heartbreaking. A lump moved from Christina's chest all the way to her throat, where it wedged itself in, causing her to swallow several times. She tried to take a step forward to ease the agony from her wife, but Phillips stopped her.

Trish turned suddenly and dashed off across the street and into a building. When she entered, Olivia was running right behind.

Moving away from the others, Christina dropped her head into her hands and cried through her sorrow.

"Christina, it's getting late. Please let me drive you home."

Twirling the golden liquid around with an unsteady hand, Christina slammed the rest of the bourbon down her throat, too drunk to feel much of its burning effects. She ignored Karen's words of concern and slid her empty glass toward the bartender.

"Christina, why don't you come home with me tonight? I'm getting ready to hand the bar over to the weekend staff." Karen rested her elbows on the bar and cupped Christina's hand in hers. "You, me, and Jason, we can have some dinner, open a bottle of wine, and get plastered together."

Pushing herself straighter on her seat, Christina leaned forward and slid the empty glass closer to the young man with spiky hair. "Don't be nice to me, I don't deserve it," she said, keeping her eyes off Karen.

"Stop beating yourself up. It's probably not as bad as you think it is."

The bartender refilled her glass before moving to the other end to take another order. Christina downed the bourbon in several sizeable gulps, following it with a wrinkle to her forehead from the potent aftertaste. She lowered the glass onto the bar. "You weren't there. You didn't see Trish's face—the suffering in her eyes. I've hurt her badly. I've destroyed us." She waved her hand dramatically from side-to-side. "It's all over, Karen. Trish has moved on."

Christina pointed to the glass, as Karen contemplated whether to allow her employee to pour her another. "Last one," Karen finally said, and told him to add several cubes of ice and soda in it as well. "I need to go call Jason and tell him I'm going to be late."

The bartender tipped the bottle above the waiting glass clutched in Christina's hand. When the liquor flowed against the frozen chunks, Christina could almost feel the snapping of the cracking ice as the clanging cubes whirled against the sides. Forgoing the soda, he gave her a wink.

"I take it you've had another hard day."

Unaware the seat next to her was no longer unoccupied, Christina jumped slightly at the woman's voice. When she turned, she felt so much anger, she couldn't help but laugh.

"Hey, what's wrong?" Janet asked, uncertain. She slid a shot glass toward her.

Christina pointed a heated finger in Janet's direction. "You lied to me. I can't believe I fell for your bullshit." Christina rotated herself away from Janet with such force, she almost became unseated from the swiveling barstool. Janet reached out to help steady her, but Christina jerked her arm away. "No, don't you dare touch me," she said. She finished her drink, pushed the glass forward, and gestured to the bartender. He shook his head no. Even more perturbed, Christina scowled at Janet. "Last Sunday, when you brought me my keys, did you go inside my house? You remember—it was the same day you took credit for yardwork you *didn't* do."

Janet stood. "Look, I simply came over here to check on you and to buy you a shot. I can see you're in no mood for company."

Christina raised her eyes mockingly. "Oh, a shot. What a dear *friend* you are." With unrelenting anger, she scooped up the tiny glass and downed the yellow liquid. "There, you bought me a drink." Christina climbed off the stool, swaying slightly on her feet. "Now, leave me alone."

She carefully pivoted and staggered her way to the exit.

"Hey, you should wait for Karen," Christina heard the bartender call out, but his voice sounded so far away. She took a few more steps, with the dimly lit room spinning slowly around in her vision. Her lips grew cold, and her tongue felt numb when she swallowed. She blinked a few times to steady herself and stumbled toward the door.

"Don't worry. We'll take her home."

Janet's words drifted beside Christina and arms encircled her waistline. Her mind flashed to Trish, bringing with it a calming spread of relief.

Christina awoke to a cramping pain in her stomach. Her head pounded, sweat covered her neck, and tiny droplets skirted along the edge of her face. With her eyes closed, she brought a shaking hand upward, the gentle movement sending spasms of soreness darting throughout her body. Her fingers wiped off the damp strands of hair from her forehead. Her entire body ached like one massive bruise, and every muscle she used trembled weakly, the aftereffects from a night filled with too much drinking.

The way she lay, curled into a fetal position, made everything about her bed feel off. The pillows, the down comforter, even the bed itself pushed unyielding stiffness into her side and hips. She adjusted her torso and tried straightening out her legs. As she did, she jerked her legs together and grunted into the pillow. The throbbing sting between her thighs was unexpected, almost frightening. She brought her arm down and cupped her hand over the area of soreness. She was naked, the tiny curls under her fingers matted, and every tiny brush of her fingertips, inspecting the rawness of her womanly crease, sent an alarm off in her head.

The moment her eyes opened, she knew at once she was not in her home. She wasn't tucked safely in her bed. She was somewhere she'd never been before. Her heart raced when the spinning room came into focus. She recognized the style of furniture. The recliner, the lamp, even the dresser were the same from her awakened memory, yet the belongings scattered on the surfaces differed from what Trish had once had in her own barracks apartment.

Trish's living area had been neat, housing items she cherished. Her mother's jewelry box, framed pictures of her and Christina, and antique items, including the collection of comic book heroes Christina had bought her two years ago, when they were friends. Whoever lived here wasn't concerned with surprise barracks inspections. Clothes lay piled throughout the floor and thrown along the recliner, empty food wrappers sat where knickknacks should have been, and various types of liquor bottles lined every surface. Even the surrounding air smelled sour, putrid. Like recent vomit which hadn't been thoroughly scrubbed away.

She rubbed at her eyes, trying hard to clear the sluggishness from her brain. She was lying in some strange bed, naked, and feeling anxious. Her subconscious shouted she should be terrified, but she wasn't sure why. She tried thinking of what she could remember, why she and Trish were here and not in their own home. Where was Jennifer? Her fingers traced the bruise line along her left wrist, and then her right. What exactly did they do last night?

Needing some answers, Christina gradually rotated her achy body around to nudge Trish awake. The second her eyes fell onto the red curls twisting out from beneath the checkered blanket, reality took over and her stomach convulsed against the intensity of it. Images of Trish and New Underwood popped up. Then she pictured herself crying as she drove to Karen's club. Karen. Karen wanted to take her home last night, but Christina didn't go with her. Why? Her eyes widened when she recalled Janet was there, talking to her. She tried remembering past that point, but she couldn't. The rest was blank.

The next wave of reality hit her so hard she had to bring a hand up to stifle her cry. She lifted the edge of the blanket and immediately turned her eyes, repulsed by her own nakedness. She used slow movements to roll herself all the way over, struggling hard not to wake Janet. What had she done? Her eyes blurred, and she pushed the awareness away, trying to concentrate on getting her things and leaving before anyone in the building noticed her there.

She slid from the bed onto her knees. Her hands and vision strained as she searched the floor for her clothes. She located her bra and underwear beside the dresser. She remained sitting on the carpet as she wiggled into them. The moment she pulled up her underwear, she knew something was off. The left side of the lacy material was half ripped and, wrapping around each ankle, there was also a bruise line. Her alertness shifted to the headboard. Her heart rate sped when she saw the rope dangling from each end. She then noticed the same twisted binding hanging from both sides of the footboard.

With a fresh wave of fear, she scurried forward to find the rest of her clothes. She spotted her jeans, socks, and shoes by the closet and quietly threw them on. As she was hunting for her blouse, her stomach clenched again. On the other side of the bed was a strap-on, and from the condition of the item and how she felt a new jab of pain when she tightened her pelvic floor muscles, she knew Janet had used the item protruding from the harness on her. Inside her.

She was going to be physically sick. The room spun wildly in her head when she stood. She steadied her balance and covered her mouth with her hand. She rushed into the bathroom, scarcely opening the toilet lid before vomiting up a sour-smelling sickness from her body. Once her stomach had given up every offering it held, she continued to heave, tasting the burning bitterness with the expelling of yellowish bile, clear fluid, then nothing.

She lowered her shaking body onto the cold tile and wiped her mouth and the bead of sweat on her upper lip with a trembling hand. She remained unmoving for several minutes until she felt confident enough to stand without puking. Her legs shook, but they held her up. She flushed the toilet and splashed cold water on her face. When she reached for a towel, she noticed an envelope discarded in the wastebasket under a food wrapper and an empty beer bottle. Her name was on it, written in cursive. She blinked a few times and reached in, knowing the penmanship was her wife's. The envelope had papers cramped inside.

She lowered herself onto the edge of the counter and removed the pages. Reading a few lines in, she clutched her chest and suppressed her cry. Trish wrote the letter not long after their last fight. How was Trish's letter in Janet's bathroom? Her eyes grew too blurry to read past the first page, but what she read was enough for her to realize, Trish had written this hoping to save their marriage. Inhaling with a shudder, she replaced the pages, balled up her fists, and grasped tightly to the envelope.

She frowned toward Janet's bedroom as pieces fell into place. Janet had gone into her house last Sunday, which was probably when she stole this. Trish was there and must have left the letter then. Scowling, Christina exited the bathroom. Janet stirred beneath the covers, but Christina was too angry to care. She found her blouse on the dresser and threw it on, just as the bedsprings gave way.

"How dare you!" Christina shouted, refusing to look behind her. She rushed to the door. The second it opened, her heart sank. Janet's apartment was on the bottom level of the old hotel and several soldiers, already dressed for the day, were moving around the open area on the far side of the indoor pool.

This would be her walk of shame if they saw her, and Trish would find out in the worst way imaginable, from gossip inside her own militia. Keeping her head turned toward the line of apartments, Christina maintained a rapid pace, focusing her eyes on the ground a few feet ahead of her.

"Christina, wait!" She heard Janet shout from behind, bringing all eyes to her.

While her achy body protested, she ran from the doors of the militia HQ. She noticed the vehicle pull up and saw Major Thomas exit the passenger seat. The woman's concerned eyes peered straight at her. Not stopping when the woman waved inquisitively in her direction, Christina tore through the cut lawn with streaks of tears sweeping across her cheeks. Whatever hopes she had of reconciling hers and Trish's relationship, she knew without a doubt, those dreams would never come true.

The half hazard jog had taken her over fifteen minutes to reach her block, but instead of rushing into her house, she hurried past, exhausted, and out of breath. She crossed over into Aralyn and Susan's yard, hoping with every part of what was left, Susan was home and not at the hospital. Leaning her weary body against the doorsill, Christina pounded hard and listened for movement. Her eyes widened when the door opened to Aralyn. Christina dropped her gaze and stumbled backward.

"Christina? What's wrong?"

In her robe, Susan poked her head around Aralyn. "Christina, is everything okay?"

"I screwed up. I'm not sure how, but I did something terrible," Christina said, her voice low, words shaking.

Both women directed her into the house, to the couch in the front room. Susan was the one who asked the questions. At first, Christina found it hard to talk with Aralyn there, but after a few minutes, with her focus directed at her lap and Susan rubbing her back, her words came pouring out. From going to Karen's bar after driving from New Underwood, to leaving the old hotel less than thirty minutes ago, Christina told them everything.

Aralyn didn't speak, but Christina could feel her judgmental eyes on her, smoldering anger seething into her skin. Susan asked her several more questions. Christina's mind was too disengaged to remember what any of them were, or if she answered correctly. When Susan left the room, Christina's worry intensified. The moment Susan returned, she drew some blood and gave Christina a cup, instructing her to head to the bathroom and fill it with urine. Susan made a call, and Christina watched, feeling numb as Susan packed the samples and asked Aralyn to rush them to the hospital. The day nurse was expecting her.

Once they were both alone and Susan passed her a hot cup of tea, Christina placed a shaking hand over her eyes and wept.

CHAPTER FIFTEEN

Lieutenant Waska crouched beside the aged man, kneeling between the man's wife and son. He could hear the hushed murmurs of the other prisoners watching from the fenced-in compound behind him. Prisoners who were too scared to protest the removal of the scientist and his family. He kept his smile fixed on Doctor Jenkins until the elderly man finally raised his eyes. "I already told you. I'm not helping Frank Webber with his vaccination. I refuse to work for a madman. Do what you will, but I will not aid terrorists."

Waska kept an amused undertone as he slowly inched his head closer to the man. "Doctor, we are your government. If there are any terrorist among us, it's you three and those two-thousand traitors locked up behind me."

Waska watched Doctor Jenkins's face transform into a scowl. His aged wrinkles resembled an old bull mastiff teetering on the verge of biting. Waska fought against his desire to laugh. "The government killed billions of innocent people and are turning those who don't condone their genocide into deranged monsters. You and your men are nothing more than delusional sheep, following psychopaths in suits."

Waska sighed dramatically and stood. "I'm sorry you feel that way, Doctor."

When the vehicle pulled forward and stopped on the gravel road, Waska waited as a woman in high heels and a sergeant wearing a well-pressed uniform stepped out. Both surveyed the area with confused expressions. "Ah, here we are. Please, Mr. and Mrs. Dixon, we've been waiting for you." Waska held his arm out, gesturing for the husband and wife. As the woman moved closer, her eyes rotated to Doctor Jenkins and the two kneeling on the ground beside him. She stopped walking and her bottom lip quivered.

"What is this?" Doctor Jenkins moved to stand, but two of Waska's men held him firmly in place.

"A family reunion," said Waska. His brow shot upward in mocked surprise. "Did you think we were going to set you free without allowing you to take your entire family? Absolutely not. That would be cruel of us. Don't you agree, Doctor?" He formed the last sentence to mimic the old medical reruns he loved watching. As if he had come to a medical conclusion about a serious illness and sought confirmation from a trusted colleague for his findings.

The woman rushed forward and dropped to her knees in front of Lieutenant Waska, bawling. "Sir, please, my husband—my husband and I are true loyalists. We're not with these traitors."

"Christal!" Mrs. Jenkins shouted. Fire filling her eyes, she withdrew into herself, too shocked and disappointed in her daughter to go on.

Waska nodded to his men. They snatched up the woman and surprised sergeant and moved them both roughly to join the three who were kneeling.

"Sir, I'm a soldier for the New United States. Me and my wife, we were the ones who informed the government they were preparing to leave the city."

Waska rolled his eyes when Doctor Jenkins's son jumped up, dove forward, and tackled straight into his brother-in-law. The soldier's wife cried louder, and Mrs. Jenkins shouted out her bitterness to her daughter. Waska pivoted from the scene and rubbed at his temples while his men forcefully got the situation under control. Once the noise settled, he signaled for his men to load up the family so he and Doctor Jenkins could speak privately.

"Children… am I right?" he asked, producing a half snicker. He gawked sympathetically at the older man, which fueled the anger in Doctor Jenkins's eyes.

Waska stood with his arms folded. He pointed an index finger at Doctor Jenkins. "You mean a great deal to me, Doctor. More than you realize. You see…I've watched the videos from NORAD, and it seems you and Patricia Webber had a close relationship." He raised his hand to clarify. "Don't get me wrong. I don't mean sexual. I know you're a better man than that, Doctor Jenkins. I'm referring to a father and daughter closeness, well from a teacher and pupil standpoint. I don't know, maybe Patricia was the daughter you always wanted." He pointed to the troop carrier they loaded Doctor Jenkins's family into. "I mean, come on, look at the one you got stuck with. We both know Christal Jenkins doesn't hold a candle to Patricia Webber."

"What does any of this have to do with Trish?"

Waska beamed brightly. "Patricia is an extraordinary woman. A special individual in ways you couldn't imagine. One who has remarkable abilities inside her. Her father, Frank Webber, wants to get a message to her under the radar. I offered him a perfect way in which to do so. By using this last experiment from the committee. Quite brilliant, actually.

"Did you know…I had to search three different prison camps to find you. I feel a message as important as this should be carried out by someone Patricia trusts. The only dilemma is, who will you be when you deliver his letter? Her beloved Doctor Jenkins, or a deranged monster that she personally kills?"

He nodded to his men, and they jerked Doctor Jenkins to his feet and loaded him into the vehicle. Waska followed and stopped beside the door. "Get comfortable, Doc. We have a long ride ahead of us." Waska smirked at the confusion on Doctor Jenkin's face, leaving the older man's parade of questions unanswered.

Olivia sipped her coffee and stretched fully in her chair. This Sunday morning was perfect. After the three days of wearing her militia bodysuit, she was taking advantage of the clear skies and soaking up all the sun she could before beginning her next workweek at New Underwood. She closed her eyes behind the dark sunglasses and listened to the beat of her radio drown out the filter of the pool.

She had just drifted off into a midmorning catnap when she heard the echoes of tires crunching on gravel close by. Grumbling quietly, she sat up when two militia vehicles pulled into the drive. Doctor Burgos' truck followed close behind.

Curious, she stood as Aralyn, Givens, Phillips, and Carlen exited the first Gladiator. The second militia vehicle emptied with faces she didn't recognize, except for Perez. Doctor Burgos was with one of the other governors of Rapid City, the one whose name Olivia had a hard time pronouncing. Josue was either ho-sway or ho-zay. Whichever she used, it always felt as if she had gotten it wrong.

Olivia leaned over, switched off the radio, and removed her sunglasses. She could tell by the grave expressions, something bad had happened. Aralyn greeted her with a stern nod but didn't say a word until the others were beside them on the patio.

"Where're Trish and the kids? Are they inside?" Aralyn asked, first peering down at the tents, then to the sliding glass door off the patio.

"No, Trish took Sam and Jennifer out to the far pasture for target practice. She has her radio on if you need me to call her."

Aralyn shook her head and pointed to the table.

"Is everything okay?" Olivia asked, worried. She took a seat across from Aralyn and the governor, noticing how everyone else remained standing. She gave Doctor Burgos a gesture of welcome, but he didn't see it. He was too busy glaring angrily toward the house, as his hands gripped tight onto the edges of his hat.

"Doctor Stonleigh, we need to ask you a few questions," said Aralyn, keeping her features unreadable.

Shifting uncomfortably in her chair, Olivia nodded. She watched Aralyn look up at Doctor Burgos before asking her first question. "How do you record the medications used by veterinary staff?"

Olivia blinked a few times, stunned by the question and also that the leader in charge of the militia and not one of the governors was asking. She straightened. "Why do you want to know?"

"Please answer the question."

Olivia wasn't sure where Aralyn was going with this, or why all these people were here, but nothing about the presentation sat well with her. "I believe I have a right to know what this is regarding."

"Damnit, Olivia, just tell her." Doctor Burgos was more than aggravated, his eyes held an emotional hurt which boarded on aggressiveness.

"James, I'll handle this," Aralyn said, not taking her attention off Olivia.

Olivia's mind flashed to each of her veterinarians on staff, the ones who had access to her locked storeroom. What had happened to warrant such a gathering? Doctor Burgos and a second governor, the leader of the militia, and a handful of her troops—had someone died? Suddenly, she thought of Tracy and Tylor. Her heart skipped a beat.

As if able to read her mind, Aralyn signaled to Carlen. Olivia watched and waited while the captain pulled out a lightweight processor and handed the device to Olivia.

Doctor Burgos stiffened and stepped a few feet away.

Aralyn said, "This is one of the video feeds taken from Karen's club Friday evening." She continued to search for any signs of change in Olivia.

Keeping her emotions in check, Olivia activated the video. Tracy was conversing at a table with a woman beside the dancefloor, a man in a ball cap was sitting off to the far side of the screen sipping on a drink. Nothing abnormal on the monitor. Tracy was always picking up strays. The woman with curly red hair was speaking to Tracy and peeking over her shoulder. Olivia felt her neck grow hot, prickly. The woman wasn't one of Tracy's weekend flings. It was Janet, the woman Trish's wife, Christina, was having an affair with. She abruptly glanced at Doctor Burgos. Christina was his daughter.

"Please keep watching," Aralyn said.

Doing as Aralyn asked, Olivia tried not to move, even though the way she was sitting grew increasingly uncomfortable. She watched as Tracy pulled out her personal tablet, and Janet placed her hand on the screen to punch in a code. Olivia swallowed. Janet was transferring credits to Tracy. These people being here, Aralyn's question, and her own gut told her why.

She had approached Tylor and Tracy two months ago and informed them she knew they had used some narcotics in storage for recreational activities. Medicine on hand normally used to put a working dog to sleep for a routine teeth cleaning, or an animal out for surgery. Both had taken small doses for use at their recent parties. Olivia had found out through April, and she had confirmed what the young veterinarian had said by conducting a full inventory of stock.

Instead of filing a report as she was required to do, she chose to handle it in-house, while giving each a second chance. She placed them both on verbal probation and performed a bimonthly inventory of stock ever since. She matched the inventory with the medical records from each veterinarian. With no further discrepancies, she thought the matter was closed.

The moment Tracy passed something to Janet, Olivia turned her eyes away. She held out the processor for Carlen, but when Carlen didn't take it, Olivia lowered the processor uneasily to the table.

"There's more," Aralyn said.

Just then, the sliding glass door to the house opened and Tracy, coffee cup in hand, stepped out. Her eyes were heavy, and she was still in her sleeping attire and robe. She halted when she registered the group of people staring at her. "Sorry, I didn't know you had company."

She moved to head inside, but Carlen called out for Tracy to wait, bringing the tired veterinarian to stare at her, confused. Carlen nodded and two of the soldiers eased their way between the patio furniture, sidestepped Tracy, and blocked the entrance to the house.

Tracy's eyes shot from the soldiers to Carlen. She scowled, but Olivia could see Tracy's concern. "What is this?"

Carlen approached Tracy. Olivia could tell by the fire in the officer's eyes, the tightening of her fist, and the stiffness of her lips, Carlen was furious and would make Tracy pay for whatever she believed Tracy had done. Clearly, Tracy saw the same thing. Knowing she had nowhere to go, Tracy raised her cup in a plight of desperation and hurled it at Carlen's head. Hot, black coffee flew everywhere. Carlen swayed slightly, the ceramic container scarcely missing her, and took two gigantic steps before closing the gap. Tracy brought a hand up to block the swing, but Carlen was too fast and exceptionally skilled. The punch sent Tracy's head jerking sideways, her flailing body landing hard on the ground.

Olivia's head snapped to Aralyn, but Aralyn was watching her and not what was happening on the other side of the pool. Olivia stood.

Carlen sent Tracy another solid jab before pulling Tracy roughly to her feet. Tracy's outraged protest mixed with a few curse words, but her tone edged close to a sob.

Olivia wasn't sure if her rising fury was from a supervisory protectiveness, never having seen Tracy cry before, or how wrong they handled this entire ordeal. "Do something," Olivia said, her demand bordering on hysteria.

Aralyn spoke evenly. "Tracy's lucky Captain Strong's the one who's arresting her. If I had let one of these other soldiers detain her, it would have been so much worse. Captain Strong has enough discipline to restrain herself."

Carlen had Tracy pressed up against the house, her hands bound within seconds. Tracy's nose was definitely broken, and her left eye was already swelling. Carlen shoved Tracy toward the table they were sitting at and forced the struggling veterinarian into a seat.

"At least let me treat her injuries," Olivia angrily pleaded to Aralyn.

"She'll live." Carlen's voice sounded like a hiss. She positioned herself directly behind Tracy, with both her hands pressing down on Tracy's shoulders.

It startled Olivia with how out of character this officer was behaving. She had never seen such venom in Carlen's features before. Maybe Olivia didn't know her as well as she thought she did. She shot Tracy a questioning glance. Whatever she'd done, surely it didn't warrant this degree of treatment. She spoke heatedly to the governor sitting beside her. "How can you allow them to do this?"

The man was just as dispassionate as Aralyn when he spoke. "Doctor Stonleigh, once the complete investigation is over, the city will enforce punishment. As of right now, Tracy can no longer practice veterinary medicine ever again. Here, or in any of our allied cities. As far as what is to become of her, she will either be incarcerated for an appropriate period of time or expelled from the city. If during the investigation we discover other offenses, the city judges may decide on a more direct means of retribution."

Olivia couldn't believe what she was hearing. "Are you saying they could execute her?"

The man shrugged. Tracy jerked up a few inches from her seat, but Carlen dug her grip into Tracy's shoulders, right above her collarbone. Face overshadowed with pain, Tracy stopped resisting.

Aralyn leaned forward to the processor, which Olivia had left discarded on the table, and opened another video. This imagery was split in two. One feed showed where Tracy and Janet were still sitting by the dance floor, and a separate one covered a group of three at the bar. Olivia recognized Karen and the male bartender beside her. A second woman slouched in her seat on the other side of the bar. By the sluggish way in which her body moved, the woman was clearly intoxicated. Olivia focused closer to the woman. Her heart raced. Christina. Was Janet buying them drugs? This would explain why Doctor Burgos and the others were upset. But surely Christina was an adult and just as responsible for her own actions.

Janet rose from Tracy's table. She headed from one video, and instantaneously emerged on the second, along the far side of the bar from where the three were located. Christina downed her drink as the bartender moved toward Janet, spoke briefly, and poured her two shots. The moment he turned to Karen and Christina, Janet put something in one of the glasses. As Janet did, she noticed Tracy in the other video. The eerie smirk on Tracy's face gave Olivia the impression Tracy had known what Janet was going to do with whatever she had sold her.

Olivia wanted to look up, to see Tracy's reaction, but she couldn't take her eyes from the shot glass. She had a sickening feeling where this video was heading, but none of it made any sense. When Karen left the video, Janet scooted closer and sat beside Christina. She and Christina exchanged a brief bout, where Christina appeared agitated, even angry. Not long after, Christina downed the tainted shot and got up to leave. Janet followed Christina toward the main entrance, and steadied the intoxicated woman before she reached the door. Janet rotated behind her, said a few words to the bartender, and nodded in a different direction. When she did, Tracy, still ogling the two from the table by the dancefloor, returned the signal and waved to the man at the other table. He stood and followed Janet and Christina from the building. Olivia tried to see if she recognized him, but with the cap on, his full face never came into view. After they left, Tracy rose from the table and headed off to a different area of the club.

The video ended and Olivia stared unfocused at the processor. She sensed no movement from those around her, and all on the patio remained quiet, waiting. She swallowed down the bitter taste plaguing her throat and didn't look directly at Aralyn when she spoke. "What was in the drink?"

"Ketamine hydrochloride, and from what I've been told, this drug is on stock here with veterinary services." Aralyn's voice did waver this time. Olivia couldn't help but peer up. She could see, even past the steadfast persona, the older woman was grappling for control.

Olivia wracked her brain, trying to grasp the reasoning. "I don't understand. Why would Janet drug Christina if they were already sleeping together?"

She regretted her words the moment she said them. Doctor Burgos stiffened, but Aralyn spoke before he had a chance. "Christina and Janet have never been together. Janet has already admitted to bribing the sergeant-on-call to destroy any messages from Christina meant for Trish and that she broke into their house last Sunday to give Trish the impression of an affair. We're investigating the surveillances of each nightclub over the last year thoroughly to see if they have done this to others.

"As far as you are concerned," Aralyn shifted her glaring eyes directly at Tracy, "you, your financial records, your practice, everything encompassing your life will be meticulously examined. Like Governor Thornton said, as of right now, you have lost your right to practice medicine and you will be placed into custody for your part in this crime. Your punishment will be decided once we complete the investigation."

Olivia's grasp on the severity of what was happening sent a shock wave washing over her. Her disgust flashed to Tracy and so did her anger. With such a small fraction of humanity left on the planet, shouldn't offenses like this have died out with the masses? "You're not stupid. You knew exactly what ketamine would do and what Janet was using it for. You're worse than a thief and a drug dealer. You're a heartless monster."

"I didn't know what Janet was going to do," Tracy protested through her tears. "I thought she would use the dose for herself, not on someone else."

Olivia turned her eyes away, feeling utterly sickened by the woman sitting across from her. "Who was the man?" Olivia asked, her limbs growing cold even in the sun's warmth. She glared at the woman whose bed she had shared less than two months ago, now wishing for a scalding shower to wash the memories away. "In the video, Tracy, who was the man wearing the ball cap?"

Tracy stopped fighting against her restraints and focused on her lap. Olivia could see Tracy was upset, not for what she had done, but from getting caught. Her bloodshot eyes held no remorse.

Olivia's mind flashed to the women who had left Tracy's bed. Had any of them fallen victim to rape? She stood, no longer able to stomach the sight of Tracy, much less hear what the woman had to say. She felt ill with disgust.

"I can give you a list of names to anyone Tracy has brought home. What else do you need from me?" Olivia asked Aralyn, moving away from the table, hoping the distance would make her feel cleaner, less infected by Tracy's filth.

"I have two soldiers here from headquarters who will need full access to your records and medications. Also, until this investigation is over, Trish isn't to know."

Olivia gripped on to the railing surrounding the patio. How could they even consider keeping this from Trish? The idea was outrageous. "Someone's got to tell her."

"If Trish finds out, I'm not sure what she'll do. This needs to be handled delicately. For everyone's sake."

Olivia squinted at the burned ash lingering in the firepit both tents encircled. She understood Aralyn's reasoning but was troubled by the misery it offered. If Trish acted on impulse, which would certainly teem with vengeance, would anyone be able to stop her from seeking justice? Would Trish be able to live with herself after? Olivia's heart plummeted. This news would be hard for Trish to bear.

Olivia concentrated on the sounds of Tracy being taken away, trying to flood out the thoughts on what this would mean for her and Trish's relationship in the future. Would there ever be anything more than friendship? "I'll get my keys," Olivia muttered.

Unwilling to focus on those nearby, she made her way into the house.

After changing into her jumpsuit, Trish left her apartment in the officer's barracks of New Underwood. She entered the mess hall, which held the aroma of cooked bacon fusing delicately with rich coffee. One she wasn't in the mood for, the other her sluggish body desperately craved. She prepared her cup and headed to where Olivia sat at a corner table, hunched over and unfocused.

Olivia's eyes came up, their glossiness taking several seconds to register Trish's presence. She forced a grin.

Trish ignored the fakeness of it and placed her untouched drink on the table. "You left the ranch before five this morning, but you arrived at the outpost after me. Was there an emergency on one of the farms?"

Both hands clasped around her cup. "Something like that."

Trish took a drink and focused her attention outside. Almost the entire team had arrived, minus Aralyn and Doctor Burgos. The two traveled together and were always here before everyone else. With Aralyn's helicopter, arriving before Rapid City's gates opened was a nice perk.

Aralyn had offered to teach Trish how to fly one, once Aralyn's first aviation class graduated next month. Trish had jumped at the chance. Yet that was before hers and Christina's separation. With not wanting to cut into her limited time with Jennifer, Trish knew she needed to rethink the offer. Maybe her godmother would be willing to teach her after hours during the week. She knew Aralyn was busy overseeing Rapid City's security and helping with this mission, but maybe Trish could ease some of Aralyn's workload in exchange. Write a few reports, attend a meeting here and there, take notes, whatever would help.

Phillips and Carlen entered and went straight for the coffee. Trish watched their body movements and how close they were to one another. Her heart sank, and she pulled her thoughts off her own crumbling love life. She sipped her coffee and pointed to the two, now ordering breakfast. "I think they're sleeping together."

Olivia grunted but didn't take her eyes from her cup. Trish assessed Olivia's unsocial mood and her standoffish body language. If anyone could respect one's need for personal space, Trish could. She excused herself from the table and headed to the infirmary to find Young and embark on her Monday morning physical exam.

By the time Young deemed her fit for weekly testing inside the vault, the time was already after nine in the morning. The way the overcast sky grew darker, without the advancement of watches, ancient humans would have guessed the day had already slipped into late evening. Just enough glow between the cracks of the darkened clouds suggested, maybe the sun wasn't quite finished with its descent. A thunderstorm was most definitely unavoidable.

Trish entered the building housing the vault and saw everyone, including Aralyn and Doctor Burgos, were present. Even Olivia was seated at one of the monitors, still looking grim but better than earlier. Trish followed Young and Doctor Burgos downstairs, and the instant she entered the vault, she spotted the contents on the table. There was no sound sensor in the room, and the six rocks and two apples sitting on the surface felt strangely familiar.

"Trish, can you hear me?"

Trish sat on the stool and gave Doctor Burgos a thumbs up through the camera. She studied the pattern, trying to decide where she'd seen this before. Five rocks stretched out along the edge of the table, and an apple sat a few inches away with the last rock directly behind it. The remaining apple stood all alone, pulling up the rear.

"Trish, I want you to concentrate your abilities on the rocks, without damaging either of the apples," said Doctor Burgos.

Trish surveyed the middle rock and apple, taking notice of how close they were to one another. They were virtually touching. Destroying the rock without hurting the apple would be hard to do. If not impossible. "All at the same time, or can I do this in sections?"

"I want you to focus on all the rocks at the same time. Trish, I'm positive you can do this."

Trish gave Doctor Burgos a half-smile into the camera for him being so optimistic about her level of skills, even though she wasn't. She turned to the table and relaxed her mind. *Five rocks in front, one behind the apple. Five rocks in front, one behind the apple.*

Her mind repeated it over and over again, trying to narrow her mental aim. Trish's breath caught in her chest when the image of her father holding a gun to Christina's head jumped in, catching her mentally off guard. Her forehead pulled downward, and she slowly rose from the chair.

"Trish is everything alright?" she heard Doctor Burgos say into the speaker, but she ignored him.

The rocks in front were her father's men, and the rock behind the apple was her father. The two apples—Christina and Givens—stood out on the table now, more than they did when she first entered the room. They were fragile, exposed. When she felt her anger flash, she focused on each rock, wanting nothing more than to vanquish them from existence. The apples, their delicacy, were everything. Her face flushed and her mind took hold. This time her ability fired with no reservations, and her eyes didn't cower in their sockets, too afraid to see what she was capable of. First, the rocks slowly vibrated, then violently shook, and with a simultaneous pop, all six crumbled.

She moved forward when the door opened and reached for both the apples. Flipping them in her hands, she could see how neither was damaged, not even bruised. She handed Doctor Burgos the apples when he entered, not bothering to answer any of Sergeant Young's questions.

"Trish, what you did that day for my daughter, I'll never be able to express how grateful I am. You will always be a part of our family, no matter what happens."

"I need to take a break," she whispered.

As she left the room, she heard Doctor Burgos tell the objecting Young that Trish was fine. She headed upstairs and went outside for a few minutes of air.

CHAPTER SIXTEEN

Lieutenant Waska waited in his vehicle until his men locked the collars around each of the prisoners. His anticipation grew. If this test proved successful, Aralyn's Rapid City would fall tonight, and Trish would join the New United States. Not at first, no. He wasn't delusional. He knew the pain from her loss would take time to heal. In a year or two, she would see things for how they were. This government was mighty, and it ruled on a planet which was lusher and more inhabitable than the last few centuries.

Her father, even though he had failed when it came to caring for his daughter, could do great things for her and her abilities. She would one day take up her position among those in authority and be the leader Waska knew she could be. He would be right there with her, to protect her, and help guild her into her rightful place.

His second signaled they were ready. Waska exited the vehicle. Ignoring the pleading from Doctor Jenkins's daughter and her low-ranking husband, Waska moved directly in front of Doctor Jenkins. The man's scowl wasn't insulting, but glorious. An affirmation of the aged geneticist's perseverance. The man would need this grit now, more than ever.

"The rules for this experiment are simple, Doctor. You and your family will run west down Interstate 90. In exactly thirty-minutes, this container here"—he waved his arm at a man , who kicked at the door of a miniature Conex positioned beside him. The metal structure rattled and banged, as screams of the infected drifted out—"will open and release two mutants."

Waska paced slowly down the line of the five prisoners. Each was silent and displayed their fear in their own ways. "Now, I won't force you to take this route, but I guarantee this direction is the best chance any of you have for survival. You see, five miles away is an outpost called New Underwood. I've timed the release of the two mutants beautifully, so maybe a few of you might make it before the creatures rip you all to shreds."

He stopped walking and gestured to his second. The second moved forward, pulled out a knife, and quickly jabbed at the hamstrings of Doctor Jenkin's son-in-law's leg. Doctor Jenkin's daughter screamed with her husband, and the second backhanded her across the cheek.

"Stop, my family has nothing to do with this. I'm the one who refused to work for you. Punish me and let them go."

Waska ignored the older man's protest. "This is a team exercise. Your group needs to stay together." He assessed the amount of blood seeping onto the pavement from the weeping son-in-law's leg. He pointed and his second wrapped a tight bandage around it. "Plus, this will be a glorious scent for the mutants to follow."

The moment he waved, his men cut the bindings on the prisoner's hands and took turns shoving them down the road. With minimal coaxing, the family finally pulled together and began to run. "Don't forget—whoever makes it, you need to give Patricia Webber the message."

Trish strolled along the doublewide street, as her mind drifted to Christina. Seeing her beautiful face every morning, the way she laughed with Jennifer, her unwavering stubbornness—Trish missed it, all of it. Observing Christina, as she sipped her morning coffee from across the room. The way Christina curled herself into her arms, seeking love and solace. How Christina had loved her in return, protecting Trish in her own way, even from the memories of Trish's troubled childhood. Now everything was gone. A love and connection she would never feel again.

If life hadn't been so perfect, this pain of loss wouldn't feel so overwhelming. Trish didn't own Christina. She was her own woman, who deserved all the joy this world had to offer. Whatever anguish Trish was experiencing, she needed to accept it, make peace with the ending of their relationship, and let her go, or else none of them, not even Jennifer, would find complete happiness.

Trish breathed in the cool air, the promise of rain filling her nose. She looked up at the clouds, closed her eyes, and prayed for strength. She thought of Christina, allowing herself to release the grip of hope she clung to, vanquishing every ounce of anger she carried, and accepting the knowledge that their time had ended. This future life of loneliness was how fate unfolded, how her destiny had taken shape, with or without Trish's own approval. She was now on an alternate path, one best walked alone.

She needed to talk to Christina, to let her know she would step aside, so she and Jennifer could live the lives they were meant for. Find the love, comfort, and stability they deserved. If Christina allowed it, she would be in Jennifer's life. If it made things more complicated for Christina's new relationship, Trish wouldn't force her parental rights. She would remain on the sideline and be there when Jennifer needed her to be.

Trish would focus fully on her work. She wanted to talk to Aralyn—today. The time they were spending in the vault needed to be redirected into working to find an immunity against this infection. Trish was better now. She no longer had headaches. She felt a level of control over her abilities, and she was able to tap into a connection she had with the Gramites. They could use this, use those Gramites in the surrounding hordes to search for a way to protect survivors against this virus. Against the transformation.

The whine from Molly brought her out of her musings. The weight, which had been pressing on her for so many weeks, felt lighter, manageable. She breathed in again, this time deeper than before. She lowered herself down and generously rubbed along Molly's coat, her companion excited for the affection she offered.

"You seem different, Trish. Content," Phillips said, dropping to his knees beside them. "It's nice to see your eyes glow again."

Trish nodded. "I do feel better. I've been fighting with factors I can't control, to the point I was losing myself. I need to accept certain things for being what they are and move on with life."

She could tell Phillips was examining her for the reasoning behind her newfound insight. His features reflected comfort and concern at the same time. Touching his arm, she did her best to silently let him know all was well. She was well.

The level of alarm jumped in so fast, the muscles in Trish's neck tightened close to a spasm. She skyrocketed to her feet. Molly raised the hairs between her shoulder blades, searching the area for the threat Trish was sensing. Trish spun to Phillips, who was anxiously viewing her. Mutants were approaching, two, maybe three, and they weren't coming to New Underwood or seeking the Gramites hordes nearby. They were hunting humans.

"Do you have the keys to your vehicle? People are in danger. We have to go. Now."

"Yes," Phillips said. He ran after her as she headed to his militia vehicle. "Trish, we've got to tell the others."

Trish waited for Molly, who climbed into the passenger seat after her. "At the gate, instruct the guards to sound the alarm." Trish activated the console. "While you drive, I'll open a link and see if anyone on the team is connected. Doctor Burgos usually is."

Panting in mouthfuls of air, Doctor Jenkins helped his wife climb to her feet. Their son bent down and examined his mother's injury. Their daughter hustled down the interstate, running barefoot beside her limping husband, while clutching her high heels tight in her hand. His disappointment in their daughter was greater now, more than ever.

"Mom, it's not bad. Can you run? If not, I'll carry you."

Doctor Jenkins searched through the opening of his wife's torn pantleg. His son was right. Blood oozed from where his wife's knee had been scraped on the asphalt. Other than the flesh wound, she was fine.

"Of course, I can run." She swatted at them both. "You go ahead. I'll be right behind you."

"Rose, I'm not leaving you," Doctor Jenkins insisted.

"Neither am I, Mother."

Doctor Jenkins looked at his son, David. He studied the face of the man before him, while giving his wife a few seconds longer to catch her breath. His eyes drifted to his wife and the pleading he saw in her features. Her unspoken begging caused a lump to form in his throat, blocking the air struggling to leave his body. He reached out and pulled his son and wife in for a firm embrace, as tears slid down his cheek and the screams behind them drew even closer.

When they broke away, he squeezed his son firmly on the shoulder. "My boy, you need to run as fast as you can. Do you hear me? No matter what happens, don't you dare turn around."

His son glared at them both. David's eyes narrowed and his bottom lip gave a slight quiver. David wasn't stupid. He knew all of them wouldn't make it. David was young, athletic. Out of everyone here, he had the best chance for survival. He and Rose…they needed their son to live.

Instead of turning and doing as his father ordered, David rushed forward, clasped hold of his mother's tiny wrists, and threw her onto his shoulder like a sack of potatoes. "Dad, if you want Mom, you'd better keep up." David shot him a challenging grin and took off, heading down the interstate.

Swelling with pride, Doctor Jenkins blinked his tears away. He stretched out his gait, taking off after his son, whom he believed had grown into the finest man he knew.

Trish pointed to the group of people running down the hill. "I see them," Phillips said, swerving around a fallen tree that blocked most of the weed-infested road.

A woman in a cocktail dress stopped when a man in a military uniform clutched his leg and fell. She shouted, gave his arm a few good jerks, then let go and ran away. Another man, who had an older woman with silver hair slung in a fireman's carry, was close to passing the man on the ground. This piggyback duo was shadowed closely by a third man, who ran with his head bowed, his arms pumping wildly at his sides, and seemed to be close to falling himself.

Trish peered over the seat the moment the two mutants broke the crest of the horizon. "Where's your rifle?" she asked. She glanced from Phillips to what was happening beyond the windshield.

"In New Underwood, same as yours." He scowled, not necessarily at her but at the thought neither were carrying firearms. "Wait, I have a high-powered rifle in the storage area. You don't have much time," he said, but she was already climbing over the first set of seating.

When she reached the storage area, she located the rifle container nestled on top of duffel bags and storage bins. She saw through the hatch window that two Gladiators were following them from New Underwood and a helicopter, its blades rising from concealment behind the surrounding wall. "The team are on their way," she shouted.

Before returning from the last row of seating, Trish removed the rifle from the case and loaded the magazine containing Jason's specially made ammo. Once she attached the scope, she scurried over, retook her seat, and peered out the windshield. The man carrying the older woman had passed the man on the ground, who was struggling to get to his feet. When the older man behind them reached the man, who was now limping over a mile away, he supported his injured side to help him move faster.

The mutants were less than a half mile behind them and gaining in speed. "We're not going to make it," Trish said. She exchanged a grim expression with Phillips.

She had to act fast if they were going to save them all. "Drive as straight as you can and try to avoid any potholes." She lowered her window and slung the long rifle securely over her head and other shoulder.

"The entire strip is full of potholes," he heatedly replied. He reached out and seized a fistful of her jumpsuit. "Too dangerous."

She shoved his hand away. "You think you would've learned by now. I really don't care. Focus on the road."

Climbing on the roof with the wind whipping against her wasn't the challenging part. Remaining on the fast-moving Gladiator without falling off was what proved to be tricky. Lowering herself into a prone position, Trish squeezed her arm through a metal strap attached to the vehicle's weaponry. Unfortunately, the laser on the weaponry tracked onto heavily armored vehicles or low-flying aircraft. It could lock onto missiles as well, under the right conditions, but could not detect organic objects, even ones as large as the mutants.

The woman running at the lead of this group spotted their vehicle, and she swung her arms animatedly about. She turned her head and shouted to those in her group, who were gaining on her slowing pace. Trish removed her rifle and took aim at the closest mutant. She held her breath, squeezed the slack out of the trigger, and fired. The mutant's head lurched, its body and legs going down with the lethal impact. Damn, these hollow-point bullets were amazing.

The woman, holding tight to a pair of shoes, moved toward the center of the road, swaying her arms above her head. Phillips blared on the horn, and Trish tried waving her away, but the bouncing woman didn't move. Trish held on tight, seconds before Phillips swerved the vehicle onto the shoulder. Trish grumbled, glared at the woman, and concentrated on those dead ahead. She tried taking aim at the next mutant. Each time she was prepared to fire, the vehicle jerked sideways or dipped into a pothole.

The creature was almost on top of the older man and soldier. Desperate, Trish focused on the mutant and tapped into her ability. She could feel her mind work its magic as heat rose to her forehead. The mutant jerked, shook its head, and rushed forward on all fours. She tried harder, but the same outcome occurred.

She brought a hand down and felt Phillips's door. The window was down. "Do you have your knife?" she shouted, trying to be heard above the wind. A few second later he passed it up, sheath and all. She lowered the rifle down to him. "I want you to slam into that ugly bastard. If the men are in the way, then slow down and drive close to it so I can jump off."

"Jesus, Trish," was all she heard.

Trish's heart raced as the vehicle closed the gap. They passed the man and older woman and were less than a minute from reaching the last two. So was the mutant. She tried her ability one last time. The mutant screamed out against it, not losing his stride. Trish gripped the edge of the weaponry frame, squatted on her heels, unfastened the sheath's clasp with her teeth, and flicked her wrist, casting the covering into the wind. Right when the mutant pushed off the asphalt with his legs and lunged at the stumbling men, Phillips applied the brakes. Trish shot from the roof, angling her body directly at the mutant. They collided with enough force that neither of his clawed hands contacted either man.

She felt the air leave her lungs when she slammed onto the edge of the asphalt, as she and the creature rolled parallel through the weeds. The reek of the infected overpowered her the moment she found her footing. A scream rang out beside her—the sound was piercing. She twisted, readying herself to block, but a rifle shot rang out and the mutant dropped into the weeds. Trish glanced in the direction of fire and spotted Carlen, who had her weapon up and was standing with Givens by a Gladiator several hundred feet away. The bullet left a hole in the mutant's shoulder, but the monstrosity was still alive. Trish took two brisk steps forward, stabbed it in the throat, and twisted the handle.

One last gurgling growl, and the mutant's fading eyes closed, its head falling lifelessly to the side. That was when Trish noticed a device sticking out of both ears. She tried pulling one free, but it didn't give way. Stitches held it in place. She had to use the knife to cut each one out. She twirled the duplicate devices around in her hand. They looked like tiny headphones, or earmuffs, without the headpiece. This ear device was probably why her ability didn't work.

"Trish Webber?"

Hearing a familiar voice, Trish spun around in shock. "Doctor Jenkins! What—where—what the hell?"

Trish was beside herself. Her lab instructor wasn't just alive. He was here, right in front of her, acting as surprised as she was. He was thinner, older, and his face was covered in dirt and an untrimmed beard, but it was him. Her heart ached at seeing him this way. Frail.

Before she could give him a hug or ask questions, a distinct pop echoed, and the injured soldier beside Doctor Jenkins fell to the ground. The woman farther down the road screamed, and Trish pivoted. The shot came from the direction this group had scurried. She pushed Doctor Jenkins to the weeded ground and covered him. Shouting and gunfire was going off around them, and Trish heard the distinct sound of a missile whistling by and spinning blades from Aralyn's helicopter.

Phillips pulled the vehicle up to them to block them from the direction of the attackers, and Trish ushered Doctor Jenkins inside. When she checked the pulse on the unmoving soldier, she saw the bullet wound above his right brow. She closed his eyes. After a few minutes of random firing, Trish watched Aralyn lower the helicopter on a weeded strip next to the interstate. She was about to move forward when she heard another cry of distress. The older woman with silver hair crouched on the road beside the body of the man who had carried her.

"David!" Doctor Jenkins shouted. He ran from the vehicle before Trish could stop him. She rushed by his side, using her body as a shield. He knelt next to the woman and clasped the young man's hand in his.

Young crouched on the other side. He checked his pulse and inspected the area where a bullet had struck the young man in the chest. "He's still alive," Young said, pulling open his bag. Trish rushed around and helped him. She applied pressure to the dressing as Young attached an IV and rechecked the man's pulse. "We need to get him to the hospital. Immediately."

Olivia was moving out from the helicopter with a stretcher. Once they lifted him on, Olivia took over applying pressure to the wound, and Trish helped Carlen and Young carry him to the helicopter. Olivia and Young loaded him into the helicopter with the rest of the survivors, including Doctor Jenkins. The younger woman was crying and motioning at the body of the other man.

"We'll get him and meet you at the hospital," Carlen told her. Once the helicopter was in the air, Carlen turned to Trish. "What were they wearing around their necks?"

Trish shrugged. "I didn't notice, but I found these," she said, pulling the earpieces from the pocket on her jumpsuit. She passed them to Carlen. That's when she noticed the acid burns on her arm.

So did Carlen. "Damn Trish, go fetch the solution out of my Gladiator."

"It's not as bad as it looks. I think my body's building a resistance to the acid."

Carlen snorted. "If you say so."

Trish applied the solution on her arms and helped the guards on her team burn the mutants. Afterward, she found Carlen with Phillips, where they were loading into Phillips's vehicle the dead man wearing the military uniform. She gave Carlen the earpieces from the second mutant. "Do you have any idea what these are?"

"Headphones of some kind. I won't know for sure until I've had time to break them apart." Carlen handed them back to Trish with a collar she'd cut off from around the dead soldier's neck. "Give these to Doctor Burgos when you get to New Underwood. Take my vehicle, will you? I'm going with Phillips to bring this body to the hospital and to stop in to speak with Susan."

"Is Susan okay?" Trish asked. Last she knew, Carlen and Susan weren't exactly seeing eye to eye with this mission.

"She's fine. We should return in a few hours."

Carlen left it at that, and Trish didn't pry. Once she loaded Molly in the Gladiator and Trish had her seatbelt fastened, they followed the guard's vehicle to New Underwood.

Christina sat on the edge of the hospital bed, grateful the last of the examinations were finally over. She was redressed and waiting, had been for over thirty minutes now. The knock on her door brought her attention off the pale-gray wall. Susan peeked her head in before entering with the female gynecologist who had performed the rape kit. The woman held a gentle understanding in her eyes, almost suggesting to Christina she had been through something similar. Before the door closed, Christina noticed how Aralyn, Carlen, Phillips, and several others were waiting outside her room, comforting her mother.

Susan stood beside Christina as the gynecologist pulled her seat closer, not losing her empathetic gaze. "Christina, would you like for us to get your mother?"

Christina slowly shook her head. The only person she wanted beside her now was her wife, but she knew that scenario wasn't going to happen. Trish didn't know about the assault. She couldn't know, not yet.

"I'm sorry, but your results showed traces of semen."

Christina's entire body felt stiff, as her brain worked to digest the news.

"Colonel Williams is asking us to release this information to her, so they can crosscheck the data with DNA swabs of all the men in the militia. I'll only do so with your consent."

Susan squeezed her hand while Christina struggled with the truth. Janet wasn't the only one on top of her that night. There had been someone else. A man was inside her. They bound her arms and legs to limit her movement. Had she resisted? Was this why they tied her to the bed, or was this merely part of their sick, twisted perversion? Christina jumped up, scarcely making it to the sink before vomiting.

The door opened. Susan moved forward and reassured Eva that Christina was fine and they'd be finished soon.

Her mother, her father. What would this information do to them?

Susan comforted her until the stomach convulsions stopped. When she finished, Christina shut off the faucet and pivoted to the doctor. "I give you my permission."

Once the woman left the room, Susan pulled Christina aside and closed the door. "Trish needs to know, Christina. I don't care what the others think. The longer we wait, the harder it will be for her. You know this better than anyone."

Christina stared briefly at Susan and swiveled away. Everything that had happened between them, the suffering Trish had gone through over the weeks, this would definitely make matters worse. Unfortunately, Susan was right. The longer they put it off, the harder it would be for Trish. "Okay, I'll do it today. After I pick Jennifer up from school, I'll head to New Underwood and talk to her."

CHAPTER SEVENTEEN

Trish laced up her boots, hung her towel up in the bathroom, and ran her hands through her semi-dry hair. She donned her utility belt and restocked the pouches from her stash of loaded magazines for her rifle before tossing her helmet in the duffel, latching it, and strapping the canvas bag and her weapon over each shoulder. Once she was ready, she ushered Molly out of the apartment.

Sitting in the Gladiator, she clenched her jaw, tightened her fist, and pictured her father. Doctor Burgos was the one who found the note tucked inside a small container on the hostage's collar. He showed the note to Trish and contacted Aralyn to tell her the upsetting news. A few minutes later, Carlen radioed to say each of the survivors had similar messages in their collars, all addressed to Trish from her father, and all bearing the same sentence: *Your mother would be proud.*

He was baiting her. They all knew it, especially Aralyn. She doubled security throughout Rapid City and ordered Trish, Doctor Burgos, and the guards to head straight to the city for the night. They would regroup later, after giving Carlen, Aralyn, and Major Thomas time to discuss steps they could take to fortify Rapid City, New Underwood, and fifty miles out in every direction. As of now, Rapid City and the two allied cities were all on high alert.

Trish directed Molly inside with her after waving to the guards who were by the other two vehicles, waiting for Doctor Burgos. Once inside the building that housed the vault, Trish found Doctor

Burgos at his desk, working on the earpieces. "It's time to go, Doctor Burgos. Bag it up and we'll take it with us."

Tiny pieces of one earpiece was scattered directly in front of him. He removed his magnified glasses, his expression grave. "Trish, they had to have been watching you for some time. They know what you're capable of. Someone delicately constructed this earpiece to sense extremely high frequencies such as yours and cancel them out. I'll have Carlen examine it, but this is complex technology. Constructing it would have taken time and talent."

Trish emptied the colorful thumbtacks from one of Doctor Burgos's small desk totes. "I used this ability on my father in NORAD. Since he apparently lived, he more than likely figured out what I did," she said, placing each device, including the one he was working on, in a four-inch square container.

"Don't you see, Trish? Today was a test. The group you rescued, these mutants, all of it was a controlled experiment." He stood and threw on his hat. "I need to talk to the survivors. Did you say your lab instructor's name is Doctor Jenkins?"

"Yes. Carlen said the man they took to the hospital is his son, David. He's out of surgery and in recovery now. Susan thinks he'll pull through. Doctor Jenkins will probably be with him at the hospital."

She handed him the parts and followed him outside. "I'll be thirty minutes behind you. I need to stop in at horde-four and check on the one who's healing from last week's injuries. I won't be long." She headed away before he could protest.

Climbing behind the wheel, she waited for the other vehicles to leave and closed the gate, activating the security panel. The next time the gate opened, the alarm would notify HQ. The guards usually did this every Friday evening. The first person to arrive in New Underwood on Monday would deactivate the alarm and call HQ to inform them all was well. New Underwood was open for business. Trish was sure Aralyn and Mayor Thomas set it up this way so Trish wouldn't stay out here by herself during the weekend.

Which was fine. Trish had no problem pitching a tent past the wall if needed. She assumed they would have figured that out by now.

Trish took the back roads to Highway 34 and headed west toward Sturgis. She left her comms link off and her helmet in the duffel bag, not wishing to be disturbed on the drive. With the way the orders had sounded, it could be several days until Rapid City opened its gates and their mission resumed. Might even be longer since her father was now believed to be alive.

Feeling an overwhelming pressure inside her chest, Trish pulled over near the motorcycle memorial she and Olivia had stopped at last week. She stepped out and took several deep breaths, not liking the way her mind was yelling at her either to pick a direction and drive, or to head to Colorado Springs and track down her father.

She squinted off toward the direction of Rapid City and wondered if this threat was as grave as Command believed. Trish figured they were erring on the side of caution. Rapid City was well-defended against the infected and the corrupt government they once followed. They even had underground shelters located around the city for added protection of the citizens during conflicts.

Molly jumped into Trish's seat and wagged her tail brutishly against the leather. Trish gave her a few good scratches, instructing her not to go too far. Molly barked out her understanding and bounced off in search of objects more interesting than watching Trish battle with her mental demons.

Hearing thunder in the far distance, Trish strolled down the side of the road and tried to picture what it would be like seeing the ocean for the first time. Or to go camping in beautiful places, like the Blue Ridge Mountains, the Grand Canyon, even braving the Colorado River in a kayak, as thrill-seekers did before the virus. To hike through the Ozarks in the Midwest, explore caves in Tennessee, scuba dive in the Gulf of Mexico, maybe even find a yacht to live on for a few months or even a couple of years. To be free like Spirit was now with no more responsibilities, just living from one day to the next.

Trish sat in the thick grass, thinking of her daughter. What she would give to do all those things with Jennifer by her side. Maybe forego the Colorado rapids, which would be too dangerous for one so young. The Grand Canyon would be okay, but from a distance. It would drive Trish's anxiety up seeing Jennifer stand anywhere near the edge of a steep ravine. The scuba diving would have to be done in fresh water, where there weren't any sharks. Still, Trish remembered reading how bull sharks had appeared in lakes and rivers. Spending time in the Blue Ridge Mountains and the Ozarks were safe enough, but the yacht was undeniably out. No, Trish couldn't chance Jennifer falling off the side or a storm appearing out of nowhere and sinking the boat with her daughter still on board. Land. They needed to stay on dry land. They could camp on the beach.

Molly came over and placed her head in Trish's lap. Rubbing Molly's muzzle, Trish realized she had turned what was meant to be a relaxing daydream into a 'how many ways can my daughter become gravely injured or killed' nightmare. She ran her fingers through Molly's coat as she studied the clouds. They needed to get this done and head to Rapid City before the storm arrived.

The moment she stood, she heard a pop in the distance, followed by a sting at the nape of her neck. She rotated to the side and raised her hand up to her hairline. Her peripheral vision distorted, as she brought her hand down with blood on her gloved fingers. She stumbled toward her vehicle and tried to focus against the spinning landscape. Her legs gave out, and she fell. As Molly licked her face, her entire mouth grew as numb as her limbs.

"Molly…run," she said, moments before her vision went completely dark, and her mind stopped working.

Christina sank forward in her seat, as Jennifer exited the building. Her daughter's normal boisterous waves of farewells to her friends had reduced over the last several weeks. Sam rushed up to her, his words lifting her spirits some, but the elevated mood didn't last. Sam stopped walking and followed Jennifer with his eyes. The seven-year-old headed to the car with her head hung low.

Turning hazily away, Christina brushed at her tears seconds before the door opened. She did her best to keep her voice light, cheerful even. "How was school today?"

Jennifer slid into her designated seat behind Christina and buckled her seatbelt before answering. "Okay."

"Just okay? Did you learn anything new and exciting?" Christina asked, trying hard to ignite any spark of conversation.

Jennifer shrugged.

Pulling away from the curb, Christina adjusted her rearview mirror for her continued line of questioning. It broke her heart seeing Jennifer unhappy. She was too young to be this sad. "How's Sam doing in school? You haven't mentioned him in a while." Or anything else.

Christina squeezed tight the leather steering wheel. Jennifer was pulling away from her a little more every day. This path they were on needed to change. If not, she would lose both her girls from her life. She knew it.

"He's okay."

Undoing the lid on her water bottle, Christina took a long drink, trying to relax the constricting muscles of her throat. She passed the bottle over the seat, but Jennifer shook her head no. Her daughter kept her head hung low with her hands in her lap. Christina placed her water in the cupholder and drove down the street by her parents' house.

"Mother, where are we going?" Jennifer asked.

Christina peered into the mirror. "New Underwood. I need to talk to your mom if she's there. If not, maybe you can hang out with your grandpa for a few hours."

Jennifer's head rose higher, her eyes wide, questioning. "Are you going to ask Mom to come home?"

Christina's eyes dampened, and her mind raced with how to answer such an innocent question. She couldn't say yes, even though she would do everything she could to make this happen, beg if needed. If she told Jennifer this, and Trish either couldn't or said no, then Christina would have placed the burden of their daughter's disappointment fulling on Trish. Even if Trish was seeing someone else, she didn't deserve more heartache. "I'm going to talk to your mom about several things, and I need to speak with Grandpa as well. Hey, maybe you guys can fly the drone again."

Christina studied her daughter carefully. She could tell Jennifer wasn't happy with how her mother answered, but her head remained up, and her eyes were now focused on life outside the window instead of her lap. The shift in her daughter's mood was minor but still an improvement.

Pulling up to the gate, she noticed the guard didn't wave her through like normal. Instead, he approached her window. She lowered it and waited.

"Destination?"

"I'm heading to New Underwood."

He shook his head. "Sorry, Mrs. Webber, but they're not there. Mutants were killed nearby, so they closed New Underwood and ordered everyone here. The last of Captain Webber's team got in a few hours ago. We're on lockdown until further notice."

Christina glanced in the rearview mirror and winked at her daughter. Trish might be at the house, but she didn't believe so. Trying to keep the concern out of her tone, she spoke with as much pep as she could muster. "I need to go to the cattle farm then, where the veterinarians live." She pointed in the correct direction.

"The Stonleigh Ranch. Yes, ma'am, that's fine." The soldier stepped away from the car and waved to the tower. A few seconds later, the inner gate opened, and Christina drove through.

Warm, blood, meat. JW bit into the dead carcass, filling her insides with the red, juicy flesh. Her claws ripped the fur, pulling it roughly away before relishing the next mouthful.

Her head shot up. She yanked her lips back, barring her teeth to the rustling sounds of trampled weeds farther away. Sending out a low growl, she signaled a threat to those nearby and dropped the meal to ready herself on all fours. She glared at the swaying of the wildflowers, the yanking of vines, the shifting of greenery seconds before the shrubs directly ahead parted.

The moment the furry creature exposed itself, it dropped to the ground. The noise it made was soft, unthreatening. Her eyes scanned the brush, waiting for the one whom the creature followed, but nothing else moved. The Gramite beside her bellowed his claim for the kill. She rotated her head and screamed out her dominating commandments. He, like the rest, remained in the lining of trees, motionless.

Her noises alerted her mate to join her, and together, they cautiously approached the creature. The beast didn't run to or away from them. Instead, it rolled on its back and exposed its belly, offering them its vulnerability. Her mate grumbled to her. She moaned to him and scanned the thick overgrowth again. Her mate towered over the creature, growled, and waited. When the furry beast whined, as if it were injured, her eyes shot to her mate, and he responded with a throaty gurgle.

Her face pulling into a scowl, she brought a fist forward and pushed persistently against the creature, sending it up on all fours. They stared directly at one another. It made a sharp piercing sound and rotated in a complete circle. The animal had come here for them. JW screamed to her followers and without waiting, the creature rushed into the thickets with her and her horde directly behind.

Drip, drip. Trish's eyes parted, her chin resting uncomfortably against her chest. Drip. She blinked several times and struggled to focus. Drip. The smell of damp earth filled her nose, while her vision was caked in darkness. The air surrounding her body was cold, and hushed whispers were coming from somewhere close by.

When she sluggishly lifted her head, stiff muscles at the base of her neck screamed out in painful protest, and a repetitive dripping echoed in her ears. She lifted her head all the way up and rested it against the same metal pole her hands were bound behind.

A beam of light stung her eyes, which forced her to squint and twist her head to the side.

"Sir, Patricia's awake."

Patricia? Her heart skipped a beat. She knew by the complete use of her first name, this group belonged to her father. They were her enemy, and she, their prisoner.

Struggling against her binding sent a sharp pain through her arms and legs. She jerked and wiggled anyway, trying to get a feel for what was holding her in place. The clanging of metal filled her ears when she tried kicking her legs outward, demanding them to separate. The effort proved useless.

Light filled the area, and the glow directed at her face disappeared. "I'm sorry for this barbaric treatment you're currently going through. With your capabilities, and your misguided mindset, I'm sure you can appreciate how these extreme measures were forced upon us."

She pressed her eyelids together several times, scarcely able to make out the figure moving beside her. This man's voice wasn't her father's, which meant her father wasn't with them. If he had been, he would have been the one to dictate the conversation. His controlling personality wouldn't allow his own voice to remain silent in the shadows of others.

She opened her mouth to respond, but harsh sounds came out. Leaning her head against the metal pole, she coughed at the scratchiness plaguing her throat. She felt the wet plastic on her lips, the cool water comforting her, as she swallowed several large gulps from the bottle.

"Sorry. The swelling is a side effect of the tranquilizer we had to use. Unfortunately, you'll be given another before we leave here tonight." The man's dark brown hair stood out, as did his caring features. "I'm positive, once you've had time to adjust to your new life, you'll look on this day with appreciation for us saving you."

She remained quiet as he spoke. She could see this man meant every word he said. His firm eyes didn't judge her with hatred, as one enemy to another, but with a great sense of admiration, even a familiarity of sorts. One which he obviously expected Trish herself would understand.

Trish inspected the other personnel around the low-ceilinged cavern. She counted ten people but heard more on the narrow stone steps directly ahead from where she sat. Some in this room held the hatred this man should have had. Others were on edge, as if waiting for her to react. All, like the man beside her, were wearing helmets, different from the ones soldiers usually wore. They were thicker and oddly shaped. Protection—used to shield them against her ability?

She tried shifting her body into a more comfortable position and winced at the pinch she felt on her outer thigh. Her eyes narrowed to the thick chains wrapped tightly around her skin. Her feet were bare, as were her legs since she was wearing shorts, and an oversized T-shirt covered her torso. She was sitting on a mixture of smooth stone and powdered earth.

Glimpsing up, she saw how his eyes were following her own. His cheeks flushed when he spoke. "I do apologize again for your treatment. Rest assured, no one else was around when I removed your bodysuit and dressed you, and I did so with great respect to your virtue and under the integrity of my own personal morals."

With a forced edge of embarrassment, Trish lightly lowered her head. "I appreciate your candor. May I have another drink?"

His chest swelled, and his eyes sparked with relief. He tilted the bottle to her lips, and she took several more swallows. She remained still so he could wipe the droplets from her chin. He shifted her shoulders to the left, and she let out a long sigh.

"Better?" he asked.

She nodded, still stunned by his worry for her wellbeing. "You know my father will have me sedated the moment we arrive in Colorado Springs."

He shook his head adamantly. "I can understand, from the information I've gathered surrounding your upbringing, why you have strong reservations when it comes to your father. He is a changed man—" His voice broke briefly when the movement to her head said otherwise. "I know. There's no reason for you to trust him. I need you to put your faith in me, if you will, and understand that I, the committee, we all have your best interest at heart. Your father's lab has been moved to New York, so the committee of the New United States can personally oversee your testing and fair treatment."

"New York? My father's in New York?"

"Yes. Once our mission is done here, we'll leave tonight to take you to your new city. I'm sorry, but we can't allow Rapid City to exist. They're too much of a threat to our government."

He motioned behind him and one of his soldiers brought over a blanket. The man wrapped it around her. She slouched herself into it, appearing grateful. He wasn't armed, but the rest were.

He gently brushed her cheek with his thumb. "You will be such an amazing leader," he said. His voice was softer, affectionate. "The gifts you carry inside, your personality...your beauty. You are truly divine, Ms. Webber."

"Will you be in New York with me?" The moment her question came out, she stiffened nervously while glancing at the soldiers behind him, acting as if she suddenly remembered there were others in the room. Trish blushed and turned away. "I'm sorry I asked. It's just, I don't want to be unaccompanied when I'm in my father's lab. He's a monster." She breathed out her last sentence.

He spoke over his shoulder. "Leave us," he ordered.

A minute later when he answered her question, they were alone. "My men and I have been assigned to you. I promise, you will always be protected, even from your father if it comes to that."

He leaned closer and stroked a finger along the rim of her chin. She could see his chest rise and fall at an elevated breath-rate, his eyes outlining the fullness of her slightly parted lips. She brought her bottom lip in, slowly brushed her tongue against it, and gently bit down. Christina could get anything she wanted with that move. He swallowed and lowered his searching eyes to her neck.

"I'm a little warm," she whispered. She averted her eyes to the right in a move of embarrassment. Dirt and rock were all she could see. She had to be in a cave.

He unwrapped the blanket slowly, while allowing his fingers to slide against her, downward, along her shoulders, and tenderly over her arm. She inhaled deeper, faster, matching him breath for breath. His eyes and hands caressed her thighs along the edge of her shorts, between the chains. She could see an erection take shape, growing firm under his bodysuit. She parted her mouth even more. He was hungry to taste her. He lowered his lips eagerly to hers.

Right before their lips touched, she brought her head back and threw it forward with all her strength. The impact was so violent, he was knocked backward on the dirt, and his helmet went flying a few feet away. Wide-eyed, he darted his arms behind him, franticly reaching for his object of protection. She focused her ability on him, while drowning out the sound of feet rushing into the room. Screaming out against the pain, his fingers fumbled with the helmet and finally sheathed his head, protecting him against her mental weapon.

The blow of the rifle butt on the side of her skull was hard, snapping her head to the left. Her body jerked painfully against the chains. She grunted and readied herself for the next blow.

"Stop," the man shouted, reeling with anger. He struggled slightly and climbed to his feet. Taking several steady breaths, he eyed her angrily. "I should have known better," he said, throwing up his hands. "You're a formidable woman, Ms. Webber. Highly intelligent and protective of those you love."

"You don't have to do this. There are many unarmed people in the city—young children, pregnant women. Hasn't humanity lost enough?"

He moved over and visually examined where the rifle impacted her head. He re-wrapped the blanket around her body, this time taking a higher level of caution than before. "I'm truly sorry for what must happen, but those inside the city are a danger to our way of life."

"Go to hell," Trish said, her voice an angry hiss. She tried to shake the blanket from her, but her ineffective efforts only caused additional pain against her restraints while the blanket remained in place. "Aralyn and our troops are a stronger force than you could dare comprehend. They'll destroy you."

"I guess it's a good thing we won't be the ones attacking." He pointed, redirecting his agitation to one of his soldiers. "You're in charge while I'm gone. If anything happens to her, anyone touches or disrespects her in any way, I will personally feed you to the infected myself." He squared his shoulders to Trish. "One day, under the right guidance, you will come to appreciate your true role in this new world we're building. Until then, you are my prisoner, and I am your warden." With that, he left the cave.

Every man headed up the steps but two. One sat on the last step and busied himself with chain-smoking cigarettes and doodling on a notepad. The other leaned forward, butt sitting on a ledge of rocks ten feet away, and glared at her. Trish ignored him, tilted her head against the metal pole, and closed her eyes.

Close to twenty minutes later, the rise and fall of her shoulders mimicked the beginning stages of sleep, as her mind focused on the chains surrounding her legs, hoping with every part of her that she could bust through metal by using her ability. The heat on her forehead increased in strength, sending a scorching burn down her thighs, knees, and both of her shins. She forced herself to physically relax against the agony, while praying those in the city remained safe against whatever these men were planning to do.

Her eyes opened with the smell of smoke, and she bit her lip against the feel of burning flesh. The closest soldier, nesting on the rock, saw the scorching hole forming on the blanket covering her lap first. He leapt to his feet and flew forward to snatch up the smoldering blanket and toss it roughly to the ground. The chains along her thighs were red hot, searing into her blistering flesh.

The other guard rushed toward her with a jug of water to douse the metal, but his companion forcefully gripped his arm to stop him. "Leave it. She did this to herself."

The man roughly shook off the hand. "Fuck you. I'm not going to piss off the lieutenant. He really will throw me in with the mutants." The man continued forward and upended the jug over the searing metal. The sizzling would have sounded comical if the pain in her legs wasn't so great.

Using his pen, he lifted the hot links away from her skin, while dousing the water until the container was empty. "The metal's still hot. Go up top and get some more." A few seconds later, he glared at his unresponsive colleague. "I'll make sure to bring up your name when Lieutenant Waska asks why she was left in so much pain."

The man glowered at them both before spinning on his boot heels. He slung his rifle and stomped his way up the stairs. The instant the soldier vanished, the remaining guard's form relaxed. His agitated mannerisms revealed how much he hated this babysitting task.

"Thank you," Trish said, trying to sound sympathetic.

"You and I have nothing to say to each other," he said.

With the sound of the first loud pop, both searched the stairs. They heard screams and rapid gunfire beyond the upper steps. The guard twisted his worried scowl to her.

She shrugged. "It's not me. Maybe Aralyn and the city brought the fight to you instead."

He focused on the flight of stairs for a few more moments before his head turned toward where he had propped his rifle against the base of the last step. Twenty feet, maybe farther. Trish paid close attention to the uncertainty in his eyes. The man feared moving toward the growing noise of battle, yet he also shifted uneasily, not liking the feeling of being unarmed. The latter of his two concerns won out, and he took a step toward his weapon.

The sickening cry was close, and so was the growling that trailed it. He froze in place, unsure of what to do. They both waited and listened as eerie silence filled the cavern.

An enormous mass bolted down the steps, halted on all fours at the bottom, and snarled directly at the man. Trish's eyes widened, and her heart leapt. The beautiful beast was Molly, looking as big and strong as ever. Trish's amazement grew as she stared at her. She was nearly unrecognizable with her front patches of white fur and muzzle stained red. Fresh blood.

Trish's eyes darted over to the movement flashing in the corner of her peripheral. The soldier swung his hand to his boot and yanked out a hunting knife. Desperate, she jerked her bound legs sideways into the soldier, her eyes tearing as she grunted against the gripping pain. The swinging momentum smacked her bound calves into the guard's lower legs, and he staggered a few steps to the right but didn't fall. With the knife raised, he readied himself for the dog, but not for the three Gramites that had leapt down the steps behind it.

The Gramites and Molly snarled in unison at the man. Terror filled him. His arms dropped flimsily to his sides, and the knife slipped from his grasp. His legs went soft with the reality of his approaching death, and he fell to his knees with a whimper. The cluster of Gramites and lone canine lunged at once, all with the same purpose.

Trish turned her head away and closed her eyes to the slaughter until the man's gurgling screams came to a sudden end.

CHAPTER EIGHTEEN

After locating her gear inside her Gladiator, which Waska and his men had left near a faded sign that read, Welcome to Wonderland Cave, Trish dressed and retrieved her helmet from her duffel bag in the car storage. Both dripping wet from the rain downpour, Trish and JW studied each other. Hoping JW understood her thoughts, Trish climbed behind the wheel after Molly jumped in, with JW looking on. Trish wanted the might of horde-four to help protect Rapid City, but whether JW would risk her clan for what may be a massacre, to defend survivors who would more than likely shoot the Gramites on sight, this decision was one JW would have to make. Either way, Trish needed to go.

With the heavy rain and the poor condition of the roads, the drive from the cave to the interstate took longer than she hoped. Knowing Interstate 90 to the south toward Rapid City was still under construction from previous flood damage, Trish weighed her options. She could head north to Sturgis and get on Highway 34 or take the bumpy ride of the train tracks, hopefully shaving some time off. While she evaluated her route through the fiercely swaying windshield wipers, Trish watched JW and those in the horde rush past the Gladiator on all fours and head south.

Without second guessing the uncertain feeling inside, Trish pressed on the accelerator and followed. The horde moved fast, determined with their course. They swerved off the interstate at Tilford and took muddy back roads, passing over a few rickety bridges and pathways that resembled small ponds in the vehicle's headlights.

At one point, when Trish had to drive through the swiftly moving waters of the flooded Antilope Creek, Molly nervously whined out her displeasure, The forceful swells slammed midway up the side of Trish's door. Halfway through the creek, JW slipped under the water. Trish was about to lower the passenger window and go out after her, but Champ yanked JW to her feet and shouted at Trish, signaling her to continue. A few of the Gramites, not trusting the watery depth, clutched tight to the vehicle and let go the moment Trish steered the armored chariot safely to the other side.

Seeing the outline of Rapid City's wall in the distance, Trish waited a few minutes for the Gramites to collect themselves before resuming their run. As their group drew closer to the outer wall, JW veered them sharply to a road heading east, running parallel with the city. She felt the danger as well, Trish reflected, knowing JW was taking them to the side by the main gate. As if answering her mental observation, JW hollered out to her, above the slapping of rain, and pressed on faster.

A streak of red light filled the sky straight ahead, followed by an explosion at the outer wall. Trish's body turned completely numb. She knew by the color from the rocket, someone had just fired an AT8 at Rapid City. She understood then, JW wasn't taking her to the main gate. They were heading instead toward the cliff surrounding the ravine overlooking the city. The same location from where the rocket discharged.

As the rain came down harder, Christina and Jennifer waited by the front door of the farmhouse, wet and close together. Although no one responded to the second round of knocking and the inside lights were off, a truck sat parked in the driveway. The outside lights surrounding the area had prematurely kicked on due to the storm, and muddy runoff flowed across the gravel road into ditches already full of rushing rainwater. Shivering on this porch until someone showed wasn't ideal.

"Maybe they're in the barn," Christina said to her daughter, trying to help Jennifer hold on to her fading hope of seeing her mom today.

Spotting the flash of worry in her daughter's eyes, Christina's stomach tightened. She knelt beside her to force their visual connection. "Will you please talk to me, Jennifer? I understand you're upset, but you need to tell me what I can do to help you through this."

Jennifer scrunched her face and looked away. Christina wasn't sure if her daughter wanted to cry, scream, or do a mixture of both. Whatever her daughter was feeling, Christina needed some type of reaction, anything other than Jennifer's continued silence. When Jennifer backed away, Christina didn't stop her. Instead, she dropped her head in defeat.

"I don't enjoy camping here anymore." Jennifer wasn't angry. She didn't cry, but the worry in her daughter's voice immediately chilled Christina.

Her mind rolled through every fear it could think of, some much worse than others. She had to work at keeping her tone calm before she spoke. "Jennifer, did anyone…hurt you?"

Jennifer peered at her feet and shook her head. "Everyone's nice here, but Olivia—" her words trailed off.

Clenching her jaw, Christina fought to stay calm. If that woman laid a hand on her daughter or uttered any unkind words—She spoke slowly, evenly. "Jennifer, you know neither me nor your mom would ever allow anyone to harm you. If Olivia did or said anything, anything at all, then I need for you to tell me."

"I don't like the way she looks at mom when she thinks I'm not watching. It's the same way you look at mom, and it scares me." Jennifer's eyes filled with tears. "What if mom stays here and never comes home?" She blurted her question out, as if fear had trapped her words inside for weeks, building pressure.

Christina reached out and pulled her close, as her heart ached with her daughter's sobs. She held Jennifer protectively, trying to think of what to say to ease her concern. "Jennifer, no one knows what the future holds, and worrying about it won't help. Your mom and I love you. Nothing will change that. Plus, your mom's an amazing woman. Olivia would be a fool not to look."

The last five weeks had been hard on everyone, especially Jennifer. "Why don't we go check the barn, and if your mom's not there, we'll head to your grandma and grandpa's house."

Jennifer nodded into her shoulder, as her whimpering subsided.

Holding onto one another's hand, they rushed through the downpour and reached the barndoor right as the wooden barrier slid open. Tylor ushered them in and hobbled on his uninjured leg to close it. He secured his crutches under his arms and headed to the tackle room for several towels.

Christina thanked him, dried her face, and worked a towel along Jennifer's damp hair.

"I'm surprised to see you both here," he said, opening the humming refrigerator positioned beside the tack room.

Christina could tell by the way he was acting, he was uncomfortable.

He passed her a cold beer and Jennifer a bottled root beer.

"They closed New Underwood earlier, so we came to see if Trish was here."

He popped open a beer for himself. "I'm not sure about Trish, but Olivia and Aralyn are in a meeting with Doctor Burgos and the rest of the governors in Rapid City."

Christina knew then what was bothering him. His downcast mood had to do with Tracy and the drugs she had sold to Janet. Not wanting any reminders, Christina passed him the beer. "Thanks anyway, but we can't stay—"

An explosion rang out, a blast so powerful it vibrated the surrounding structure. Christina pulled Jennifer into her arms, as the horses kicked up a ruckus inside their stalls. Tylor placed the bottles on top of the refrigerator and hobbled to the door. He opened it, inhaled sharply, and tightened his grip on his crutches. "It's the wall," he said sharply to Christina. "Someone blew up part of the wall."

Christina rushed forward, Jennifer right beside her. Tylor was right. The next hill over, less than a mile away, a section of the wall was completely gone. "We need to head inside the city. Is anyone else here?"

"They won't open the gate. It's grown too dark, and Justin has the truck in the far pasture. With this rain, he could be stuck somewhere."

"Yes, they won't open the main gate, but in an attack, the guards monitor the smaller entrances to bring people into—" An animalistic scream rang out, interrupting Christina's words. They stared at one another.

Christina felt her blood turn to ice. She picked up Jennifer, as a flood of creatures fanned out through the opening. They were mutants, and several were veering toward the farm. Knowing they wouldn't make it to her car in time, Christina reached out for Tylor. "We need to hide," she said.

Fear masking his face, Tylor slammed the barndoor closed and engaged the latch. He scanned the barn and motioned for her to follow.

Gripping tight to Jennifer, Christina headed with him past the row of horse stalls.

As the rain died away, the wind kicked up along the top of the ravine. Waska watched the scene below through his binoculars, under the swaying of the canopy. The infected spilled into the opening of the outer wall, screaming so fiercely they could be heard from his position of safety, several miles away. Like always, their vicious battle cries both thrilled and frightened him.

Rapid City sounded their alarms. Numerous soldiers lined themselves along the top of the inner concrete barricade and began firing relentless rounds at the creatures from behind perched walkways.

He signaled one of his men to release the last container of mutants and another to target the inner wall, hoping the missile could reach the intended barrier several miles away.

Right after his soldier took aim and fired, the explosion impacted the earth, raining a cascade of dirt and rocks less than a hundred feet from the inner wall. He spun to his trooper. "If you miss a second time, I'll shoot you and do it myself. Aim higher!"

The private pointed the AT8 nervously toward Rapid City, and Waska squinted into the eyepiece. The second missile struck the target beautifully, sending chunks of rock and pieces of Aralyn's troops outward in a fountain of heightened chaos.

A helicopter rose from Rapid City, closely followed by another. They glided toward the outer wall, their spotlights searching the area below. Their forward momentum shifted to hovering, which was followed by rapid, high-powered rounds, drumming out past the thunderous uproar of screams and snarls. Various explosions rocketed rough ththe valley between both walls.

His eyes dropped to the opening in the inner fence line to the might of the mutants rushing on all fours straight for it. Aralyn's soldiers formed up quickly, filling the gap with both rifle fire and grenade rounds. His hands tightened firmly on the eyepiece frame. They needed the requested air support he had requested from the committee to complement double the mutants at his disposal.

He knew why they had shot down his request. With giving him an attack force of a hundred mutants strong, they didn't see the necessity for additional support. The leaders of the New United States had learned the hard way with their city in Seattle, Washington, that once one mutant entered inside the city walls, it bit and clawed its way from one person to the next. A chain-reaction occurred, and the infection took over. In Seattle, family, friends, and neighbors had transformed within minutes, and turned on each other. Hours later, the city had been lost. It had taken two military battalions and several long weeks for the New

United States to kill the mutants within Seattle and reclaim the city. Now, Seattle remained unoccupied, with less than a hundred troops to oversee security and the large number of prisoners tasked with burning the infected carcasses, removing the rubbish, and sterilizing everything within.

Nevertheless, this city wasn't like the unprepared Seattle. This was Rapid City. Aralyn and her troops were expecting and ready for an attack. He pointed to the helicopters. "Bring them down," he snapped at the private, feeling his temper rise. Must he do everything himself?

"Sir, the committee's online. They're requesting to speak with you."

Waska frowned from his second-in-command to the two soldiers filming the battle, relaying the confrontation straight to the New United States' satellite. He passed his second the binoculars and headed to the holographic display. Every member of the committee was positioned around the long table, with Frank Webber sitting at the very end. Waska's chest tightened at seeing the man. As far as Waska was concerned, Doctor Webber was the single brilliant mind at the table and the one man who truly frightened him. The patch covering his hollowed, right eye-socket added to his fearsome demeanor.

General Princeton was the first to speak. "Lieutenant Waska, explain to me why we're losing."

Thankfully, Frank Webber came to his aid. "General Princeton, Waska informed this committee what he needed, and none of you listened. I warned you all, this committee wasn't taking the threat seriously. Aralyn is a skilled commander who's as proficient at training her troops as she is with leading them." He motioned to the video feed at the center of the table—the one Waska's men were capturing for their entertainment, or lack thereof. "Princeton, this is exactly what happens when you grow too arrogant to heed the warnings of those who you consider inferior."

Waska spotted the missile in the video feed shoot off, monumentally missing both helicopters. He bit his tongue and waited. He knew what was coming.

"If his men were better trained, maybe this fight wouldn't be an epic failure," Princeton said.

Unable to keep down his temper, Waska spun toward the imbecile holding the AT8. He was prepared to kill one of his own. He stood motionless, his mind struggling to comprehend what was happening. A creature had its teeth around the private who fired the rocket, while the rest of his men stood fear-stricken, watching the same unbelievable scene. Coming out of his mental daze, Waska abruptly barked out orders.

Before his men could react, the area surrounding the trees exploded with fierce screams, as a swarm of enraged Gramites rushed in. With powerful swings and sharp, snapping teeth, they lunged for his men. The agonizing screams and cries sickening his soul.

Ignoring the harsh questions and intense gasps from the holographic display behind him, Waska ran forward to where his rifle lay. The moment his fingers brushed the muzzle, something knocked him violently off his feet, landing him face first into the mud. Wiping the dripping filth from his eyes, he spun his head around but couldn't see his attacker. What he did witness was a Gramite, face drenched in human blood, picking up Waska's robust, second-in-command easily off the ground, as if the man's two hundred and twenty pounds of solid frame were nothing. With the man flailing over his head, the Gramite slammed him to the ground so hard, Waska was certain he felt the earth shake beneath him. The creature looked straight at Waska, screamed, and snapped the sobbing soldier's body in half in a way the spine was never meant to bend. Waska dropped his head toward the mud and vomited more violently than he ever had in his life.

A pair of black boots stepped into his line-of-sight. He wiped his hand across his face to remove the mud and sickness from it and looked up. Patricia Webber stood towering above him, hair soaked, yet looking as powerful as ever. He wasn't surprised to see that she was no longer his prisoner.

"I'm not the only formidable woman here," Trish said, and the female Gramite beside her leaned her sneer inches away from Waska's face. Her throat gave a gurgling-grumble, and Waska closed his eyes, waiting for the attack.

The seconds ticked slowly by. It felt as if time itself had stopped the rotating clock of his life, purely to draw out his final moments of existence with misery.

"Ms. Webber, I'm glad to finally meet you." When Waska heard General Preston speak, he opened his eyes. Trish was leaning over the hologram, the female Gramite directly beside her.

Trish ignored him. "Father, you're responsible for this. You all are. One day soon, I will hold each and every one of you accountable for your crimes."

The female Gramite shrieked at those in the hologram right before Trish powered it off.

He remained motionless as Trish turned toward Rapid City, donned her helmet, and activated her wrist processor. "Aralyn, I have horde-four with me. My father's troops are dead. Where do you need us?" Waska tried but couldn't hear what Aralyn was saying inside Trish's helmet. "Okay, we're heading in. Make sure you spread the word to the troops not to shoot the Gramites."

The moment Trish deactivated the link and removed her helmet, she signaled to the female Gramite. The female growled, not to him, but to those behind him. A second later, Waska felt powerful claws rip at his face and neck. He jerked forward, and tried to crawl away, but several were on him, ripping into every part of his body. Before he took his final breath, he continued to scream out, begging for an end to the creatures' razor-sharp slashing.

Christina closed her eyes and prayed. Jennifer wrapped herself in her mother's arms, as the shadow moved along the crack underneath the door. "I'm scared," Jennifer whispered, and Christina held her tighter.

The mutants were in the barn, smelling the air, searching for where they were hiding. The horses shrieked and kicked inside their stalls, but their flesh wasn't what the mutants were seeking. The infected hungered for the taste of humans.

Placing a hand gently on the wood, Tylor bent closer, listening. Christina wanted to tell him to move away from the door, but she was too worried the mutants would hear. Instead, she whispered hushed sounds in her daughter's ear, trying her best to comfort her.

No other explosions had gone off for close to twenty minutes, and the gunfire was drifting farther away in the opposite direction. They were out here alone with no militia support, while several mutants roamed the farm, hunting. They needed to get a signal out to let Rapid City know they were here. Smoke could work, but she didn't know how to do it safely without giving away their position to the mutants.

Her head shot upward with the sudden penetrating squeak inside the room. She locked eyes with Tylor. He stood stationary beside the large freezer he had been attempting to push in front of the door. Of all the stupid things to do—why? Both their frightened eyes darted toward the direction of the growl they heard from the next room, as the sounds of heavy scampering drew closer. The growl pitched into a cry, alerting the others.

Placing Jennifer on the box beside her, Christina jumped up, rushed forward, and helped Tylor slide the heavy appliance over to block the entrance. At once, a bang rang out when something struck hard against the wooden barrier. Christina took several steps backward, as Tylor stacked items on and around the freezer.

"It's not going to hold," he shouted.

Christina spun to where her daughter sat, wide-eyed, too frightened to move. She spied a small opening above her. "The window!" she screamed, rushing forward. "Tylor, help me move the shelf!"

Jennifer shifted to the side, as her mother and Tylor threw off the items resting on each shelf, shimmied the large wooden container over, and tilted it against the wall. Christina climbed up to the opening first. When she was situated, Tylor passed Jennifer to her. "I'm going to lower you down. Once you're on the ground, stay in the shadows and don't move."

The pounding on the door grew forceful, shaking several items off the freezer and onto the floor. Jennifer's eyes shot to her mom. Her head shook, and her grip tightened on Christina's arms.

"It's okay, Jennifer. It's just like playing hide-and-seek."

Jennifer reluctantly released her grip. Christina helped Jennifer glide her legs and head through the opening. She clasped Jennifer's hands, holding her upper body farther out the window before letting go of her daughter. She pulled herself into the room, as they heard more banging against the door. This time the lock snapped, and the freezer shifted. Tylor rushed forward and pushed his weight against the makeshift barricade. "Go!" he shouted. "I'll be right behind you."

Christina grasped to a roof brace and wiggled her body through the opening. Right as her legs were clearing the gap, a sharp nail stabbed through her jeans and penetrated her left leg. She felt the painful sting as the nail sliced down her flesh when she dropped to the damp ground below. Stumbling against the throbbing ache, she hugged Jennifer in her arms, backed up a few paces, and waited for Tylor. She watched his head and then his arms poke out. She took a few additional steps to give him more room to drop.

Suddenly, everything happened at once. His eyes widened, an animalistic scream echoed out, and his face distorted in either pain or horror. Christina dropped Jennifer and rushed forward, jumping up and reaching for his hand. When their fingertips touched, he gave an ear-piercing cry and was yanked vehemently back inside the building.

Her tears fell as she heard his blood-curdling screams and the loud thumping coming from inside the barn. She swallowed down her urge to be sick, scooped up Jennifer, and rushed through the pasture toward the gravel road, which snaked along the acres to the north. The muscles in her calf cramped where the nail had pierced her, but she had to ignore the pain and push herself forward in order to get her daughter to safety. Jennifer was all that mattered now.

She heard the barn door smash open behind them, and she knew they wouldn't make it. That's when she saw her one bit of hope. Spilling water from an overflow pipe connected to the pond. It was big enough for her daughter to crawl inside, possibly even herself if she hurried. The circular concrete outlet was sticking out of the side of a five-foot drop-off in the terrain, with the gravel road running a foot above it. The screams grew closer, and her heart pounded loudly in her ears. Gripping tighter to Jennifer, she hurried toward the outpour. The nearer she drew, the muddier the ground became. She lowered Jennifer, reached out, and opened the thick grating covering the opening. Her feet were sinking down in the mud, legs growing tired from the added exertion. She helped Jennifer first, lifted a foot from the sucking mud, and pulled higher on the metal.

Jennifer's shriek was sharp, as was the cry that emanated behind Christina. She knew she was too late. She slammed the grating, pushed her body against it, and yelled for Jennifer to crawl farther in.

"Mother." Jennifer sobbed, her tiny hands pressing hard on the grating.

"No baby," she said, and she pried her daughter's fingers from the slats. "Crawl inside, and stay there," she insisted, her tears stinging her eyes.

Wishing to draw the beast fully onto her and away from the pipe her daughter was in, she fought against the sludge and stumbled up the side of the muddy pit as fast as she could. Once clear, she stood, mentally readying herself for what was to come. Christina rotated, preparing to fight and protect her daughter until her last breath. Gripped with fear at seeing the hatred in the distorted features of the mutant rushing at her, less than half a minute away, Christina bit down on her lip and shuddered.

"Mother!" Jennifer screamed.

"No, Jennifer—go back," Christina cried, as her daughter climbed from the pipe and struggled in the mud. She could see in the mutant's eyes, the monster was readying itself to lunge at her daughter, and not at her. Christina swung her arms in the air and screamed out swearwords at the beast. She was too late. The mutant was preparing to pounce.

The moment Jennifer grabbed hold of her arm, the scene exploded around them. An item flew out from above, and smacked the mutant hard in the face, spinning the bright-orange glower away from them. The object of attack, a militia helmet, dropped to the ground and rolled a few feet away. Equally surprised, the creature skidded in the mud, its eyes darting ferociously around. A scream echoed out, followed by a solid mass, another infected flying for the mutant.

Before Christina could work out what was going on, a figure covered in filth rushed in, and slid into the mud-puddle beneath the drainpipe, like a baseball player stealing home. Its arms reached out for Jennifer, and Christina yelled, while pulling her daughter to her.

"Christina, it's me," Trish insisted, this time securing an arm around Jennifer's waist. She lifted the grate and placed their daughter in. Trish held out her hand, and when Christina took it, Trish practically pulled her off her feet. Trish directed Christina inside the opening after Jennifer. "Stay in here until I come for you."

Frantically, Christina tried to pull Trish in after them, but she wasn't fast or strong enough. Trish's head stretched upward. She whistled and cried out, mimicking the infected. From the gravel road, another creature jumped into the mud beside Trish. Frightened, Christina pushed on the grate to help her wife.

Trish spun sideways and pressed her shoulder against it. "Damnit, Christina, stay with our daughter," Trish yelled.

As if agreeing, the female creature beside Trish rotated to the pipe and snapped out a screech. Christina's eyebrows shot upward. This female was a Gramite, not a mutant, and it, like the Gramites joining the one attacking the mutant, was aiding her wife.

A few seconds later, a large animal, a dog, caked in both blood and mud, jumped down from the road and stood in the puddle beside the Gramite. Trish's Saint Bernard, her wife's dog!

Trish told Molly to stand guard, and she stumbled off through the mud to join the other Gramites. Christina and Jennifer both shifted closer to the grate until the female Gramite groused at them. Jennifer and Christina both backed away.

Two other mutants rushed into the mix, and at least a dozen more Gramites arrived. The boisterous impacts they heard, as bodies slammed fiercely into one another, were frightening. Having the two types of infected creatures so close, Christina was now finding it easy to tell who the Gramites were, and who were the mutants. The mutants were larger, both in height and mass, and their distorted features, arms, legs, skin, even the green scales of their face, were more beast than human in both appearance and form. Trish fought side-by-side with the Gramites, matching them both with fury and strength, yet she moved quicker and was more agile than either.

Arms pounded, claws slashed, and teeth ripped into flesh, as the area filled with shrieks and screams from the brutal battle. The trampled pasture after the hard rain left the area slick with earthy filth. Escalating patches of mud caused some to slip and others to fall, while Gramites and mutants fought to gain the upper hand, each trying desperately to defeat the other.

After a powerful blow to her upper body, Christina saw Trish stumble a few feet forward. Trish reeled, stretched out the soreness of her neck, and rushed back into the fray. Christina's heart gave a worried flutter. Molly whined at Christina and so did the female Gramite. Were they reassuring her?

One mutant captured a Gramite and flipped him upward, high in the air. The Gramite gripped onto the mutant's ears, and the female beside the pipe cried out in distress. Trish rushed forward, smacked into the mutant, and they all tumbled to the ground together. When the Gramite stood, it held out two black devices in its hands, as if it were showing Trish what it stole. Trish spun to the mutant and glared.

Christina squinted as the mutant clawed at its head and screamed out in agony. She covered her daughter's eyes right before a dark, thick goo exploded from every orifice and the mutant dropped to the ground. *NORAD*, Christian thought, gripping her hand tight to the metal links, as she sought to reassure herself that Trish was fine. Not only was she uninjured, but she was moving briskly toward the next mutant.

Christina was unsure how long the battle lasted before the last mutant fell. She didn't take her eyes off Trish and the Gramites, even when the helicopter flew above the pasture. She was too mesmerized by how this night had revealed so much she had been blind to.

Trish moved forward and retrieved the helmet. When the helicopter circled around, preparing to land, Trish waved her arms outward, signaling to the helicopter to leave, while reassuring the restless Gramites the helicopter was friendly.

The female Gramite beside Trish's dog, both covered in mud, gave a low moan and opened the grate. When she did, a familiarity of the subtle sound sparked inside. Christina pulled her daughter backward. The Gramite sent out another moan, louder this time.

Trish rushed forward and moved beside the Gramite. She held out her hand to Christina, her features soft, sympathetic. "Christina, it's okay. Take my hand."

"Adam, Gabe—"

Trish nodded. "I know. It's okay."

Christina looked at the Gramite and her wife. Slowly, she inched herself and Jennifer forward and reached out for Trish. The female Gramite took a few steps away, and Trish pulled Jennifer into her arms and led Christina from the muddy trench. Jennifer snuggled her upper body into a ball in her mom's arms, as Trish held their daughter protectively and led them to the gravel road.

When Trish noticed the way Christina was limping, she lowered Jennifer and bent closer to inspect the gash past the ripped opening of her jeans. "As soon as the Gramites leave, we'll head to the hospital and get you checked out. I'll have Aralyn send a few teams here to get your car and come deal with these bodies."

They headed to where Trish had left her vehicle by the barn. She placed Jennifer and Molly inside and opened the car hatch. After passing Jennifer a sleeping bag for warmth, Trish thoroughly cleaned and wrapped Christina's leg, who marveled at how her wife tended to the injuries on the Gramites. Once she finished, Trish turned to the female Gramite from their past. After a few minutes of staring without verbally or physically communicating to one another, the Gramite moaned to Trish and called out to the horde with a deep bellow. At once, the female spun and rushed off, leading the Gramites away from the area. Christina sat on the tailgate motionless, trying hard to grasp the perplexing way life's events were unfolding right in front of her.

Trish lowered her visor and connected to Aralyn. She spoke to her godmother again, telling her the Gramites were a safe distance away. They could now move troops into the area. Once the call ended, Trish removed her helmet and placed it in the duffel bag.

Christina jumped up so Trish could close the hatch and touched her hand to gain her attention. "Tylor's in the barn. He didn't make it."

"I know. I found his body before locating you," Trish said. "Do you want me to have someone radio Janet to meet us at the hospital?" she asked.

Without warning, a wave of grief caught in Christina's throat and her eyes watered. Hearing Janet's name was bad enough, but having her wife say it, and in a way which intimated that Trish had come to terms with them being romantically involved—the agony was sharp, penetrating.

"Trish, I've never been—" Christina couldn't go on. What was she supposed to say? What words could she use to tell Trish what happened over the weekend? Feeling overwhelmed by so many painful emotions, Christina couldn't fight her tears.

Trish wrapped her gently in her arms. "Christina, I'm sorry for my anger the other day. If you need Janet there for support, then it's okay. I want you to be happy, even if it's with someone else."

Shaking her head, Christina sank into Trish's body. She didn't want Trish to continue. Even if her words were meant to be supportive, they still hurt. Trish loosened her grip, but she didn't release her. The moment Christina brought her hand up, and placed it onto Trish's chest, Trish broke her hold and backed away.

Trish stared at her, uncertain. "Why were you both out here? Why'd you leave the city?"

"I was heading to New Underwood to find you, but the guards told me the outpost had been closed and that you all came back to the city. I assumed you were here." Christina brushed at her eyes, inwardly forcing herself on. "I've handled everything so wrong. All of it. You, my father, what you're trying to accomplish here, and I'm so sorry."

Trish shifted to the side, and Christina moved with her, reaching for her arm, preventing her wife from turning away. "If I could take it all back, I would. But I can't."

"Christina—"

"No, please listen. I was hurt, angry, and I feared losing you. Not like when you were in the coma, but forever. I know it doesn't make this right, but I was desperate. I wanted to keep you safe, but instead I ended up hurting you—hurting us in the process."

Christina glanced at the area where the battle had occurred. "I didn't understand any of this. What you were trying to do here. The importance of it. But I do now." Christina took a step closer, her eyes pleading. "Please come home, Trish. I love you." She motioned toward the vehicle. "Jennifer and I miss you. I know I've screwed up, but I also know we can work through anything as long as we're together."

When Trish shook her head, Christina's heart dropped. "You kicked me out of your life, almost out of Jennifer's."

Christina kept her eyes low, feeling too ashamed to look at Trish. "I never wanted to lose you. I was trying desperately to get you to rethink your choices. I know my actions were wrong, but I can't change what I've done. I can promise it'll never happen again."

"Janet—" Trish glared up at the sky, as a shudder passed through her. "The thought of even kissing someone else is unfathomable. What you heard Olivia say the other day, she wasn't talking about us—"

"I know," Christina said, touching Trish's cheek. "Perez told me. I left messages for you twice a day, but Janet bribed the sergeant at headquarters to make sure you never got them. The day you came over to mow, my mother had given Janet her spare keys to drop off at the house. That's how she got inside. Trish, I never let her in. She told me she was the one who mowed, and she stole the letter you left for me. I found it Saturday morning in her apartment at the old hotel."

A flash of bitterness crossed Trish's face, but just as fast, her resentment disappeared.

"No, I—" Christina said.

"You don't need to tell me," Trish said, cutting her off. "It's not my business what you do—"

"It is," Christina insisted. She felt desperate, seeing the distant look in Trish's eyes. Christina knew that look. She'd seen it the day after Trish woke up from her coma, when she thought Christina was with someone else. Trish was trying to pull away, ease her emotional anguish. "Trish, I'm your wife, and you're mine. I would never knowingly sleep with someone else. Ever."

Trish's head spun to her so fast it reminded Christina of how Trish had acted last week in New Underwood. Like Aralyn, Trish had learned well on how to control her emotions. But this sudden shift of anger on Trish's face, the unexpected way her body tensed, the rawness was unexpected, frightening even. Had she done this to her wife? Was the stress she had placed upon Trish the reason for Trish's lack of restraint?

She took a step to increase the distance between them, but Trish moved with her. "What do you mean 'you would never knowingly sleep with someone else'?" Trish grasped her arms, her deep tone demanding answers. "Christina, what happened?"

This rage was why Aralyn didn't want Trish to know. Would Trish hunt Janet and Tracy down? Kill them? Uncertain what to do, feeling for the first time lost when it came to her wife's reactions, Christina lowered her forehead onto Trish's chest and sobbed. Trish was motionless at first, but as Christina felt her limbs go numb, unworking, Trish wrapped her tightly into her arms and protected her.

As they stood under the barn light, Christina continued to release her tears. Trish lovingly stroked her hair while telling her repeatedly everything would be okay. Several minutes passed before Trish asked her again what happened. Feeling her wife was more in control of her anger, Christina told her. She talked about going to the club after leaving New Underwood, and how Janet had bought her a drink. She explained what happened when she woke up the next morning in Janet's bed, about going to Aralyn's and Susan's house, and how, thanks to Susan, they discovered someone had drugged her. Christina felt Trish's muscles tighten, but not enough to cause her to worry. By the time she told Trish how Janet hadn't been the only one involved, that a man had also taken part in the rape, Trish, too, was in tears.

They stood, wrapped in each other's arms, even when the vehicle door opened and Jennifer climbed out. Their daughter didn't ask questions. Instead, she encircled her arms around their damp, muddy legs and silently waited.

CHAPTER NINETEEN

Trish scanned her hand over the screen, paid the credits for the multiple containers of food and drinks, and headed to the waiting room with Jennifer and Doctor Burgos. Jennifer held out one drink she was carrying to Karen, the other one she gave to Givens. Trish handed Givens the warm food containers and helped get Jennifer situated on the chair with her food and drink.

"Are you sure you're not hungry?" Trish asked Eva, who was pacing close to the exam room door. She declined.

Concerned by why the exam was taking so long, Trish peered through the window slit on the door. Christina was still in the exam room with Susan and a female doctor. When they first arrived, the emergency room doctor had cleaned and stitched up Christina's leg injury. Not long after, another doctor showed up with Susan and asked to speak with Christina alone. This couldn't be about her leg.

Doctor Burgos was trying to get his wife to sit and eat something by the time Aralyn and Carlen arrived. Aralyn observed her goddaughter briefly before making her way into the exam room. Trish turned away from the door and those in the gathering. She headed through the hall to clear her rising resentment.

"Are you doing okay?" Carlen asked, coming up behind her.

Trish waited until a few nurses passed before answering. "Why didn't anyone tell me?"

Carlen's tone held empathy. "Believe me, we all wanted to, but we couldn't. Aralyn, Doctor Burgos, hell, even I was worried you'd go off and kill someone, and all of us knew what that would've done to you. We needed to investigate this fully, figure out who was involved, and remove them from the city."

Trish's head snapped around. "Janet's gone?"

"Yes. Janet, Tracy, and the man who took part in the assault. Perez and two guards are taking them to Salt Lake now to stand trial."

"Tracy? How was she involved?"

Carlen was every bit surprised. "I'm sorry. I thought you knew. Tracy was the one who sold Janet ketamine. This isn't the first time a drug-induced rape has happened in our community. Unfortunately, Tracy and the owner of the nightclub that's across the street from Eva and Christina's restaurant, have been doing this for over a year. Christina wasn't the first. Tracy provided the drugs, and the owner of the nightclub set up the rest. Olivia, the governors, and HQ are still investigating this matter. So far, they've found three other victims and two additional assailants."

Trish couldn't believe what she was hearing. That explained why Olivia was so detached that morning.

"What Tracy did for Janet was more to hurt you."

"But Janet…I thought she actually cared for Christina," Trish said. She worked hard to keep her anger down.

Carlen shrugged. "Maybe, in her own way. Janet said she was chatting with a group at the club about how her pursuit for Christina was a lost cause. The owner of the club overheard and suggested maybe getting Christina in bed would seal the deal. He told her about Tracy and the ketamine, offering Janet the opportunity to recoup her credits, and then some, if she let him record it. Apparently, he ended up paying her triple to join in. She said she had made a spur-of-the-moment decision, one she regretted soon after."

Feeling her control snap, Trish slammed her fist straight through the closest wall. A nurse down the hall gasped, and Carlen anxiously tried to settle Trish's enraged emotions. The control of Trish's anger didn't come from Carlen's motherly words, though, but from a warm, familiar touch on her arm. She spun, not sure what to say or do. Trish felt completely lost.

Christina placed a hand over Trish's heart and curled herself into her arms. The contact was soothing. Trish closed her eyes and swallowed. "I did this. You went to the bar because of what I said."

Christina brought her head up, her eyes set firm, her willfulness unmoving. "Don't you dare blame yourself for the vile actions of others," Christina said. She stroked the tears of anger off Trish's cheek. "No matter why I was at the bar or how drunk I was, nothing gives someone the right to do what they did. Normal people don't violate others like this."

Christina stopped talking when Jennifer made her way over. "Mom, can we go home?" Jennifer asked, pulling on Trish's arm.

Trish picked her up. Her daughter was exhausted. Like her and Christina, Jennifer was completely covered in dried filth and ready to leave the commotion of the hospital. "Do you want me to drive you both home?" Trish asked Christina.

Christina's lips pulled slightly downward. "Are you not going to stay at the house?"

Before Trish could respond, Jennifer's arms encircled her neck. "Please, Mom. At least for tonight."

Keeping her concerns to herself, Trish nodded. "When does Aralyn want us to report in?" she asked Carlen.

"The team's meeting at HQ Wednesday morning at seven. Christina, do you want me to tell your parents you're leaving?"

"I'll do it." Christina sounded defeated. "Give me a moment," she said to Trish.

With a heavy heart, Trish waited. She wished she could take Christina's pain away. Ease her soul from the darkness which had forced itself into her life. Trish had her own demons to face, though, and she needed to do so alone.

Trish awoke Tuesday early morning in the spare bedroom of Christina's house, thirty minutes before her alarm went off. She snatched up the camouflage militia outfit she had pulled from her duffel bag the night before and headed to the downstairs bathroom to shower. After everyone washed up and ate, Trish tucked Jennifer into bed. Since it was so late, they left the needed discussion for this morning.

Entering the kitchen, Trish smiled at seeing Molly with her head in Christina's lap, as Christina stroked behind the dog's ear. Christina motioned to the coffee cup sitting on the counter. She looked as if she had gotten little sleep herself. "I figured you could use it."

Trish dropped her bag beside the counter. "Thanks."

"I scrubbed your bodysuit and hung it in the laundry room to dry."

Trish prepared her coffee and took the empty seat beside Christina. "You didn't have to, but thank you."

"Are we over?"

The question was straightforward. It needed to be asked, yet the suddenness was unexpected. Trish's gaze lowered with her cup. The warm touch of Christina's hand on hers brought Trish to focus her attention on Christina. They stared at each other, their nonverbal messages expressing volumes of information to one another. Soon Christina nodded and gently pulled her hand away.

"I'm not doing good, Christina," Trish said, her voice just above a whisper. "I go from crying one minute, to a flash of uncontrollable anger the next, to feeling completely numb inside. Half the time I don't even know who I am anymore, or if I ever did to be honest."

"I'm guessing you think being around me won't help you figure this out?"

Trish could feel herself pulling away, protecting her heart from the pain she was causing them both. "My life, our relationship, everything inside me is turning unhealthy, toxic. I don't like the person I'm becoming." Trish rubbed her hands on her pantlegs. She needed to be honest. Christina deserved to hear the truth. "I've got to take a break from all of this, Christina. I have to find some confidence in myself without outside interference."

Christina covered her mouth with a trembling hand and closed her eyes.

"Christina, this has to do with me. Even before we met, I had a hard time believing I was good enough to be loved. When you came into my life, you, our relationship, every part of this experience was a blessing. Your self-confidence, your emotional strength, the woman you are, even now you take my breath away. You loved me so fiercely, and I finally felt like I belonged."

"But now you don't?"

Trish struggled to take a few sips from her coffee, wishing to clear the lump rising in her throat. "Last month, when everything I loved was ripped away, I was lost. Bitter, jealous, angry. I resented myself for believing I was actually deserving of happiness in the first place." Seeing the argument in Christina's expression, Trish touched Christina's arm. "No, all of this happened for a reason, Christina. Don't you see? I need to find my inner strength. I can't keep going through life thinking I'm good enough solely because you or others love me." Trish pushed her cup away and leaned closer. "I love you, Christina, but I've got to find love in myself before I can expect to receive it from others."

"What do I tell Jennifer?"

Trish stood. She felt herself add a few more bricks to the wall around her heart. "That I'll be here whenever she needs me." She grabbed her items and called Molly to her. "I'll always love you, Christina," she said.

No longer able to see the pain burdening Christina, Trish left the house, with Molly following close behind.

Doctor Jenkins motioned to three locations on a blown-up map of North America lying on the conference room table at HQ. The three cities, San Francisco, El Paso, and New York, each were circled with a bright red marker. "These here are the three cities with prison camps that I know about, but overhearing the guards talk, I'm positive there are more."

Trish scowled from Doctor Jenkins to Aralyn. Hearing the cruel treatment of those who the New United States caught fleeing their corrupt rule brought her anger to new heights. From the faces of the others in the room, she was not alone with her resentment. Those in the bunkers who had heard the warnings from her mother's video, who realized the ones in charge were to blame for worldwide genocide and wanted no part of it, they were now prisoners being tortured, and they needed help.

Doctor Jenkins tapped on a blue circle which surrounded Seattle, Washington. "When one of their experiments got loose, they lost the city to the infection. Last month they sent in troops to kill all the mutants. After they cleared the city, they brought in over a thousand prisoners to remove the bodies and work on cleanup."

"We should start there," Aralyn said. "I don't want to stretch our personnel in Rapid City thin, so I asked Salt Lake to give us some additional troops to help. Kansas City is sending teams out to these other cities to gather intel." She spoke to everyone around the table. "I understand the importance of our mission in New Underwood, but for right now, once the walls are repaired and fortified, we need to turn our focus to freeing these prisoners. With that being said, we'll still have Doctor Burgos, Olivia, and our newest member of the team, Doctor Jenkins, working at the labs in New Underwood. They will study samples and information already collected and develop an agreed upon operating procedure to combat the infection. The rest of you, I'll need your experience elsewhere."

Olivia's head came upward, and she asked, "Are you leaving us any guards?"

"You'll have four, and I'm giving you Staff Sergeant Young as well. Trish, once we've taken control of Seattle, if everything goes as planned, I'll want your team to return to New Underwood." Aralyn took a few seconds to consider the map and those seated at the table. "Placing New Underwood on the backburner isn't ideal, but we have no other option."

Trish's mind turned to the image of her father and those he worked for. "What about New York?"

"Too dangerous," Aralyn said, peering at the city circled in red with a star following the city's name. "New York is their stronghold. We don't have the strength for an attack of that magnitude. For right now, let's keep our focus on the prison camps we know about, claiming Seattle, and building up our numbers. Phillips, we're doubling recruit training for the next two cycles, so you and Givens will stay behind and help HQ. If everything goes like we hope in Seattle and San Francisco, I'd like to hit Colorado Springs early next year. After we control the west half of America, we'll revisit striking New York."

Once the meeting ended, Olivia made her way over to where Trish was gathering her things. "Trish, about Tracy…"

"Nobody blames you, Olivia."

"If I would have reported Tracy and Tylor's drug use two months ago—"

"Then they would have been given a warning, but it wouldn't have changed what Tracy had done. You know this, everyone here knows this, even Christina. She doesn't blame you."

This did seem to alleviate some of Olivia's uneasiness. She changed the subject. "Did Doctor Burgos tell you the city awarded you Spirit?"

Trish nodded. "I was actually going to talk to you about him. When I'm gone—"

"He'll be well cared for."

Trish smiled. "Thank you."

"Your room at my place is also available if you should ever need somewhere to crash."

Trish shook her head no. "Since Doctor Burgos is living with Eva again, I asked him if I could stay at his lab for a while. I appreciate the offer, but I'm enjoying the solitude."

"Then it's true? You and Christina separated?"

Trish shoved the last of the papers in her backpack. The speed at which news traveled throughout the city was grossly exasperating. She knew she had to steer her reply on the right course, especially if she and Olivia had any hope of a continued friendship. She was as honest and direct as she could be. "Yes, but not because I'm not in love with her. I have some issues to sort out on my own."

Olivia didn't respond right away, and when she did, her tone held a sliver of masked disappointment. "I understand. If you ever need to talk, I'll be here."

Thanking her, Trish left HQ and headed to her Gladiator. She tossed her backpack in the passenger seat, waited until Molly settled, and read through the list of additional Gramite samples Doctor Burgos asked her to collect over the next few days. Most were blood draws and stool samples. Even though gathering feces wasn't on her list of exciting things to do, leaving the city for a few days of quiet camping with Molly and horde-four was.

With a heightened sense of freedom, she drove through the last gate and headed toward Sturgis, South Dakota.

TO BE CONTINUED IN
BOOK THREE OF THE ALPHA EVOLUTION SERIES

ACKNOWLEDGMENTS

A big thanks to my editor Lori Lake for the hard work and dedication you put into this manuscript. Another big thanks to my publishers at Launch Point Press.

ABOUT THE AUTHOR

Michele Coffman is an author who also moonlights as a Journeyman Plumber in the Kansas City, Missouri, area. She's an Army Veteran with fifteen years of service where she froze in Germany, sweated in Kuwait, unknowingly bedded down with a tarantula in Nicaragua, almost got bit by a poisonous snake in Ecuador, and even sought shelter from the noon rainstorms of Panama.

Michele has two wonderful children and is a proud grandmother of one incredible granddaughter. She is a passionate writer, has an untamable imagination, and enjoys writing sci-fi, conspiracy thrillers and—well, just about anything that strikes her fancy. You can find out more about Michele's work at her website: www.michelecoffman.com.

NOTE TO READERS:

Thank you for reading a book from Launch Point Press. We have made every effort to edit this book. However, typos do slip in. If you find an error in the text, please email publisher@launchpointpress.com so the issue can be corrected.

We appreciate you as a reader and want to ensure you enjoy the reading process. We would like you to consider posting a review on your preferred media sites and/or your blog or website.

For more information on upcoming releases, author interviews, contests, giveaways and more, please sign up for our newsletter and visit us as at Launch Point Press: www.launchpointpress.com and "Like" us on Facebook: Launch Point Press.

Bright Blessings